A DARK AND SECRET PLACE

Also available by Jen Williams

The Winnowing Flame Trilogy

The Poison Song
The Bitter Twins
The Ninth Rain

The Copper Cat Trilogy

The Silver Tide
The Iron Ghost
The Copper Promise

Short Story

Sorrow's Isle

A DARK AND SECRET PLACE

A NOVEL

JEN WILLIAMS

CROOKED LANE

NEW YORK

This is a work of fiction. All of the names, characters, organizations, places and events portrayed in this novel are either products of the author's imagination or are used fictitiously. Any resemblance to real or actual events, locales, or persons, living or dead, is entirely coincidental.

Published in the United States by Crooked Lane Books, an imprint of The Quick Brown Fox & Company LLC.

Crooked Lane Books and its logo are trademarks of The Quick Brown Fox & Company LLC.

Library of Congress Catalog-in-Publication data available upon request.

ISBN (hardcover): 978-1-64385-574-5
ISBN (ebook): 978-1-64385-575-2

Cover design by Nicole Lecht

Printed in the United States.

www.crookedlanebooks.com

Crooked Lane Books
34 West 27th St., 10th Floor
New York, NY 10001

First Edition: June 2021

10 9 8 7 6 5 4 3 2 1

For Juliet, the devil on my shoulder who
whispered: ‘write a scary book’

CHAPTER

1

BEFORE

Light from the doorway fell across the boy's face, and for the first time he did not turn away from it. His arms and legs were too heavy, the cuff at his throat too solid, too tight. And it wasn't as though turning away had ever saved him before.

The figure in the light paused, as if noting this change of habit, then knelt to undo the leather strap with sharp, jerking movements. The cuff fell away and she reached for his head, grasping a thick handful of his black hair, close to the roots.

Years later, he would not be able to say what had been different about that particular time. He was starved and tired, his bones heavy and his flesh bruised, and he had thought that every inch of him was resigned to the reality of his existence, but that time, when her fingers twisted in his hair and her fingernails scraped against his scalp, something in him *woke up*.

"You little brute," she said absently. She filled the cupboard doorway, blocking out most of the light. "You filthy little brute. You stink, do you know that? Dirty little shit."

Perhaps at the very last moment she did realize what she had woken, because for the briefest second a flicker of some emotion animated her pale, doughy face; she had caught something in his eyes, perhaps, a look that was alien to her, and he saw quite clearly the panicked glance she gave the cuff.

But it was too late. The boy sprang to his feet, his jaws wide and hands hooked into claws. She leapt backwards, yelling. The landing stairs were directly behind her—he dimly remembered this, from the time before the cupboard—and they went crashing down them together, the boy howling and the woman screaming. It was so brief, that moment of falling, but for years he would remember several sharp impressions: the hot searing pain as she ripped a fistful of hair from his temple, the yawning sensation of falling into space, and the wild delirium of gouging her skin with his claws. His nails.

They hit the floor. There was silence. There was, the boy realized, no one else in the house; no raised voices, no sharp fingers, no alarming flash of red. The woman, his mother, lay underneath him in a collection of strange angles, her throat cocked and bared as though she were trying to appease him. Her right arm had snapped halfway down her forearm, and a bone, shockingly white against her grayish skin, pointed toward the window. The sleeve of the yellow smock she wore was caught on it.

"Muh?"There was a thin stream of blood running from her nose and mouth, and her eyes—green, like his—were looking at point above his head. Carefully, he put his hand over her mouth and nose, and pressed, watching with fascination as her flesh slid and wrinkled. He pressed harder, leaning his whole weight on his arm, feeling her lips mash against her teeth and split and . . .

He stopped. He needed to be outside.

* * *

It was a cold, gray morning, he guessed autumn. The light hurt his eyes, but not as much as he had been expecting. In fact, he seemed to drink in the light, staring around at the bleak landscape and the sky with a growing sense of peace. There were the woods; he had played in them once, and the leaves were turning brown and red. There were the fields, dark now with recent rain, and there were the old out-buildings his father had let fall into disrepair. Somewhere beyond them, there was a paved road, but it was a long walk. His mother's body, which he had dragged out onto the scrubby grass with him, looked more beautiful already—away from the house she was something else. Taking hold of her ankles, he dragged her a little further, across the dirt track and into the fallow field opposite.

"Here." He opened his mouth to say more, but couldn't. The grass was wet, framing his mother and cushioning her, and he could feel the life of it; tiny flies and beetles, the bright interest of worms. The boy moved so that he was kneeling next to her, and he felt his body fill with an anger that was so flat and so enormous it was like a landscape inside him, a rage that filled his every horizon. For a time, he came untethered from himself, seeing nothing but that flat, red rage, hearing nothing but thunder. He did not come back to himself until a polite cough from behind him made him jerk with surprise. His arms were bloody to the elbow, and his mouth was thick with the taste of pennies. There were things in his teeth.

"What is this then? What do we have here?"

There was a man in the grass, tall and sharp-angled. He was wearing a hat and he was watching the boy with a kind of gentle curiosity, as though he had come across someone making a kite or playing conkers. The boy went utterly still. The man wasn't from the house, but that didn't mean the boy wouldn't be punished. Of course he would be punished. He looked down to see what he had done to his mother, and the edges of his vision went gray.

"Now then. Don't take on so." The man took a step forward, and for the first time the boy saw that he had a dog with him, a huge black dog, covered in shaggy black fur. It steamed slightly in the cold morning air and looked at him with yellow-brown eyes. "You know, I had completely forgotten the Reaves had a boy, but there you are. There you are, after all."

The boy opened his mouth and closed it again. The Reaves, the Reaves were his family, and they would be angry with him.

"And what a creature you are." The boy winced, remembering how his mother had called him *brute* and *beast* and *filth*, but the man sounded pleased, and when the boy looked up, he was shaking his head gently. "You're to come with me, I think, my little wolf. My little barghest."

The dog opened its mouth, letting loose a long pink tongue. After a moment it began to lick the blood from the grass.

CHAPTER

2

COLD AND TIRED and in no mood for awkward pleasantries, Heather forced a polite smile on her face. A moment later she reconsidered, and just as forcibly removed it—smiling too much at a time like this would be seen as inappropriate, and she was already well aware that she was about as welcome as a turd in a swimming pool.

"Thanks, Mr. Ramsey, for waiting in for me. It's very kind of you."

Mr. Ramsey glowered at her.

"Well, if you had been around here more often, I dare say you would have had your own set of your mother's keys." He sniffed, communicating in one bronchial sound everything he thought of Heather Evans. "Your poor mother. It's . . . well, it's all very sad, I'm sure. Very sad indeed. Just a terrible situation all round."

"Yeah, it's definitely that." Heather hefted the keys in her hand, looking at the towering bushes and trees that hid her mother's house from the road. "Don't let me keep you, Mr. Ramsey."

He stiffened at that, the pouches under his eyes turning a slightly darker shade of gray. She kept quiet, letting the silence spool out into the overcast morning, and soon she could see him wondering if he shouldn't give her a piece of his mind. But in the end, he turned and marched back to his own house.

Heather stood for a moment longer, taking a deep breath and listening to the quiet. Balesford was a place of residential sprawl, of detached houses and high fences, of eerily similar faces and the same accent everywhere you went. It was technically London, nestled as it was on the very border of Kent, but a very anemic strain of it—no color, no life.

She sighed, jangling the keys in her hand before taking a deep breath and marching up to the gate, half hidden by the vast, evergreen bushes. On the other side was a neat lawn with slightly overgrown flower beds and a gravel path that led to the house. There was nothing special about it, certainly nothing unusual, and yet despite this Heather felt her stomach tighten as she walked up the path. It was not a welcoming building, never had been; the bleak pebbledash merged with the blank windows to suggest a place that was closed and would be closed forever. The door was painted a dreary magnolia, and on the ground next to it was a fat terracotta pot. It was filled with black soil, and on the smooth orange surface a rough heart had been scratched, the lines jagged and overlapping. Heather frowned at it slightly—she'd never thought her mother as one for the rustic look—and why was it empty? It was very unlike her mother to leave something unfinished . . . which was ironic, given how things had ended. For a long wobbly moment Heather thought she might cry, right there on the doorstep, but instead she gave her arm a swift pinch, and the tears retreated. *No time for that.* There were a few gray feathers on the doorstep, probably belonging to a pigeon. Grimacing, Heather kicked them away with the toe of her trainer and pulled the right key from the bunch.

She let herself in to a hallway ticking with silence and dust, a few letters and a slippery pile of junk mail skittering away as she pushed the door open. It was late morning but the gloomy September sky and the tall trees outside meant that the place was busy with shadows. She hurriedly flicked on all the light switches she could see, blinking at a chintzy lampshade that leapt into pastel life.

The living room was tidy, and dusty. There were no dirty cups, no half-read books propped on the sofa. There was an old red coat slung over the back of a chair, its thick wool pilling at the sleeves. The kitchen was in a similar state; everything cleaned and put away. Her mother had, Heather noticed, even turned the page over on the calendar to show September, despite knowing she wouldn't be seeing the rest of the month.

"What was the point, Mum?" She tapped her fingers against the slick pages, noting that there was nothing written in the little boxes, no notes saying: "cancel milk/kill self."

Heather stomped up the stairs, her footfalls muffled by the thick carpet. The main bedroom was as tidy as the rest of the little house. Her mother's dressing table was clean and neat, glass jars of cold cream and bottles of perfume in rows like soldiers, while a pair of brushes lay next to an old-fashioned hand mirror. Heather sat down and looked at the brushes. Here, her mum had been less careful, less fastidious. There were strands of hair caught in the bristles, wisps of blonde and the occasional streak of wiry gray.

Organic material, thought Heather. For some reason the phrase seemed to settle in her chest, heavy and poisonous. *You left behind organic material, Mum. Did you mean to?*

The only thing out of place on the dressing table was a screwed-up ball of slightly yellowed paper, covered in a close-set typeface. In an effort to distract herself from the hairbrushes, Heather picked it up and smoothed it out, half expecting to see a page from one of her own articles—her mother might not have been in touch very often but Heather was sure she still kept a critical eye on her daughter's career—but she quickly saw that it was a page from a book, possibly quite an old one, judging from the texture of the paper and the font. There was an old, woodcut illustration that at first she couldn't get her head around—it seemed to show what looked like a goat, or possibly a lamb, standing over another animal. A dog, perhaps? The dog's belly had been cut open, and smaller goats were pushing rocks inside the suspiciously clean opening. Heather's eyes skipped to the text, which informed her that when the wolf woke up, he was thirsty, and he went to the river to drink . . .

It was a page from a book of fairy tales, but what her mother was doing with it, she had no idea. Colleen had never liked the older, gorier tales; story time when Heather had been little had involved a strict diet of happy ponies and girls at boarding school.

The page made her feel uncomfortable: the strange picture, the way it had been crumpled up and left on the table. Did her mother even mean for her to see it?

"Who knows what you were thinking, right? You must have been . . . you must have been out of your mind, I don't know . . ."

Suddenly, the room seemed very warm and close, the silence too loud. Heather stood up, a little shakily, crashing hard enough into the dressing table that a bottle of perfume fell over—the stopper tumbled from the bottle, startling her further.

"Shit."

The scent filled the room, flowery and thick. It made her think of the morgue, and specifically of the waiting room, which had featured several tasteful flower arrangements, as though that could distract you from what you were about to see. She shook her head. It was important not to fixate on it, that's what her housemate Terry had said. Don't think about the smell, don't think about the wind whipping along isolated cliffs, and definitely don't think about the particular effect that a very long drop will have on the *organic material* of a body . . .

"Shit. I need some air."

Heather shoved the crumpled paper into a drawer where she couldn't see it and headed back downstairs. She was on her way to the backdoor when the doorbell rang out through the house.

Instantly, the sick, tight feeling in her chest was replaced by anger. It would be someone selling something, or collecting for a charity, or chattering about god. Or it would be Mr. Bloody Ramsey. She swept to the door, already savoring the look on this interloper's face when she said *can't you see I'm grieving, how dare you*, and was startled to find a tall, well-dressed older woman on her doorstep. She didn't have a clipboard or a donation box, but she did have a covered casserole dish in her hands and an expression of sympathy.

"Er, can I help you?"

"Heather? But of course it is." The woman smiled, and Heather found her anger fizzling into nothing. She had very short gray hair, cut into a style that would be quite unflattering on most people, but she had strikingly good cheek bones and a long, handsome face. Heather could not guess her age; she was clearly old, older than her mother, but her skin was largely unlined and her bright eyes were clear and sharp. *Mary Poppins*, thought Heather wonderingly. *She reminds me of Mary Poppins.* "I'm Lillian, from up the road, dear. I just wanted to pop in and make sure you were coping." She lifted the dish up, in case Heather hadn't spotted it. "Can I put this down somewhere?"

Heather jumped back from the door. "Sorry, of course. Come in."

The woman moved smoothly down the corridor, heading straight for the kitchen, her confidence suggesting she was familiar with the place.

"It's just a stew," Lillian announced as she put the dish down on the counter. "Lamb, carrots, onions, and so on. You're not vegetarian are you, dear? No, I thought not. Good. Heat it slowly in the oven." Catching the expression on Heather's face, she smiled again. "I know what it's like when you're dealing with something like this. It's very easy to forget to eat properly, but that will do you no favors at all. Make sure you get something hot in your stomach, every night. Colleen was a dear friend. She'd be pulling her hair out if she knew you were wasting yourself away over this."

Heather nodded, trying to catch up with the conversation.

"It's very kind of you to think of me, uh, Lillian. You knew my mum well? Colleen, I mean. You said you live round here? You must have moved here in the last few years?" She was trying to remember Lillian from her own childhood, or her infrequent visits as an adult, but she couldn't place the woman.

"Just round the corner," Lillian was looking around the kitchen, as if she could spot every bit of dust Colleen would have been mortified about. Although Mr. Ramsey had instantly inspired Heather's contempt, the idea of disappointing Lillian was oddly alarming. "Colleen and I used to spend afternoons together sometimes, drinking tea and talking about old lady things."

Heather nodded, although it was strange to think of her mother as an "old lady".

"How did she seem to you? Over the last month or so?" The question seemed to bring Lillian up short, so Heather uncrossed her arms and tried to look more relaxed. "I didn't see her as often as I should have, you see. All this has come as a bit of a shock."

"She was a strong woman, your mother. Surprisingly so. But it's a generational thing, you see. People my age, well, we don't talk about our feelings." Lillian smiled thinly. "It's not the done thing, and I'm afraid if Colleen was struggling, I had no idea."

Heather thought about the screwed-up page on the dressing table, the pained face of the police officer as he passed her her mother's wedding ring.

"So, nothing she said struck you as strange? No odd behavior?"

"Goodness," Lillian looked down at the countertop as if Heather had just said a rude word in front of the vicar. "Colleen mentioned you were a journalist, but . . ."

"I'm sorry, I . . ." Heather looked away, half smiling. *I can't even do small talk properly. Mum would have found that funny, probably.* "Look, can I get you a cup of tea?"

"No, thank you dear," Lillian flapped a hand at her. "I wouldn't dream of intruding, not now. I just wanted to drop that off and get a look at you. Colleen used to talk about you all the time, you know."

"Really?" Heather smiled again, but it felt forced this time. We didn't always get on so well. I was a pain in the ass when I was a kid, as I'm sure she told you."

"Oh not at all," Lillian brushed a piece of fluff from her sleeve. "Nothing but praise for her golden girl."

Heather had the sudden impression that Lillian was lying, but she nodded anyway. The woman made to leave, squeezing her arm briefly as she came past.

"If there's anything you need, dear, just tell me. Like I said, I'm very close, always happy to bake or cook or even do laundry if you're feeling overwhelmed . . ." Heather followed her down the corridor like an errant schoolchild; she suspected people were often following Lillian about like this, dragged in her wake.

"Oh, would you look at that?" Lillian had stopped at a small side table in the hallway, where Colleen used to stack her post and keys each day. On it was a framed photograph of Heather. It showed her as a teenager, sitting on her bed in her old room. Tall and gangly, her dark hair hanging in her face, she was holding up a certificate of merit she'd been awarded at school; for an essay, a short story, Heather couldn't remember. Seeing the photo made her stomach turn over—it had been taken just a few weeks before her dad had died and everything between her and her mother had started to turn to poison.

"That's my favorite photo of you," said Lillian, sounding pleased for reasons Heather couldn't guess. "Isn't it charming?"

Heather opened her mouth, uncertain what to say. In the photo she was wearing a black *X-Files* T-shirt that was too baggy on her, and she looked sulky. She had no idea why her mum had even framed it, let alone why this stranger was so taken with it.

"Anyway, I'll let you get on." The woman was already out the door, her neat white shoes crunching on the gravel. "Remember dear, anything you need, just let me know."

* * *

Heather gathered up the post from the hallway carpet and chucked it on the kitchen counter. Lots of shiny leaflets, a few bills, several takeaway menus. Frowning, she separated out the stuff that would need attention, then dumped the rest in the bin. Something in the bottom of the bin had gone bad—some old bit of food, probably, the remains of her mother's last dinner—and the waft of rotten meat made her stomach roll uncomfortably. Suddenly very close to being sick, Heather headed to the back door, sure that fresh air would make her feel better.

Tall evergreen trees obscured the view of the neighbors. When she had been a kid—when she had lived here, too, getting under her mum's feet—those trees had been shorter, friendlier even. Now they threw the garden into shade, hiding Heather from view and keeping the outside world firmly out. There was a little square of concrete by the back door, with two ironwork chairs and a table on it, and another clay flowerpot with empty soil in it. *Empty.* Out in the cool air, she felt a little better. She wondered why she had gone wandering around the house in the first place, looking in rooms and staring at photos. Poking around on dressing tables. *Because I'm checking she's not here,* she thought, wincing. *Part of me still expects to find her in the bathroom, scrubbing the loo, or in the living room, watching Countryfile. I'm checking for ghosts.*

"Fucking hell." She took a long, deep breath, waiting for the nausea to retreat. "What a bloody mess, Mum. Honestly."

Her mind turned back to the screwed-up page, thinking of her mother's mental state in the days before she took her own life. What had she been thinking? It was hard to imagine her mum—a woman with near religious feelings about the use of coasters and bookmarks—tearing out a page from a book, let alone crumpling it up like a piece of rubbish. But that was the dark heart of it all, the frightening truth Heather didn't want to look at directly: her mother hadn't been in her right mind. Something had stepped in and taken her reason from her; some cruel, lethal stranger had taken up residence inside her mother's head. "None of this makes any sense to me. None of it."

Shortly after she'd been called to take possession of her mother's body, the police had put her in touch with a counsellor, who had been very kind and spent a lot of time talking about shock, about how people with severe depression could be very good at hiding it, even from their closest loved ones. Heather had listened patiently, nodding through her own numbness, and though she had understood perfectly what the counsellor had been saying, even then it had felt . . . wrong. Those old instincts had started to twitch, the ones that told her when a story was bunk and when a story had legs.

"You're being ridiculous," she told herself, listening to how cold and small her voice sounded. "Paranoid."

Somewhere out on the road in front of the house, someone beeped a car horn, and she jumped. There were hot tears on her face, which she wiped away irritably with the back of her hand. After a moment, she slid her phone from her pocket to see a text message notification winking up at her.

Hello stranger—word is you're back in Balesford. Want to meet up? I was so sorry to hear about your mum, I hope you're ok xxx

Nikki Appiah. She looked around at the dark trees, wondering if the neighbors were watching and reporting on her somehow from between their net curtains. She sniffed, blinking rapidly to clear her eyes before typing a reply.

Are you on the neighborhood watch or what? Yeah I'm back for a bit. Are you around now? Spoons? I need a drink.

She paused, then added a green-faced vomit emoticon.

Nikki's reply popped up almost immediately.

It's eleven in the morning, Hev. But yes, let's meet in town. It's been too long, and it would be good to see your face (even if it's green). See you in an hour? Xxx

Heather slipped the phone away. It was growing darker, and the air was beginning to smell sharp and mineral—it would rain soon, and it would be good to be elsewhere. The wind picked up, rattling through the tall bushes and making them sway, and for the barest moment it seemed to Heather that there was too much movement there, as though something was choosing to move with the wind, to hide its footsteps. She peered at the darker shadows, trying to discern a shape, then turned to the back door, dismissing it as her imagination looking for things to be scared of. The house still looked blank and unknowable, a little box of mundanity.

"What were you thinking, Mum?"

Her own voice sounded sad and strange to her, so she wiped away the last of the tears from her cheeks, and headed back through the house to the rented car.

CHAPTER

3

THE WIND HAD freshened through the morning, driving away the clouds and leaving behind a scrubbed-clean sort of sky—chilly yet cheering. Beverly was pleased. Her grandchildren, Tess and James, would get a few hours out in the garden at least. Like all kids these days they were obsessed with their phones and their gadgets, but Beverly was proud to note that they could still be tempted out into her garden when the weather was fine, and with that in mind she shrugged her coat on—still the thin one, autumn hadn't quite started to bite yet—and made her way out the back gate. Her garden was beautiful, but it had no horse chestnut trees, whereas the fields out back had two very fine ones, and she wanted to see if they were dropping yet.

Ahead of her were the line of trees that cupped the field, the two huge horse chestnuts and a cluster of oak, birch, and elm. Under the sunshine the leaves were as bright as stained-glass, green and yellow, red and gold, and yes, there were the thorny green casings scattered on the grass, spilling open their milky pale insides. Beverly began stuffing her pockets with fallen conkers, picking up only those that had survived the fall unscathed, and keeping an extra eye out for cheese cutters—conkers with a flat side, which were especially good for destroying your opponent. Once or twice, she found casings that had only partially split open. These she pressed on one side with her boot, smiling with satisfaction as the conkers popped free, all smooth and newly born. One of these produced a particularly fine cheese cutter.

"I'll keep that one for myself, I think." Beverly slipped the conker into an inside pocket. Conkers was no fun at all if she couldn't beat at least one of her grandkids. It was the conker immediately after this, plucked from the grass close to the roots of the big old tree, that felt wrong in her hand. Grimacing, she held it up to the light, not quite registering the crimson smear on her fingers until she caught the smell of it: the back step of the butcher's shop on a hot day.

Beverly yelped and dropped the conker. The grass by her feet was dark: saturated, she belatedly realized, with blood.

"It'll be that bloody dog," she said hotly, holding out the dirty hand as though she had burned it. "Bloody dog got hold of something again."

But there was no eviscerated rabbit that she could see, or even a big bird—both of which she had seen on the fields in the past. Instead, as she drew closer to the trunk of the old conker tree, she saw that the blood was flowing from the roots, as though the tree itself were bleeding. The big hollow at its base, normally clogged with old leaves and mud, had been filled up with something else.

"Oh God. Oh God no, oh *God* . . ."

Beverly's arms fell to her sides, her fingers numb. There was a face in the hollow, a woman's face with her eyes closed and mouth open as if in prayer. Her cheeks were waxy and flecked with dark matter, and there were flowers poking out from between her teeth. *Pink ones,* noted Beverly, who would never allow pink flowers in her house again. *Dog roses, by the looks of it.*

Crushed beneath the woman's head were a pair of feet, bare, save for a silver toe ring and pale pink nail polish, and there was an arm, too, the hand laying palm up on the grass as though she were reaching for help, or, beckoning for someone to join her. Incongruously, she could also see the sleeve of a red jacket, the wide buttons on the cuff dotted with beads of moisture. It was all crammed in so tight that Beverly couldn't see the color of the woman's hair or anything of her torso, if indeed that was in there with her, but she could see a soft wall of purplish rope-like things, falling softly to either side of the arm. In the bark above the hollow, a heart had been scratched; some pining lover's romantic gesture, no doubt.

Suddenly aware she was very close to passing out, Beverly stumbled away from the tree and began to run back to the house, her face wet with tears.

CHAPTER

4

"THIS PLACE WAS always a shit hole."

Heather settled the two glasses on the table and dropped three packets of chips next to them. Nikki picked up a packet of salt and vinegar and peered at it critically.

"You chose it," Nikki pointed out mildly. She looked, annoyingly, much as she always had. Her hair was in neat black braids and her glasses were slimmer, more fashionable versions of those she had worn in school. She was even wearing a chunky knitted navy jumper, reminding Heather inevitably of their old school uniform. "I know Balesford isn't heaving with trendy spots, but I suspect we could have managed better than Wetherspoons."

"Oh, for old time's sake." Heather took a sip of her drink and grimaced. Once at the bar she had fallen back into old habits and ended up with a dark rum and coke—the drink she most associated with school. Nikki had ordered a white-wine spritzer, although she seemed more interested in the chips. "I'm sorry I didn't let you know earlier that I was back in the area, but . . . everything has been such a mess. How did you know I was back, anyway? Do you have spies watching the house? Are you with MI5 now, is that it?"

Nikki shook her head, smiling. "My auntie lives on your road, you know that. And she basically *is* the MI5 of Balesford. They were all waiting for you to turn up, once Mr. Ramsey had told everyone you didn't so much as have a set of your mum's keys." Nikki's smile faltered. "I'm sorry, Hev. Really sorry. How bloody awful. Are you all right?"

Heather shrugged and popped open a packet of chips, not quite meeting her friend's eyes. Nikki had always been the nice one, the kind one, and having to look at real sympathy on another human's face was too much to handle at that moment, especially after her wobble at the house. *Organic material.*

"I'm as well as can be expected, I guess. Looking around the house earlier, I half expected her to still be there, you know? Like it was all some sort of, I don't know, clerical error. It's . . ." Something moved in her chest, and the room felt unstable, as though the floor were about to drop away. "It's been a while since I've been back to the old place. And, well, you know she wasn't a huge fan of mine, anyway."

"That's not really the point."

"Yeah, I know." Heather took a sip of the rum and coke, blinking as the burn hit her throat. A headache that had been brewing fizzled away, and some of the tension left her shoulders. "Why would she kill herself, Nikki? I can't get my head round it. There's something . . . it doesn't feel right. It doesn't make sense."

Nikki looked faintly uncomfortable, shifting in her chair. The pub was starting to fill up with lunch trade, people coming in for the five-pound curry deal. "Auntie Shanice wouldn't believe it at first. Said that Mr. Ramsey must be talking out of his ass . . . Heather, suicide is difficult to understand. Your mum must have been very unhappy, troubled even, possibly for a very long time, and it's possible that no one even knew she was suffering. Mental illness can be devastating like that."

"Yeah. And I'd be the last person to know, wouldn't I? It's just . . ." Heather shrugged. "You remember my mum? I know you do. Never wanted a fuss, preferred everything to be as quiet as possible. It feels like such a gesture, like she was telling me something, or she wanted to, I don't know, punish me maybe."

Seeing the look on Nikki's face, she sighed. "I know, I sound like a bloody cliché. Refusing to accept what's right in front of me because the truth is a little too uncomfortable. Making it all about me, for Christ sake. But I can't shake the feeling I'm missing something. Did your aunt notice anything wrong with her? Recently, I mean?"

"Hev . . ." Nikki reached over and squeezed her hand briefly, and again Heather found she couldn't look at her friend's face. "Some things . . . Some things can't be figured out, or reasoned away."

Heather nodded, looking down at the sticky table top.

"Anyway, let's not talk about this, shall we? It's rubbish. How are you? It's been a little while since we last did one of these random booze ups. What are you up to now? Still teaching, I assume?"

"I am, and I can tell from the face you make when I say that, that you're horrified." Nikki smiled and took a sip of her spritzer. "I'm teaching at a college now, which you would know if you ever paid attention to my Facebook updates. I'm covering the English and History departments. Are you still at the newspaper?'

Heather winced, then tried to hide it by eating several chips at once. "It didn't work out. I've been freelancing for a while and it suits me better." More bad memories. She downed the rest of her drink, and raised her eyebrows. "Another?"

They spent the rest of the afternoon in the pub, both switching to soft drinks when the edges of the room started to blur. At some point, one of them suggested getting food, and soon the table was crowded with plates, with smears and blobs of alarmingly bright yellow curry sauce and scattered bits of poppadum. They talked about school, dredging up all the old stories that must by tradition be dredged up at such times. Eventually, the evening crowd began to arrive, and they agreed that it was likely time to make their way home—spending all day in the pub was not, Nikki pointed out, a great look for a teacher.

"Suit yourself, professor."

Outside, the day had grown gloomy and cold, and as Nikki called them a cab, Heather found that the small cache of good spirits she had built up over the afternoon were leaking away into the shadows. She wasn't going home now, to her untidy yet cozy room in a house shared with other untidy people; she would be going back to her mother's empty house, no doubt to a long night of trawling over bad memories and unanswered questions. Something must have shown on her face, because once she slipped her phone back in her pocket, Nikki touched her arm softly.

"Hey. Cab's going to be a few minutes. Are you all right?"

Heather shrugged. The fizzy drinks were a sour slick in her stomach, and she felt too weary to pretend.

"The suicide note was really weird. Did I tell you that?"

Nikki shook her head, her brown eyes somber.

"I mean, like you said, she was in a bad place, and there's no real reason to expect a suicide note to make sense, I suppose." Heather tried to smile, but it twisted into something sickly on her lips, so she stopped. Instead, she opened her satchel and slipped a piece of paper from out of her notebook. It was pale lilac, with a picture of a wren at the top next to a banner reading "*notes to you*". For reasons she didn't want to look too closely at, she'd kept it with her since the police handed it over along with her mother's belongings. Her mother's cramped handwriting hunched in the middle of the page. She passed it to Nikki, who frowned and smoothed it over carefully with her fingers.

"To you both. I know this will be a shock, and I'm sorry that you will have to deal with all this mess, but I can't live with it anymore—not knowing what I know, and the decisions I have had to make. They say this is the coward's way—well people who say that don't know what I've lived with, this awful shadow I've lived under forever. All those monsters in the wood never really went away, not for me. And maybe that's what I deserve. I truly am sorry for everything to come, for what it's worth. Despite what you might believe, I love you both, and I always have."

Nikki didn't say anything, instead pursing her lips and looking down the high street. After a moment, she touched a finger to the corner of her eye and sniffed.

"Oh, Hev, that's awful. Your poor mum."

"Don't you see though?" Heather took the note back, folding it away into her bag. She was glad to have it out of sight. "*To you both*. I love you both. What does that mean? There's only me. She had no other family left. And what is she talking about, these *decisions*?"

Nikki shook her head slowly. "Okay, it is weird. But maybe she meant you and your dad? If she was very unwell, she might have forgotten that he'd died already, somehow. Or . . . or, she could be talking to whoever found her body."

"But both sounds so specific. Like she had two people in mind. And *monsters in the wood?* What the hell does that mean?" Heather sighed. "You're right, she could be talking about Dad, I suppose, but I hate not knowing. Like I'm going to spend the rest of my life wondering what she was on about—as if dealing with all this shit wasn't bad enough, she had to leave a vague and cryptic suicide note." Somewhere up the street, a dog was barking, and a light rain had started to fall. The road was mostly deserted as people hurried to get out of the drizzle, but up toward the bus stop, a shadowy figure stood, unmoving. A bus thundered past, not stopping, and the figure turned their face away from its light.

"I know. You'll feel better after the funeral, I think. They're supposed to give you closure, aren't they, funerals?" Nikki pursed her lips, as though she wasn't sure this was true. "Have you started . . .?"

"Oh, it's mostly sorted." Heather smiled a little. It was good to see Nikki, to have someone steering her back toward the practical things. "People are really helpful in these situations, you know? Her phone though, she had it with her, and it . . . well, it didn't survive. So, I need to find her address book, if she had one. Do people even do that these days, write down phone numbers? I suppose if anyone does, it would be my mum."

"Well. Mum and Auntie Shanice are ready and willing, just say the word. Anything you need. Here, look." Nikki nodded toward the curb. "There's our cab."

* * *

Several hours later, Heather woke up in the spare room of her mother's house, eyes opening onto utter blackness. Panicked, she grabbed her phone off the side table and the light from it threw the room into a collection of grayscale shadows. *Just the spare room*, she reminded herself, *just the stupid, thick curtains*. The window in her own bedroom looked out onto a street light and the place was never properly dark. Here, with the trees outside and the long, heavily embroidered curtains, she had woken into a kind of blindness. Trembling slightly, she snapped on the bedside lamp and sat up, phone held loosely in her hands.

A noise. A scuffling from directly overhead. Heather rubbed at her eyes, reminding herself that she was a grown adult in an unfamiliar house—she should expect strange noises, and she should expect to be creeped out. The scuffling became a kind of flapping, and goose bumps broke out across her skin.

"Okay,' she said aloud. 'There's a bird in the attic. A pigeon got in there, or there's starlings nesting or something." Her voice was familiar and normal, and she nodded to herself. "A bird is just a bird. Nothing to worry about."

She lay there for a few more minutes, listening to the faint noises and getting more and more irritated. Eventually, she threw the duvet back and stomped out of the room and down the hallway. Perhaps, she reasoned, the noise of her footsteps would startle the bird into leaving. The landing was especially dark after the lamplight, and Heather blinked repeatedly, waiting for her eyes to adjust. It was cold, the carpet under her bare feet oddly frigid.

"Bloody place."

The door to the loft was a barely glimpsed shape on the ceiling. As Heather came to a stop underneath it, the scuffling and flapping noises stopped abruptly, as if they had been listening for her. Still curious, and much more awake than she had been, she stood for a time underneath it, just listening and occasionally rubbing the tops of her arms. It was cold enough, and she was half convinced she could see her own breath.

The house was utterly silent; even the thumps and creaks of a building settling seemed to have stopped.

Heather turned to go and caught sight of the window down the far end of the landing. Just for an instant, she saw movement out there, as though something was watching from the thick line of the trees. Eyes, wide and bright and utterly inhuman, peered in through the darkened glass.

"What—"

A second later a gust of wind blew through the trees and whatever had been causing the illusion was scattered into nothing. *Because that's what it had to be,* she told herself, *your eyes playing tricks on you. You idiot.* Even so, she went over to the window and peered out. There was nothing but the street lights filtering through the branches of trees, the moonlight creating strange shapes and half glimpsed forms.

Annoyed with herself, she went back to bed. The lamp light stayed on until morning. And although she didn't hear the noises again that night, her mind kept returning to them, and when she did sleep, she dreamt of feathers, downy and brown, and her dad's round face, scarlet with rage.

CHAPTER

5

THE NEXT MORNING was not a pleasant one for Heather.

She had known that staying in her mother's house would summon a lot of uncomfortable feelings, and so it was with no great surprise that she felt a shroud of misery settle over her when she woke up in an unfamiliar bed. Once this room had been her dad's box room, full of his random junk—old car manuals, big plastic buckets for home brewing beer, and a massive chest freezer, which mum had filled with frozen ready meals and tubs of Neapolitan ice cream. As a kid, Heather had loved the room, convinced it contained all her dad's secrets. Now, the guest room was small, and neat, and entirely without personality, but even so Heather couldn't help but feel her mother there still—in the pile of towels on the footstool, on the doily on the windowsill, the empty vase. It was too quiet, and too cold, so she got up and put the heating on as high as it would go, and put on both the television and radio. Once there was a comforting level of noise, she made herself a strong cup of tea, sat at the kitchen table, and began making a list of things that needed doing.

To her surprise, she found her mother's address book almost straight away—it was sitting in a wooden magazine rack in the living room, half forgotten—and as quickly as possible, she called everyone who needed to be called, passing out bad news, and taking in condolences. When that ugly business was done, she found herself wandering back upstairs, her hand resting on the doorknob of her old room. Holding in a sigh, she stepped inside. It was still possible to recognize it as hers; the duvet cover on the bed, neatly turned down and clean, of a color only a teenager would choose, and the wallpaper that still had a series of tiny bald patches from old Blue Tack, to hold posters in place—the posters her mother had taken down and rolled into tubes not long after she'd left home. During her visits over the years, Heather had gotten used to the fact that this wasn't her room anymore, but for the first time she noticed that her mother had apparently started using it for other things—there was a small card table in the corner, covered with crafting materials.

Half smiling, Heather sat down on the foldaway chair and sifted through the bits and pieces. It looked like she'd actually rescued an old abandoned crafting set of Heather's, one of the expensive packs of multicolored clay she had campaigned for one birthday, and with it she'd been making jolly napkin holders festooned with holly and snowmen. Next to the finished pieces was a Post-it note with the address of a nearby old people's home. Had she intended to give them to the retirement home as part of their Christmas fair? They had gone to it many times when she was a kid, buying cakes and talking to the old dears. Heather picked up one of the napkin rings and slipped it on to her finger. She'd done a lot of work on these, had been halfway through making another. What made someone put down their cozy crafting project and think about ending their life instead?

The texture of the smooth clay against her fingers reminded her of the times she had tried to make things herself. The clay was tough to mold straight out the packet, so you had to warm it up in your hands, but Heather's small fingers had never been much good at it. Abruptly, she remembered sitting in this very room with her mother, newspapers spread carefully over the carpet, and small plates in front of them both. Her mum had taken each piece of colored clay and warmed it in her own hands first before passing it over to Heather, so that she could make something out of it . . .

Heather put the napkin ring back, her hand shaking. *Nikki was right*, she told herself. *I can't know what Mum was going through. I'm seeing mysteries where there are none.*

Even so, as she left the room, turning back to look again at the industrious little table, the sense that something somewhere was deeply wrong wouldn't quite leave her.

* * *

Heather spent the next day moving around the house, making notes and wondering at how much stuff people accumulate around them. At lunchtime she heated up the stew Lillian had left her, eating it from a big bowl in front of the television. It was tasty and thick, but by the end of it she felt faintly ill, and she wondered if she'd waited too long to heat it up—if some ingredient in it had gone off. She washed up the dish diligently, just in case Lillian called back for it.

There was so much to think of with every room; what to do with clothes, knickknacks, old photographs—even boring things like bed linen and curtains. And with every room came a new cascade of memories, as though every space was packed with ghosts from her childhood. Most of them were not as pleasant as playing with modelling clay on the floor of her bedroom, either. And as she stood in the door of the bathroom, remembering a blazing row that had resulted in Heather kicking the bath so hard she had to go to the hospital, she wondered why on earth she hadn't brought someone with her to do this. Terry, her housemate, had even offered to help, but she had turned him down automatically. Nikki, too, she was certain, would have been glad to shoulder some of this unpleasantness.

What was that about? Was she worried Terry would have judged her for this ordinary, suburban childhood? Or, was she more afraid of him seeing her in a vulnerable state?

Going through the paperwork and shifting things around had tracked dust all over, so she dragged the hoover out and pushed it—somewhat unenthusiastically—around the living room. As she was chasing down a few errant hairs, the edge of the nozzle smacked against something solid underneath the sofa. Reaching down, she tugged the blockage out and was surprised to see it was a book, and quite an old one by the looks of it. She rubbed the dust and fluff off, and frowned at the cover. It was a collection of fairy tales, a battered old paperback, and on the front was a large black wolf, its jaws agape to reveal every one of its lethal teeth.

"Weird." She chucked it on the sideboard and finished up.

Dumping a sack of recycling outside, by the front door, Heather took a deep breath of cold, autumnal air. Out here, when she had been around seven or eight, she had sat with her new magnifying glass, burning little holes into dried leaves and pieces of paper, whatever she could get her hands on. Ants, she had discovered, popped when you burned them with the magnifying glass, and she'd spent an entertaining afternoon creating lots of tiny shriveled bodies on the path until her mother had come outside and caught her at it.

Heather had been banned from the garden for a week, at the height of summer, and she still remembered her simmering fury so clearly it made her cheeks feel hot. Trapped in her room, she had taken to other petty forms of destruction—breaking the plates her sandwiches arrived on, tipping her mother's perfume down the bathroom sink. She had been so angry then—and that had only made things worse.

That's why I didn't want Terry with me. Who would want their adult friends to see the child they once were? Standing in the cold, Heather felt a fresh wave of anguish move through her.

"The ghosts are just too bloody loud." She wiped her hands down the front of her jeans and went back inside.

* * *

It was after a few hours of sorting and cataloging that she remembered the attic. There had been no more strange noises, but passing under it again with a mug of tea clutched in both hands, she found her eyes drawn to it. *The man in the loft*, she thought to herself. *When I was little, granddad used to blame the Man in the Loft whenever anything went missing.*

It wasn't a reassuring thought, and Heather knew she would have to go up and check it out, or be doomed to lie in bed that night, listening for the Man in the Loft—or even worse, the soft footsteps of her mother.

"Christ, what's wrong with me? There are no monsters in the attic. A couple of days alone in the house and I'm behaving like a hysterical five-year-old."

An hour later and she was sitting, legs crossed in the surprisingly comfy space, sorting through a box of old vinyl records.

There was a lot of dreck—a lot of bands and singers in strange suits that she did not recognize, and a handful that were promising: Led Zeppelin, Siouxsie Sioux, David Bowie. Her dad's, no doubt. He'd told her once that when he and her mother had been dating, he had been trying to form his own band; he had been learning the bass guitar, but never quite got the hang of it. Smiling faintly, she put the records to one side, thinking that she would either keep them or put them on eBay, and when she went back to the box, she saw that they had been hiding an old, battered biscuit tin. She levered it out and popped the lid, wrinkling her nose at the dust. Tightly packed inside were two fat bundles of letters, secured with elastic bands.

Each one was addressed to her mother, and the ones in the first bundle looked very old indeed, the envelopes stained and creased, the ink faded to shadows. The ones on the top of the second bundle looked right up to date—she even recognized a recent set of stamps featuring old *Doctor Who* villains. Unable to resist, Heather pulled out one of the letters from the second bundle and began to read. The correspondent had untidy, expansive writing, and the black inky scrawl stretched from one edge of the paper to the other. The spelling was extremely erratic.

Dear Colleen,

Today has been quiet. So still. I have very little to do here, and when I have done the jobs they ask of me, I feel the emptiness closing in on me on all sides. Its in the yellow lights and the cleen floors, an emptiness that is more than emptiness, it is nothingness. A place that is so sour with man made things has no real life in it so I think of the time we spent together. On the grass and in the feelds thats how we were best. I cant see the grass here, or any trees.

Heather blinked. Without reading further, she plucked another, older letter from its envelope, and recognized the same messy handwriting immediately.

You discribe these places so well. That you would still do this for me after all these years just tells me that I was always rite about you. Your joining us at the commune changed my life.

"Commune?"

Another, to find the same. All of these letters were from the same person. And her mother appeared to have replied to them. The handwriting was not her dad's, she knew that straight away; he had only ever written in neat, block capitals, a consequence of his construction work and a need to write legible receipts. Who was this person with such strong feelings about her mother?

"You never mentioned a pen friend, Mum." The words sounded odd and flat in the warm air of the attic, as though they, too, were covered in dust. Because underneath her surprise, and even her slight amusement, a cold feeling was settling in Heather's gut. "I don't think I ever heard you talk about writing letters at all."

Its so noisey here at night. Do you remember how quiet it would be in the feelds, under the stars? When we were in the woods. Like we were the only people in the world even though we werent. The other people who came and lived under the stars, they didnt feel it like we did Colleen."

Heather scanned to the bottom of the page and squinted at the name there. A Michael? Next to the scratchy signature was a green tick stamp, and then printed next to it in a different pen and handwriting were the words REAVE and APPROVED. Reave, thought Heather. Michael Reave.

Her stomach turned over slowly. The name felt oddly familiar, although she couldn't say why. She stood up, putting the letters back in the biscuit tin, and took them with her down the ladder. Back in the kitchen, she spent some time making a quick sandwich and a pot of very hot coffee.

She removed the elastic bands from both piles, and for the next hour read through twenty or so of the letters. By the end of it, her throat felt hot and her head was thumping steadily, the sandwich abandoned on its plate. With a slightly shaking hand she put the letters back in the tin, and thought about all the things she knew about her mother, and all the things she didn't.

* * *

Quiet, well-to-do, respectable Colleen Evans had been writing to a man in prison for the last twenty-five years. She had, in fact, been writing to this mysterious man even before that—while Heather's father had been alive, all through the early years of their marriage. It also appeared that in the '70s, her mother had been a part of some sort of hippy commune, somewhere up north.

Heather rubbed her hand across her eyes, trying to make sense of this new information. Her mum had never been the type for reminiscing, and Heather had never questioned it. Now it was apparent there was a whole stretch of her life that had never even been hinted at. As far as she'd ever known, there had been no other serious relationships with anyone other than her dad. Yet here was this man in the letters. This man who, it seemed, was in prison.

And in all the letters Heather had read, her mother hadn't mentioned that she had a daughter. Not once.

Who was this man? Reluctantly she thought of the suicide note again, the strange phrases her mum had used—as though she was talking to someone as well as Heather.

"Oh, shut up," Heather murmured to herself. "You're jumping to conclusions now."

She gulped down the last of the coffee and pulled her laptop from her bag. Her mother had always been something of a technophobe and had refused to get even dial-up Internet, so Heather had to piggyback off the Internet data on her phone, and within seconds she had the Internet browser page up. She looked at the name, Michael Reave, sitting in the search box.

She paused before clicking search. "There could be nothing at all, right?" she said to the empty kitchen.

The first image that came up was his mugshot, and of course she knew it—it was as familiar to her as the hateful, lax faces of Myra Hindley and Ian Brady, as familiar as the snarling goblin face of Fred West. For a moment the bitter taste of coffee lapped at the back of her throat, and she wondered for an agonizing second if she was going to be sick on the kitchen table, but then her stomach croaked and settled. In the photo, Michael Reave was looking straight at the camera, his tousled black hair not quite meeting his collar. There was none of the blankness you often saw in these sorts of photos; Michael Reave looked aggrieved, even faintly rueful, as though the arresting officers had made some sort of foolish mistake that they'd feel bad about soon. He was unshaven, but it suited him, and the little lock of white hair at his temple only made him seem appealingly quirky. As pictures of serial killers went, it was a reasonable one.

A serial killer.

"Fucking hell, Mum. Fucking *hell*."

There was a Wikipedia page, which in the little introductory paragraph explained that Michael Reave was a convicted serial killer from the UK, known in the British tabloids as "the country ripper," "Jack in the Green," and, more popularly, "the Red Wolf." He was finally caught in 1992, but not before murdering five women in Lancashire and Manchester, with another possible ten victims elsewhere. The article noted that it was widely thought he was responsible for a great many more missing women, but that Reave had always protested his innocence, and continued to do so. The page was oddly truncated; Heather knew Wikipedia well enough to know that anything involving grisly murders tended to have paragraph after paragraph of lovingly researched detail, but here there was little to go on. She scanned through what there was, her lips pressed into a thin line of revulsion. Michael Reave was known for leaving flowers with his victims, sometimes planting them in wounds—Heather looked away for a moment, trying not to picture that—and sometimes winding blossoms through their hair or placing them in their mouths. The "Red Wolf" nickname was one he had apparently given himself; he had left a note with one body reading simply: "the red wolf hunts."

Heather clicked back to the search page. Under the image tab there were pictures of some of his victims. They were young women mostly, their old-fashioned haircuts catching them in time like flies in amber, their images forever linked to the man who had killed them.

The house was very quiet. Heather sat, thinking about her mother, sitting in this kitchen, probably at this table, writing letter after letter to a man who had butchered women. Her daughter in the other room watching television, her husband out at work, while she wrote letters to a killer.

She thought about her mum sitting at the kitchen table, writing a suicide note.

Monsters in the wood.

Feeling sick, Heather picked up her cell phone, her thumb hovering over Nikki's number. She felt cold, and untethered somehow, but she also couldn't help noticing a certain tension in her stomach, a kind of delirious excitement that was oddly familiar; it was a little like the feeling she got when an enormous story landed in her lap. Biting her lip, she pressed the number. When her friend's voice came on the line, it was suddenly difficult to say anything, but she forced the words out.

"Nikki, can I come over? I need to talk to someone."

CHAPTER

6

PUTTING THE MARKING aside finally, Fiona smiled at the little pile of cards and presents on her desk. Her A-level girls had been working on old exam questions, and she was half convinced that their sudden interest in her birthday was all a way of buttering her up, but there were worse things to find on your desk at the end of the day—plenty of teachers had horror stories about that. Besides, Fiona was in a generous mood and willing to forgive a bit of outright bribery; she had about as much interest in reading essays on "Opportunities for and the Effects of Leading a Healthy and Active Lifestyle" as they had in writing them.

Next to her, the radiator ticked on, and she shuffled her chair a little closer to it. No doubt it would be warmer at home, and the cat would be annoyed that she was taking her time, but the girls would be disappointed if she didn't have all the cards opened on her desk first thing in the morning.

She made her way through the pile, smiling faintly at "Happy Birthday Miss Graham" and "Have a great one, Red!!!" Having any sort of distinguishing characteristic as a teacher could be disastrous—a facial mole, a lisp, bushy eyebrows—but Fiona felt like she'd gotten off lightly with red hair. There had been a few less than pleasing nicknames, such as "ginger minge," a gift from a group of especially charmless year eights, but the more grown-up ones seemed to consider it a feature to be admired. Not surprising since they were all in the habit of dying their hair a different color every week.

The presents were small things: little boxes of chocolates, a set of flavored lip balms. One girl, Sarah, had given her a Boots voucher, of all things.

"When I was a kid, teachers were lucky to get an apple," she murmured to the empty classroom.

One of the presents didn't have a gift tag on it and wasn't attached to any of the cards. The wrapping paper was curious; a slightly old-fashioned paisley print, like the lavender smelling paper from her nan's wardrobe, and there were two wilted pink flowers set on top of it.

Frowning slightly, she unwrapped the parcel only to find a large, smooth pebble. It was cold to the touch and made her think of the seaside. Someone, not very artfully, had scratched the shape of a heart into one side of it.

"Huh." Fiona's frown deepened, trying to think of who might do something like that. You did get the occasional artistic kid, the child who savored the role of being the one to do something shocking or different. But then, in all honesty, very few of them ended up in an A-Level PE class. They were all doing Art or Drama.

In the end, she lined up the cards along the front of her desk, and set the pebble down next to them, scratched side facing the class. And then she went home.

CHAPTER

7

BEFORE

THE MAN TOOK the boy to his house, although it was not a house in the sense he knew. It was a vast, sprawling place with shining floors and old, dark furniture, warm with polish. It was clean and cold and silent, with no marks on the walls or dirty cutlery lying around. The big black dog trotted across the wooden floor briskly, its claws clattering the quiet into pieces, and the man came in behind them, taking off his hat and hanging it on a hat stand.

"You can stay here now, Michael. It *is* Michael, isn't it?"

The boy didn't reply. He was watching the dog, which had passed in front of a tall mirror on the wall, and briefly there were two black dogs, eyes like amber fires. The boy followed the animal and saw another creature in the mirror—a filthy stick figure with a shock of black hair, a dark thing smeared with dark matter. Abruptly, he could smell himself, and the thought of being in this clean place and making it dirty forced a noise of distress from his throat. His skin felt hot and prickly.

"*Nuh. Unh . . .*"

"Come on. I'll run you a bath." The man came up beside him and looked down, and for the first time the boy saw that one of his eyes was wrong—the white was a little too white, the brown of his iris too smooth. "You'll feel better, lad."

The man left him alone in a bathroom with a bathtub filled with hot, soapy water. He circled it for a time, unnerved by the slippery white enamel and all the unfilled space in the room. Crisp, yellow light filtered in through a frosted window, and he felt exposed. He did not look in the mirror over the sink. Eventually, after listening at the door for a time, he peeled off his sodden shirt and shorts—chucked in a pile on the floor, they didn't look like clothes at all—and sank into the bath, making small huffing noises as the hot water inched up over his chest. He stayed there until the water was utterly cold, and a thick brownish film had ringed the sides.

Later, he sat at a long table in a set of pajamas that were slightly too big for him, while the man put plates of food in front of him. Soft white bread and pink bacon, crispy brown at the edges; a pat of yellow butter, a jar of pickles, half empty and filled with mysterious murky shadows. A tall glass of milk.

"When I'm away, the woman who cleans the place brings her son to stay," he said. "He's about the same age as you, I'd say, but he's got a bit more meat on his bones. I don't reckon he'll miss a set of pajamas, do you?" The man's voice was warm and soft, unconcerned. The boy thought of how he had smiled at him in the grass, smiled down at the ruined body of his mother. "You can eat the food, lad. It's safe."

Was it safe? The boy wasn't sure. Hesitantly, he curled his hand around the glass of milk but didn't pick it up. Food was a tease, a punishment, a myth.

"How did you get those scars on your neck, Michael? The marks around your wrists."

The boy looked up. The man was still smiling, but the light from the big windows collected in his false eye, turning it into a flat piece of opaque glass. There was a clatter of claws against polished wood, and he knew that the big black dog was behind him again.

"There's always a family everyone whispers about, in every town," continued the man. He sounded faintly amused. "I know that better than most. A family that keeps its secrets, keeps to itself. Rumors and tales grow from those families, like ivy on a house, and most of the time the stories are just nasty gossip, a load of vicious nonsense from old women with too much time on their hands. And then, sometimes, the stories are true, aye, Michael? Something else I know a little about." He took a slow breath in through his nostrils. "You're safe now, lad."

"I can't stay here." It was the first complete sentence he'd said in months, and it felt strange in his mouth, alien. "They'll come for me." He didn't say who.

The man's smile widened.

"Just do as I say, lad."

"They'll come."

* * *

It was three whole days before they came.

In that time, Michael had had four more baths—the smell of the prison cupboard seemed to hang around him—and he had slept in an old-fashioned room with big windows, filled with a blank, white autumnal sky. At night he kept the light on and slipped out of bed repeatedly to check that the door hadn't been locked. He couldn't keep it open, because he could see a sliver of stairs beyond it. During the day he had been allowed to wander the house, feet moving silently out of habit, and he quickly realized that the man was alone here, apart from the dog, and that the rooms seemed endless. Some of them were locked, which gave him a bad feeling in the pit of his stomach, but Michael put his back to those doors and headed elsewhere. Sometimes, he would catch the big black dog watching him, an indistinct shape at the top of stairs or across the landing, and he would beckon to it, but the dog did nothing but grin wetly at him.

When they came, Michael was in the room where he slept, his hands full of a pack of cards the man had given him. There was a crunch of boots against gravel and *he knew*, he knew immediately who it would be, and for a few dangerous seconds his eyelids flickered and his fingers went numb, suddenly close to passing out. But a sharp bark from the dog somewhere in the house acted like a slap, and instead he scrambled over to the window. A doorbell rang.

His father, a bow-legged man with thinning black hair, was standing in front of the porch, but he was alone; no red coat against the gravel, no sharp white fingers. His sister wasn't here.

Michael leaned heavily against the sill, briefly too relieved to think or move, even though he knew that if his father spotted him in the window he would be dead. And then his father vanished from view, and a door slammed.

There was some shouting. Michael thought of his mother's body. They had left it in the lively grass, and he imagined her eyes filling up with rain water, slugs tracing their delicate dance across her yellow smock. Eventually, he became aware that the voices had grown quieter, and without thinking too closely about what he was doing, he crept out onto the landing and peered down through the bannister struts. There was the man, his hands clasped behind his back as though he were admiring a painting, and there was his father. He was wearing a dirty blue rain mac, and he looked strangely small.

Snatches of conversation drifted up the staircase toward him. *You know as well as I do*, and, *sordid business*, and *better left unsaid*.

Michael thought of other words: *beast, dirty beast, animal*, but when he looked up he saw that the dog was there, watching him.

Eventually the door slammed again, and when he looked back his father was gone. The man spoke without moving, knowing somehow that Michael would hear.

"You don't have anything to worry about now, little wolf."

CHAPTER

8

When Heather stepped through into Nikki's living room, she was pleased to see several bookcases rammed with books and a television so enormous it dominated one wall. The décor was soothing and pleasant and clearly chosen by someone without much interest in interior decorating. Heather paused by one small cabinet, smiling.

"I remember these from your mum's house. Is it genetic or something?"

Nikki grimaced. The cabinet contained a little collection of pastel colored ceramic figures, including swans, shepherds, milk maids, and ladies with frothing dresses.

"Don't. Mum buys me a new one for every birthday and every Christmas. I don't know what to do with them. Do you want a cup of tea?"

"Go on then." She followed Nikki into the long kitchen at the back of the house, which smelled pleasingly of some recent spicy dinner. "How was school?"

"Fine, the usual dramas." She was pouring hot water over tea-bags, fragrant steam filling the kitchen. "Are you ok? You sounded weird on the phone."

Heather opened her satchel and pulled out the biscuit tin. Now that she knew what was inside, it felt heavier, like she was carrying around a severed head rather than a bunch of letters. She opened the lid, already looking at the scrabbly handwriting with a sense of dread.

"I found these letters in Mum's attic, under a pile of old records."

"Letters? What sort of letters?"

"Well, I . . . Maybe it's better if you just have a look."

Nikki took the proffered bundle and began reading. Heather watched her face. As Nikki's brows drew together in an expression of confusion, Heather got up and finished making the tea. When she came back to where Nikki stood at the worktop, her friend was holding the paper in her hand as if it might bite her.

"Is this what I think it is?"

Heather half laughed, although she felt very far from amused. "I know, right? I might have been a bit out of touch with my mum over the last few years, but this? This is a bit of a shock."

"Michael Reave. The Red Wolf." Nikki was shaking her head slightly, as though to clear it. "Heather, have you not heard the news?"

"No? What do you mean?" Heather blinked. Normally she was all over the news—since she laughingly still liked to refer to herself as a journalist, she took it as part of her job to keep up with current events—but for the last couple of days she had been, she realized now, avoiding the world. Listening to her mum's old CDs, watching old movies. It was easier to do with no Internet in the house.

Nikki put the letters down and went back into the living room. She returned with a newspaper, which she held out to Heather. The headline read "THE RED WOLF STRIKES FROM WITHIN PRISON," while the lead underneath stated: "Police are concerned a copycat may be at large." Feeling oddly light, as though her head might float up to join the ceiling at any moment, Heather read on.

"Are you fucking kidding me?" she said eventually. Nikki, meanwhile, had gotten her laptop out and was reading rapidly through the same Wikipedia article Heather had seen. Her eyes had grown very wide.

"Hev, this bloke was a monster. He used to arrange the pieces of these poor women's bodies in these elaborate displays, all interlaced with plants and . . . bloody hell, I'm sure I've seen the *CSI* episode based on it. There were bits of their bodies they never found. They still think there are victims they don't know about yet. Hev, did your mum know? Did she know what he was doing before he was caught? Do you think this could have anything to do with her, you know. . ."

Heather shook her head. "I've not read all the letters, but in the ones I've seen, they don't talk about him killing anyone. But I mean, what do I know? Did I even know her at all? This man, currently serving life for chopping women up into bits, apparently knows a whole different side to my mum I've never seen." Heather picked up her hot mug of tea and put it back down again. "She must have known him while he was killing those women, but was she aware of what he was doing? I've no idea. Plus, I don't have any of her letters. Who knows what she was asking him? I mean, did he even know she had a family? A husband? Did my dad know what she was up to?" She half laughed, feeling abruptly sick again. "Oh god, was my mum one of those mad women who gets fixated on prisoners because they think they can change them?"

"Heather, I don't know what to say."

"And then there's the note she left behind. *To you both. The monsters in the wood?* I mean, I thought that was weird enough before I found the letters, and now . . ."

There was a second's silence. Heather could hear a clock ticking in the hallway. She shook her head. Spilling it all out to Nikki only seemed to be making it more unbelievable.

"And he's in the news *now*? What's happened?"

Nikki brought up one of the more reputable news sites on her laptop and pushed it toward Heather.

"An old lady found the body in a field in Lancashire, or at least most of the body. It had been dismembered and placed inside a tree. It's everything the Red Wolf used to do, except that the Red Wolf has been safely packed away in prison for decades." Nikki paused, her lips pressed into a thin line. "And it's not the first one. Do you remember, a few weeks ago, that young woman who went missing from Manchester? Everyone was looking for her."

Heather's stomach turned over. "Sharon Barlow. They found her by a river, didn't they? I remember . . ." Except that the horrible thing was, she didn't remember much. Once the frantic search was over, media attention had faded away and Sharon Barlow became one more woman lost to an unknown monster.

"The police seem to think it was the same guy."

"There will be stuff they haven't told the press, stuff that links the two cases together." Heather thought of her days on the newspaper, sniffing after every tiny detail the police let slip. "Christ, I dread to think.' She looked away from the laptop, trying not to picture what had happened to Sharon Barlow. "So, what? He has a tribute act?"

"He's always said he didn't do it, you know," said Nikki. "Even twenty odd years later, he still says he didn't. What if they have the wrong man after all and maybe . . . your mum knew that?"

Heather curled her hand around the hot mug of tea, trying to find some comfort in the familiarity of it. A new serial killer on the loose, or a miscarriage of justice. Did this man, who had known a side to her mum completely invisible to Heather, also know why she had killed herself? Either way, these were questions she desperately wanted answers to.

"Hev," Nikki said eventually. "Hev, you'll have to take these letters to the police. There could be stuff in here that might be useful to them. Look, there's a phone number here for anyone with information.'

Heather nodded slowly. She thought of the man in the mugshot and wondered what he looked like, twenty-five years later.

"Nikki," she said, "do you think they'll let me speak to him?"

"What?"

"This man knows more about my mother than anyone else on earth. Christ, they could have been phoning each other, Nikki! She could have been visiting him, and I wouldn't have known. I'm sure if anyone knows why she killed herself, it's him. Maybe that's what she was getting at in her note. I want to talk to him."

Nikki placed her hands flat on the worktop and sighed. "I don't know, I really don't. I doubt they let just anyone rock up and talk to these people."

"Well, I'm not just anyone, am I?" Heather picked up the biscuit tin lid and turned it over and over in her hands. She still felt sick, but it was mixed with a tight feeling of excitement in her chest. There could be answers here. "I'm the only daughter of his only friend in all the world, it turns out. Nikki, I need to know. I have to find out what happened to my mum."

"Hev," Nikki met her eyes steadily, and again there was the expression of sympathy Heather found so hard to look at. "Sometimes there are no answers. Sometimes awful shit just happens. All I mean is . . . don't get your hopes up, okay?"

* * *

Heather walked home that night half in a trance. She had phoned the police from Nikki's phone, and had eventually spoken to a man who introduced himself as DI Ben Parker. At first, he had sounded impatient, harassed even, but as she spat out the details of what her mother had hidden in her attic, his voice took on a quiet, musing tone. She had photographed a few of the letters and sent them to him, being sure to include those that had been received before Reave was in prison, and he had thanked her for her help. When she'd asked if she could come to the prison and meet Reave, he had shut the suggestion down immediately, if politely. Standing at the door to her mother's house, wrestling with unfamiliar keys, Heather shivered and glanced uneasily at the tall trees looming on all sides.

"As if this wasn't all creepy enough already."

Halfway up the corridor to the living room she paused, a cold hand curling around her heart. Her mother's perfume hung in the air, strong and unmistakable; violets and lily-of-the-valley, strange and sweet—the same scent from when she'd knocked the bottle over in her mother's bedroom. Every Christmas, Dad had bought her a new bottle of it, and when he'd died, she bought it for herself. It was the only perfume she would ever wear, despite the old woman fustiness of it.

Heather stepped into the living room, sniffing, and just as abruptly the scent was gone.

Perhaps I'm having a stroke, Heather thought as she threw her satchel on the sofa, wincing at the clank as the biscuit tin crashed against something else in her bag. Sighing, she sat down next to it, sinking into the overstuffed cushions. "They say you smell odd things as your brain is turning off the lights."

Thanks to the chintzy pattern on her mother's sofa it took her a few moments to spot the three brown feathers, lying against the soft fabric. Three feathers, small and faintly downy looking, their ends speckled with darker spots. Heather jumped up and looked around the room, although she couldn't have said what she was looking for.

"Is someone here?"

She left the living room and quickly skirted around the house, poking her head into the kitchen, the downstairs bathroom, the utility room—nothing. Upstairs was a similar story, each room sitting in its own little pool of silence, everything undisturbed. Was it possible she had just missed the feathers before? It seemed unlikely. Without her mum to tell her off, she had eaten most of her meals in the living room, a plate propped on her knees and some old film on the television. After a moment's further thought, she went around and checked all the windows, but they were shut, too. It seemed unlikely that a bird could get in, shed a few feathers on the sofa, then find its secret way back out again. Eventually, she returned to the living room and stood looking down at them.

"It doesn't mean anything," she said aloud. The house kept its silence, only the faint hum of the fridge breaking it. But they were brown. Brown feathers, the rounded ends speckled with black. She couldn't help feeling like she'd seen them before, years ago—that these were the exact same feathers. . .

Heather shook her head sharply. The image of her mother, her head all caved in and wet sand on her shirt, gleefully leaving these feathers for her to find, was too sharp and clear. Her mother, still smelling of violets and lily-of-the-valley even though her brains were trickling down her neck, had held the brown feathers stiffly between her broken fingers.

Heather made a small, gagging noise in her throat. Her mouth turned down at the corners, she went back into the kitchen to get a bit of kitchen towel. She used that to pick up the feathers, and then she threw them in the toilet and flushed them away. Once that was done, she washed her hands and turned all the lights on, before pouring herself a large glass of lemonade to settle her stomach.

Calm down, Heather. It's just your imagination and an afternoon spent googling serial killers. It's ok. There's no such thing as ghosts, she told herself.

She had just started to convince herself that she had been overreacting when her phone rang, startling her badly enough to slop her drink down the front of her shirt. Going to the sink to put down her dripping glass, she pressed receive on the phone. It wasn't a number she recognized.

"Yeah?"

"Miss Evans? It's DI Parker again." He cleared his throat, clearly uncomfortable. "Thank you for sending through the images so quickly."

"No problem." Heather licked a drop of lemonade from her hand. "Are they of any help?" She and Nikki had spent some time trawling the Internet for more information, and a woman called Elizabeth Bunyon had been named as the latest victim of the so-called Red Wolf copycat. They had looked at the same photo of the woman, on so many news sites, until Heather felt she'd never forget her face.

"Yes, and no. We have copies of some of them already, of course, as everything Reave sends and receives in prison is monitored."

"I saw that," Heather broke in. "The stamps."

"But the earlier letters are interesting, at least. Miss Evans, I think the key to this isn't in the letters, but more his reaction to them. He didn't know your mother had passed away."

A cold shiver walked down the back of Heather's neck. "You've told him? What did he say?"

There was a beat of silence as DI Parker took a breath. "Very little, really. Michael Reave rarely says anything much, which has long been a source of frustration. But we need him to talk, and quickly. I'm sure you understand why."

In the kitchen, Heather frowned, wondering where this was leading.

"I can imagine."

"He didn't know about you either, that Colleen Evans had a daughter. When your name came up, his behavior changed. I . . ." DI Parker cleared his throat again. "I know we spoke about it briefly earlier, but would you really be willing to come in and speak to him? It's not something we ask lightly, I promise you."

Heather blinked. This was exactly what she had wanted, when she had initially brought up the idea with Nikki, but now that it was being presented to her on a plate, she felt wrongfooted.

"He'll talk to me?"

"He *wants* to talk to you." Parker gave a small grunt of wry amusement. "You're the only one he will talk to. And as I said Miss Evans, we desperately need to find out what he knows about these new . . . incidents. If he knows anything at all."

Heather looked up at the kitchen window, catching sight of her reflection. Her face was pale and her eyes were lost in dark shadows. She found herself thinking of her last day on the newspaper, and the feelings of strength and rage she'd had before it all went to shit. That Heather wouldn't even hesitate.

"Can I see the other letters? The ones my mum sent to him?"

There was a pause on the other end of the phone. ". . . That may be possible."

Heather nodded to herself. It was a start.

"When can I come in?"

CHAPTER

9

THE FIRST THING that was wrong was the cat.

Normally, when Fiona let herself in after a long day of persuading sulky teenage girls to throw a netball at each other, Byron would be immediately on ankle duty, curling himself enthusiastically around her trainers until opening cans of cat food was the only option. But as she let her shopping bag collapse onto the hall carpet—sloppily ejecting a rogue cabbage—the slinky devil was nowhere to be seen. The house was quiet. No ugly rattle of cat litter from the kitchen, and no guilty thump as he removed himself from the kitchen units.

"Byron?"

Muttering to herself, Fiona wrangled the shopping into the kitchen, flicking on lights as she went. Byron was a housecat, much too fancy, expensive, and, let's face it, stupid to be allowed outside unsupervised, but he did occasionally find some new hiding place in the house, vanishing for hours. Once he had managed to squeeze himself into the open suitcase rammed underneath her bed. It was unlike him to pull a fast one at dinner time, however.

Fiona began rattling around in the cupboards, making more noise than was necessary to remove a can of shredded chicken and empty it into a plastic bowl. Normally, these exact noises would bring Byron out of his hiding place at light speed, but the house remained quiet. She placed the plastic bowl on the floor and waited. Nothing.

"Byron? You little sod."

At that point she thought of the wonky window she'd been meaning to fix for the last few weeks. He shouldn't have been able to wriggle his way out of that, but what if he had? Pushing that thought from her mind, Fiona headed upstairs. May as well check everywhere before she started to panic.

The second thing was the smell. It hit her on the staircase, a wild and unnerving funk, like cages at a zoo. She frowned on the landing, thinking that perhaps Byron was ill and had thrown up somewhere, although cat sick was never nearly so powerful.

"Byron, you little sod, are you all right? That food is expensive you know, I'd appreciate you not puking it up every . . ."

The words dropped into nothing, eaten up by silence and the stench.

"Byron?"

She stood by her bedroom door, a sick feeling building in her stomach at the sight of the evening's deep shadows. The smell was worse in here. It was too easy to imagine terrible things waiting for her in the darkness—Byron dead on the bed, his little kitty brain overheated and his fur covered in vomit. Or something else, something worse. A figure in the dark perhaps, watching her.

Abruptly annoyed with herself, Fiona flicked the light switch, watching with no small relief as the big ramshackle room was revealed; cupboard doors half hidden under hanging clothes, the huge bed that was far too big for her, covered in cushions; the nightstand with its pile of dog-eared romance novels. She crossed to the bed and sat down, yanking at the laces on her trainers.

"You've found a mouse, I expect," she said aloud to the room. "You killed it and made a mess, and now you're too guilty to face me. That would explain the stink."

Free of her trainers, she leaned down to pick them up—just in time to see a hand sneak out from under the bed and curl around her ankle.

The fright and the shock were like a hammer blow to her entire body. Fiona made an odd, *whuffing* sound—terror seemed to snap her lungs closed in an instant—and she tried to jump clear, but the hand around her ankle had a strong grip, and it yanked back viciously, causing her to lose her balance and crash to the floor. She hit the floor chin first, padded only slightly by the thick carpet, and as she opened her mouth to scream, she was aware of a great weight on the back of her legs. Whoever it was who had been hiding under the bed was climbing out, crawling up her rapidly. Fiona bucked wildly, attempting to throw them off, but they were bigger than her, stronger. She turned, catching a glimpse of a face hidden in a black woolen mask, and then there was another blow to her head, turning the edges of her vision dark and uncertain.

"NO, no, no . . ."

She brought her arms up and struck him again and again, horrified by the strange weakness in her shoulders. Fright had sucked all the strength from her, and he pushed her back onto the carpet, using his weight to pin her there. For an odd, elastic moment, Fiona remembered putting the benches away with her year seven's: they did it in teams of three, but Fiona could lift one herself, because she was strong, so strong despite her height, everyone said so, everyone said . . . With another clench of horror and shame, she realized she'd wet herself.

"Get OFF of me!"

She landed a blow finally, pushing the man's face back and away from her, but he lunged back and bit her, sinking his teeth into the flesh of her hand just as though he was a rabid dog. The stink, that had never really gone away, increased to the point that it seemed to stop her breath in her throat.

"Get off, help, HELP . . ."

Fiona wriggled backwards frantically, her wrists and her lower back burning fiercely against the carpet weave. If she could just get free of him and down the stairs, there could be someone in the street. Her hand was bleeding and her heart was trying to thump its way out of her chest. He lunged again, and this time she saw that he had a white pad in his gloved hand, which he crushed into her face. A number of smells mingled together, sending spikes of pain into her eyes.

"Listen," he said, quietly, as though they were talking softly together in a library. He pressed his face close to her ear. "Listen. I've come to take you home."

Later, when both the humans were gone, Byron crept out of the trainer cupboard, belly close to the floor. The house still smelt strongly of the stench that had frightened him in the first place, so he slunk downstairs to the front door, which smelt only of blood.

CHAPTER

10

"ARE YOU SURE you want to go through with this? You can still back out."

"Yes, I'm sure," said Heather immediately. If she could get out of bed with this cloud of foreboding hanging over her, if she could get dressed and come here, all the way to this prison and to this anonymous little room without turning around, then she certainly wasn't going to chicken out now.

DI Ben Parker looked at her gravely, as though trying to spot her doubts. He was about an inch or so taller than her, on the stocky side, with sandy hair and hazel eyes—not her type at all, generally, but there was an untidiness to him that was faintly endearing; the knot in his tie slightly skewwhiff, a sense that he had tried to make his hair do something impressive, then given up because he had other things to think about. "Are there any tips you can give me? Any rules? Should I avoid making eye contact or anything like that?"

"He's a serial killer, not Tom Cruise. We're not *monsters*." He gave her a smile that was more eyebrows than teeth. "Just remember, you can leave at any time. He can't reach you and you're not on your own. And, you know, see if you can get him talking. But don't provoke him. Don't deliberately lead him toward conversations that you can't handle. And if I tell you to leave the room, do so immediately."

"Right. Great. Anything else?"

"You'll be fine. If you're ready . . .?"

Heather nodded, not quite trusting herself to say anything that wasn't sarcastic. DI Parker led her into a small room with pastel yellow walls. Inside there were a pair of burly looking prison guards, watching her with interest. And sitting at a wide table, was Jack in the Green, the Red Wolf. Michael Reave.

She had been preparing herself for him to seem pathetic, smaller in real life and somehow pitiable—or at least, she had been hoping for such. But in the flesh, he seemed even more vital and threatening. He was tall and broad across the shoulders, his black hair dusted with salt but still thick, and although he was pale he looked healthy enough. He was wearing a simple white T-shirt and a pair of black tracksuit bottoms—socks but no shoes—and there was a pair of handcuffs around his wrists.

"Michael, we've brought you a visitor."

Reave had been looking at the table, and as he lifted his head, Heather had the strangest sense that he was bracing himself for something. And indeed, as they made eye contact, an emotion flitted across his unshaven face that she couldn't identify. She watched him blink several times as she sat herself down opposite him. DI Parker stood nearby, his arms crossed over his chest. There was a small black box on the table which she took to be a recording device of some sort.

"Mr. Reave, thank you for speaking to me today."

She had an envelope with copies of the letters, which she placed on the table.

"You're Colleen's girl." It wasn't a question. He spoke with a soft northern accent that ordinarily she would have found appealing. "She had a little girl."

"She did. I'm Heather, Mr. Reave, and my mum . . ."

He twitched, as though she had struck him. "Michael. It's Michael, to you."

For reasons she couldn't name, the hair stood up on the back of her neck, and she found herself looking at his hands—big powerful hands, scarred across the knuckles. Despite all her bravado and her certainty that she was going to ace this like some big-time journalist, the idea of being on first name terms with a serial killer had turned her stomach to ice, and she couldn't think of anything to say at all. Bizarrely, it was Michael Reave that saved her.

"I'm sorry, lass," he said. "I mean, I was sorry to hear about your mum."

Heather nodded, contemplating the strangeness of being offered condolences by a serial killer. It all seemed too outlandish to be true; her mother's body crushed against rocks, decades of correspondence with a convicted murderer. This small, yellow room and the man who sat in it. She cleared her throat and shifted in the chair, trying to ignore the compulsion to shiver.

"Thank you," she said. "I hadn't seen much of her over the last few years, but it's been a bit of a shock." She knew that DI Parker hadn't told Reave how she had died—his idea was that hearing it from Heather might provoke some sort of reaction. "She took her own life."

Michael Reave nodded slowly, not looking away. There wasn't a trace of surprise on his face at all, and all at once Heather was glad she had had the guts to face him. He *had* to be linked to it all. There were answers to uncover here.

"You don't seem shocked?" When he didn't reply, she continued. "Did she tell you she was going to do something like that? In her letters?"

"No, lass," Reave's eyes were steady, his gaze not leaving her face. "But life is hard, and some people get . . . all torn up by it."

"Torn up is an interesting choice of phrase." Heather felt rather than saw DI Parker shift behind her. "Mr. Reave, can you tell me anything about why she killed herself? Judging from the letters, you knew her quite well." The idea that he might know the answer, that he could make her mother's death neat and somehow understandable, and yet could choose to withhold the information from her . . . was unbearable. She took a slow breath, focusing on what was in front of her. What had her editor Diane told her, years back, when she'd been an assistant on the paper, fetching coffees and taking lunch orders? *Ears and eyes open, always, Heather. That's the first part of your job.*

Michael Reave tipped his head slightly to one side, regarding her with something that looked suspiciously like pity.

"You're her girl. I reckon you'd have a better idea than me, what was going on in your mum's head."

Heather nodded slowly, conceding the point. "Fair enough. It's hard to lose someone that way though, with all these unanswered questions hanging over you. Maybe it's the hardest way of all."

Michael Reave said nothing. His eyes, she noticed, were a deep dark green; the color of pine needles against snow.

"Why did my mother write to you?"

"She was a friend. A good friend."

"You knew each other for a long time?"

He shrugged. "I suppose we did."

"I had no idea." Heather forced herself to smile, although it felt strange and small on her lips. "Such a long correspondence, and she never once mentioned it to me. I . . . perhaps you can help me understand that?"

"Everyone has secrets, lass." He was still watching her, so closely her skin was crawling. "It's hard for kids to understand, I reckon, but even parents hide stuff sometimes. Your mother had a life before you were born, Heather."

Her name on his lips felt like a threat. Heather looked down at her hands, suddenly desperate to get the conversation away from her.

"Did you confide in my mother, then? Was she that sort of friend? You see, the mum I knew never had any interest in crime, or murders. She wouldn't even watch the news because it was too depressing. So why was she talking to you?"

"She was my friend. An old friend. And I have no one else to talk to here, lass."

"I'm not sure I believe that." An expression of surprise flitted over his face briefly, and she felt like she'd won a small victory. "Not now that your name is back in the news. Surely lots of people want to talk to you about the murders happening up north?"

He smiled slightly, and tugged gently at the chain between the handcuffs, so that they clinked together. "I know nothing about that. How can I? I've been sitting in prison longer than you've been alive, I reckon. How old are you? Everyone looks young to me now," he nodded toward DI Parker, "like that one. He hasn't even started shaving and there he is, giving me the evil eye."

"Once I start, I'll be sure to ask you for tips," said Parker dryly.

"Ok then," Heather leaned forward, catching Reave's eye again. He smiled slightly, and she had to suppress a shiver. There was something in the way he looked at her; like a magpie that had spied something shiny in the grass. He was pleased by her, and she didn't know why. "What about your own past? Can you tell me about the old murders, instead?"

He leaned back in his chair, stretching his arms out in front of him.

"Shall I tell you a story?"

Heather sat up straighter in her chair. Where was this going?

"If you like, Mr. Reave."

"Michael, please." He touched his hand to his mouth, hiding his expression for a moment. "Once upon a time, there was a brother and a sister whose mother died, leaving them in the care of their stepmother, who was secretly a witch. She beat them and let them starve, so the brother and sister ran away, far into the countryside, where they hoped to find their own happiness. But it was a hard journey, and they didn't think to take anything with them, so soon they were so hungry and thirsty they could hardly think straight. Eventually, they came to a stream, and they bent to drink from it, but just before they did the girl heard in the babbling and running of the water a voice, and the voice said, 'whoever drinks of me will become a tiger. Whoever drinks of me will become a tiger.'"

Heather blinked. The strangeness of the situation and his words were making her feel like she was sleeping through a particularly unsettling dream.

"Mr. Reave . . . I'm not sure . . ."

"The witch, you see, had cast a spell on all of the streams. The little sister said, 'oh brother, do not drink from that stream, or you will become a tiger and eat me.' The brother agreed to wait, but when they came to the next stream, she heard the water again, and this time it was singing 'whoever drinks of me will become a bear. Whoever drinks of me will become a bear.' Again, the sister told her brother not to drink, and this time he agreed reluctantly. 'We'll have to drink soon,' he told her, 'or we'll die.' Eventually they came to a third stream, a wide and welcoming one full of sparkling clear water, and they fell to their knees desperate with thirst, their lips all cracked and their mouths all dry. This time, the little girl heard, 'whoever drinks of me will become a wolf, whoever drinks of me will become a wolf.' She begged her brother, and pleaded with tears in her eyes, but there was no stopping him this time. The boy drank the water, and became a wolf, and he tore his sister into pieces."

There were a few beats of silence, into which one of the guards coughed. Behind Heather, DI Parker sighed very quietly.

"Huh. What a charming story." Heather cleared her throat. "Mr. Reave, I'll be honest, telling stories about little girls being eaten isn't the best way to convince anyone of your innocence."

Michael Reave chuckled, his face lighting up in apparently genuine amusement. "I know. Most of the old stories, the ones collected by the Brothers Grimm, sound like they were written by murderers. That story was called Brother and Sister, and it was one of the ones your mum collected. She had loads of them, copied out of old books or written from memory."

"*My* mum?" Heather half smiled in disbelief. "There's no way. Mum didn't like me watching television after 9 PM. All the picture books I had when I was a kid were about flower fairies worried about their pet unicorns. You must be thinking of someone else."

But even as she said it, she was thinking of the torn crumpled page on her mother's dressing table. And the book, the old book she had rescued from under the sofa and discarded.

Michael Reave shook his head slowly, still smiling. "You wanted me to tell you about your mum, didn't you? She loved those stories. Back then, she loved the countryside like I did—wanted nothing more than to be under the sky, to walk in the woods. Those stories were, for her, a link to the time when that's just what we did. When we were rightly afraid of the forest, and we knew the rhythms of the world. My point is, there's likely a lot you didn't know about your mum, lass. That's what people are like. Lots of layers, some of them darker than others. Your mum, she was good at hiding things. Better than anyone."

Heather realized that she had her hands clasped together tightly under the table; tight enough that her fingers were turning white. With some difficulty she untangled them. Her memories of the day at the mortuary seemed very close, as though she might turn to her right and see a cold white table, the cold white faces of the morticians. She squeezed her hands into fists under the desk, concentrating on the dull pain of her nails digging into her palms.

"The countryside, that's right. In the letters you talk about a place where the two of you lived for a while, a sort of hippy commune up north. I thought that sort of thing died out in the sixties, but it sounds like it went on for some years. Is that where you met? What can you tell me about it?"

Michael Reave looked down at the table. All of the animation that had entered his face while he had told his grim fairy tale seemed to seep away.

"I don't see why I should talk about that. It's all ancient history."

"Why not? Everyone getting back to nature, escaping the rat race and so on. In the letters you call it Fiddler's Mill. What was it like?"

He turned his head to look at the far wall, just as though there was a window there he could look out of.

"I think I'm done," he said quietly. "I think I want to go back to my cell now. No more talking for me." Heather blinked, surprised by his sudden change of attitude. As DI Parker touched her shoulder, inviting her to leave, Michael Reave met her eyes one last time. "Did you understand the story, Heather? Do you see what the sister should have done?"

Heather didn't answer.

"She should have drunk the water, too," he said.

* * *

DI Parker offered her a lift back since he was going that way anyway, and she took it gladly, pleased to be avoiding buses as the skies turned dark with rain. The interior of his car was untidier than she'd expected of a police officer—hollow McDonalds cups, empty Tupperware, a few screwed up chocolate bar wrappers—and she spotted a faint pink flush cross his cheeks as she chased a plastic bottle top off her seat. It was sort of adorable.

"Sorry about the mess," he said, grimacing faintly as they pulled out onto the rain-slicked roads.

"Don't worry, you should see my place." Heather paused, both amused and horrified by the way the sentence seemed to hang in the air between them. *Inviting him back to my place already. Bloody hell.* "Do you have a siren hidden in here somewhere? Zipping home like I'm in *The Bill* would mean this day wasn't a total write off."

DI Parker grunted. "Those things are literally for emergencies, Miss Evans. And listen, don't take it so badly. You did well in there today."

"I did?"

He shrugged one shoulder. "It's a start. It's certainly the most I've ever heard him say to someone. He's interested in talking to you, and we have to hope that will open up some new threads. Maybe he'll let something slip. I'd like to put you back in there, if that's all right with you."

Heather glanced out the window. Raindrops had turned the outside world into something uncertain, smeared with red and yellow lights. Despite her description of the session as a write off, she had to admit that it had been fascinating; both Reave and his unsettling confidence, and the morsels of information he had dropped about her mother.

"It's quite the thing, speaking to . . . someone like that. If you saw him in a pub you wouldn't look twice, yet I can *feel* he's holding stuff back. Stuff about my mum." She looked at Parker briefly, feeling vaguely embarrassed. "Hark at me, been in one interview and I think I'm Miss Marple, right?"

DI Parker gave her a brief lopsided smile.

"Anyway. He's scary, Inspector Parker, but the fact that he's been talking to my mother all these years, that there's this whole side to her I knew nothing about, and *then* she commits suicide out of nowhere . . ." She shook her head slightly. "And this new killer. Did you already check out Fiddler's Mill? I mean, back in the day."

"It was searched when Reave was arrested. As best they could, anyway—it's a big piece of land. And Lancashire CID had another look when they realized the link with these new disappearances. It's all very different now, you'd hardly know there had been a commune there." Parker tightened his grip on the steering wheel. "The information on Reave's background is incredibly sparse. Everyone who might have known him when he was a child is dead now, and there's hardly any record of him from those years, and nothing from adulthood. There's a birth certificate, enrolment in an infant's school, and then he seems to just drop off the face of the earth."

Heather pursed her lips, taking this in. "He has got to know something. When do you want me to go back?"

"Give him a day or so to think about it, but otherwise, as soon as possible."

"You really think it could help? With the current murders, I mean?"

"There's every chance Reave has vital information." Parker drummed his thumbs against the steering wheel briefly. "Whoever this new person is, we think he has a personal tie to Reave. The murders are just too similar."

"*Stuff only the killer could know*, things like that?"

He snorted a little and pushed a hand back through his hair. Abruptly Heather could see how tired he was, and how young. Certainly no older than she was.

"I can't really comment on that, but yeah. The original Red Wolf killings were, well, uniquely weird. Michael Reave is a particularly strange monster, and it's a very good thing that he's in prison. But whoever this new guy is? He has certainly done his research." He cleared his throat, apparently realizing he was being unprofessional. "Anyway, Elizabeth Bunyon and Sharon Barlow weren't found in London, of course, but our biggest source of information so far is sitting in a cell at Belmarsh. I'm liaising with Lancashire CID on this, giving them all the assistance we can but . . ." Outside, a set of traffic lights turned green, and for a moment the car was filled with the sound of purring engines. DI Parker apparently drove faster when he was agitated. "Serial murderers are their own kind of unpredictable."

"You're sure it's a serial killer? Is he taking souvenirs?"

"What is it you do for a living again, Miss Evans?"

"Uh, well. I'm a writer."

"*Oh*."

She laughed. "Just bits and bobs, you know. Freelance. Copywriting mostly . . ." She smiled. "Film reviews sometimes. A lot of proofreading at the moment."

"Well." He looked thoughtful now, and Heather got the impression he was talking something through out loud, almost as though she wasn't there. "He's taken a lot of time over the bodies, and there are things—things that were not released to the press about the original Red Wolf murders—that strongly suggest he intends to keep going." He cleared his throat, looking faintly embarrassed again. "I studied criminal psychology. Wrote some pieces about serial murder. The Green River killer, Shipman. Bits and bobs, like you say."

"If he's doing stuff that matches up with the original murders that the public never even knew about . . . *is* it possible it was someone else all along?"

For a long second, Parker said nothing. When he spoke again, he sounded newly sure of himself. "No. Ultimately the evidence against Reave was strong, and while he's been in prison, we've had no more murders like it."

"Until now."

He grimaced. "Until now."

"I'd love to hear more about it, if you have time."

The traffic had slowed, and he had a moment to look over to her. "It's not normally an appealing subject for conversation, Miss Evans."

"Then you can't know many writers. Call me Heather, okay? Bloody Michael Reave thinks it's fine to call me Heather, so I reckon you can."

He chuckled reluctantly at that. "Fair enough."

When they reached the outskirts of Balesford, Heather asked him to drop her off by a row of shops—for reasons she couldn't put a finger on, she didn't want him to associate her with her mother's house. Leaning back to close the car door, she made herself meet his eyes directly.

"I meant it, you know, about having a chat. Balesford is a shithole but there's a decent Chinese restaurant a few minutes from here. Really good Peking ribs."

"Well . . ." To her faint surprise he smiled. "I'm not sure that's really appropriate, Heather." She noticed it wasn't a yes or a no, technically, so she smiled back.

"You've got my number, DI Parker."

* * *

Back inside her mother's house, Heather went into the living room and picked up the book she had found earlier. A book of fairy tales, a wolf on its cover. She thought of the creepy story Michael Reave had told her, of the child that turned into a wolf when he drank from an enchanted stream.

Reave was right, then. Her mother had been interested in this stuff. But why would it be here, lost under the sofa? As though someone had kicked it there.

Remembering the torn page she'd found on her mother's dressing table, Heather began to flick through it, looking for the story it had been ripped from. But quickly she realized this was going to be harder than it looked; many pages had been ripped out and apparently thrown away. There were still illustrations of round cheeked boys and girls, of bears and castles and soldiers, of fairies and goblins and boggarts, their capering figures appearing every few pages.

No wolves though. No wolves left at all.

CHAPTER

11

"NIKKI, IT WAS so fucking creepy I can't even tell you."

"It sounds like it."

They were in Nikki's living room again, the remains of a Chinese takeaway strewn across her formerly pristine coffee table. It was late, and the windows looked too dark to Heather. She was glad her friend had put all the lights on, and even the television with the sound off was a reassuring presence.

"He wasn't what I expected. But what do you expect? I don't know. People like Fred West—he looks like he's crawled out from under some bridge somewhere. Ian Brady has the most amazingly punchable face. Or he did. Jeffrey Dahmer looks like he has creep written through him like a stick of rock. But Michael Reave was like . . . I don't know. A pub landlord from up north who looks after himself. Or," she snorted with sour amusement. "Or the dubious love interest in a Mills and Boon. He broods."

"You think those people look evil or unpleasant because you know what they did," pointed out Nikki. She was sitting on the sofa with her feet tucked under her. She had changed out of her shirt into a big purple jumper, but was still wearing her work tights. There was a ladder in the knee. "Look at Bundy, or Harold

Shipman. They looked normal. Shipman looked like a kindly old man, and he's our most prolific serial killer."

"Hmm." Over the last couple of hours, both she and Nikki had taken a crash course in serial killer research. "Bundy. What a cunt."

"My mum would murder you herself if she heard the language you're using in front of my porcelain figures. That story though . . ."

"I know, right?" Heather snatched up one of the remaining prawn crackers and munched on it. "What a weird thing to come out with. And he reckons my mum was a huge fan of these things." She paused, wondering whether to tell Nikki about the book, then decided against it.

"It's hard to imagine your mum having much time for grisly fairy tales, I have to admit."

"Huh. Yeah. And the thing is, it's a real story. As in, it's a fairy tale that exists. More or less."

Nikki paused with a prawn cracker on its way to her mouth. "It is? How do you know?"

Heather pursed her lips. "I've been reading up on the subject—there are a lot of people on the Internet who spend their time analyzing these things. Anyway, the Grimm's tales have mostly been Disneyfied these days, covered over with sugar and lace and made more palatable, but it seems that once they were every bit as unpleasant as the story Michael Reave told me. The thing is, the Brother and Sister story exists, except he's changed the ending. In the real story, at the third stream the brother is turned into a deer. And then there's a lot of quite complicated stuff about kings and princesses, and eventually the witch herself is torn apart by wild beasts. His version was a lot snappier, it has to be said.'

"Oh." Nikki dipped another prawn cracker into the little plastic container of sweet and sour sauce. "Why do you think he changed it?"

"Lots of these stories got changed, like I said, although not many were changed to be even more violent. Maybe he remembered it wrong, or maybe he was trying to tell me something."

Catching Nikki's raised eyebrows, Heather shrugged. "He said he'd told me that story to demonstrate that I don't know everything about my mum. But maybe there was another message, too."

"That message might well just be 'I want to freak you out.' Are you going to go back?"

Heather nodded.

"He knows something, Nikki. He wasn't surprised at all when I told him what happened to Mum. Maybe they had a pact or something, maybe they were writing in code in the letters." She trailed off, looking at the darkness outside the windows. "Whatever it is, I need to bloody know."

* * *

Walking back to her mother's house later, Heather found herself thinking of Michael Reave's unpleasant fairy story again. It was true that her mother had been strict over her television and reading habits, to the point where Heather had often stayed late round friend's houses, watching all sorts of horrors on VHS tape—the fact that her mum had banned them only made her more determined, obviously—and there had been an entire box in her wardrobe, carefully hidden under old shoes, containing books and comics her mum definitely wouldn't have approved of. The idea that she had once collected especially ghastly stories, sharing them with a future serial killer, seemed impossible; a piece of a puzzle that would not fit together. Yet . . . there was something familiar about the story, even so.

It's just Red Riding Hood, she told herself. *Whether you had an overprotective mum or not, all children become familiar with stories about little kids being eaten by wolves, and maybe you never really forget that first little thrill of horror you felt when you realized that the Big Bad Wolf has eaten Grandma and, ghoulishly, is wearing her nightie. That feeling of wolfishness, that creeping fear of the beast, sinks its teeth into all the old tales.*

"It's all one story," she muttered to herself. "Fear the beast, for the beast is hungry."

Inside the gate, Heather stopped. She had left the living room light on so it wouldn't seem so spooky when she came back, but somehow that blazing square of yellow light, fuzzy and indistinct through the net curtains, only made her feel worse, like it was a portal onto something she didn't want to look at. The pieces of one of Michael Reave's victims scattered on the grass of a remote field perhaps, or her mum sitting at the kitchen table with her head all crushed in by rocks, dutifully scratching out another letter to a murderer while bits of her brain dripped onto the paper.

Shaking her head at herself, Heather went to the door and let herself in. The house was quiet and still, and she made a note to leave the radio on when she went out next time; the silence was too expectant somehow, too eager for her to fill it. She went upstairs to the spare room and changed into her pajamas and then went across the landing to the bathroom. In the seconds before she opened the door, her hand on the handle, she had a flicker of something wrong—a smell, a tiny noise—but it was too late. The door opened and something quick and dark flew at her face.

Crying out, she jumped back, but the thing was already out in the landing, flying hectic circles around the light fitting and crashing repeatedly into walls. It was a bird of some sort. Heather bit down on the shriek that was building in her chest and thumped a fist angrily into the bannister.

"Fucking bastard thing!"

Her heart still racing, Heather went to the airing cupboard and extracted one of her mother's old brooms. With some difficulty she attempted to push the bird toward one of the bedrooms, or back into the bathroom, but it just flew more frantically, making sharp, panicked calls as it hit the ceiling, the lampshade, the walls. Heather swore at it repeatedly, feeling her own fright simmer and ignite into a quickly growing rage. The thing was moving too fast to see it properly, but it was brown, with speckled wings and a slightly oily cast to its feathers.

A starling, she thought bitterly. *Of course it's a fucking starling.*

Eventually, seized with frustration and impatience, she smacked the bird squarely with the thick end of the broom, and it dropped to the carpet with a thump.

"Oh. Oh shit."

Dropping the broom, Heather went over to the bird and looked down at it, grimacing. The tiny chest was rising and falling still, and its beak was open enough that she could see its sharp black tongue. It was stunned. Quickly she went back to the airing cupboard and grabbed a towel, which she wrapped around the bird. It was light, barely any weight to it at all, and as she brought it up to her chest, a flood of memories threatened to overwhelm her; a bird wrapped in one of her old t-shirts, its heart beating against her heart; her dad's face, pink and hectic and somehow afraid. And then later, her mother's hands so white against a black dress, curling into fists.

She shook her head and ran down the stairs to the front door. Outside, the cold air felt shocking against her flushed face and all at once she felt dangerously close to crying.

"Bloody bird," she muttered, walking over the grass to the trees. Instantly her socks were soaking wet and freezing. "Stupid bloody creature."

Crouching by the bushes, she unfolded the towel. The bird was still stunned, but its legs were moving a little, and Heather thought it was going to come to its senses soon. *Best put it down right now,* she thought. *Put it under the bush and maybe a cat won't get it.*

Instead she crouched and stared at it, remembering. She had been taking the long walk home from school, dawdling in the park with the usual suspects. Going home hadn't been particularly appealing at the time, because every conversation with her mum seemed to derail into an argument—arguments about her clothes, about what she was studying, or whether she was really "doing her best" or just coasting along. Nikki and the others, Kirsty and Aaron and Purdeep—she smiled slightly, remembering their names—had been talking about some boy band or other that she wasn't interested in, so she had wandered off, over into the tree line. It had been quiet there, and she had felt at home; certainly more at home than in the house, with her mother prowling restlessly from room to room.

That was where she had found it, the bird. A broken thing in the grass. And she had taken a t-shirt from her bag and carefully picked it up, feeling the flutter of life under her fingertips as she did so.

Shame and guilt, as painful and as unexpected as a punch to the gut, washed over her. Dwelling on old memories suddenly seemed very stupid. Heather stood up, filled with the need to wash her hands, and saw a dark figure standing over her. For the second time that evening she yelled and jumped backwards, slipping on the wet grass, but when she looked again the figure was gone—if it had ever been there in the first place. Angry and tired, she left the bird under the bush, still on its towel, and went back inside the house.

C H A P T E R

12

BEFORE

ONE NIGHT, MICHAEL woke up in a darkness so complete it hummed. The safe, warm electric light that burned from the shaded bulb in the ceiling had vanished, casting him into the black; sending him back, in an instant, to the cupboard. Suddenly it was impossible to know where he was, who he was, which way was up. He gasped in great whooping breaths of hot, fetid air, air that tasted of musty clothes, of old food and fresh shit, of the red coat, the red coat, the red coat . . .

He flung his arms out, and when his fingernails skittered against old splintered panels he began to shriek over and over again. Soon his mother would come storming up the stairs to see what the noise was about, her doughy arms trembling with rage, or his father, already whipping the belt from his trouser loops, or worse, perhaps *she* would come, smiling and kind, her sharp hands seeking his skin . . . but the noises from his own throat wouldn't stop—he was a wounded animal caught in a trap, tearing itself to pieces. Abruptly he felt a hot muzzle press itself into his hand, a wet blast of breath through his fingers, and the sensation surprised him so much he clamped his mouth shut, his teeth nipping the end of his tongue.

A second later and the man was in the doorway, the beam from an old electric torch chasing away the confines of the cupboard to reveal the room, exactly as it had been. The dog wasn't there.

"It's nowt but a power cut, lad." In the dazzle from the torch, the boy couldn't see the man's face, but the shape of him was so unlike anything from home—*the red coat the red coat the red coat*—that he felt the air transform, becoming clear again, slick and clean and free of terror. "Come downstairs if you're going to take on so, I've all the candles out. Is your mouth bleeding?"

* * *

The next day was wet and blustery, but the man made him put a coat on—again too big, the bottom of it came down to his knees—and they went walking outside. The area around the house was green and isolated; Michael could see fields and hedgerows, and a tangle of dark woods. It was this that the man led him toward, their trousers quickly becoming heavy with water from the tall grass, and as they passed under the dark twisted trees, Michael shivered and blinked, feeling more awake than he had for days.

"This is Fiddler's Wood," said the man. "It's ancient." There was a clear note of pride in his voice. "Primrose, wood anemone, yellow rattle, dog roses. Bluebells, in the spring. Flowers that mean a place is old, that a place is a leftover from the ice age." He looked down at Michael, his false eye dull. "You don't care for flowers none, I expect, but that's not what I'm going to show you."

Not far from the wood's edge, they came to a small domed building, sunk deeply into the black dirt. It had been built from red brick once, but the colors of the woods had leeched into it. Green moss and yellow lichen covered it, until it looked like a natural thing, a growth on the forest floor. There was a low padlocked door set into the front of it.

"This is an ice house," said the man. "A lot of big old houses have them. I want you to think about your mother, lad." He dropped his hand onto Michael's shoulder, and Michael felt cold fear move through him like a shower of stones.

"What's in there?"

"Your mother was not a good woman, but I imagine you know that better than most. Your whole family is . . ." He stopped and pushed the boy forward slightly. "But I don't want you to remember that, lad. I want you to remember the last time you saw her. You got that? Are you listening to me, boy?"

He stepped forward, smoothing a key from his pocket, and he unlocked the door. Cold air moved across the boy's face. It smelt brackish and strange, like water left to stand in a bucket for weeks.

"Are you thinking of it, lad? The last time you saw her?"

The boy did not move. He was remembering the odd feeling of weightlessness in his stomach as they'd fallen down the stairs, the delicious sensation of hurting that which had hurt him.

"Remember the time when you had complete power over her," said the man. He settled his hands on Michael's shoulders again and gently pushed him through the door of the ice house. The ground sloped away ahead of them, and Michael felt his over-sized boots moving through a gritty kind of sludge. The daylight from the door revealed a dank room, the walls smeared with creeping black mold, and it was cold, much colder than outside. There was a shape in front of them, resting on a long, low stone bench. Michael looked at it. The man squeezed his shoulder.

"Remember the *power* you had then, lad. Remember it."

The shape was his mother. She looked small, curled in on herself. Her limbs were dark, as though her skin were one big bruise, and he could still see the flash of white bone poking through her arm where it had torn itself free. The yellow smock was no longer yellow. Her face was turned away from him, but he could see the jut of her jaw and her cheekbone, which looked larger than it had. He imagined her staring at the far wall, imagined her whispering into the dark. *Dirty beast, filthy little shit.* Michael made a small strangled noise in the back of his throat.

"No,' said the man, firmly. "Look at what she is now. She's nothing. Do you see?"

He pushed the boy forward sharply, so that he almost fell onto the corpse. All at once Michael was inches away from the torn flesh of his mother, her rotten fingers like small brown sticks.

And he saw it.

He saw that she was a small pitiful thing, a broken shape on the landscape of his rage.

"That's it, my lad. That's it. When you are the wolf, the likes of her are just meat. Bad meat."

CHAPTER

13

If Heather had one good habit, it was that she was early to everything. Arriving at Belmarsh a good hour before she was needed, she had taken root in a greasy spoon in Thamesmead. Heather had a begrudging sort of affection for Thamesmead; like Balesford, it clung to the bottom of London like a sort of crusted canker, but it at least had the good sense to be cluttered with lots of brutalist architecture—looming gray concrete wherever you happened to look, and that vague sense that once this urban landscape had existed only on the design sheets of an extremely optimistic architect.

She ordered a bacon and egg sandwich and a cup of tea, and sat near the window, looking out at a high street crammed with betting shops and fried chicken places. Eventually, she pulled out a folder of scanned letters. Ben Parker had given her a few copies of the letters her mother had sent, and these she had already read feverishly, rigid with indignation, but ultimately, they hadn't told her much at all. Mostly the letters were short and polite, talking about inconsequential things like the changing of the seasons, the weather, or her dinner plans. Heather couldn't make head or tail of them; you would never guess that the woman was writing to a convicted serial killer. Every now and then they would drift slightly, mentioning a place she had visited in her youth, but always her mother brought things back on track quickly. Heather had asked Parker why she couldn't see all the letters, and he'd reluctantly explained that even murderers had rights—although Reave's mail was monitored, they only made copies when they felt the letter contained something that might be useful. Mostly they didn't. That could change as the investigation progressed, but for now, they wanted Reave on side.

Inevitably, Heather found herself turning back to the letters of Michael Reave himself, the ones apparently so precious to her mother she had hidden them carefully away in the attic.

. . . I know you couldnt be with me Colleen. I am happyer here under the sky. Would be happyer with you, but I cant have everything. Ive always known that . . .

. . . in all my life Ive never been close to anyone but you . . .

Heather put the letter down. The foundations of her life seemed weak and ghostly, something that could vanish entirely in just the right shade of moonlight. She thought again of the bird that had managed to trap itself in her bathroom. Even in a busy café, smelling of bacon and coffee, it was hard not to think of that as an omen . . . At that moment, the woman arrived with her sandwich and tea, and she seized on this normal interaction desperately, nodding and smiling at the woman so much that she looked quite put out. When the waitress had retreated back to the safety of the counter, Heather returned to the letters.

. . . Ive never seen a storm like it. They said on the television that it would pass over without damage, but they couldnt have been more wrong. You should have been out here Colleen where it gets really dark. The howling of the wind was so loud it was like a voice. And so many trees down. It hurts me to see the woods so broken . . .

. . . Theyre selling the big house at Fiddlers Mill. Its going to be a retreat for the rich can you believe it? Men and women who want to get out of the city and be in the green but don't understand why, so they wear dressing gowns and get massarges . . .

Heather put the letters down and pulled her laptop from her bag. There was, unsurprisingly, no wi-fi in the café so she piggybacked off her phone again. A quick bit of googling told her several things: that a big stretch of land known as Fiddler's Mill had indeed been the location of a commune in the 1970s, outstaying its welcome slightly but still supposedly dedicated to the ideals of peace, free love, and copious drug use. Now the big house known as Fiddler's Mill was partly home to a fancy spa complex, which had been in existence since the early '90s. The land and the spa were partly owned by an environmental charity called Oak Leaf, and indeed the emphasis was on the environment, healthy living, detoxes, and other things Heather was naturally repelled by. It looked, to a woman recently booted out of a modest salaried journalism job, mind-bogglingly expensive.

She opened a new page and delved a little deeper into the old Fiddler's Mill, the one that existed before the fancy spa. Very quickly she found herself down a rabbit hole crammed with erratically written blogs and ugly webpages awkwardly chucked together by people too old to be comfortable online but too keen to share their memories to give up. At first it seemed fairly innocuous, with most recalling a lot of music, a lot of drink, a lot of young people having a good time. There were a few photographs scattered about, showing people with long hair and a relaxed attitude to grooming, more acoustic guitars than Heather thought was healthy, and a lot of food being cooked outdoors. There was the central building, a reasonably impressive eighteenth-century house and its grounds, and a number of tents and caravans, a few temporary shed-like things thrown up, and lots of cars.

There was an edge to it all, though. Perhaps it was because they had left the '60s behind and were ensconced in the grottiness of the '70s, but in the photographs Heather saw a lot of hard eyes, a lot of people who were thinner than they should have been. She saw one photo of a pregnant woman sitting by a campfire, one hand resting on her distended belly; far from glowing with maternal satisfaction, her face was hard and distant, as if carved from flint. Heather wondered, looking at the photographs, if weed was the only drug of choice at Fiddler's Mill—she doubted it. And in the blogs and diaries and articles, she unearthed a line of discontent that spoke of poor facilities, abuse, and even fraud.

"My mum was here," she muttered to herself. Saying it out loud seemed to edge it closer to reality. "*My* mum. She must have been very different back then."

Following back some of the more outraged accounts, she found a handful of posts by a woman calling herself whytewitch59 who seemed to be claiming that all sorts of shadowy things went on at Fiddler's Mill in the '70s and even the '80s, although she never quite managed to name them. There was a picture of the woman in the top right-hand corner of her webpage, revealing a ratty face topped with a woolly hat that had to be home made. Heather combed through these accounts, looking for the sorts of details that a story could be built on, but ultimately came away with the impression that the woman had probably been looking for a place to find connections, and instead had done a lot of drugs, only to end up lonelier than before.

Her pictures, though, were something else. Clicking on a "gallery" tab at the top pulled up a long page of photographs and paintings, all of which appeared to be of the countryside and, specifically in some cases, Fiddler's Mill. Heather recognized the looming eighteenth-century house in some of them, either dominating the frame or appearing as a blocky shape in the distance. All of the photographs were in black and white, lending them a gloomy air, and there was something unnerving about them. Fields of wheat under a blank, blind-looking sky, and close-ups of grass, focused on stones and sticks placed in odd, concentric patterns. There were lots of photographs of trees, too, many of them dark and deeply shadowed, as though taken at the very tail end of the day, as twilight soaked up through the ground, or in the middle of a very dense forest. There was something claustrophobic about those photos, and Heather found herself frowning as she looked at them.

There were paintings, too, in a similarly limited palette of blacks and grays, greens and yellows. Trees like grasping fingers tore at a jaundiced sky, shadowy white figures moved through a field lit from within with green lights. In one of the paintings, Heather recognized the solid shape of Fiddler's Mill House crouched alone at the top of a hill, and far to the right, emerging from the woods, a figure dressed in a shapeless red garment. This last painting Heather looked at for some time, until the café woman came and took her empty plate away. Her tea had gone cold.

Heather put whytewitch59's webpage into her favorites, for no other reason than the sense she would want to look at the pictures again. Impulsively, she went to the "contact me" page and sent whytewitch a quick message—"Hi, my name is Heather Evans, how are you? I really love your work and would love to chat about it and your time at Fiddler's Mill. I'm happy to talk online, or if you're London based, maybe we could grab a coffee—on me." She added her email address and clicked submit.

When she'd done that, another thought occurred to her. Taking out an old USB stick from her handbag, she spent some time saving a few of the photographs and paintings on to it. There was a small Internet café, a few doors down, that offered printing—she'd seen it as she'd wandered up the road. Perhaps Reave would be more willing to talk about Fiddler's Mill if he could see it.

* * *

HMP Belmarsh looked more like an industrial estate from the outside, but up close it was an impressive monstrosity of brown brick. DI Parker wasn't there to meet her this time; instead she was greeted by a short man with an overly orange tan who introduced himself as DC Turner, giving her approximately three seconds of his attention before turning back to his phone. Parker, he explained with an absent expression, was up north again. Heather was surprised by the genuine pang of disappointment she felt.

"What's happened? Has there been another murder?"

He jerked his head up and stared at her, as if only just realizing she was with him at all.

"I can't really comment on that, love."

"Okay then. Don't call me love, yeah? Thanks."

He turned away from her with a long-suffering sigh, and she knew immediately that she would never form a long and lasting friendship with DC Turner. In truth, she generally didn't mind people calling her love, or honey, or even treacle, if they didn't look like a miserable piss-pot dickhead with a tanning bed fixation. *DI Parker, with your charmingly messy hair and hazel eyes, come back, all is forgiven.*

"Anything you want me to try and get him to talk about?"

They were outside the small interview room, and Heather could see Michael Reave already, sitting with his hands clasped in front of him on the table. DC Turner raised his eyebrows at her.

"Just do what you can." He opened his mouth, and she could feel the "love" dangling there, half formed. ". . . Miss Evans."

This time when they entered, Michael Reave lifted his head and watched her sit down. There was a plastic cup of water in front of him, and his hair had been carefully brushed back from his forehead. He had also shaved, but Reave appeared to be one of those men whose five o'clock shadow could only be chased away by the razor briefly. He wore a long-sleeved navy jumper, and he leaned forward as she sat, his elbows on the table.

"Hello, Mr. Reave."

He smiled lopsidedly. "What do I have to do to get you to call me Michael?"

"Not have murdered a load of women?" The answer was out before she could stop herself, but to her surprise his smile turned into a grin—it was brief and then gone, an oddly boyish expression.

"I didn't, but I can hardly blame you for thinking that." He tipped his head to take in the tiny room, the chains at his wrists, the burly guards behind him. "They're letting us have another chat, lass. You must have impressed them."

Heather shrugged. "I reckon you did that, Mr. Reave. What would you like to talk about today?"

"I thought of another story to tell you. It's another one your mother liked. Would you like to hear it?"

Heather paused. "I do want to talk about my mother. And Fiddler's Mill. I'd love to know what she was like when she was there—and what the commune was like, too."

Reave looked away, staring at the door. His hands, she noticed, were covered in little white scars; the hands of someone who worked outdoors, who worked with knives.

"I'll tell you a little about that place," he said eventually. "If you listen to my story."

"All right then." DC Turner hadn't offered her a cup of tea, or anything to drink, and she felt she had nowhere to put her hands. Self-consciously she rested them on the table. "Tell me a story."

"Once upon a time," there was a flash of that boyish grin again, "there was a king, who had a beautiful daughter. The princess sought a husband, but she insisted that any man who married her must love her so much that on the event of her death, he must agree to be buried alive in her tomb—"

"They told these stories to kids?"

Reave was still smiling, but there was a coldness to his eyes, and she suspected he did not appreciate being interrupted.

"These stories were told around the fire, at night. They told people how to live right, how to see the dangers in the forest." He sat up a little straighter and continued. "The king was rich, and the princess was beautiful, but all her suitors had been scared off by the terms of the marriage. Eventually though, a young soldier in the King's army, known for his bravery and strength, met the princess and fell deeply in love. He declared that he was not afraid of her conditions, and they married. For a while, they were very happy. The whole kingdom was happy."

"Well, that's good. I don't suppose they all lived happily ever after?"

"After a few years, the princess grew gravely ill, and after lingering a while, she died. The soldier, now a prince, remembered with horror what he had agreed to and thought of fleeing the castle, but the king put guards on every door and window, and had the soldier watched every moment of every day. When the day of the funeral came, the soldier could do nothing but be marched to the princess's tomb, and he was sealed in there with her corpse."

"So, the princess is a loon, clearly, but it sounds to me as if the whole family was nuts. Surely the sensible thing to do would have been for the king to say, all right, she had her funny ways, we will miss her terribly, and now let's never speak of it again." Heather watched his face closely, interested to see if she could provoke a reaction—a man who cut women into pieces would surely have a temper, she reasoned—but Michael Reave just nodded slightly, as if he agreed with her, and carried on.

"They had given him candles, so he lit one and waited for death, watching the body of his beloved. There were flowers entwined in her hands, dog violets they were, and they matched the color of her lips. Soon he grew hungry, and thirsty, but there was nothing he could do. Eventually, a little snake crawled out of a hole in the wall—small and green and quick. Thinking it meant to bite the dead princess, the soldier leapt up and cut the snake into three pieces, killing it dead."

Reave paused, brushing his fingers against his lips as if remembering something.

"A little while later, another snake slithered out of the hole, and seeing its dead brother, immediately retreated. However, it soon returned carrying three leaves in its mouth. These it placed over the severed pieces of the other snake's body, and in moments, the dead snake was alive again. They disappeared back into the wall together, leaving the snake-leaves behind. The soldier, barely hoping to believe it could be true, retrieved the leaves and placed them on the eyes and mouth of the princess, and in half a breath the blood flowed again to her blue lips, and she leapt up, full of life. Together they banged on the tomb doors until the guards came and let them out. The soldier and the king were both so happy, and the kingdom rejoiced for seven days and seven nights."

"Does this have a point, Reave?" broke in DC Turner. "We didn't bring this woman all the way here for creepy story time."

"I brought myself, actually, and I want to hear the end."

If Reave appreciated her support, he didn't show it. Instead he carried on as if neither of them had spoken. "But the princess had come back changed. With her new blood red lips came a new power, and new appetites. She would haunt the kitchens, stealing pieces of raw meat and eating them. The castle's dogs and cats began to go missing, and then, the beggars that waited by the back gate found their numbers lessening. There are gifts, and then there are prices that must be paid. There is a becoming, we . . ."

He stopped, and met her eyes again. "One day, the princess went to the armory and dressed herself for war, and she went directly to the king's chambers, and killed him. She did not kill the soldier, but kept him obedient in her room, and ruled over the kingdom herself for the rest of her days."

An uneasy silence seeped into the room, while DC Turner coughed and sighed behind her. Heather thought it likely that this story had been given a new ending, too, just as the story of the brother and sister had—surely even the unpleasantness of the Grimm's stories could not end with so much implied strangeness.

"I'm not sure if that's a happy ending or not."

Michael Reave shrugged. "Colleen . . . I mean, your mum, enjoyed that one. The roles of women in these stories were interesting to her. They were witches, and people hated them, but they had power."

"Did she talk about these stories at Fiddler's Mill?"

He looked up at her almost admonishingly, seeing through her ploy easily enough. "Aye."

"And is that where you met? How old were you when you were there?"

Reave lowered his chin to his chest, letting out a slow breath.

"My family lived nearby there, and I just . . . drifted to the place as I got older. I did odd jobs for the man who owned it—tidying the place up, mending things. It became my home. Colleen turned up there in . . . the spring of 1977 I think it was."

"In 1977, my mum would have been fifteen . . . She was just wandering around the countryside? She was a kid. What about school?" She stopped, realizing she sounded like an outraged aunt and Michael Reave was laughing at her.

He shrugged. "Things were different then. Colleen, she was wild, she didn't get on with her dad, she didn't get on with school . . . It was easier for kids to just get up and leave. No cameras watching, still wild places to hide. And the man who owned the land, he was good at making problems go away."

Heather blinked, trying to imagine her mother as a rebellious teen. A few weeks ago, that would have seemed laughable, but now her mother seemed to be a shifting presence, someone that could change at any moment.

"This man. Who was he? The owner?"

"I don't remember."

That was an obvious lie. Heather ignored it.

"I've done some research into the place, read blogs and articles. It sounds like it was quite the party central, if you were part of the gang. A lot of drugs and free love?"

Reave shrugged. She could tell he was losing interest in her.

"Did you meet a lot of people there, Michael? A lot of women?"

"A few."

"A lot of people think you're responsible for a number of missing women we don't even know about yet. Do you want to tell me about that?"

This time he didn't even shrug, and the expression on his face was flat and very still.

"Mr. Reave . . . Michael, look, everyone believes you murdered those women. The whole country thinks of you as the Red Wolf." She thought she saw a flicker of some new emotion in his eyes at that. "Maybe you can think of me as a neutral party." She shrugged slightly. "Before I found those letters, I didn't really know anything about you. Not anything beyond the tabloid headlines, anyway. Maybe you could take this as an opportunity to tell me how *you* saw things. Tell me your story."

He watched her now, a tiny crease appearing between his eyebrows. He shifted in his chair, and Heather saw that he was considering it.

"My story?"

Heather nodded.

"My story." Reave leaned back in his chair and looked at the wall. The prison guards shifted; one of them crossed his arms over his chest. They both looked bored. "I was a poor country kid. My father did odd jobs for people, some of them less than legal, I reckon. My mother was an angry woman. She didn't like me much, but then I don't think she liked anyone much. She was cold and turned inwards on herself, wouldn't speak for days sometimes. I remember her stoking the stove up until it was fair spitting sparks, and she would sit by it for hours, until one side of her was all red and mottled, just staring at nothing. When she was angry with me, she would shut me away." He cleared his throat and met Heather's eyes again. "When a doe rabbit has kits, Heather, she has to feel completely safe. If she doesn't feel safe, lass, if she feels that there is a predator in the woods, do you know what she'll do?"

Heather shook her head.

"She'll eat her young to save herself. A kit is all scent and hot blood, Heather—it doesn't know that it's like a beacon for hungry things. It'll lead the predator to the mother rabbit, and she can't have that. She'll eat her own babies to save herself."

The prison guard had uncrossed his arms, and was now staring at Reave with a look of open dislike.

"I— "

"It sounds monstrous, but some things are just not born with maternal instincts. Some things are born scared, rabbits being one of them."

"Was there a predator in your house growing up, Michael?"

He smiled then, a really genuine smile, and she found herself recoiling in confusion, because he looked *vulnerable*. He looked lost.

"No one cares about my story, lass. No one cares about poor kids growing up in dirty houses that are never warm, or about what they have to do to live. What they have to do to get out. Not even you, girl."

I do care. The words were on her lips for the briefest second, but she couldn't quite bring herself to say them. Those words might be the key to getting the rest of his story, yet she found she could only think of the photos of the girls that were forever linked to his name. *I do care*, she thought. *I care about them and my mother. I care about Sharon Barlow and Elizabeth Bunyon.*

"Was Fiddler's Mill your way out, Mr. Reave? Is that where you escaped to?"

He said nothing to that.

Not taking her eyes off him, Heather reached into her bag for the folder in there and pulled out the prints she'd had made. Each of whytewitch's pictures and photographs had been blown up to A4 size, a little larger than the file could take, it turned out, but something about the graininess of the images made them more impressive. The first photograph she slid across the table toward him. It showed bleak fields, a cluster of tents off to the right, and Fiddler's Mill House in the distance.

Reave looked down at the picture without moving or speaking. Heather couldn't be sure, but she felt like he was holding something back again, as he had when he had first laid eyes on her.

"Do these bring back any memories?"

He tipped his head to one side; a noncommittal answer.

"I guess you spent your formative years there, it's difficult to forget." She placed the second picture on top of the first; another photograph, this one of more tents, slightly blurry people coming and going, smoke coming from several places. "I found these online, taken by a woman who calls herself whytewitch, would you believe. She was there at Fiddler's Mill in the '70s, too. Do you remember her at all?"

He looked away, a flexing in his jaw that told her he was not happy. *Not happy.* Heather thought of her mother's body lying broken at the bottom of a cliff, of the faces of the women who came up on a Google image search under *his* name. With a flourish, she produced more pictures, dumping them one on top of the other. Reave looked at them impassively, as though they were a work colleague's boring holiday snaps.

"She took a lot of photos back then, and she was an artist, too. She found it a very inspirational place, I guess. What did it mean to you, Michael? What did it mean to my mum?"

"Lass, I understand your pain over your mum, I really do," said Reave, his voice slow, a soft parody of compassion. "You want to understand what she did. But perhaps there's no understanding something like that. No understanding the fear that makes you eat your own babies, or the fear that makes you kill yourself."

Heather said nothing.

Images of whytewitch's paintings were next, and the one of the figure in the red coat emerging from the woods went skittering across the slippery pile, almost landing in his lap. Michael Reave looked down at it, and abruptly he was yanking on the chain around his wrists, pulling hard enough that Heather felt the bolted table jump under her hands. She yelped and scrambled back even as Reave was standing, still repeatedly yanking on the chain, apparently trying to pull the whole thing up by the roots.

"That's enough."

DC Turner's hand was on her shoulder, gripping it none too gently, and before she really knew what was happening, she was being propelled out of the room. Just before the door slammed shut, she saw the two guards moving in toward Reave, and she caught the expression on his face; he was furious, points of color high on his cheeks. And then the view was cut off.

"What . . .?"

Abruptly, Heather realized her legs weren't holding her up properly, and she fell against the wall. DC Turner was glaring at her and rubbing the back of his neck.

"I think that's going to be your lot, Miss Evans."

"I . . . what happened?" It was difficult to breathe—she felt roughly the same as the time a car had turned a corner unexpectedly on Peckham high street and nearly run her over. His sudden eruption from calm boredom to violent rage had made her dizzy.

"You pissed him off." Turner shrugged. "You can't predict people like that, love, so don't feel bad about it."

"But we were getting somewhere!"

"It costs money, stuff like this. Did you know that? I didn't expect you would." He curled his lip, then made an effort to arrange his features into a sympathetic expression. "Me watching over you, those guards in there. We've all got better things we could be doing—me especially, given we've got another nut like him on the loose."

"Hey, you people asked me to do this." Heather pushed herself away from the wall. "Where is DI Parker? I want to talk to him about it."

Turner laughed and gestured down the corridor. "Now, DI Parker definitely has better things to be doing than talking to you, I'm afraid. It's time to go."

"Can I at least get those printouts back?"

Turner sighed dramatically again, and Heather wondered how well he'd be sighing if she slammed her elbow into his nose. The incident at the newspaper loomed large in her thoughts—the sound of gagging, blood dripping onto a biscuit-colored carpet—and she clenched her fists instead.

"If he hasn't torn them up, you're welcome to them."

An hour or so later, as Heather sat in a bar in Lewisham nursing a shot of whisky to calm her nerves, DI Parker called. She cleared her throat and answered, willing herself to sound cool and professional.

"I was sorry not to see you today, DI Parker. Belmarsh is a lot more appealing with you in it. Plus your mate Turner is a waste of skin."

"How did it go? With Reave?"

"You mean you don't know?"

There was a beat of silence before Parker replied.

"You've got to expect him to be temperamental. Difficult to understand. But even how he reacts to things can be useful to us."

"He knows more about my mother's death than he's telling, I'm sure of it." Heather picked up the glass of whisky, picturing her mother's face briefly, creased and stern, as it often was. "I'd like to keep going, if that's possible."

Parker made a noncommittal noise. "Our priority has to be your safety."

"Aw, I'm touched. But he's chained to the table, and you've got your giant blokes there. What could he do?"

"Not all damage is physical, Miss Evans."

Heather took a sip of whisky, grimacing against the burn in her throat. She thought of the morgue, and her mother's broken body. She hadn't seen it, of course—ultimately the body had to be identified with her dental records and the engraved wedding ring still on her finger—but it was funny how little phrases stayed with you, particularly when you had a vivid imagination. Her mother's bones, shattered into lethal shards; her mother's hair, heavy with sand and pieces of rock. *Physical damage. Organic material.* The bar, just starting to get busy, dipped and weaved around her as if she was on the deck of a boat, and she forced herself to focus on Ben Parker's voice. He was speaking again.

". . . no way to know it's related, but it smells like it is to me. It'll be in the papers by now."

"I'm sorry, what?"

"A woman called Fiona Graham appears to have been taken by force from her house. There are reasons to believe this is our copycat again."

"Fiona Graham?" Heather blinked. It was like being dunked in cold water. "I feel like I know that name."

"You do? Where from?"

"I'm not sure." She willed herself to remember, but despite a strong sense that she'd heard the name before, no other details came to mind. "I'll have to think about it," she finished lamely.

"If you do remember, let me know."

"Sure. Listen . . ." She bit her lip. The familiarity of Fiona Graham's name had brought back some of the tight excitement to her stomach despite her unpleasant afternoon at the prison. There were clues here, pieces to a larger puzzle, and she just had to get them all lined up to get her answers. Maybe, in fact, she was the best person to do it. "Are you up for a drink at all? A chat? Today has shaken me a bit, and I could do with looking at a friendly face."

"Heather, we've got our hands full here, and I'm not even in London . . ."

In the bar, Heather closed her eyes, wincing.

". . . but maybe when I'm back?"

She put the glass down. "Absolutely. Give me a shout."

From there the conversation became awkward, and she sensed him mentally retreating from her. Standing in the bar, her cheeks were warm with embarrassment, but she couldn't feel entirely bad about asking him out so blatantly—later she would go back to an empty house, with nothing to think about but murdered women and the mystery of her own mother's death. Was it so terrible to want company? The whisky was sour in her throat, and after she said her goodbyes, she downed the rest without pleasure.

CHAPTER

14

BEFORE

MICHAEL LIVED AT the big house, but Fiddler's Wood was his home.

He spent most of his days out there, whatever the weather, tramping through the undergrowth, sitting with his back against a tree or following half-hidden paths to places that seemed significant; a dead tree, blasted black and white by lightning decades ago; a deep ditch riddled with dog roses; a trio of birches, growing up together, twisted and light-dappled. Under the rain and wind and ever weakening sun, he grew taller and stronger. The marks on his wrists and neck faded, and the hair at his temple grew back, although it was the color of moonlight now.

There were still nightmares most nights. He dreamed of the cupboard, or he dreamed of his mother's thick fingers twisted in his hair, her face contorted with rage, or slack and absent. Sometimes, he dreamed of a flat, red landscape, the sky the color of dusty roses, and there were things on the land, desperate, howling things, and from these dreams he still woke screaming, but the knowledge of the wood outside his window—dark and cool and green—was a balm to him.

Michael did not go to school, although he could not really remember ever going to school. He had some very vague memories of being left at a place with lots of children who did not want to speak to him, and he had an impression he had not been there for long. Instead, the man let him look at the books in the one room in the house that was full of them, and to Michael's surprise he found that the words did make some sort of sense. The man largely left him to his own devices, providing food when Michael reappeared from the woods, covered in mud, or sometimes walking out with him across the fields, the big black dog somewhere in the grass ahead.

One day in the spring, the man caught him at the door just as he was hopping into a pair of boots.

"I've got something to show you today, lad," he said. "Come on."

He whistled between his teeth and the dog skittered across the wooden floor, and then they were out under a sky the color of cornflowers. Instead of heading to the woods, the man took them toward an old shed. Michael had always ignored it. A shed wasn't the woods, after all.

"Here. Come look over here. Stand on that bucket."

It was a large shed that clearly didn't see a lot of use. There were tools and boxes stored in it, enormous rusty spades and sacks that had turned discolored at the bottom. The rafters holding the roof up were blistered and old, and there was a sizeable hole there, a chunk of sky staring through. Michael climbed up onto the overturned steel bucket and looked at the corner just below the hole. There was a bird's nest, complete with three little chicks. Belatedly, Michael realized he had been hearing their peeping cries since they had entered the shed.

"Now look down there." The man pointed. On the floor, in the dust and some curls of sawdust, was the body of a plump female blackbird. Its neck was at a strange angle and its eye, like a tiny bubble of ink, stared up at nothing.

"A cat must have got at it," said the man. Michael knew instinctively that this was a lie. He had never seen a cat here, not in the fields or anywhere near the house, or even in the woods, and besides, he felt certain that the dog wouldn't have tolerated it. As if it had been summoned, the dog trotted over to them and stuck its nose into the body of the bird, panting loudly in the small space. "These chicks will die in a day or so. What will you do about it?"

"Me?"

"They're yours now. Here." The man reached up and scooped the chicks into his big, shovel hands, and then pressed them on Michael. Shocked and somewhat repulsed, Michael gathered them into his jumper. Their outraged peeping grew louder, and they struggled weakly in his arms, oversized heads weaving back and forth.

"I don't know what to bloody do with them."

"Do whatever you like," said the man. Michael looked at him. "That's the point. Touch them, feel that they are living things, then do what you like."

The man and the dog left him, and unsure what else to do, Michael took the chicks to the woods. As he walked, he contemplated a few different outcomes, the sorts of ideas that occur to children of that age—perhaps he would find a blackbird family in the woods willing to take on a few extra babies, or he could dig up worms, and feed the chicks himself, by hand. Eventually they would be his own pets, and they would come when he called them. The idea pleased him.

Eventually he came to one of his favorite spots: a grassy bank next to a small, muddy stream. The tree cover broke a little here, allowing for a small sunny patch, turning the stumpy grass a brilliant, almost supernatural green, while the space beneath the bank provided a hidden spot of cool thick mud and the occasional toad. Michael put his chicks down on the grass and watched them as they wriggled about. The peeping had mostly stopped, as if they sensed that they were no longer in the safety of their home—as if they knew that there were predators around.

Gently, he pressed the end of his finger to the chest of one. He could feel its tiny heartbeat, impossibly fast and frantic, and the slightly clammy warmth of its skin. He imagined the blood surging around its body, getting ready to push out feathers, even as the bird knew nothing of where it was or what it was. It was just a life, waiting to happen.

Michael picked up the baby bird and, carrying it in one hand, climbed down the little hillock to the shadowy bank of the stream. The mud here was soft and only a little stony, and it took only a few moments to scoop out an empty pocket. A tiny grave.

He placed the bird in it, and paused, watching it wriggle. For some reason, his heart was beating very fast—as fast as the bird's, almost. He pressed his fingers to the bird, pushing it into the mud, and felt very aware of his own strength—how easy it would be to push until tiny bones snapped, until newly formed innards became a paste. The brutal red landscape was very close. If he closed his eyes tight, he was sure he would see it.

Frowning slightly, he picked up a handful of the discarded mud and squashed it down on top of the chick. The peeping stopped. He gathered more mud, packing it in tightly, and then he sat with his hand pressed to the wet earth, counting seconds in his head. When two full minutes had passed, he dug back into the mud. At first, he couldn't find it, as though the earth had just absorbed the baby bird back into its heart—the idea excited him—and then his probing fingers met a squishy resistance. He pulled it out and was shocked to see that it was still alive; the thing had black mud in its throat and one of its little legs was bent the wrong way, but its head still weaved back and forth pitifully. Michael held it up, both annoyed and full of wonder.

"No," he told it. "It's up to *me.*"

He packed it back into the earth.

* * *

When he returned to the house hours later, the sun was just sinking toward the horizon and the man was gone. This wasn't especially unusual. The man had a car and sometimes he would be gone for hours, returning in time for dinner, or bringing back bags of groceries. Michael did not pay much attention—it didn't seem important. He slunk back up to his bedroom, where he moved restlessly for an hour or so, unable to concentrate. He looked down at the thick black dirt under his fingernails and thought about how each chick's heart had stopped. Eventually.

When he heard the man come back into the house, he did not stir from his place on the bed until a sharp bark summoned him downstairs. There, the man looked him over, seeming to take in the mud soaked into his trousers and the dirt ground into his palms. He smiled, his fake eye flashing with the orange light of sunset.

"I've something else for you."

There was a sack on the dining room table—a rough hessian thing that had been printed with the single word: DARTS. It was moving slightly. Without needing to be told, Michael went to the sack and opened it, revealing four tiny kittens, all still with their eyes shut, and all a piebald mixture of black and white. He reached in and picked one up, feeling the hectic warmth of its body against his skin. So alive, and so powerless.

"Michael, lad, have you ever heard of the barghest?"

He curled the kitten against his chest.

"The what?"

"It's a great demon dog, a wolf really, that haunts lonely roads and stiles. An old legend of the north."

"Like . . . a fairy story?"

The man smiled, exposing his long, yellow teeth.

"Not really, lad. The barghest is an omen, but it's also thought of as a spirit of the land, a symbol of death and rebirth. Where it walks, it makes no sound and leaves no mark, but if it bites you, the wound will never heal."

"All right,' said Michael, uncertain of what he was supposed to say.

"The wolf has an important role, lad. You know that? He gives life to the land, because the land is always hungry." The man went to the sack, where the other kittens were clinging together, mewling at each other. He covered them over with a piece of hessian. "There are people who don't recognize the power of that. Your dear old mother, for one. Women, lad. They have a different role to play."

Michael winced.

"But you already solved that problem, didn't you?" He turned to the boy, and his face changed again; an onlooker would have taken him for a kindly uncle, pleased to be treating his nephew. "The kittens are yours to play with."

Michael nodded.

CHAPTER

15

FEELING A LITTLE shaken and more than a little tired, Heather opened the door to her mother's house, half expecting more trapped birds. Michael Reave's reaction had frightened her, but more than that, she felt haunted by dead women—by Sharon Barlow and Elizabeth Bunyon, by all the women butchered decades ago, and most of all, by her mum. Reave, with his scarred hands and green eyes, was connected to all these deaths, and if she could just figure out how . . . Perhaps she could end it. And that might just ease some of her relentless guilt.

Instead of birds, she was greeted by the gentle sound of the radio and the faint smell of the coffee she had brewed that morning. The normality of the situation reassured her, and she made herself a pile of scrambled eggs on toast and wolfed it down in front of her laptop, eating for once at the kitchen table.

Reading the names of his victims, seeing the photos of them while they were still alive, none of it had really conveyed the monstrousness of what he had done. She and Nikki had skirted around the edges of it with their own serial killer research, but there had been an unspoken agreement between them not to unearth anything they couldn't handle. Well, today she felt she had caught a glimpse of the beast Michael Reave really was, and perhaps it was time to face that.

She revisited the brief Wikipedia page, but there was very little information there about his background, or details on the murders themselves—all of which backed up DI Parker's comments about Reave's past being a mysterious blank space. She would have to look elsewhere for the information she wanted.

Back when she had worked on the newspaper, she had picked up the skills required to explore the murkier bits of the Internet, and taking sips of wine every now and then, her plate empty save for a few scraps of egg, she began to look for the raw reality of the Red Wolf murders. Quickly the screen was filled with some very basic looking websites, all favoring vaguely unpleasant color schemes of black, green, and red. There were titles like "nightmare fuel," "dead lovers," and "corpse faces."

These forums were created and curated by people who regularly sought out the bloodiest details of the worst side of humanity, and it wasn't long before she found a long thread detailing the Michael Reave case. There were pictures of crime scenes, and of bodies. In some cases, just pieces of bodies. Judging from the clinical lighting and lack of dramatic angles, some of these at least seemed genuine, photographs snuck out from police archives or from the investigation in the late '80s and early '90s, and in the face of them something, some barrier she hadn't been aware of, was broken into pieces. She thought of the images of Reaves' victims she had already seen, their faces caught smiling or uncertain in photographs that would go on to become infamous—this was where they ended up. Because of Michael Reave.

One of the first pictures showed a young woman lying naked and face down in a field. Her arms had been bound behind her back, and she had long red hair, glossy and loose, across her shoulders and across the grass. Her skin looked painfully white, and around her body was a rough garland of bedraggled wildflowers, clearly placed there with some thought and care. Heather, who knew virtually nothing about plants and nature, thought she recognized some of the blooms—bluebells, daisies, pale yellow primroses, and the nodding heads of foxgloves, pink and purple and somehow obscene. Next to her was an item of clothing that was difficult to identify, both because of how it lay against the grass, and the fact that it had been soaked with blood.

The next picture had also been taken outdoors, and the woman was lying with her eyes to the sky. In the center of her chest there was a large, almost round hole, and bursting up through it was a young tree, the sort you could buy from garden centers, small and ready to plant. Heather could see the dark wetness of the inside of her chest, although the hole itself was relatively clean. She wore what looked like a white shirt, unbuttoned, but it was stained a dark, brownish red; only a small patch on the collar gave away the fact that it had ever been white at all.

"He dresses them," she said, feeling her stomach turn over. The eggs felt heavy and unwelcome. "He dresses the bodies, arranges them. He cares more about them dead than alive. He cares about this picture he's creating."

She scrolled down, already wondering why she had decided to do this to herself. Hadn't today been enough?

There were a few posts from people speculating on the Red Wolf's motives, talking about possible links to paganism and devil worship. The hearts, someone claimed, had never been found, along with other soft tissues—the poster was of the opinion that he might have eaten some of them, like Jeffrey Dahmer or Albert Fish. Heather got up to refill her wine glass, glancing uneasily at the windows. It was fully dark now, and they showed her nothing but her own reflection.

The doorbell rang, startling her into putting down her glass. Snapping the laptop shut, she went to the door, peeking out the spyhole before opening it.

"Lillian?"

"Hello dear," the older woman stepped past her smoothly into the hallway, then as if catching Heather's aggrieved look, held up a tote bag. "Sorry, I know it's quite late. Just come for my casserole dish, if that's all right? I need it for tomorrow's dinner. I hope you've eaten it by now or it will have gone peculiar."

"Oh sure, no problem. It's all washed and ready. Come through to the kitchen . . ."

Except that Lillian was already there, locating her blue casserole dish and placing it carefully into her bag. Heather eyed the washing up from the day before—she'd always been lazy about chores—and felt her cheeks grow warm.

"Would you like a glass of wine?" She cleared her throat, feeling ridiculously formal.

Lillian raised her eyebrows at her and smiled. As before, she was dressed smartly, in a fitted green tweed suit, a brooch in the shape of two intertwined silver fish on her lapel, and her black leather handbag shining expensively. She wore pearl earrings, tiny and discreet flashes of white on her earlobes.

"That would be lovely, dear. Just a small one, if you don't mind." When Heather had handed her a glass, she took the smallest sip imaginable. "How are you getting on? Holding up all right?" Her gray eyes were kind. "When is the funeral? I would dearly like to attend. Colleen was such a good friend."

Heather took a long gulp from her own drink to hide her discomfort. She had been trying not to think about the funeral at all; most of the arrangements had been made as soon as her mother's body had been released from the mortuary, and since then she had done the bare minimum.

"Next Wednesday, at one o'clock, Baleford crematorium. I invited everyone I could find in my mum's address book, I must have missed you." She forced herself to smile. "You're very welcome to come along, of course. I don't imagine there will be many of us there—Mum didn't have any family left, and she tended to keep to herself."

"Oh, I think you'd be surprised." The knowing tone made Heather look up, but Lillian already seemed to be thinking about something else, her thin mouth creased with displeasure. "A cremation? Is that what Colleen wanted?"

Heather shrugged. "She was very clear about it in her will."

Lillian made a small noise, then gestured with her glass to the printouts on the table. "Are you working on a story? I would have thought you'd be too grief stricken for such."

With a lurch, Heather realized she had left whytewitch's images out, but before she could sweep them away Lillian was picking up one of the photographs with her free hand. She nodded slightly.

"Fiddler's Mill? Goodness, this must be a very old photograph."

"You know it?" Heather couldn't keep the surprise from her voice.

"Me? Not personally, dear, but your mother talked about it a lot. It was a memorable time for her, I think."

Heather put the glass of wine down. "She did? That surprises me, to be honest, because she never even mentioned it to me."

"Well." Lillian shrugged gracefully. "There are things you don't want to talk to your daughters about, at least, not while they are young."

"Perhaps you could tell me what you remember?" Heather nodded to the stools at the kitchen counter, and they sat together. "Anything she said about it would be useful."

"*Are* you writing a story about it?" Lillian asked. "Colleen talked a lot about your career as a journalist, too."

"Not really." She assumed that her mother hadn't mentioned that she'd been thrown off the newspaper in disgrace. "I'm just curious about, you know, her life, her past. I feel like I missed out on some things that were important to her."

"Well, I'm not sure that I can help you." Lillian sipped from her wine again, looking across the kitchen to the back door as though the memories were waiting out there for her. "My memory, you see, it isn't what it was." She smiled brightly at Heather. "Don't get old dear, it's quite tedious."

Heather smiled back, thinking of the photos of the women with their bodies left dismembered in fields. "It's better than the alternative. Is there nothing you can tell me?"

"She mentioned communing with nature, eating a lot of very bad food. There might have been a boyfriend." Heather sat very still, trying to ignore the creeping dread settling over her with every word. "Maybe more than one." Lillian chuckled. "As I said, these aren't the things you talk about to your daughter, not if you want to be setting an example. Perhaps you should go up there, dear. Have a look around."

"Up there?"

"To Fiddler's Mill. It could be," she shrugged one shoulder, "what is it young people say? Closure. A way of dealing with your grief. To go and see this place that was so important to your mother."

Important to Mum, thought Heather. *And important to a notorious serial killer. Great.*

As Lillian was leaving, she paused at the front door, appearing to peer out at the sky—it had been threatening to rain.

"Do you have far to go? Did you want to borrow an umbrella?"

"Thank you dear, I'll be fine. Just up the road." But as she turned back, her face was serious. "I don't want to worry you, but I thought I saw someone hanging around your trees earlier today. A man."

"When was this?" Heather thought of the figure she thought she had seen the night before, when she'd been putting the bird out. She had half convinced herself she was imagining it, but perhaps . . .

"This afternoon. You haven't left any spurned lovers behind, have you?"

Despite herself, Heather smiled at the archaic phrase. "Hardly. I'm sure I'll be fine, Lillian. Thanks for dropping by."

But she watched the old woman to the end of the path, and when she was gone, she stood for a time, looking at the darkness that surrounded the lawn. Could it be someone from the newspaper? There was at least one person there who would be keen to upset her, if not actively harm her. Eventually, the rain began to fall, the thick heavy rain of autumn, and she closed the door.

* * *

Later, Heather crashed on the bed in the spare room and opened her laptop. Waking up her phone, she popped off a quick message to Nikki, asking how she was and giving a swift rundown of her day at Belmarsh, and then she checked her emails. To her vague surprise, there was one there from whytewitch59, who apparently possessed the somewhat more prosaic name of Pamela Whittaker—she was happy to meet up for a chat, and wanted to know if this week would suit her? She emailed back, suggesting a time, wondering as she did so if she was setting herself up for an awkward half an hour of paranoid hippy nonsense.

Browsing a news site, she saw that DI Parker was right: news of a missing PE teacher in Lancashire had broken, and there was an appeal for information on the front page. Next to the headline was a photo of her, taken during some sort of school sports day, and that seemed to turn on some obscure light in the back of

Heather's head. She went out into the hallway and retrieved one of the boxes she'd brought down from the attic. This one contained a heap of loose photographs—photos that her mother had never gotten around to organizing or pressing into her many sets of leather-bound photo albums.

Taking it to the bed, she made herself comfortable and began to sift through the pictures. She knew which one she was looking for, and she knew it would be in the box. Her mother wouldn't have put it in an album, she was sure of it.

Images of the past slipped across her lap; the older ones slightly grainy to the touch, the more recent glossy and cold. There were lots of photos of the parties her dad used to throw for his construction firm, filled with anonymous red-faced men drinking punch and looking worse for wear—in a few she caught sight of her dad, and these ones she paused to look at for a moment longer, her fingers lingering over his ruddy face. And then, there it was, nestling at the very bottom. The single photo of a summer fête she'd attended when she was about six years old.

Heather lifted it out of the box and peered at it carefully. It wasn't a great photo really, a touch overexposed, and a few of the children had picked up that unnerving red-eye effect. There was a bunch of them, kids and adults, crowding around a picnic blanket covered with egg sandwiches and packets of biscuits. Heather picked herself out immediately; a pale and slightly solemn looking kid with dark hair and a pink lunchbox clutched to her chest. There was her mother, her expression closer to a grimace than a smile. And there: a little red-headed girl, perhaps a year older than Heather had been, standing up in a pair of bright blue shorts and grinning straight at the camera. There was a smear of cream on her cheek from where she'd been eating cake.

Fi. Heather remembered her name clearly, because she had been so certain that Fi wasn't a name at all. Fi was the first bit of the giant's rhyme in Jack and the Beanstalk. *Fee-fi-fo-fum, I smell the blood of an Englishman.* And she remembered the day so clearly because her mother had started crying and shaking quite abruptly in the middle of it, and they had had to go home.

She never had been told why her mother had broken down like that, but she did remember that she had been sad to leave Fi, who was boisterous and sturdy and very keen on climbing trees. They had exchanged names, repeating them over and over so that they might be able to find each other again in the future—when you were a child, names still seemed like magical things. Fi. Fiona Graham.

Of course, she had only ever seen her that once, and they had never gone back to that particular summer fête. Perhaps she was imagining it. She looked at the little girl with the red curls and the freckles and remembered the hot grasp of her hand in her own.

Now, she looked at the photo on the news site and her stomach clenched. They certainly looked like the same person to her. Fiona Graham, it seemed, had grown into a good person, a teacher. A woman who had done nothing wrong aside from go about her life as normal, and then someone had broken into her house, and likely hurt her. Fiona Graham had probably helped countless kids more than she could know; had mopped up their tears and taken them to the nurse's office when they'd grazed their knees. Her students probably thought of her fondly, or would, when they were far away enough from school to have positive feelings about their teachers.

And none of that had saved her.

There was a video clip of Fiona's parents at a press conference, asking for anyone with information to come forward, and they looked shell-shocked and fragile, as though they had been hollowed out overnight and now the slightest breeze could tatter them to pieces. It was difficult to see how they were related to the vibrant, laughing red-head standing with a group of school girls in shorts. Inevitably, Heather's mind turned back to the images she had seen earlier that night. Was this the fate of Fiona Graham?

She was shoving the photos back inside the box when her phone pinged back with a message from Nikki.

Sorry, was finishing up some marking. Scary stuff. Why wasn't DI Parker there? How did your mum hide all this stuff? Do you think it's true? Are you okay, Heather?

Was she ok? Putting the box back on the floor, Heather pulled the bed covers up over her legs, thinking. On the one hand, she certainly did know more about her mother—she never would have suspected that she was the wild child type, that she had run away from home at the age of fifteen, or even that she had a fascination with eerie fairy stories. Yet somehow all this new knowledge had only exposed more holes in what she had thought was real, leaving gaping absences that seemed to lead to something darker and more terrible—like the awful wounds in the bodies of the Red Wolf's victims.

Whether or not the police would let her speak to Michael Reave again, she would need to fill in some of those holes.

CHAPTER

16

ABI PULLED HER hood up and gathered her arms around her, cursing the thin material of the sports top. If she'd been thinking clearly, she'd have grabbed her coat as well, but the perpetual itch of withdrawal didn't leave much space for clear thinking, and she'd been anxious to get out of her brother's house so she could give him and his date some space. He had said more than once that she didn't have to go out, of course not, but she had seen it on his face clearly enough: few things would put a potential girlfriend off faster than your junkie sister sleeping on the sofa.

She wandered to the end of their road and stood for a moment, considering which way to go. Her lower back ached faintly. She was too old for sofa-surfing, but she'd lost her third job in a row and had little choice about that. It was too cold for wandering the streets, too, but she didn't have enough money to do anything else. Abi chose to go right, and started walking again.

It was the run-down end of town, where most of the shop fronts were either boarded up or displayed posters for betting shops, and one or two of the street lamps were dead. There was a pub called the Joiners on the corner, and Abi looked longingly toward its dimpled windows, but the thought of standing in there just for the warmth was humiliating; the thought of hoping someone would buy her a drink, even more so. She hadn't had the heart to tell David that she didn't have the money to "amuse herself" for the evening and that his cozy date would be condemning her to a night of slightly cold boredom.

Abi walked on past the pub, pretending that she didn't have an end destination in mind. She turned another corner, heading down an even seedier road, wondering already if anyone would be there. She could see the park at the end of the street, obscured by a chicken wire fence and an ugly steel gate. There were the swings and the rusting roundabout, the looming shadow of the slide, but she couldn't make out any figures. Sometimes, she reminded herself, when it was cold, they would sit underneath the slide and pass out their goodies.

She was so intent on reaching the park, Abi almost missed the figure coming toward her, a tall stocky man also wearing a hood, his face in shadow. Despite the itch, she felt abruptly afraid, and she kept her head down, wishing she had been paying more attention, wishing that she had thought to cross the road. As he came closer, she caught a whiff of something rotten and feral, and for the briefest second she was sure he was going to shout at her, or grab her—he smelled mad, inhuman.

And then he was past her, and gone, his footfalls thumping rhythmically away down the street. Abi stopped by the mouth of an alley, watching him go. The stench was still with her, making her wrinkle her nose and cough, and she had just started to figure out that perhaps the smell hadn't been coming from the hooded man at all when a dark shape stepped out of the alley and curled a strong arm around her neck.

CHAPTER

17

Whytewitch59, or Pamela Whittaker as she was likely known to her Whist buddies, lived in a council flat in Elephant and Castle. As she made her way up the stairwell, Heather checked her phone again, but there were still no missed calls from DI Parker. When she had phoned him that morning his line had gone to voicemail, and she had left a somewhat rambling message about the photo of Fiona Graham, before taking a snap of it on her phone and emailing it to him.

When she reached the second floor, she knocked at flat number 87 and the door opened to reveal a tall woman in her early seventies, much less rat-faced than her profile picture had suggested, although she peered at Heather with faintly anxious eyes. She was wearing a khaki-green knitted cardigan that came down to her knees, the sleeves of which were dotted with flecks of paint. Her hair, which was a solid gun-metal gray, was held away from her eyes with a pink plastic Alice band.

"Miss Evans?"

"Heather, please." Heather smiled warmly and shifted the strap of her bag to sit more comfortably over her shoulder. "Are you still okay for a chat, Ms. Whittaker?"

Pamela Whittaker waved her in. The flat was cramped, the orange and brown wallpaper peeling away from the walls where it wasn't covered in picture frames.

"Tea? Coffee?" Pamela Whittaker waved her toward a sofa. The living room was crowded with the usual stuff, chairs and cabinets and coffee tables, all supplemented with easels and rolls of paper, palettes crusted with browns and greens, mugs turned rainbow-like with daubs of paint. On an occasional table near the sofa Heather caught sight of a large framed photo, clearly given pride of place among the general chaos, showing a younger Pamela Whittaker with her arms around a short, curvy woman. Somewhere in among the mess a television screen held it all within its single black eye. "Squash? I have some cordial somewhere here . . ."

"Tea would be great, thank you."

Pamela vanished through a narrow doorway, then reappeared almost instantly with two mugs of steaming tea—she must, Heather reasoned, have had the pot brewing already. Pamela seated herself on a chair opposite, sitting forward with her mug clutched between her hands.

"I saw your work online, Ms. Whittaker, and I thought it was great. Very compelling, atmospheric. I'm putting together a story about Fiddler's Mill, and I thought it would be really interesting to get an *artist's* point of view."

A variety of emotions passed over Pamela's face, and Heather watched closely, trying to match them up. Pleasure at the praise of her work. Uncertainty, maybe even fear, at the mention of Fiddler's Mill. And pride at being called an artist. Pamela leaned forward, staring down into her tea.

"Yes well, thank you. I, well, I am entirely self-taught, you see. Parents couldn't afford to send me to art college, so I did it on the side. It's been, it's been my life's work. Capturing, capturing the true face of nature, you see. The rawness of it."

Heather nodded seriously, as though she had any idea what she meant by this. She had interviewed a few people when she'd been working at the paper, and the key was heavily loading the front end with flattery—people always liked to talk about themselves. It was the subject they knew best, after all.

"That's *so* interesting. You continue to work, I'm glad to see. Do you still largely work with the pastoral landscape? Was Fiddler's Mill the beginning of that for you?"

Pamela curled her fingers around her mug. "Yes, yes, I suppose it was. You are very perceptive." She flashed Heather a brief, shy smile. "I was there in my early thirties. I'd been travelling for a while, across Europe, surviving on beans and waitressing jobs, but there was so much to see, you see. And I ended up back in England, and a lot of my friends were talking about this place in Lancashire that was supposed to be about getting back to earth, to the soil, and it seemed to feed directly," Pamela nodded, as if confirming something to herself, "seemed to feed directly into my work."

"The pieces you produced from that period are so atmospheric," said Heather. She sipped her tea. "Did it inspire you?"

Pamela's face seemed to close up again, and she looked away toward the window, although it faced out onto the walkway and there was little to see there. While Heather waited for Pamela to fill the silence, she found herself looking at the clutter of the living room instead; there were lots of little framed drawings and prints, some clearly of her own work and others by artists Heather didn't recognize. One, which Heather found particularly unnerving, showed a naked male figure scrawled in thick strokes of black and red, his head replaced with that of a snarling wolf.

"You could say that," said Pamela eventually. She reached up and nervously fiddled with the Alice band. "It's a place of great energy. You really have to go there to feel it . . ." But all the previous enthusiasm had drained from her voice, and instead she went back to staring at her tea.

"So, what was it like? What did you do?" Heather smiled encouragingly. "Smoked some weed, listened to music? Some sort of nature worship? I've read some bits and pieces online."

Pamela frowned. "There was a group, and I was on the fringes of it I suppose, but yes, they were very much concerned with nature worship. The idea of the haunted landscape, of returning to an earlier time when people always carried the earth under their fingernails, when we knew the rhythms of the forest . . ."

Heather thought of Michael Reave, sitting in his little yellow room in prison, saying similar things.

"Forgive me Ms. Whittaker, but what does that actually mean? Were there rituals? Did you sing hymns, cast spells? That sort of thing?"

Pamela looked up sharply, clearly expecting some sort of mockery, so Heather kept her face carefully blank.

"Sun up, sun down, chanting . . ." She was becoming vaguer, staring at the window again. "There was dancing, and drugs, yes. There were the two priestesses, thought they were better than everyone else, lording it about. But it was, that was, the softer fringe of it. If you got close to the center . . ."

Suddenly Pamela Whittaker's demeanor changed completely. She shook her head and crashed the mug down on the coffee table, causing little waves of tea to splash over the sides, soaking an embroidered tea cloth.

"Ms. Whittaker, are you—"

"I saw things! Terrible things. Women being used, and hurt, but when I complained about it, they told me that I was imagining it, or even worse, that I was just jealous because I wasn't part of the inner circle. They told me I just didn't understand, because I was . . ." Her sallow cheeks had turned a hectic pink. "I saw blood, in the woods, but we weren't supposed to talk about it."

Despite the close warmth of the living room Heather felt a chill travel down her spine.

"Didn't you go to the police?"

Pamela Whittaker shot her a pitying look over her glasses. "A strung-out hippy lesbian, talking about abuse in the woods? They would have dismissed me out of hand, Miss Evans. That's if they didn't just arrest me for being a pot head."

Heather found herself reassessing whytewitch59. Yes, she had the flighty neurotic artist persona, but there was a steely streak of realism to her, too.

"It was an evil place," Pamela looked down at her hands, an expression of hate twisting her features. "*Evil.* Like I said, you have to be there to feel it, I think. If there's one thing I still believe from those days, it's that the landscape remembers—deep down in its stone roots, the landscape remembers all the terrible things, all the blood shed on it. Fiddler's Mill is a place like that. You couldn't pay me to go back there now."

"Ms. Whittaker, would you be prepared to tell me exactly what you saw? If there were crimes, then we should get justice for them. I could help you do that. Can you describe what was going on out there?"

All the anger and certainty seemed to bleed out of the older woman, the line of her mouth becoming wet and infirm.

"It was so long ago . . . Even with the best will in the world, things get clouded. I painted some of it, and some of it I couldn't. Babies crying, blood in the earth . . ."

"I'm sorry? Blood in the earth?"

Pamela Whittaker shook her head but didn't say anything.

"Pamela, are you aware that Michael Reave was there, at the commune?"

The older woman went very still, like a rabbit in the grass when there's a dog in the woods.

"Do you know who I mean by Michael Reave? The Red Wolf?"

"I thought you said you wanted to talk about my art." Pamela Whittaker's voice was a small thing now, and vaguely petulant. "I feel I've let you in here under, under false pretenses. You're a journalist, I know that, or you used to be. I can use Google, you know."

Heather shrugged a little, feeling all her previous admiration for Pamela Whittaker dissipating. She didn't want to think about her old job, or how she had lost it.

"Don't you think it's interesting though? Here you are telling me that Fiddler's Mill is evil, that you saw some terrible things—and all the while there was a serial killer there. I reckon that makes your story even more believable, but you don't seem very willing to actually talk about it. Why is that?"

Pamela Whittaker pressed her thin lips together. "He was there. There were others, too. I told the police later, when all that came out . . . I can't talk about it now."

"What happened? Did they threaten you? Who else was part of this circle?"

The old woman shook her head slowly, her face creased with distaste. "There were always rumors flying about. Rumors about sex parties in the woods, what those led to, the aftermath. I got to know a young woman called Anna. She was very fragile, very vulnerable, and she should not have been in a place like that . . . I didn't realize until it was too late, of course."

"What happened to her there?"

"Truly? I don't know. But she left Fiddler's Mill deeply changed. I won't lie to you, Miss Evans, Anna wasn't entirely well to begin with. In the head, I mean. But when I saw her afterward she told me that she had gotten pregnant at the Mill, and she had had it, out in the woods. And then creatures came and took the baby away, stole it from her."

"Monsters stole her baby? That's what she said? Did you see her pregnant while you were there?"

Pamela Whittaker heaved her thin shoulders into a shrug. "I wasn't always there. I drifted in and out for a while, looking for work in the area, but I do remember there was a time when she seemed happy. She wouldn't tell me why, but she kept her hand on her stomach a lot then. I should add," she looked at Heather from under her eyelashes, "she didn't look pregnant to me then, and she was a tiny slip of a thing. A pregnancy would have stuck out like a bowling ball."

"Didn't she go to the police, if she thought her child had been stolen?"

"You don't understand. Anna was . . . unreliable. A woman like her now would get help, be on all sorts of medications, but then . . . She fell through the cracks, and Fiddler's Mill made her worse. I felt so sad for her. Still do."

Heather sat back a little in the overstuffed sofa. There was no way to tell if anything she was being told was useful at all. "Did Anna know Michael Reave?"

Pamela Whittaker turned her head away. "Not that I saw. But he was an enigma. He would come and go all the time—I've no idea who knew him there, not really. This is all very upsetting, you realize. Bringing all this back up."

"Pamela, I'm sorry, but I think my mother was there, too, and I really need to know why. Would you have known her? Her name was Colleen, she would have been in her teens at the time. Skinny, blond."

"Your mother? Is this what it's actually about? I have no time for liars, young lady."

Abruptly, Pamela Whittaker stood up and stalked from the room. Heather watched her go, wondering if she was going to come back with a rolling pin and chase her out of the flat. She pursed her lips. She'd gone in too strong, as usual, and frightened the woman off.

Instead Pamela returned with what looked like a thick black photo album, which she passed to Heather. Her face was closed again, the hectic pink of her cheeks sunken back to the color of old cheese.

"I didn't know anyone called Colleen, but there were a lot of us there. Here, this is my work from that period, I had copies made. This is how I file things, how I keep track. Perhaps you'll find something in there."

Heather opened the album. Instead of family snaps, it was filled with decent quality color prints of paintings and photographs, most of which were A4. There was a date painted on the leather cover in white Tippex: 1978–83.

"Take it, borrow it. Anything I have to say about Fiddler's Mill is in there. It might help you, with whatever it is you are doing, Miss Evans." She took a deep breath, hovering over Heather, clearly wanting her to leave. "And go and speak to Anna. I've written the address on a Post-it on the inside. I don't think you'll get much sense out of her—I haven't been able to, not for a long time—but I don't know, maybe it'll do her good to think that someone cares about her *baby*, or whatever it was." She suddenly looked to be on the verge of tears. "Terrible things happened there, Miss Evans, but forgive me, I don't want to expose myself to that again, not even to remember the details you want." She shuddered all over. "It's a wound that never heals."

Heather looked up, but Pamela Whittaker was already turning away. She thought of her mother's suicide note again: *monsters in the wood.*

"Now, if you wouldn't mind, I have a lot to be getting on with."

* * *

On her way back down the cold concrete steps, Heather's phone rang. Pausing by a battered and ancient telephone box, she pressed receive.

"Miss Evans?"

"Oh, DI Parker. Hello."

"I got your voicemail. You have something on Fiona Graham?"

"Yes, I sent you an email. It's not much, but there's a photo I think might be her. My dad took it, years ago."

"Do you think your parents knew Fiona Graham?"

The question threw her for a moment. What was he suggesting?

"Well, I don't know. It's probably nothing."

"Would you come in to the office tomorrow? I'm back in London."

"Here I was thinking I'd lost the chance to see you again."

He made a small noise of amusement, and Heather was surprised by how much it pleased her to have amused him, even a little bit. It was good to smile after her unpleasant conversation with Ms. Whittaker.

"No such luck," he continued.

"Does this mean you've found Fiona Graham?"

There was a pause, and within it Heather imagined all manner of terrible fates for the girl she might have met fleetingly in her childhood. She stood very still, staring unseeing at the scratched glass of the telephone booth.

"Listen, I'll tell you what I can tomorrow. If you can make it then?"

"It's a date." She waited for another laugh, but there was nothing this time.

* * *

When Heather arrived back at her mother's house, it was to find Lillian standing at her gate, a large Tupperware box in her arms. Catching sight of Heather's bemused expression, the old woman had the grace to look embarrassed.

"You mustn't think I'm poking my nose where it isn't wanted, dear, but you look thin and I'm worried you're not eating properly." When Heather opened her mouth to object, Lillian held her hand up. "I know, interfering old baggage, it's not the role I wanted to play either but here we are. I can't help worrying." She hefted the Tupperware box in her arms. "Just a traybake. Something to line your stomach. I whipped it up this morning, and then blithely assumed you would be in. I was just dithering out here, wondering if I should leave them on your doorstep like a good fairy."

Heather thought of the pile of washing up from the night before, the lines of empty tumblers and wine glasses. She winced.

"That's very kind of you, Lillian. Please, come in."

Once inside, Lillian took the box through to the kitchen and deposited it on the side, only glancing briefly at the chaos around the sink.

"There you are. Just bread pudding, but it's good and stodgy and if you pop some ice-cream on the side it's actually pretty good, if I do say so myself." She paused and laid one warm hand on Heather's arm. "I'll leave you be now, I promise, but if you do need anything at all, you will let me know, won't you? Are you holding up, Heather? I would hate to think that you were struggling, and I know your mother would be horrified."

The old woman's gray eyes were sharp and steady, searching Heather's face avidly. For a moment, Heather felt close to weeping; close to telling Lillian about everything—the bone freezing terror when the police had called her about her mother's suicide, the unending guilt she'd waded through every single day since her dad had died, even the haunting presence of Michael Reave. She opened her mouth, ready to spill all of it, and Lillian's eyes widened, just slightly. For some reason, the eager expression on her face broke the spell, and instead Heather just smiled lopsidedly.

"Thanks for checking up on me, Lillian. And for the bread pudding."

The woman nodded, smiling as she gathered up her handbag, but Heather had the distinct impression she was disappointed.

"Any time, dear. Perhaps you should think of getting away for a while, after the funeral. Some space by yourself, somewhere quiet. It'll do you the world of good." They walked to the door together, and just as she stepped outside, she added, "the Tupperware is dishwasher safe, if that helps at all."

When she was gone, Heather served up a large portion of the bread pudding, reheated it, and then poured herself a large glass of wine. It was early enough that the sky was still light, but caught within its trees and bushes, the house itself was already growing the darker shadows of evening. Deciding to take her cue from this, Heather changed into her pajamas and sat on the sofa with the bowl of pudding, a pile of notes, and her laptop next to her. She ate steadily, getting through another serving and another large glass of wine, until she began to feel increasingly dozy. Soon, it was difficult to focus on her notes from her talk with Pamela Whittaker, and the pages of news websites were increasingly difficult to look at—all emblazoned with images of Fiona Graham. Heather yawned hugely.

She checked her phone and saw that there were a few missed messages from Nikki, but the thought of attempting to type out any sort of answer added to her increasing sense of nausea. Instead, she chucked her phone back onto the sofa—it bounced onto a cushion—and she stood up, a decision she immediately regretted.

"Shit." Her stomach and the room seemed to be rolling in opposite directions. Two glasses of wine weren't normally enough to make her drunk, but she had had only a sandwich for lunch. She chalked it up to low blood sugar. "Early night, I think."

Uneasily she made her slow way upstairs to the bathroom. Blinking slowly at her reflection in the cabinet mirror, it was possible to see why Lillian had been so concerned; her skin was chalky white, and there were dark smudges under her eyes, like elderly bruises. Even her hair was greasy, strands of it stuck to her forehead. Grimacing, she went to grab her toothbrush only to find it wasn't on the sink where she habitually left it, nor had it fallen on to the tiled floor. Assuming she must have chucked it in the medicine cabinet that morning, distracted by thoughts of meeting up with Pamela, she swung the door open—only for something to flutter out into the sink.

It was a piece of lilac paper, and a handful of brown feathers. Bile rising rapidly at the back of her throat, Heather hooked the paper out of the sink before it could absorb any more droplets of water. Turning it over, she saw the little printed wren at the top of the page—the same paper, she realized, her mother had written her suicide note on. There was a small note written on it in black ballpoint pen, printed carefully in block capitals.

"So?" she said to the room at large. "Just a bit of paper she left lying around. And the feathers are from that bloody bird. That's all."

Even so, her stomach was churning before she read the words.

I KNOW WHAT YOU ARE, AND I THINK YOU DO TOO

And underneath that, a tiny black heart.

CHAPTER

18

BEFORE

MICHAEL GREW TALLER and stronger at a tremendous rate, putting on a layer of muscle and shooting up to be almost as tall as the man. If he was starved of human contact, he did not mind, or even think about it very much—he spent his days outside in the woods, or in the man's library. He did drawings sometimes, although he was very careful to hide them, slipping them under his mattress in the early hours of the morning. Sometimes the woman who cleaned the big house came, and he would stay out of her way, listening for the sounds of her hoover or the faint sigh as she polished some piece of silver, and every now and then other men would come to the house; big, brash country men who brought a trail of cigarette smoke and the faint sour smell of beer. When they came around, Michael made sure to leave the house entirely, staying out in the woods all night sometimes, watching the lilac dawn light filter through the trees and tending his graves.

One afternoon, he returned to the house to find it filled with a new presence, something he couldn't name. He hung in the doorway, sniffing carefully—there was a scent, something floral and exotic, and a different energy. The dog appeared across the hall and then was gone, and a second later he heard the man call out to him.

"Michael! We have guests. Come and meet them."

It was summer. The living room was hot and still. Motes of dust hung in the air, making Michael think of old water moving slowly in a forgotten fish tank. The man was sitting in one of his wooden chairs, leaning forward eagerly to see Michael's face. On the large green sofa two women were sitting—they were both older than Michael, but not as old as the man. One had chalky white skin with glossy pink lips, and her eyebrows looked as though they had been drawn on with a pen. She wore a tight blue dress with holes in the side; her pale flesh poked through like uncooked bread. The other had a lot of yellow hair that she had pinned up on top of her head and somewhat incongruously she was wearing a thick white fur coat over a short black skirt and a top with spots on it. Michael could tell from looking at it that the fur wasn't real; it fluffed up around her as though she were sitting in the arms of a big white bear. This one smiled at Michael, revealing small neat teeth.

"This is your boy, is it? He's a big lad." The other woman laughed at this, raising her pretend eyebrows at some meaning Michael couldn't grasp.

"Come and say hello." The man waved him over. "These are friends of mine."

Michael did not move. The weird floral scent was coming from these women, and in the confines of the hot living room it was overwhelming. There was too much to take in about them, and he could feel his heart starting to beat too fast; thick silver rings on bony fingers, shiny red shoes with heels like knives, the soft pouches of flesh that seemed to be seeping out from everywhere he looked. The girl with the eyebrows leaned forward, threatening to spill out of her tight top.

"He's not frightened, is he? Not of us."

"Of course not," said the man, and Michael caught the look he gave him; interested, close to being angry. There was a path Michael was supposed to take here—just like with the chicks—and he was close to missing it. But quite abruptly, he didn't care. He was disgusted by these strange colorful women and their strong smells. They were disrupting his home, turning the air strange and charged. For the first time he felt a flare of anger toward the man, a sense of betrayal. This place was supposed to be *safe*.

He left the living room, ignoring the trill of laughter from one of the women, and headed back outside into the lengthening afternoon. He walked and walked, taking himself down the paths he was fondest of, through Fiddler's Woods and down through the fields and further, out past the hedgerows and thickets until he came to paved roads. He walked these, too, walking further than he ever had, with the sun pressing hot on his head and his mind carefully blank.

The sun was inching toward the horizon when he came to the outskirts of a small village. There were cars parked outside cottages set back from the road, and a little further in, he could see a pub sign swinging from a black and white building. There were people here, he realized. People who might wonder what a fourteen-year-old stranger was doing wandering by himself; people who might even know his family. Jumping as though he had been doused with a bucket of water, Michael turned to head back to the fields, suddenly feeling terribly exposed—he was the mouse out after dark, caught in the shadow of the owl—and that was when he saw her.

A figure in a red coat, standing just by a low drystone wall. She was leaning back, her pale face tipped up to the last of the sun, grinning. Her sharp white fingers were spread against the stone, but he knew that they could move fast. They could be touching him in moments.

He ran.

There was movement as he passed her, and he sensed her turning her head to look at him, sensed her sharp hands reaching out, and he knew that if he felt the feathery touch of her fingers he would faint dead away, and that would be it, he would be back there, in the cupboard, at the mercy of his family again—at the mercy of his mother, who beat him, his father, who hated him, and his sister . . . who came to him at night, with her red coat and her sharp smile.

She did not catch him. Instead he ran wildly out into the fields, running until he was back under the blessed trees again, and eventually his terror became something else. Something red. He rubbed his face angrily, outraged at the tears he felt there and the slow throb of the stitch in his side.

It's not right.

It wasn't right that they could come with their smiling faces and sharp hands and take his safety away. It wasn't right that they could make him weak like that, when he was the strong one. They were soft, after all, he had seen it; the weakness of their flesh, seeping out of their clothes—had tasted their prey-scent in the flowery perfumes they doused themselves in. Women were dangerous, and difficult, just as the man had said they were. They would always be lethal to him, a thing to be feared.

When he returned to the house, the man was nowhere to be seen, but the living room door was open and Michael could see one of the women still sitting on the sofa. It was the one in the white fur coat, and she looked bored, picking at a loose thread on a cushion. The other girl was gone. Michael went down to the kitchens and picked out one of the long meat knives; he had seen the man cooking with it sometimes, cutting up steak or carving a pork joint. When he returned, the girl was still there, and in the lengthening shadows of the evening Michael realized that she couldn't see him just outside the room. He imagined himself as he was in the woods, silent and at home, a predatory force. He thought of all the little ghosts he had packed neatly away in the black earth, how they knew him from his silent footsteps as he passed over their graves.

The knife held loosely in one hand, he went into the living room and closed the door.

* * *

Later, much later, Michael became aware of the man standing in the doorway, watching him. He blinked rapidly. The room appeared to have changed; it was a different place, a room in a red landscape full of silence.

"Michael." The man's voice was very soft. "We can't leave her here, lad."

He shook his head. "We'll take her to the woods."

"No," the man came a single step into the room, then seemed to think better of it. "Even that's too close. We'll have to take her far away, Michael, just to be sure."

"But that's what I promised her, a place under the trees." Michael didn't recall making the woman any such promises, but the last hour or so was already fusing into one strange fever dream, and it seemed right enough. She belonged in Fiddler's Woods with the rest of them, so she would feel his silent footsteps walking over.

"That can't be, lad," said the man, and there was an edge of danger to his voice now. Michael dragged his eyes away from the mess on the carpet and looked up. The man was a creature of black and gray shadows, the light from the single lamp winking out of his dull, false eye. "You've done well, but you've got to bloody listen to me now, right? Every word, you pay attention now, and learn something. Right?"

In the end, they gave her heart to Fiddler's Woods. The rest of her they loaded into the man's battered old van, and they drove a long way, the hot, sweet smell of her flooding the cab and making the man grimace. Eventually, when they had found a good, remote place, they took her out of the van and placed her in the grass. By that time, the sky in the east was turning a burnished silver color, and the man was eager to be gone.

"A lot of tidying up to be done lad, and don't think you'll be getting out of that. It's important you learn it. A proper good clean will save your neck."

Michael ignored him for the moment. The woman in the grass looked oddly serene, her eyes turned up to the brightening sky, everything below her collar bone a churned, butcher-shop mess. He knew why she looked so peaceful; because her heart was in the cold, black dirt, deep in the roots of the ancient wood. With a single gloved finger, he drew a heart in her blood on one of the few patches of her skin that wasn't ruined.

"A heart for a heart," he said.

And her coat. Her coat, which had been so white before, was a deep and sopping red. He smiled at that, drinking in the sight, before getting back into the van.

CHAPTER

19

IN THE SPARE bedroom with the lights still on, Heather sat in the bed with her knees drawn up to her chest, waiting for the nausea to pass. There was a bucket on the floor next to her. She had screwed up the note and thrown it in the bin in the bathroom, but she couldn't stop thinking about the words, so neat and so damning. It hadn't looked like her mother's handwriting, but then how familiar was she with it, anyway? Not to mention the fact that it had been written in big, uppercase letters, much closer to the way her dad had used to write his notes: Post-its on the fridge for more milk, or receipts for building work. Nikki had said, she reminded herself, that suicidal people were very ill, that they might not be thinking clearly when they wrote their notes—perhaps this message had been her mother at her most unwell, writing accusing letters to no one in particular, or perhaps even to herself. She wanted to believe that, for the shred of comfort it gave her, but she didn't.

She knew the note was for her.

It made sense. It was too close to all the barbs her mother had thrown at her in the months before she had finally moved out. Back then, in the dark days following her dad's funeral, the two of them had been in a state of war, all the conflicts between them finally exposed by the loss of the one person that had kept them together.

There had been hours of silence, long periods where they kept out of each other's way, but inevitably something would cause the other to erupt—one of dad's old trainers wedged under the fold-away table, or a tub of the ice cream he especially liked left in the freezer. And then, like splinters working their way under the skin, these little reminders of his absence—*of what Heather had done*—tore all the wounds open again.

Reluctantly, Heather remembered bringing the injured bird home in her arms, still carefully wrapped in her t-shirt. She had hidden it in her room, finding an old shoe box and stuffing it with rags. She had filled up a little pot of water, stolen a handful of breakfast cereal, thinking it might eat that. Looking back, she was amazed she had done it—obviously she couldn't have kept it hidden for long, and she hadn't the faintest idea of how to look after animals; she had never been allowed any pets, after all.

Even now, after life had supplied her with a number of terrible memories, the look on her dad's face when he'd found the box was still one of the very worst. He'd snatched the box up from its place by the bed—the bird had looked dead then, Heather remembered, its head curled round to its breast and its eyes glassy—and a look of sheer terror had passed over his face. Then, slowly, anger had replaced it; a rage so unexpected and complete that thinking of it as an adult still frightened her.

He had turned red in the face, and they had shouted at each other, a rising chorus of outrage. Even then, Heather had been taken aback by the heat of her own anger, a lot of it fueled by sheer surprise—in their little family dynamic, her dad was the soft touch, and mum was the rod of iron. And besides which, it was just a bird. A poorly bird. And he was acting as though she'd been out murdering babies.

She had told him that, she remembered; had screamed it in his face. White blotches appeared on his red cheeks, his eyes wet and shining, and he had marched from her room, the bird box still in his hands. He had died around forty-five minutes later, a sudden and apocalyptic heart attack while he was in the park, putting the bird back where it had come from. It had been getting late, the sun going down, and there had been no one there to help him, or to phone for an ambulance, and that was that.

Sitting alone in the spare room of her mother's empty house, Heather looked down at her hands. She felt sick to her stomach and so tired she couldn't keep her eyelids from slipping down every few seconds, yet her heart was skittering in her chest.

"You know what you've done." It was what her mother had hissed at her, a day or two after the funeral. She had never seen her mother drink before that, but she had been drinking then, taking small sips from a glass of vodka and coke, her eyes red and the skin around her mouth pinched. "You know what you've done." It was the icy truth of it, the freezing water between them that could never be bridged again. And was it really so different from *I know what you are*? Heather found she could imagine her mother writing that note. Could imagine it very easily, her lips pinched together with hate and the hand holding the pen clenched so tightly her fingers were white.

Abruptly, Heather leaned over the bed and was noisily sick, snatching up the bucket just in time. A hot curd of bread pudding and sour red wine splashed wetly against the plastic bottom, her stomach clenching and flexing until it was all out of her. After that, some vital energy seemed to leave her and she finally slept, despite the smell of sick and the brightly burning lights.

She woke up at around 4 AM, sitting straight up in the bed. *My toothbrush was in the cabinet*, she thought wildly, with no idea why the information was important. It was only when she'd stepped out to turn the light off, then slipped back into bed, that she realized what it meant: if she'd put the toothbrush in the cabinet that morning, then why hadn't the note and the feathers fallen out then?

She lay awake for some time after that, until the rancid smell of vomit forced her out of the bedroom and onto the downstairs sofa.

CHAPTER

20

"SORRY ABOUT THE mess."

Heather stepped around a stack of box files as DI Parker led her through the chaotic office. It was remarkably shabby for a police station, to her mind, mostly filled with people frowning at pieces of paper or eating Subway sandwiches, but it was at least very lively.

"Like I said before, you're busy, right?"

Ben Parker gave her a quick smile over his shoulder. "Always. But as it happens, part of the ceiling collapsed in the east side of the building, so a lot of stuff that was over there is now being found a home over here," he waved at the overloaded desks. "It's also where we'd normally interview people, so you'll have to make do with my office today."

At the far end of the open plan space they came to a row of small, closed off offices, the glass partitions dotted with Post-its and pale dots of old Blu Tack adhesive. Parker led them inside one and set down the two coffees he'd been carrying on a crowded desk. As Heather sat down, she found herself trying to see everything on the desk at once; there were handwritten reports there, printouts of emails, and a few large photographs of what looked like someone's bedroom.

"Is this an interview then? I mean, that sounds very official."

"Ah, no." Parker sat down, the chair squeaking slightly. He ran a hand through his hair, also looking at the chaos on his desk. He seemed to have briefly forgotten why they were there. "Just a chat. The photograph you think might be Fiona Graham. You have it with you?"

"Yeah, I . . ." Heather hauled her bag up onto her lap, ready to delve into it for the photograph, when something else on the desk caught her eye. It was a series of clear plastic evidence bags, each containing what appeared to be a cheery birthday card. On the far end one contained something else entirely: a smooth gray rock about the size of the palm of her hand. It was polished and shiny, with a rough heart shape scratched into the surface. Heather stopped, her own heart doing something like a somersault. "What is that?"

Parker saw where she was looking, and grimaced. "Sorry. Like I said, everything is a mess here at the moment." He stood up and moved around to the front of the desk. Heather, guessing he was about to put the evidence bags away, glared intently at the rock.

"Evidence collected from the school Fiona Graham worked at. Works at." He sighed, going to put the tray out of sight. "The forensics is faster down here, so we're doing what we can to fast track everything."

"The rock, it's— "

"This? One of the presents from her schoolchildren."

She wanted to snatch it up, to feel the weight of it. It was probably nothing. Hearts drawn on objects was hardly rare, but she couldn't help thinking of the empty flowerpot in her mother's garden. The crude renderings appearing on a murdered woman's belongings. The note left in her bathroom. Hadn't someone on the Internet claimed that the Red Wolf ate the hearts of his victims? A chill ran down her spine. Part of her wanted to point this out to Parker, to leap on something that smelt like a clue, but at the same time she couldn't help seeing herself through his eyes: a recently bereaved woman, raving about her mother's terracotta plant pots. She'd sound like a crazy person. And if he thought she was crazy, he might not let her talk to Michael Reave again, and with that would vanish any chance of her getting some answers about her mother.

"Found anything? I mean," Heather cleared her throat. "I mean, do you think the killer sent Fiona Graham a birthday card?"

Parker shrugged. "Violent criminals have certainly done weirder things. And naturally, we have to check everything. Which is why . . ."

He raised his eyebrows at her, and Heather remembered the bag on her lap.

"Oh yeah. Well." She pulled the photo from the front pocket, glancing at it quickly before she handed it over. On the way to the station she had started to worry that her hunch was ridiculous, that she was seeing things in the photo that just weren't there, but the stone heart on Parker's desk had changed all that.

"Hmm. We have the photo of the photo you sent, but as you can imagine, it's better to see it in the flesh." He smudged his thumb across the surface. "It certainly feels like a real photograph."

"You think I'd fake it?" Despite herself, Heather was slightly amused by the idea.

Parker glanced up. "You'd be surprised at the weird stuff people do, Miss Evans, especially around cases like this. Do you know where this was taken?" Parker was frowning at the photo now, looking troubled. She had half expected him to immediately dismiss it, but he was turning it around in his hands, looking for a date that wasn't there.

"As best I can remember, a little summer fete somewhere outside of London." Parker glanced up at her. "I know, but you can see how old I was. Having said that," she tipped her head to one side slightly, trying to picture her infrequent childhood day trips. She couldn't stop thinking about the roughly scratched shape of the heart. "We tended to go to Kent or Essex on days out. Southend maybe. Places like that."

"Fiona Graham's family were from Manchester. What would they be doing down here?"

"I don't know, but I've heard that even Northerners like to leave their icy lands occasionally."

That got a smile. "All right. And, this certainly looks like our girl to me." Parker shuffled some papers on the desk and came up with an old school photo. It was a typical school portrait, still housed in its brown cardboard frame. In it, Fiona Graham looked a couple of years older than she had been at the fête, and she was grinning widely at the camera, wild corkscrews of ginger hair framing her face. She was wearing a school uniform—dark green cardigan, shirt with light green checks.

"I'll pass this on to Fiona's parents, and see if they can confirm it." Parker put the photos down and took a sip of his coffee. "This is your mother in the photo? And you say that your father took it?"

"Yeah, that's right." It was on the tip of her tongue to tell him about that day; how her mother, normally so icy and distant, had suddenly broken down in tears, shaking and hiding her head in her hands. How her dad had herded them away from the happy picnic area, his own face oddly pale around the jowls.

"Any idea if your parents knew Fiona Graham's parents?"

She shrugged and picked up her own coffee. It was vile, but it was a good distraction. "I've no clue."

"Still, quite a coincidence, isn't it? A connection to Reave, a connection to Fiona Graham . . ."

"You don't even know yet that Fiona is a victim," Heather pointed out quickly. "She might have just wandered off. People do that, sometimes—life gets a bit too much, or she's in debt, or fallen out with her family." She smiled. "I left home as soon as I could, didn't think too closely about what I was doing. I'd just had enough of it all. Maybe she just had enough of it all, too."

Parker was nodding, but not smiling.

After a moment he picked up one of the photographs she'd seen earlier—the one of an untidy bedroom. He passed it to her over the desk. It was clear immediately that something terrible had happened in the room. Shoes and bags were scattered on the floor, and there were dark patches of what was clearly blood on the carpet—not a huge amount, but enough to imply a certain level of violence.

"This is Fiona Graham's bedroom," Parker said, somewhat unnecessarily. "There's more blood on the landing, on the stairs. Pictures knocked off the wall, stuff like that. She didn't leave under her own steam, Heather."

"No. No, I guess not." Heather stared at the photo, trying to take in every detail. "Inspector, if there *is* a link between my parents and Fiona Graham . . . what would that mean? What if my mother was sitting on something, something she knew and felt she couldn't tell anyone, not even me? I mean, my mother killed herself just as these murders started and now this?"

The sad, scuffed trainers, the pile of dogeared paperbacks on the bedside table. It could be her room. There was a story here, the sort of story that could get her back onto any newspaper she wanted, but more and more it looked like writing that story would mean discovering a side to her mother she couldn't have guessed.

Parker stood up suddenly.

"Listen, the coffee here is bloody awful. Do you want to go and, uh, get some lunch?"

Looking up, she saw that there was a faint blush across the tops of his cheeks. Smiling, she put the photo down.

"Let's do that."

* * *

They went to a place around the corner, a small cozy restaurant that Heather guessed wasn't a regular police hangout. Parker ordered a kind of complicated sandwich that promptly fell apart when he tried to pick it up. Heather stuck to a pasta salad, from which she picked out all the bits of meat. To her surprise, he ordered a beer, and when she raised her eyebrows he just smiled.

"So, what's your history with Michael Reave?" she asked, when she was halfway through her demolished salad. "You've had to deal with him before, I'm guessing."

"I'm too young to have been involved in the original investigation—as my DCI keeps reminding me—but I had to talk to him about another case a few years ago." He tapped his fingers against the neck of his beer bottle. They sat with their back to the large window at the front of the restaurant, and a shard of autumn daylight fell across the shoulder of his shirt. "It was relating to a cold case, a woman who went missing in 1979 that we had always thought he was responsible for. It turned out she had links with an old East End gang, and suddenly it seemed possible that she'd gone missing for entirely different reasons, so I went in there to talk to him about it. This was back when I had just moved up to CID. It was a small, probably pointless job, so they gave it to the newest recruit." He smiled lopsidedly. "It *was* pointless. He barely said anything at all. But he did listen, he didn't show off or shout. As these things are measured, that was almost a success in itself. So the case moved on. But I didn't forget Reave."

"He made an impression?"

"I'd read all about him during my degree. It was quite the thing, to meet him face to face. A serial killer as strange and as singular as him. He's a real outlier, as strange as Bundy was, really."

He was warming up now, she realized, getting into the subject. She thought of the notebook in her bag, and with it came a pang of guilt. He was opening up to her, when she hadn't been entirely honest with him—all those notes she'd been making all along were looking more and more like an article.

"Bundy?"

"Ted Bundy. They're not similar, not really, but Bundy was remarkable in the way he was able to shut himself off from what he'd done. Like he was two different people, living in the same body. Right up until the end, he was trying to explain it all away, as though he wasn't responsible."

"And Reave is the same?"

"Reave is *very* certain he's not responsible." Parker smiled grimly. "But with him it's the ritualization of what he did to the bodies, the care he took to lay them out. It's hugely risky, what he did—spending so much time with them was only ever going to make it easier to find and convict him—but every victim we know of was arranged in these strange, I don't know, displays. *Tableaus.*

And there are so many other identifying marks of the Red Wolf. The flowers, often in the mouth. The item of clothing soaked with blood. And their hearts."

"Their hearts?" Heather felt her hand tighten around her fork, and she forced herself to relax. "What do you mean?"

"None of them were ever found. He took them out, hid them somewhere or bloody ate them, I don't know." He stopped, glancing down at the remains of her lunch. "Sorry. Christ, sorry, this really isn't appropriate lunch conversation is it?"

Heather shrugged and took a sip of her drink. *Hearts.* Perhaps the article could examine the overall mythology of the Red Wolf. She could already see how it would hang together; pieces on his sketchy background, his time in the commune at Fiddler's Mill, and sections on the details of the murders—people loved that stuff. And interspersed throughout, her own impressions of the man himself, drawn from the interviews. Her mother wouldn't even need to come into it. And it could wait—the papers would still be interested once this new killer was safely caught and behind bars. Even more so, perhaps. She could reach out to Diane, let her see some of her notes. For the first time in weeks she felt a little sliver of hope; a brightness in a long period of dark. She'd forgotten how much she had enjoyed her job.

"It doesn't bother me, honestly. You wouldn't think it to look at him, would you? I know that's a daft thing to think, but to be able to do something like that, you picture someone completely unhinged."

"You want to try talking to him again?"

Heather blinked, surprised he had offered it so readily. "I want to help. And I think he knows more about my mum than he's letting on."

On their way out, she pressed her hand to his sleeve; the arm underneath her fingers was firm and warm, and she fought against the urge to squeeze it.

"Hey. Thanks for the lunch. It's a grim subject but the company is good."

They paused in the doorway, and for a moment they stood close together. She looked at the collar of his shirt and the patch of tanned skin just above it, wondering what would happen next, when his phone made a shrill noise. Turning away slightly, he thumbed the screen.

"I'd better get back," he said. "But if you can make it tomorrow, we can try again with Michael Reave?"

Heather nodded, faintly disappointed. "I'll be there."

* * *

By the time Heather was back at her mother's house it was full dark, and the terracotta pot by the doorstep was almost completely lost in shadows. Trotting up the path, Heather was half convinced she had imagined the whole thing, but as she reached it, kneeling down in the dark to pick it up, her fingers brushed over the scratched surface and a tingle moved up her arms and across her back: *the heart*.

Inside the well-lit kitchen, she turned the pot back and forth under the lights, examining the shape she'd first noticed just after Mr. Ramsey had given her the keys. It still looked rough and strange, and it was very much like the heart scratched into the rock in Ben Parker's office. And there was something else, some other dim memory she couldn't quite grasp . . .

Heather took the pot to the sink and gently tipped out all of the black dirt, sifting through it with her fingers, but there was nothing more to be found. Standing back, she looked up to see her reflection in the window; she looked pale and drawn, her dark hair falling forward across her cheeks and forehead.

"It has to mean something," she said aloud to the empty kitchen. "It's not a coincidence, it can't be." There was a connection here. A connection between not only her mother and Michael Reave, but between Heather and the new killer. Which had to mean she was in real danger. *The story*, she reminded herself. If there really was a connection between her and the Red Wolf, it meant that any article she wrote would be truly explosive. She would have to play this very carefully.

Movement in the darkness outside the window. Heather gasped, nearly dropping the pot, which she slammed down on the counter. There was a figure out there, a dark shape against the lawn. Without thinking she snatched up a knife from the kitchen drawer and ran to the back door, ramming the key home and turning it so violently that later she would realize she had almost sprained her wrist. Outside, the chill of the autumn evening filled her lungs like ice blocks and she could see almost nothing. Confused thoughts shot like comets across her mind: *what if I catch the killer, what if he kills me, what if I kill him . . .*

"Who are you? What do you want?"

Light from the kitchen windows cast yellow squares across the lawn. Whatever had been moving out there was gone.

CHAPTER

21

BEFORE

Michael stood on the driveway looking out across the fields below, narrowing his eyes as another vanload of young people drove up. They were greeted by a group who had already set up their tents, and he heard their bright voices drifting across to him. A soft pressure next to his thigh let him know that the dog was with him, and he heard the squeak of a pair of wellington boots moving across the foyer floor.

"I thought the rule was, not on our doorstep?" He spoke without turning around. The man chuckled from behind them, then appeared, pulling on a pair of thick gardening gloves.

"Your problem, lad, is that you've got no vision." The man sucked in air through his teeth. It was early spring, and still very cold in the mornings. "I'm setting up a septic tank for them. Want to help?"

Michael crossed his arms over his chest. Down below, a pair of women were walking together across the field, one of them carrying a guitar case. They both had long blonde hair the color of wet straw, perfectly straight, and they walked arm in arm, their heads bent together in conversation. They looked like they could be twins, at the very least, sisters. He knew, instantly, that they, like all women, were not to be trusted.

"Why are you doing this? You've never wanted company here before."

"Company? It's hardly company, lad." The man grinned his long toothy grin. "Oh no, this is something else altogether."

CHAPTER

22

SHIVERING OUTSIDE THE gates waiting to be taken inside the prison, Heather glanced back at a small strip of green across the road. In the summer it would be thick with trees, but thorough winds had stripped all the leaves from the branches and it looked exposed and raw. A figure was standing there, his back to her, a hood up over his head and his hands deep in his pockets. She thought of Michael Reave, so dedicated to the landscape and things that grow. Unwanted, one of the images she'd found during her Internet searches floated through her mind's eye; a woman, her face pale and waxy looking, her mouth full of blood and her head garlanded with primroses and small white flowers Heather couldn't name. What did Reave do now, trapped in an antiseptic little cell? Did they have schemes to keep the prisoners busy? Did they let him do gardening? The thought of it made her grimace, and it took her a moment to summon a smile for the guard who collected her and took her through.

"Inspector Parker. It's good to see you." And she meant it. She had spent the morning making notes and searching her memories for any other links between her family and Michael Reave, but the thought of the slightly awkward, slightly sweet lunch she'd had with the detective kept slipping to the front of her mind.

The slightly ruffled looking detective glanced up from a ream of papers, eyebrows raised.

"Likewise." They stood outside the interview room, just out of sight of the small reinforced window. "I, uh . . . thanks for coming in again. I know it's not easy."

"Yeah, well. Last time I saw Reave, he lost his temper with me. Is he . . . is he happy to speak to me again?"

"Very much so. In fact, he's been asking about you." Seeing the expression that passed over her face, Parker continued. "I know it's weird, but . . . this is a man that carted parts of bodies around the country then planted flowers around them. His behavior isn't necessarily rational, or predictable. It's worth remembering that while you're in there. Are you ready?"

Heather straightened up, lifting her chin a touch. Her head was thumping steadily, but she had spent a good half an hour in the shower that morning, trying to wash away her tiredness and the lingering anxieties of the night before.

"Let's do it."

The interview room was still small, oppressive, yellow. Michael Reave was still a larger than life presence, hulking in his seat, yet there was no mistaking the brief expression of pleasure that passed over his face as Heather entered the room.

"You came back."

"How are you . . ." Heather steeled herself, internally apologizing to a score of lost women, ". . . Michael?"

He smiled, and he looked briefly younger.

"As well as I can be, lass. What's the weather like out there?"

It was such an oddly polite question, so wildly out of place, that for a brief moment it was all Heather could do just to sit down and gather her wits.

"It's cool, getting colder. Really starting to feel like autumn. There's that freshness, you know."

"Fresh air is good. It's good for the soul. I wish I got more of it, but . . ." he shrugged, a rueful expression on his face. "I'll never get as much as I need."

There was no sign of the anger he'd displayed in their last meeting.

"Do you get outside?" she asked, thinking of the strip of green she'd seen outside the prison. She had no envelope of images today.

"He gets to spend time in the yard," said DI Parker.

"And is there grass? Can you see trees, or anything?"

"It's not much more than a concrete hole," said Reave, dryly. He glanced at the guards. "I can see the sky, though, which isn't nothing. And I'm glad of anything I can get."

"It's important to you, isn't it? The natural world, the countryside.'

"Where I grew up . . ." He paused, as though he was going to say something else, then changed his mind. "When I was a kid, that's all there was. We lived in a remote place—I spent my days in ditches and fields, caked in mud. There's a peace to it, you know, especially when you don't have anything else." He looked up, his face briefly alight with anger. "We're connected to the land, all of us. It's not natural to be apart from it."

"The women they say you killed." Heather heard Parker clear his throat, uncomfortable with the turn in conversation. "They were found in the middle of green places, weren't they? With flowers and trees and plants. Green things. Were they disconnected from the land? Were you trying to put them back?"

Heather sat very still. She was expecting an outburst, or at least for Reave to demand to be taken back to his cell. But instead he sat quietly, his gaze rooted to the table.

"Your mother knew. She knew about how important the real world was," he said eventually.

"What else did my mother know, Michael?"

When he didn't say anything, she continued.

"You can read a lot about your case online. I mean, you have to go a bit beyond Wikipedia, but it's there, if you look. God knows how much of it is accurate, though . . . It was the last victim that got you convicted. Your van was seen in the area where her body was found, and a few strands of her hair were found on a blanket in the back. Not all that much to connect you to the previous victims apart from the similarity of the way they were killed and the bodies were staged. It must have been a lot of work, and you were very careful."

She paused. From somewhere down the hall she could hear a phone ringing and ringing, no one answering. Reave had gone very still. One hand rested against the edge of the table, and one thick, callused thumb pressed against it, turning the flesh white. His eyes, which would still not meet hers, looked haunted.

"When I saw you the other day, we talked about this being a chance to tell your story. Was there someone helping you, Michael? Someone who helped you grab the women, and get them in the van?"

"My story." He smiled tightly. "I told you lass, no one cares about my story."

"*I* do." She managed to say it this time, and with enough feeling behind the words that he looked up, his eyebrows raised. "If it's my mum's story, too, then I want to know about it. You think no one cares, but they would, Michael, if your story helps to stop someone from hurting more women. I care, if it means I can understand a bit more about my mum's pain, and what made her do that to herself."

She stopped, and for a long moment there was silence in the room. Heather reached for her bag, and after a slight hesitation, she pulled her mother's suicide note from inside her note book. She smoothed it down with her fingers, trying to ignore the crushing feeling of guilt—*What are you doing? Why would you show this, this painfully private thing, to a killer like Reave?* And then she passed it over to him. Reave took it carefully, as though he was handling a baby bird.

"This is the note she left behind. It's . . . I wondered if you could make anything of it."

She watched his face carefully as he read it, hoping for something obvious—shock, anger, sadness, even amusement. Instead he looked at it steadily, his big hands making the note look like a tiny scrap of paper. He swallowed once, and then he passed it back to her, nodding slightly as though she had done him a big favor by letting him read it.

"Well?" Heather paused and bit her lip, trying to remove the desperate tone from her voice. "Does it mean anything to you?"

When Reave spoke again, his voice was softer than it had been.

"Your mother. She was different to the rest of them. Kinder, more innocent. She was a doe in those woods."

"My mum was? Different to who?"

He snorted. "The rest of the commune. They were there because their friends were doing it, or they wanted to take drugs and get drunk, but your mother, lass. She was different to *everyone*, to all other women. She knew how important the woods were, she knew . . ."

When he didn't continue, Heather leaned forward again. "*What did she know?*"

He's going to say she knew about the murders, she thought wildly. *That my mother stood by and waited for him to come back every night with blood on his hands.* The idea was horrifyingly appealing. If her mother had been a terrible person all along, she'd be free of her guilt.

"She was innocent, but strong, too. I didn't think it, not back then, but that just shows what I knew, doesn't it? Like a rock under snow. I got her wrong, in lots of ways. She defied me, in the way that only a woman can."

"What do you mean?"

He shook his head, and Heather experienced a moment of pure despair. They would talk in circles forever, the two of them, and he would always dangle this information just out of reach.

"Michael? Please. Tell me what you mean. Did you . . . did you love her?"

"I wanted to tell you another story," he said. "Would you let me?"

Heather pressed her lips together and swallowed down her frustration. Parker had moved so that he was standing behind her chair, and she wondered if she was close to being removed from the room again.

"There was a king, and he was known for being the wisest king that ever lived. He was truly the . . . father of the land, and seemed to know about things almost before they'd happened. It was a mystery, but the people, his children loved him anyway. They didn't ask how. They just trusted that he would always know.

"Every day, he would be served dinner in his royal dining room, and the final course would be served on a covered silver platter. No one knew what was in the dish, as the king always dismissed his guests and servants before he ate it, and the servant who brought it was always instructed never to lift the lid."

Reave took a slow breath. Something about the telling of the story seemed to have calmed him.

"One day though, the servant couldn't resist any longer. When the king had finished and asked for the dishes to be taken away, the servant took the mysterious silver plate to his own room, and locking the door, he removed the cover. Lying on the plate was a little white snake, it's eyes red like drops of blood. Curious, the servant sliced a slither of snake flesh from it and put it on his tongue. Instantly, the room was filled with strange whispers and hushed conversations. Voices all around—it was the fleas in his bed clothes, the ants under his bed, the birds at his windowsill. They were all talking, talking, and he could understand them. He could understand them all, those little souls."

Reave cleared his throat, and glanced at the note, which was lying between them on the table.

"Eventually, the king found out what had happened, and the servant was certain he would be executed for such a crime. But instead, the king took him, alone, into the heart of an enormous dark forest. They rode together for three days and three nights, until they came to a deep hole in the ground. The bottom of it, Heather, was littered with animal bones, and there were many white snakes, slithering across the dirt floor—so many, it was difficult to tell which were snakes and which were bones. 'You see the price?' said the king. 'For such knowledge as we have, the land demands meat. It demands flesh and blood, for it is always hungry.' And with that . . ."

"The king pushed the servant into the pit?" Heather completed it for him.

Reave stopped. A slow smile spread across his face. His hands were now lying loosely on the table, palms facing the ceiling.

"There you go, lass."

Heather swallowed hard. She was beginning to think like him. When the silence between them had spooled into something less than comfortable, she leaned forward on the table. She forced herself to meet his eyes. "Was there someone else, Michael, someone you trusted to know how to handle everything? Do you know the person who is murdering these women now? Who was he to you?"

Reave shook his head. "I'm telling you my story, Heather, over and over. But I don't think you're listening."

Michael Reave would say nothing more. However, when the two guards moved forward to escort him from the room, his head snapped up, life returning to his face.

"There will be a funeral? For Colleen? Or have you already . . .?"

"It's on Wednesday," said Heather.

"Are you putting her in the ground?"

It was almost too easy to relax around Reave, to believe he was no longer dangerous, but the eagerness with which he asked the question caused the hair to stand up on the back of Heather's neck. She picked up the note from the table and slipped it back into her pocket.

"No, it's a cremation. She asked for it in her will."

He looked down, hiding his face, his big shoulders heaving as he struggled with something. The hand still resting on the table opened and closed convulsively.

"And her ashes?"

DI Parker stepped forward and pressed Heather's shoulder, briefly, and she found herself ridiculously grateful for it.

"You know very well that's none of your business, Reave."

The big man looked away from them. Heather was shocked to realize that he was genuinely upset, his strong features constricted with grief. "She would want to be somewhere out in the open, lass. Just remember that."

* * *

Later, in the murky little prison canteen, Parker sat opposite Heather, frowning and fiddling with paperwork again. Both their beakers of tea stood untouched.

"I'm not sure what good this is doing us. While it's true that this is the most he's ever said to anyone, including his array of shrinks, I'm not sure what the world's creepiest episode of Jackanory is achieving."

"Have you thought about it? The possibility that he wasn't the one actually doing the killings all those years ago?"

He sighed.

"He's not the best example of a serial killer, you do realize that?" When Heather looked at him blankly, Parker continued.

"The vast majority of them are nasty idiots who got lucky for a while. Inadequate men with low IQs and messed up sexual appetites. Sad little men who feel nothing unless they are dominating someone. A case like Michael Reave is extremely rare, and I don't want you to be taken in by it."

"You mean, he's unusual for a serial killer."

Parker shrugged one shoulder, picked up his tea, and put it down again. "He's articulate. Even charming. You can have a conversation with him and not feel your brain cells dying, which believe me, is unusual for that group. He doesn't look like a monster. But," he cleared his throat, "aside from the van and the evidence in it, he was living an itinerant lifestyle at the time, travelling around a lot, and he has no real alibis for any of the murders. His mother disappeared when he was a kid, did you know that?"

"Are you suggesting he killed her, too?"

Parker shrugged. "Maybe she just left, but we have every reason to believe it was an unhappy, abusive home."

"That proves nothing."

"True. The hairs and the location of the van are what prove it."

"I'm not arguing with you," said Heather. Her face was growing hot, and she felt angry. Parker was suggesting she had been taken in by Reave, like those bizarre women who wrote letters to convicted killers and ended up marrying them. She thought of her mother, and her stomach rolled violently. "Ben, you have someone out there right now who seems to know an awful lot about the Red Wolf case. Who seems to know too much."

He reached up and rubbed the back of his neck. "Listen, we appreciate your help. *I* appreciate it. I know it's grim, sitting in that room with him." He stopped, sighing suddenly. "We've found Miss Graham's body."

"Oh."

Unable to stop herself, Heather thought of the photo she had given Parker, of the little grinning red head with the smudge of cream on her cheek. The idea that such a fate was waiting for her, a few years down the line, was unspeakable.

"Was she . . . was it like the rest?"

Parker shuffled his paperwork back into a pile, signaling that the conversation was over.

"It's best I don't tell you about it, to be honest. You'll come back? Try again?"

"You don't think it's pointless then?"

"I will take anything I can get at this point. We have to find this guy and stop him. Soon. Plus," he glanced away, looking to see, she suspected, whether any colleagues were in earshot, "I'd like to see you again."

Heather grinned. "You know, there are other ways to ask someone out. Ways that don't involve a third-wheel serial killer. Call me old fashioned."

DI Parker smiled ruefully at her. "Like I said, I take what I can get."

C H A P T E R

23

HEATHER SAT CROSS-LEGGED on her mother's sofa, the terra-cotta pot in her lap. She turned it around and around in her hands, her fingers occasionally brushing over the ragged heart-shaped scratch in the clay. Nikki was pouring more wine into their glasses as she sat on the floor.

It was a heart. It was nothing. She could wander into any department store in London and find some sort of rustic crap emblazoned with hearts—coasters, toast racks, plates. Probably everyone had something with a heart on in their house, whether you were stylish or chintzy or utilitarian. They were weirdly hard to avoid.

Yet.

"My mum never liked this sort of thing, you know."

"What?" Nikki took a sip of her wine and raised an eyebrow. "Flower pots?"

"Hearts." Heather turned the pot around so she could see the scratched heart. "My dad was always so careful about what Valentine's gifts he brought home for her. He always said she was *fussy*. But the more I think of it . . ." she frowned. "He gave her all sorts of presents, my dad, but never love-hearts and flowers. When it was her birthday, he'd get chocolates in her favorite flavors, candles that smelled of things like fresh laundry and sea breezes, jewelry and perfume and books. No teddies clutching hearts or massive bouquets of flowers."

"Okay," said Nikki. "So what? Lots of people don't do the whole Valentine's thing. And would that have been so out of character for your mum? She never struck me as soppy, exactly."

"Yeah, I know what you mean. But . . ." Heather turned the pot over again, racking her memory. There had always been plants around the house when she was growing up, fat green plants with lustrous, shining leaves, the sort of plants that you could ignore most of the time without them dying. But flowers? Had Dad ever just brought home a bunch of tulips from the gas station? Sitting in her mother's chintzy living room, the faint smell of coffee and air freshener in her nose, Heather thought not. "She didn't like flowers, I'm almost sure of it. No daffodils in a vase on the table, no roses on Valentine's Day. Nikki, what if flowers had bad associations for her? Perhaps she had looked at cut flowers, fresh blooms already dying, and had remembered that the man she had once spent so much time with—*the man she was writing to in prison*—had used flowers to decorate the corpses of his victims."

"You're reading too much into it," said Nikki, but she looked uncertain, all the same.

"I don't know if I am. Because there's clearly loads of stuff about my mum I never had a clue about. It's like I'm being shown a whole other side of her now." Heather sighed. "Maybe I'll find out more tomorrow."

"You're going to see this Anna woman?"

Heather nodded. She had phoned the number Pamela Whittaker had given her and spoken to the receptionist of the Twelve Elms Centre. Heather had sensed a fair amount of surprise from the woman that Anna had a visitor at all, but they had been eager enough to book her in.

"She might have known my mum, so it's worth a try."

Nikki swirled her wine in her glass thoughtfully. "Hev, do you really think Fiddler's Mill is the key to all this? That something that happened so long ago could have caused your mother to . . . do this to herself?"

"I do." As soon as she said it out loud, she realized it was true. "I really do think something happened at this place, something mum kept secret for the rest of her life."

Heather stood up and left the living room, heading for the kitchen with the pot still in her arms. She was halfway across the tiled floor when a memory dropped into her mind like a blade of ice, and she jumped, the terracotta pot slipping from her arms. It shattered, scattering shards of orange clay all over her feet and sending pieces skittering under the fridge and the oven, but Heather hardly noticed.

The card.

"Heather?" Nikki appeared at the kitchen door, her eyes wide. "Are you all right?"

It had been left outside their door when Heather was thirteen or fourteen. She had found it as she'd stepped out to nip to the shops, and she remembered the weird combined feeling of embarrassment and pleasure as she'd knelt to pick it up. At the time, she had been nursing a crush on a boy called James Thurlow, who was in her science classes, and thanks to a wild combination of hormones and optimism she had been dropping huge hints about Valentine's Day for the last few weeks. The card itself had been quite a classy one; simple white background traced with gold lines, a big red heart in the middle. Inside, somewhat disappointingly, there were just the printed words "always thinking of you" with a heart hand drawn in ballpoint pen underneath.

"What is it? What's wrong?" Nikki took her hand and squeezed it, and with some difficulty Heather dragged herself back to the present.

When I was a teenager, someone left a Valentine's card on our doorstep. I thought it was for me, but . . . Mum saw me pick it up, and Nikki, she went batshit."

Her mother had grabbed her by the shoulder, yanking her back into the hallway and slamming the door shut. Her face had been so pale, and Heather could clearly picture the dark smudges that had appeared under her eyes, almost like bruises.

"She yanked the card out of my hands and she tore it up, just like that. When I shouted at her, said that it was mine, she had asked me if it had been addressed to me, and it hadn't, but you know, I was a kid, it never occurred to me that anyone could have been sending my mum a Valentine's card. She was old, and married, and to kids that basically means dead, right? But . . ." Heather looked at the shards of the pot littering the floor. "When she was done shouting at me, she started crying. Locked herself in the bathroom. We never spoke of it again."

"What do you think it means?""

"I don't know." Heather rubbed her hands over her face. They smelt like the dirt that had been inside the pot. "Probably nothing. Come on, I can't be bothered to clean this up now. Let's go and finish our wine."

Heather watched Nikki walk back into the living room. It was cold, too cold. She rubbed vigorously at her arms, and a violent shiver worked its way down her spine.

The card didn't mean anything, except that her mother was paranoid about something, even at a time when Michael Reave himself had certainly been in prison, and in no position to leave cards on doorsteps—unless there was someone on the outside, performing little tasks for him. Tasks like romantic gestures. And murder.

Heather kicked one of the bigger shards of pot under the fridge, and went to join her friend.

CHAPTER 24

THE TWELVE ELMS Centre was a pleasingly gothic building, with white windowsills shining against dark gray brick, and all the more imposing under a sky filled with rain clouds. Heather walked up the path through the gardens, noting that they were well kept and neat, while the sign outside the building was narrow and discreet: Twelve Elms Centre for the Treatment of Anxiety Disorders and Trauma. Inside a cozy reception area she spoke to a sturdy looking man with kind eyes, who shortly introduced her to Doctor Parvez.

"You're here to visit Anna Hobson?"

Dr Parvez was a tall willowy man with an advancing bald patch and large, old-fashioned glasses. He wore a beige cardigan that was both too long and too big for him, making him look a little like an absent-minded grandma.

Heather smiled. "Yeah, a favor for my friend Pamela. She used to visit quite often, I think, but has been rushed off her feet lately. You've probably met her?"

"Ms. Whittaker, yes. Well, thank you for taking the time. Anna doesn't get many visitors, and they really do help. News from the real world always goes down a storm."

He led her down a series of pleasant corridors, all smelling faintly of disinfectant and floor polish. Heather caught sight of a few people here and there; a young man with an old- fashioned haircut reading a newspaper, an older lady sitting in an armchair, rubbing her hands together over and over.

"Did Ms. Whittaker tell you much about Anna?"

"Not so much. Only that she's been through a tough time."

Dr Parvez nodded seriously. "She has, at that. She might lose her train of thought a little, but generally Anna is delightful company. Here you go."

He stopped at the doorway to a wide, spacious room, tastefully decorated in magnolia and a faint, anemic pink. There were several tables, each set with pairs of chairs, and a handful of people talking quietly. The tall windows looked out across the gardens. Despite the pleasantness of the surroundings, Heather found herself thinking about her visits to Belmarsh to see Michael Reave.

"The people here," she said suddenly. "They don't have . . . a history of violence or anything, do they?"

A flicker of annoyance passed over Dr Parvez's face, and Heather immediately regretted asking.

"We treat a variety of problems here, Miss Evans—depression, anxiety, various personality disorders—and one of the few things they all have in common is that the patients are much more likely to hurt themselves than anyone else. Shall I introduce you to Anna?"

He took her over to a table in the far corner. Sitting there was a tired looking woman with lank, brown hair and a deeply creased face. Heather found she could not guess at how old she was; she seemed all ages at once. She was wearing a soft hooded top and a T-shirt, and she looked up at Heather with watery eyes.

"Good morning, Anna," said Dr Parvez, brightly enough. "Pamela sent someone to have a chat with you. Are you feeling up to it today?"

Anna's eyes wandered back over to the doctor, as if seeing him for the first time, and then she nodded slowly.

"Great." Dr Parvez turned to Heather and smiled. "I'll get someone to bring you both a cup of tea."

Heather seated herself at the table. She felt slightly foolish. What was she supposed to say to this woman? A soft murmur from the corner of the room revealed a television set no one was watching.

"Hi Anna, how are you? I'm Heather Evans. Pamela said I should come and have a chat. Would you like that?" Heather cringed inwardly at the patronizing tone in her own voice. It was because the place felt like an old people's home; she half expected to have to raise her voice, or avoid talking about politics. The woman sighed heavily.

"A chat. Yeah. That would be good," she shifted in the chair, bringing her arms up around her chest briefly, as though hugging herself, and then dropped them again. "It's very boring here," she said, some animation coming into her eyes. "Not much to do. I'm allowed to go for a wander, usually, but I got into trouble last time."

"How come? What happened?"

Anna shrugged and looked away, a slightly shifty expression moving over her features, when a short young woman came over with two polystyrene cups of tea for them. Heather thanked her, and she moved to the far side of the room, where an old man was playing checkers by himself.

"So. This seems like a nice place. How did you end up here?"

"Referrals, one place to another, that's me. They said I have mild paranoid schizophrenia," she pronounced it carefully, as though reading it off a card in her head. "With long-term delusions, occasional hallucinations." Then, as an afterthought, "probably exacerbated by drink and drug abuse."

"That's a lot to deal with."

"You're telling me." With this out of the way, Anna seemed to brighten a bit. "It's hard, and I take so many pills I rattle, but this is a nice place. Better than others. Pam sent you, did she?"

"Yeah. I chatted to her about her art work, and she helped me out, so I said I'd come and talk to you." She cleared her throat. "She says she's sorry she hasn't been lately."

Anna shrugged again. "Poor Pam, she worries a lot. She thinks a lot of this is her fault, when it's not. It's just the way my brain is made, but she . . . she finds it hard to see me when I'm going through a bad patch."

"Why would Pam think your problems are her fault?"

Again, Anna seemed reluctant to answer. Instead, she took a sip of her tea, grimacing as she swallowed. "Christ, this stuff tastes like piss. That's the worst thing about being in these places, I think. The bloody tea. There's no tea quite like the stuff you make yourself at home, is there?" As she put the cup back down, Heather got a glance at the top of her forearm; she only saw it for a second, but there was a tangled knot of scar tissue there, white against the woman's heavily freckled skin. It was roughly heart-shaped.

Heather forced a smile onto her lips even as her stomach turned over. "You're definitely right there. So how do you know Pam?"

"We met when I was a girl really, travelling round Europe, getting into all the wrong things." She grinned briefly, revealing at least one tooth that had turned black. "She was older than me, so I followed her for a bit, and we ended up at this commune place in Lancashire. She loved it at first, Pam did."

"The commune?"

"Oh yeah. All that nature stuff, she loved it. She was one of those real committed hippies, you know?" Anna smiled, although it looked pained now. "I was there for the drugs, mostly. They had some good shit there."

"Fiddler's Mill." Heather said it carefully, somehow convinced that the name would upset the woman, but she didn't show any particular reaction. "Pam mentioned the place. Said that you had a hard time there."

The unspoken question hung in the air for a moment. Anna lifted her arms again in the slight, almost hugging motion, then laid her hands on her stomach instead.

"There were some bad people. Good drugs, bad people. Funny how that works, isn't it? I . . . I had some fun there. It's a strange place, that bit of the countryside. I grew up in a flat on a council estate and the closest we got to green stuff was the scrubby grass in the swing park but that place . . . there's so much of it. You go out there and stand in the middle of the woods, it's like it could be any time. Like, a hundred years ago, three hundred years ago, I don't know. Maybe even before people were around, you know? That sort of place. So quiet, so lonely." She shrugged. "I got lonely there, I made myself less lonely. That's how drugs work sometimes—they make it easy not to be lonely."

"A lot of free love?"

Anna smiled wanly, although there was an expression about her eyes that worried Heather. She glanced around and saw a portly nurse come into the room, the first person she had seen in any sort of uniform. The woman paused at a table to pick up an empty cup.

"Not sure free is a good word for it. Certainly bloody costly to me. But yeah, I suppose."

"Anna, while you were there, did you know a woman called Colleen?"

Heather pulled an old photograph from her satchel and laid it on the table between them. It was a photo of her mother at a birthday party, standing next to a cake covered in unlit candles. Heather guessed she was in her late-twenties at the time, and she looked, as she did in all photos, slightly uneasy. The tops of her cheeks were flushed pink.

"Colleen?" Anna was peering at the photograph.

"Yeah. She might have been at Fiddler's Mill at the same time as you. Do you recognize her at all?"

"Why? Why are you asking about this?" Anna looked confused. She touched her fingers to the photograph and then brought them away quickly, as though it had burned her. "I thought you were a friend of Pam's?"

"Oh, just curious. It turns out I knew someone who went there, too. Weird coincidence, isn't it?" Heather smiled, watching Anna's face for any sign of recognition, but there was only bafflement.

"There were lots of girls there," Anna said eventually. "And a lot of drugs. I don't know. It's a miracle I remember Pamela, to be honest." But as she turned away from the photo, Heather thought she saw another expression in the set of her eyes, and the corners of her mouth; guilt.

Heather picked up the photograph and put it back into her satchel.

"Was there other stuff going on, Anna? Weird stuff, I mean." For a second she considered asking about the scars on her arm, but Anna had turned her chin up to the ceiling and narrowed her eyes, as if looking up at a bright summer sky.

"They grabbed you so hard sometimes, it bruised. Would wake up in the morning with these dark smudges all up my arms, you know? I would think it was dirt, but it wouldn't wash off."

"Who? Who would grab you?"

"They said it all had to go back to the land, it's what they always said—that the land was hungry, so thirsty, and we had to make it better again. I think that's where . . ." Her chin and lower lip crumpled, as if she were about to cry. "I think that's where they put her." She spoke her final words in a whisper.

"Put who, Anna?"

"My baby." She dropped her head and looked directly at Heather. Her eyes were abruptly full of tears. "My baby. They *took* her."

"You were pregnant at Fiddler's Mill, and gave birth there?"

"He *took her.*" Anna's voice had risen, becoming wavery and shrill. Heather felt rather than saw the other occupants of the room turning to look at them. "I gave birth to her in the woods, in the mud, and they ripped her from me while she was still covered in my blood."

"Anna, it's okay, you don't have to talk about this —"

It was too late. Anna was on her feet, the seat behind her knocked to the floor. "They stole her!" she howled. "Stole my fucking baby and no one will believe me!"

The nurse appeared at the table, moving so quickly and quietly Heather was half convinced she had materialized there.

"Anna honey, it's okay. Maybe it's time to go back to your room?" To Heather's mild surprise the nurse had an American accent—somehow this only made the situation more surreal, and she found herself looking at the corners of the ceiling, wondering where the cameras were. Anna wasn't mollified by the nurse.

Instead, she stumbled away from the table, tears running freely down her face.

"Where did she go? Why don't you fucking believe me?"

Dr Parvez appeared at the entrance to the communal room, and at a nod from the nurse he took Anna's arm gently, easing her away from Heather.

"Come on Anna, let's get you settled, shall we?"

The woman shuffled from the room, her head down and her hair hanging in her face, still muttering about her baby, how she had been taken, how no one believed her. Heather watched her go with a tight wad of distress in her stomach. The nurse turned toward her, her mouth pursed with displeasure.

"Why would you go and talk to her about that? She'll be like that for the rest of the day now."

"I didn't know," said Heather, not entirely truthfully. "Is it true, that her baby was taken from her? That seems like quite a wild story."

The nurse rolled her eyes theatrically, but the hostility in her posture seemed to fade a little. "Honey, Anna isn't well, not well at all. She has lost babies, but not because any boogie man snatched them from her." She cast her eyes downward and lowered her voice. "Two babies carried to term, but stillborn. It's been very hard for her. It would be hard for anyone, but for Anna . . ." She shrugged one rounded shoulder. "The illness makes it worse, because she doesn't just suffer the grief, her mind provides all sorts of strange reasons for it. Listen," she picked up Anna's half-finished cup of tea and peered into it critically. "It's best if you go now. Dr Parvez will be trying to calm her, and you'll not be able to speak to her again today. If you come back to see her again, do me a favor and think of better conversation starters, okay? The food, the local news, the weather. You people love your weather."

Heather agreed that she would, and left, walking back down the gravel path with the big building looming behind her. Just before she turned the corner that would take her to the main road, she looked back, peering up at the blank windows. She wondered if Anna was watching her leave, or if she was in a sedative induced sleep now, dreaming of giving birth in the woods. But the daylight had turned the windows opaque, and if there was anyone looking out, she couldn't see them.

* * *

The next day was bright and bitterly cold, a blameless blue sky apparently letting the chill of the universe in. Heather stepped out of the cold into a busy central London coffee shop, immediately soothed by the warmth and the gentle chatter of office workers munching through their paninis.

"Hi Diane. How are you?"

It took the older woman a moment to look up from her latte. She did not look much different than when Heather had seen her last—the haircut was a little slicker perhaps, the clothes a little more sober.

"Heather, sit down. I heard about your mother." Diane turned in her seat and made a complicated gesture at a nearby barista. He nodded and set about making a fresh pair of coffees. "How are you holding up?"

"About how you'd expect, really. Thanks for seeing me. I know that with the way things ended at *The Post*, well . . ."

Diane flapped her hands dismissively. They both paused as their coffees were brought over.

"Listen, Diane, I have a story," Heather looked down at her hands. "I think it's going to be pretty big."

Diane raised one perfect eyebrow. "And what? You want to give it to me?"

"Yes. Well, no." Heather grinned. It was good to see Diane again. Her no-nonsense attitude made everything seem saner than it had ten minutes ago. "I want you to run it, eventually, but I need time. It's about the Red Wolf."

"Heather, every paper is dripping with the Red Wolf at the moment, if you'll forgive the phrase. Do you really have a new angle on it?"

"Would speaking directly to Michael Reave himself count?"

It was satisfying to see the look of surprise that passed over her old editor's face.

"Let's say you have my attention. How did this come about?"

Heather dumped a couple of extra sugars into her coffee. "First of all, you have to promise me you'll wait, okay? I can't mess up the investigation, or my current . . . arrangement, so the story needs to wait until I have everything. And I want to write it. All right? This is *my* piece, Diane. More than anything I've ever written, okay?"

Diane raised her eyebrows. "Are you going to tell me what this is all about?'

After a sip of much too sweet coffee to steady herself, Heather told her. About the letters, her mother's apparently close relationship with a serial murderer, and everything she'd gleaned about the new murders so far: that Fiona Graham had been taken directly from her bedroom, that the police had been going through her personal belongings at the school where she worked, that hearts, or heart shapes, seemed central to the killings. She gave Diane her impressions on Reave himself, and watched as her old editor's face grew hungry—a look she'd seen whenever a big story was about to break. She left out the note left at her mother's house, and her own crawling suspicions about her mother's role in everything; in the story she told, the letters were simply the catalyst that got her access to a murderer. She said nothing about Anna Hobson's wild claims of stolen babies—she didn't want to push her luck.

"I'm picturing maybe a series of articles," Heather said, her voice low. "About Reave, and when they get this new bastard, him, too. From my unique perspective. Do you see? I'm the only person he's spoken to in any detail."

"Apart from your mother." Heather winced at this, but Diane carried on speaking. "You're right. It's a unique angle."

"You have to promise me, Diane, that I get to write it. I'll come back to you when I have everything I need."

"Heather, the way things ended before . . . Well, it leaves me without much space to maneuver. There are people I work with now who wouldn't be thrilled to see a story from you gracing our paper."

"Does that really matter? Or, do you think I've somehow lost the ability to write in the last few months? Come on, Diane."

"Tell you what, since I'm fond of you. Send me over a few pages." Diane sipped at the foam on the top of her coffee. "Give me a solid idea of what you're going for. It'll make it easier for me to get it in."

Heather sighed and leaned back in her chair a little. This was risky, and she knew it, but just seeing Diane again had brought back a lot of memories; memories of how much she had enjoyed her job; memories of how, at one time, it had been enormously important to her.

"Fine. I'll send over some notes."

"It's a deal," Diane gave one of her rare smiles, like sun breaking through on a winter day. "This feels like dangerous ground though, Heather. Be careful. Stay safe."

CHAPTER

25

"THERE'S BEEN A complication with today's visit."

Heather curled her hands around the warm polystyrene cup, watching Ben Parker's face for a clue. Today he was all business again, no hint in his manner of the cozy lunch they'd shared, but he flashed her a slightly pained smile as they walked down the corridor.

"Oh?"

"An incident with another inmate." Seeing her look, Parker shook his head slightly. "Nothing serious, but alongside a bit of a cock up with communications it's messed up Michael Reave's schedule. So. Now he's in the yard for the next hour, when he's supposed to be chatting with you."

"You can't just get him out?"

"I could," Parker conceded. "But the warden isn't keen. If there's one thing Reave does like to complain about, it's his yard access, or lack of it, and the warden doesn't want to provoke more belly aching. So you've got a bit of a wait. Shall I get you another tea?"

Heather glanced down at the brown liquid in the cup. It smelt like it might have been near some tea once. "No. Thanks. Listen, can't I see him in the yard?"

They had reached the door that led to the small interview room. Parker stopped, rubbing the back of his neck with one hand.

"That's very much not allowed, Heather . . ."

"But it's urgent, isn't it? And you'll have your guards there. Besides, he might be more amenable in the fresh air. I think it's worth a try."

Parker sighed. He looked tired, she realized, the skin under his eyes shadowed and thin.

He rolled his eyes at her and a small smile crept in at the corner of his mouth. "I'll see what I can do."

Five minutes later Heather was being escorted down more anonymous corridors by a pair of burly men in uniform, Parker bringing up the rear. Eventually they passed through a series of gates, the clunk of locks and buzzing of various alarms ringing in her ears, until they stepped out into a bleak square courtyard. The ground was a mixture of dirt and gravel, and the stone walls were chipped and scratched here and there with graffiti—someone had painstakingly carved "FUCK PIGS" just to one side of the door. In the center of the shabby square was a series of large wooden planters, filled with some anonymous green bushes, and to the sides of those were two metal stands for cigarette butts, both of which were overflowing. The smell of stale tobacco and ash was powerful, but directly overhead was a bright square of blue sky and Heather found she was glad to see it.

"Heather. You're a sight for sore eyes, lass."

Standing by one of the walls was Michael Reave. He was wearing a dark blue long-sleeved jumper and black tracksuit bottoms. His hands were cuffed behind his back, but as he moved toward her, he was smiling easily enough. Outside, under real daylight, he looked somehow larger than he had earlier, more vital. In contrast to DI Parker, he didn't look tired at all; he looked awake and calm, even younger than he had, and Heather felt a tremor of unease move through her. He might be caged up and constantly watched, but he was still a tall, powerfully built man, and she was sure that if he wanted to do her harm in this space—or any space—he could.

"This is where you have your breaks? Your exercise?"

Reave looked around, as if seeing it for the first time. He shrugged. "It's one of the places. I take what I can get. And it's a sunny day." He smiled, and she realized this was the happiest she'd seen him. "And I have company for once."

Taking care not to get too close, Heather took a few steps forward. Parker was just to her left, the two burly officers just behind her. "I wondered, Michael, if you could tell me some more about what my mum was like. When she was young. Now she's gone, I feel like . . ." She made a point of looking down at her feet, then back up at him, the sun in her eyes. "I don't know, I feel like I've missed a lot, you know?"

He nodded slowly, his face softening a touch. For a long moment, no one said anything. From somewhere behind them Heather could hear the harsh buzz as doors were unlocked and locked again, deeper in the building.

"Colleen," said Reave eventually, "was kind. Softhearted. She was an educated woman. At least, she was to me. I liked to listen to her talk about stories, about what they meant to her." He paused, and turned to look in the direction of the planter, although Heather didn't think he was seeing it. "It didn't matter to her that I hadn't had no schooling to speak of. She never judged me for it. She would just share things. That was what your mum was like."

Heather crossed her arms over her chest, trying to keep a neutral expression on her face. It was proving difficult to match up this vision of her mother—forgiving, sweet natured, kind—with the woman she had spent so much of her teenage life having bitter arguments with. Talking about Colleen seemed to have warmed Reave up, and he took a step toward her. Heather felt cold fingers walk down her spine as the officers shuffled closer in response, clearly uncomfortable.

"Do you know the story of Briar Rose, lass?"

"Another one of the Grimm's tales?'

"Aye. You'd know it, I reckon, as Sleeping Beauty." He smiled, and this time it was without humor. "Probably the Disney version, all singing and kind woodland animals."

"It's the one with the three colorful fairies," said Heather. "Flora, Fauna, and Merryweather." To her surprise, she felt her cheeks turn pink. There was something surreal and vaguely embarrassing about naming cartoon characters in a prison yard. "They bless the princess at her christening."

Reave looked amused now. "That's right. But in the original story, they were wise women, or witches, and there were thirteen of them in the kingdom. The king only had twelve gold plates for them to eat off—witches being fussy, I suppose—so he decided not to invite one of them. When the thirteenth wise woman arrived at the christening, furious at being snubbed, she cursed the princess to prick her finger on a spindle in her fifteenth year, and die."

"I remember," said Heather.

"But the twelfth witch, she hadn't had a chance to give her gift yet. Although she couldn't undo the sentence of death . . ." Reave paused, his eyes abruptly far away. "She couldn't stop the killing, the twelfth witch, but she could soften it."

"To a hundred years of sleep instead."

Reave nodded. "Your mother was like that good witch, lass. She softened things. She took some of the pain out of this world. Like a tiny piece of light in a forest of shadows."

"And how long was she at Fiddler's Mill?"

"I'm not sure I could say." Reave turned away slightly, no longer meeting her eyes. "I didn't keep an eye on her every movement."

"But you were close?"

"We were *friends*." Something in his tone made Heather's stomach turn over. "She is—was—my oldest friend, I suppose. The only one who still thought of me, twenty years after Fiddler's Mill. Her soul was too kind to just let me rot in prison without another thought. Every letter she wrote to me was out of the kindness of her heart—I never asked her to do that."

"Did you know a woman called Anna Hobson while you were at Fiddler's Mill, Michael?"

"Anna Hobson? Should I have?"

"She was a young woman who got involved in drugs when she was at the commune. She claims that she got pregnant there, and that the baby was taken from her shortly after it was born. Taken against her will."

Michael Reave chuckled warmly. "Never heard of her. Doesn't surprise me that people are making up strange stories about the place, though. What do you think, lass? Do you think that sounds at all likely?"

"I don't know," Heather said, unable to keep the sarcasm from her tone. "A lot of stuff I thought was pretty bloody unlikely now seems to be true."

He nodded at that, conceding the point. Heather decided to try a different approach.

"Did she—did my mum believe you were innocent? Did she think you were a victim of a great injustice or something? Is that why she kept on writing to you?"

"She thought I was good. Knew I was good, I mean. The only person who valued me . . . In my whole life. Do you know what that's like?"

Somewhere far above them, a seagull called. Heather pursed her lips, biting down her immediate reply, which had a lot of swear words in it and largely concerned the injustice of her mother's loyalties. Colleen Evans had believed Michael Reave was *good*, apparently; had given him unwavering support through his years in prison. Colleen Evans had also watched her sixteen-year-old daughter walk out the front door and not come back; had let her relationship with her only child atrophy into something cold and weak. But it had never been too much effort to pick up a pen and write to her old friend, the Red Wolf.

"Michael," she said quietly. "Do you have any idea who is killing these women? Do you know who is such a fan of your work? Any thoughts at all?"

Reave shrugged and shook his head, smiling slightly, as though Heather had made a particularly poor joke. Heather took a step forward, ignoring the tension in her own gut.

"How did you choose them? At least tell me that, Michael. Was it random? Or were you looking for something in particular? The person who's taking them now—does he know what you were looking for?"

"I told your mother once that I was sentenced and found guilty years ago," said Reave. His voice was soft, dangerous. "Long before any women died, long before I even left the place where I grew up. I was destined to be found guilty, because of who my family was, and what they did to me. Even *he* . . ." Reave stopped then, an unreadable expression passing over his face like a summer storm. Heather opened her mouth to ask who "he" referred to, but Reave continued. "I've been judged because of what they did to me, what they made me, and they'll never see any blame for it."

"Who? Who are they?"

He shrugged as if this didn't matter. He gestured around at the dirty walls. "I've been trapped all my life. I told Colleen that once, and she tried to give me a way out, I think. It was her who showed me the sky, but here I am, stuck here, forever, even so. What I am isn't my fault. And listen," he turned back to her, his face stern. "I understand you wanting to know about your mother, but I'm no fool. You ask too much about other things, you'll get yourself in trouble. I don't want that for you."

"What—?" Heather thought of the heart scratched into the terracotta pot, the sense she was being watched. What did Reave know about that, exactly? "Michael, what do you know? Am I in danger?"

He shook his head, not looking at her.

"Don't go up there. There's nothing for you, there. Don't poke around in stuff that doesn't concern you, lass."

But DI Parker had stepped forward, lightly touching the back of Heather's arm, signaling that today's session was over. Later, as they walked back to the prison entrance, Heather found herself thinking about Michael Reave's final words. They had only left her with more questions.

"What about his family? Are any of them still around?"

Parker shook his head. With another session over no closer to any answers, he looked distracted again, impatient to be somewhere else.

"All dead. His mother, as I mentioned before, vanished when he was a kid, and if she's still alive she'd be very old now, and she certainly wouldn't fit our profile. There was a father and an older sister, both of whom have a few scattered reports on social services—suspicions of sexual abuse in the family."

"Jesus."

"But they're both dead now, too. Some distant relations, but nothing that leads anywhere."

Outside, under the cold blue sky, Heather stood alone at a bus stop, still thinking about her mother and the mysteries she had left behind. It was clearer than ever that Colleen Evans had been of enormous importance to Reave, had represented something to him that Heather couldn't begin to understand. And she had to believe that Colleen had had a similar attachment to him, yet nothing about that fit in with the strict and unbending woman Heather had grown up with. There was something else, some other connection. There had to be.

When the bus eventually came along, Heather got on board without looking at the driver. She found a seat at the back of the bus, got out her notebook, and began writing.

CHAPTER

26

BEFORE

Early mornings in the woods were full of birdsong and light. The muttering from Michael's graves was at its quietest but he still liked to visit each one, letting them feel his wolf-shape as he passed over—it was important that they knew he was there, no matter how far he travelled these days. On this particular morning, the wood was awash with bluebells, a near-purple haze that peeked around every corner. Michael was considering picking some to take with him on his next outing—he had taken to placing flowers in the mouths of his women, so that a little piece of Fiddler's Wood would rot with them—when he heard a soft voice calling.

"Is someone there?"

He lent his shovel against a tree and moved toward the sound.

"Hello?"

He saw her long before she ever saw him. There was a girl in the woods, wearing tight blue jeans, mud spattered green wellies and a diaphanous white shirt that floated around her arms. She had pale blonde hair that fell in soft waves across her shoulders, and a pale, slightly pinched-looking face. There were two spots of hectic pink blush on the tops of her cheeks, and she was carrying a battered looking paperback book under one arm. When he stepped out from the trees near her, she startled, almost dropping it.

"Oh," she laughed, her face turning pinker. "I thought I heard someone else walking here. Sorry."

"You're from the commune?" Michael cleared his throat. He didn't much want to speak to anyone, not with mud on his hands and the graves so close, but right from the very start there was something about her—something that provoked him.

"Yeah." She hugged the book to herself. "Are you not?"

"Did you get lost?"

She shrugged and looked away. "I wanted to see the woods in the morning. I didn't think anyone else would be here, because . . ."

When she trailed off, Michael nodded. The other young people from the commune wouldn't be here because they spent every night drinking and smoking weed, staying up until the small hours, talking and laughing before sleeping until midday in their fetid sleeping bags. Or grunting together like animals. Michael had heard them himself, from his room in the house, or from the woods.

"I can walk you back there." It was clear she didn't want to go back just yet, that she'd come here with the express intention to wander a little longer, but she bent to his will easily enough, nodding once so that her hair bobbed up and down. "What are you reading?"

She looked down at the book in her arms as though she'd never seen it before. "Oh, this is my old Grimm fairy tale book." She held it up for him to see; the brown cover was covered all over in white creases, and in the middle was a stark woodcut of a huge black wolf, its jaws open wide to reveal lots of white teeth. Its feet were tangled about with ivy, and it stood against a stark white sky. Michael's heart began to beat faster at the sight of it. Who was this woman who carried what he was in her arms?

"It doesn't look much like a children's story," he said, uncertain what else to say.

"They're not, not really, or not how we'd think of them." The girl shrugged, half smiling. "They're very old, passed down from family to family. An oral tradition. But I love them," she added with sudden feeling. "They're just so *honest*, you know? It's all about the dangers of the wild world, and good and bad, and doing the right things . . ." She trailed off. "I thought it would be good to read them out here, as if they . . . as if they would be more real out here." She flushed a darker shade of pink, clearly embarrassed. "Anyway."

They had come to the edge of the woods, and the commune stretched away in front of them. It still wasn't huge but, as the man liked to put it, its citizens were enthusiastic. From where they stood, Michael could see the man—he looked so much older among all these young people—standing over a group who were mostly sitting. There was a fire going, and the smell of coffee drifted toward them. Most of the men and women looked barely awake, but there were the two Bickerstaff sisters standing with the man, and they looked alert enough, their long blond hair recently cut very short, into identical pixie cuts. The man called them his "Hitchcock girls," although Michael had only the vaguest idea why; the one time he had been to the cinema, he had panicked when the lights had gone down and he had had to leave rapidly—the cupboard had seemed very close, that day.

"He's good, isn't he?" The woman sounded uncertain as she said it. Michael just nodded. "They love hearing him talk, about the countryside, the vital importance of the rural landscape, about freedom from domesticity and the rat race. Some of the stuff he says, makes me wonder. . . "

She trailed off again and Michael wondered if she ever did finish a thought out loud. They were closer now to the group, and he found his eyes going to a couple on the edge of the circle; the man had his hand up the woman's jumper, and she was yawning, not quite paying attention to him. All at once he realized that the girl was looking at them, too, and when she glanced up at him he saw something in her eyes—fear, excitement. The white length of her neck seemed to shine in the morning light, and he felt a powerful surge of emotion toward her; protectiveness and lust, all tied up and tangled. *She is the hare that lays down for the teeth*, he thought, abruptly dizzy.

"I should go back," she said doubtfully. "It's my turn to wash out the breakfast pans."

"What's your name?" His voice seemed to come from very far away.

"Colleen," she said.

CHAPTER

27

THE DOORBELL RANG just as Heather was finishing typing up her notes from the last few days. Standing up, she moved down the hallway as quietly as she could, her eyes rooted to the panel of warped glass in the center of the door. There was a figure standing there, and she was fairly sure it wasn't Lillian. Feeling half foolish and half sick, she snatched up a heavy wooden ornament from the side table and, holding it to one side, peered out the peephole. The figure outside shifted, and she caught sight of messy sandy hair and an unbuttoned collar.

"DI Parker?"

He looked pained as she opened the door, as though he'd been half hoping she wasn't home. Smiling sheepishly, he held up a bottle of wine.

"I know. This is all kind of wrong. But it's been a rough day and . . ." He shrugged. "If I tell you I looked up your mum's address now, will that save you throwing me out later?"

"Come in." Heather stepped to one side, settling the wooden ornament back down on the side table as she did. "You're bloody lucky, as I ordered takeaway about twenty minutes ago and I habitually order enough for six people. Can you eat three people's worth of Chinese food?"

"I'd consider it an honor and a challenge."

Later, when the Chinese food was largely demolished and they had started their second bottle of wine, the conversation had moved inevitably back to the Red Wolf copycat. Parker threw his disposable chopsticks into the plastic carton.

"Another body today. I didn't tell you, but . . ." He shrugged. "This is escalating. The original murders took place over the course of several years, but this bastard? Four women in what? Just over a month? We're sweating bullets over it."

Heather shifted in her seat, blinking rapidly. They were on the sofa, having dragged the coffee table over to put the dishes on, and it was very tempting to slip into the doziness summoned by a stomach full of noodles, but Parker was mildly drunk and suddenly talkative.

"Was she . . . the same as Elizabeth Bunyon? And Fiona Graham?"

For a long moment Parker didn't say anything, and she felt a pang of sympathy at the expression of sorrow that passed over his face. Eventually he nodded. "Their hearts missing. Mouths filled with flowers. Graham was found by a dog walker out before sun up. When we got there, the grass was still frosty, and it was like . . . like she was made of ice. Her blood all crisp on the grass." He shook himself. "The new girl was a junkie called Abi. That's terrible isn't it, reducing her to that? But that's what happens. Victims become a line of summary while we trip over ourselves trying to figure out who *he* is. Abi was cut here," he slid his hand across his stomach, "severing her in half. And there was a hole in her chest, soil inside it, things buried. The photos are something else."

Heather shivered, thinking of the terracotta pot on her mother's doorstep. She wanted to ask if they had found anything heart-shaped near the body, but that would be coming too close to revealing her own thoughts.

"Christ. I'm sorry, Ben. I can't imagine what it's like to have to see that stuff, and just carry on with work. Did you find anything on Fiona yet? I mean, forensics stuff?"

She expected him to shut down at this; to realize that he was sharing too much. But instead he shrugged and sipped at his wine.

"Nothing useful yet. Whoever this bastard is, he's careful not to leave anything of himself behind. But the other stuff—the flowers, the insects . . . Back when the original killings were happening forensic entomology wasn't such a big deal. I'm hopeful something will come out of that, some clue as to where he's based perhaps . . ." He trailed off, then said, blankly, "I shouldn't be telling you any of this."

"Hey, better than keeping it all bottled up." Heather leaned forward and began stacking the empty plastic dishes, and together they carried them into the kitchen and began dumping them in the bin.

"Even so," he leaned with his back against the counter. He'd taken off his blazer and rolled the sleeves of his shirt up to his elbows, which had revealed a thin white scar on his forearm. "It's the last thing you need."

Heather shrugged. She was wondering what Ben would think if he knew why she had lost her job in the first place—or that she used to be a journalist. Her stomach turned over slowly—he wouldn't be here, getting cozy with her on the sofa, that was for certain.

"What's your gut feeling?" she said suddenly. "You've studied serial killers, you've spoken to Michael Reave before. You've had access to everything, all the files and photos. If you had to guess now, what would you tell me?"

Parker grinned a little crookedly. "I'm not an FBI profiler, Heather."

She came closer, leaning on the counter next to him so that she had to look up into his face. His cheeks and forehead were a little flushed, contrasting nicely with his hazel eyes—in this light, they almost looked green.

"Come on. You must have thought about it?"

Outside, the wind picked up, throwing dry autumn leaves against the windows. Parker cleared his throat.

"Well, a white male in his thirties, maybe. Has a job that allows him to move around, probably lives alone. If he does have a wife, she'll know nothing about it. And he'll be someone with a troubled background, just like Reave. Abusive or absent parents, most likely. Not everyone who is abused as a child grows up to be a serial killer, but almost all serial killers have experienced abuse."

"Is that like how not all bastards vote Tory, but all Tories are bastards?"

That surprised a laugh out of him. "I thought politics were off the table until at least the third date.'"

"Well you're already at my place, so . . ." Unhelpfully, memories of the trapped bird, of the note in the medicine cabinet, the scent of her mother's perfume, all rose up at once. Suddenly, Heather wanted Parker to stay—while he was here, the house felt safer, less bleak. Catching the killer seemed like a wild fantasy, something she had been using as a distraction; even understanding her mother seemed like an impossible task. And she was tired of feeling sad. It would be so good, she thought, to feel something else for a while. "I think technically that counts as the fourth or fifth date."

She looked him in the eyes as she said it, hoping he would get the hint. He looked away, smiling, but made no move to step away from her.

"Uh. I think the killer chooses his victims very carefully, maybe has them chosen well in advance, because he knows how to take them with the minimum of fuss. There *has* to be something that links them, but I can't bloody see it. They're all roughly the same age, thirty-four, thirty-five, that's it."

"They're all roughly the same age as me." She frowned.

"Heather, we showed the photo you gave us to Fiona Graham's parents."

"Oh." She rubbed a hand across her forehead, trying not to imagine Fiona Graham's grief-stricken mother, sobbing over a picture of her daughter that she had never seen before. "They must be devastated."

"It wasn't pleasant. All they want at this point is to be left to grieve, but . . ." He paused, and Heather got the impression that he was once again telling her more than he should. "They identified the little girl as their daughter, and they do remember the occasion. Fiona had been taking part in a sort of junior conservation scheme, and there was a little presentation of certificates at the fête. It was called the Young Nature Walkers prize, or something. That's why they were there."

"Huh. I don't remember anything like that."

"As far as we can tell, they didn't speak to your mother, or your father, and there's no obvious connection between them."

Heather shook her head. "Isn't that weird though? I mean, it's a huge coincidence that they went to a fête and sat and ate cake with the woman who used to know the man who . . ." She squeezed her eyes shut; shifting all the facts into place was giving her a headache. "The man who *inspired* the killer who murdered their daughter?"

"The woman who had been writing to Michael Reave for decades," he corrected her, and Heather shivered despite the warmth of the kitchen. "Yeah, we think it's a strange coincidence, too. We're going back through the letters you gave us, and the ones Reave has from your mother, in case we can draw any more connections between your mother and the victims."

"What do you mean?"

"I'm sorry to ask this, but . . . what was your relationship like with your mother?"

Heather leaned back, almost laughing then swallowing it down hard. "Do you think that's a fair question to be asking me right now?"

"I'm sorry, I really am, but I've got women being . . . Look, I had to talk to another father about his daughter today, and we had to ask him to identify her belongings, only there were spots of blood . . ." His voice was tight with emotion, and Heather felt a swift pang of desire for him. "He's going to do it again, and probably very soon. We need to get the jump on him."

"You're right." She looked down at the kitchen tiles. "Look, I left home when I was sixteen, not long after my dad died. I barely spoke to my mum after that—just the occasional awkward phone call when a relative died, that sort of thing. We weren't close. She sent me Christmas cards." Quite out of nowhere, it became difficult to speak. Her throat felt stuffed with feathers. "Christ, it was a bloody mess, if you want the truth."

"Do you think it's possible she was picking the victims somehow?"

For a long time, Heather didn't say anything at all. There was a rushing noise in her ears, and a terrible thumping behind her eyes. *I know what you are, and I think you know too.* She could picture her mother, crouched over a terracotta pot with a knife in one hand, her face twisted with some unknowable emotion.

"Heather?"

"I don't know what to say to that, Ben. Of course, I don't think she was picking these women. I can't believe my mother was involved at all. But what if the link *is* my family? My mother?" She bit her lip. "I don't want to think that way, but that photo, and my mum's suicide . . ."

He turned slightly toward her, looking concerned. "If there is a link, Heather, we'll find it."

"I know, you're right. I just . . ." She pushed a strand of hair behind her ear, thinking hard. *What if this was a story for the paper? What questions would you ask?* "All right, what else? What other things can we reasonably assume about this new killer?"

"He takes them away somewhere to kill them, he doesn't kill them at their homes or in any sort of public space. He likes to be in control. I . . . I don't think he kills in a frenzy. It's about power, about exercising power over them, and the presentation of the bodies is all about that, too."

Heather nodded.

"I thought that," she said absently. "That he cares about the bodies. He cares about them beyond death."

Parker looked at her sharply. "Cares isn't quite the way I would put it."

"No, but . . ." Heather tapped her fingers against the marble top. "Does he care about the way they're displayed because he wants them to look as much like the original Red Wolf murders as possible? Or because he himself needs them to be that way?"

"That's the big question isn't it?" Parker sighed. "Does he know Reave, or is he just a very enthusiastic fan?"

"Yeah. I'm sorry that my chats with Reave haven't helped much."

"They do help, though." Parker turned toward her. "We might not see how yet, but I'm certain —"

A noise outside made them both turn to the window. It was dark, the glass reflecting back the image of the two of them stood closely together, when a sudden streak of movement made them both jump.

"Was that a fox?"

Heather laughed nervously, her heart suddenly racing. "A dog, maybe?" Something in her voice must have been off, as Parker touched a hand to the small of her back.

"Are you all right? You look like you've seen a ghost."

"Yeah, I . . ." She took a breath, embarrassed at how jumpy she was. "God I'm all over the place at the moment. Sorry, I'm probably terrible bloody company."

"I think you're pretty great company, actually."

Again, she had the powerful sense that she didn't want him to leave. As if he had heard her thoughts, he bent his head toward her, an uncertain expression on his face mixed with something else. Without thinking too closely about what she was doing, Heather took hold of the front of his shirt and, pulling him toward her, kissed him.

There was a second where he didn't move—Heather could almost hear him questioning his own judgement—and then his arms were around her, his mouth pressed firmly to hers. He tasted of wine and something else she couldn't place, and his hands as they slid up the back of her shirt were pleasantly calloused. Together they bumped against the kitchen table, and as she kicked off her trousers, her hands busy at his belt, she briefly wondered what her mum would think.

All things considered, I think me fucking a policeman on your kitchen table is fairly small beans, Mum.

"Are you . . . Is this okay?"

Heather looked up into Ben's flushed face and realized she'd laughed out loud.

"God, yes. Don't bloody stop."

* * *

Afterward, they stumbled upstairs, laughing quietly, and had a slower second round in the guest room. When they were lying together in the dark, finally exhausted, Heather found herself listening to his breathing, slow and steady and somehow comforting. It would be easy to lie here, listen to him go to sleep, let tonight become a pleasant memory, eased and turned fuzzy around the edges by too much wine and sleep—but the images of the bodies he had described, the words he had used to describe the killer, were floating in her head like buzzing neon signs.

"Hey," she nudged him with her foot, and he gave a delicate sort of grunt. "Ben?"

"Mhm?"

"I hate to say this, especially after . . . But you can't sleep here. I have to go to my mum's funeral in the morning."

He grew very still in the bed, and then turned over. In the half light from the hallway, she could see the firm muscles of his stomach and the soft thatch of hair on his chest, slightly darker than that on his head. It was tempting suddenly to see if she could get him to stay for longer after all, but it was clear from the way he sat up that the word "funeral" had scattered all chances of that.

"Ah. Shit. You didn't say anything."

"What is there to say?" She sat up, too, her arms around the tops of her knees as she watched him climb out of bed, looking for his pants. "They're by the door. Sorry, it's just . . . I doubt I'm going to be good company in the morning. You know?"

"Do you have someone to be here with you?" He turned toward her in the doorway, enough light on him that she could see the genuine expression of concern on his face, and abruptly Heather felt dirty, ashamed and more painfully attracted to him than ever. It was too easy to imagine what her mother would say if she were still alive, the "disappointed but not surprised" tone of voice.

"My friend Nikki is going to go with me, and half her family, I think. I'll be fine."

"I can come. I . . ."

She made herself face him and tried a smile. "But thank you, anyway. I mean. For being here tonight."

* * *

When he was gone, Heather put on a dressing gown and went back down to the living room. It was very late, and her body ached in a number of different ways, but even so she fired up her laptop and began typing. The story was coming together.

CHAPTER 28

THE DAY OF the funeral dawned bright and sunny, although the house was still chilly and saturated with shadows. Heather, who had been up for hours, found herself caught in a state somewhere between exhausted and wired, repeatedly washing her face and drinking strong black coffee in an attempt to focus.

She chose a pair of jeans that could still charitably be called black rather than gray, and a simple black blouse, laying them out on the bed and then avoiding them all morning. Over and over she found herself going to the windows and looking out at the row of dark trees at the edges of her mother's lawn, half expecting to see someone waiting there, and her mind kept returning to the note: *I know what you are, and I think you do too.* She told herself that it was important she go to the funeral. It was closure, a way of putting her mother and her spiteful notes behind her. But when she returned to the windows, she got the sense that she was missing something; that there was a message, kind or otherwise, that she was failing to get. In an attempt to take her mind off it, she emailed Diane the notes she had so far, along with the comment "this is a very ROUGH DRAFT, so don't judge me too harshly."

By the time Nikki called for her, she was desperate to get out of the house, and squeezed herself into the back of Nikki's aunt's car gladly. Nikki's mother was there, too, sitting in the passenger seat, and she reached over the headrest to pull Heather into an alarmingly fierce hug.

"How are you, Heather? How you doing?"

"I'm fine, Mrs Appiah, honestly. Will be glad to get this out of the way, though."

There was a larger group at the crematorium than Heather had honestly been expecting—more neighbors like Nikki's aunt, a couple of very distant second cousins that she only recognized from old photographs. Lillian was there, too, wearing a very smart black dress suit and a small black hat with a crisp flourish of black lace. Seeing her, Heather felt a flush of shame; someone who had lived down the road from her mother had made more of an effort than her own daughter.

"Come on, Hev," Nikki took her elbow lightly. "We're going inside now."

Slowly, the tiny group of people shuffled into the little red brick chapel, their heads down, their eyes dry. As they passed under the arch and moved down the pews, Heather felt a shiver of dread move through her—there was a large wooden cross on the far wall, dominating everything else, and her mother's coffin lay in front of it, a spray of white flowers draping the warm toffee colored wood.

For a long moment, she felt herself almost pulled backwards, as though the room itself was repelling her, and then she remembered; of course, this was the same chapel where they had said goodbye to her dad. How could she have forgotten that? Except that in some weird automatic act of desperate self-preservation, she *had* forgotten most of it. Her father's funeral now only existed in her memory as a series of painful images and impressions. The smell of leather from the coat she was wearing; the sound of her mother's painful sobs; and her own grief and guilt, a bright shard of glass lodged so deep in her throat she had spent the ceremony in a kind of stunned silence.

Nikki looked up at her, concern creasing a line in between her eyebrows.

"Hev?"

She nodded rapidly, forcing herself to smile.

"Come on," Mrs Appiah slipped her meaty arm around her waist. "We're sitting with you."

Nikki's family ushered her to the front pew and sat around her, fussing and handing out handkerchiefs. They were at home in churches, completely unfazed by the smell of old flowers and the looming cross, and Heather felt a surge of gratitude for them that threatened to make her cry before the service had even started. However, when the vicar stood and cleared her throat, she found herself oddly calm. She glanced around once, and spotted Lillian sitting at the back by herself, her hands folded over her large handbag and her eyes focused intently on the coffin.

"Thank you all for coming here today to celebrate the life of Colleen Evans." The vicar smiled around at them, and Heather wondered what she thought—about the small turn out, about the circumstances of her mother's death. There had been an awkward conversation over the phone where the vicar had asked lots of questions about Colleen, clearly trying to glean enough information to be able to talk about her confidently at the service, but Heather had found she had had very little to tell her. If her mother had had hobbies in her later life, she hadn't known about them, and most of her memories concerned a distant and uneasy childhood. At one point she had been seized with the compulsion to tell her about Michael Reave. *My mother used to knock around with a murderer of women. Can you get that in somehow? Perhaps mention how she wrote to him for decades and never mentioned it to anyone. Or you could talk about how she used to live on a hippy commune and probably took loads of drugs. That makes a good anecdote, doesn't it?* In the end she had cut the whole thing short, and now she could see the vicar struggling to build an image of someone she had known nothing about.

"Happily married to her husband Barry for many years, Colleen was also extremely proud of her daughter Heather . . ."

She made a small noise in her throat at that. Thinking that she was crying, Mrs. Appiah patted her knee gently.

Heather found herself staring at the coffin, inevitably remembering her conversations with the people at the morgue, when her mother's body had been retrieved and identified. They had been kind people, solemn and attentive, and they had explained to her that it would not be possible for her to see Colleen—the damage, when someone falls from a great height (jumps, Heather had added silently, *jumps*) was too extensive. Instead they had introduced her to a police officer who had given her Colleen's handbag. Inside it had been her mother's battered purse, her bus pass, and handfuls of rose hips, as though she had picked them and shoved them in her bag on her walk to the cliffs. It had also contained her suicide note.

"The rose hips, are they important?" The officer had asked. She had been very young and earnest, with big brown eyes, and she had put two large sugars into Heather's tea even though she had asked for it without. For the shock. "We didn't throw them away, just in case you wanted to keep them."

Heather hadn't known what to say to that, so in the end she had just taken the handbag, rose hips and all, and emptied the thing out into the bushes outside the mortuary. Were they important? She had no idea. That was the problem that was becoming more and more obvious: she knew barely anything about Colleen Evans and everything she'd found out since her death suggested she never would.

"Colleen loved her family, and she was a very giving woman. Very generous with her time . . ."

So generous, thought Heather, the misery inside her suddenly flaring into anger. *Generous to a bloody fault, really.*

With a start she saw all the heads in her pew turn to her, and she realized she had spoken out loud. Turning scarlet, she bowed her head, but it was like a dam had opened up; unwanted images and thoughts tumbled through her mind, pressing in on all sides. Sitting in this same chapel as a teenager, numb with pain and guilt; the look of fear that had passed over her dad's face when he'd found the bird in her bedroom; her mother stepping over the edge of the cliff, perhaps regretting it at the last moment and feeling terrified on the long drop down, before her head was smashed and her bones turned to powder . . . She thought of Michael Reave and his infuriatingly steady voice, of all the women whose lives he had cut short.

Before she knew what she was doing, she was on her feet. The vicar's words dried up in her throat, and they all looked at her expectantly. Someone just behind her coughed.

"Hev!" Nikki's voice was an urgent whisper. "It's all right, sit down. Please."

It was impossible. Impossible to stay here a moment longer, just yards away from the box containing the broken pieces of her mother. She shook her head, and shuffled down the pew, gently brushing off the hands of Mrs. Appiah and her sister.

"Please, carry on," she said, trying to make her voice sound as normal as possible. "Carry on, I just need some air."

She left through the side door, stepping out into the small remembrance garden beyond. A long section of it was paved over, with small areas filled with white gravel and small succulent plants, and on a low wall someone had thoughtfully arranged all the floral tributes. She spotted her own immediately, a wreath of white and yellow lilies, and she made herself go and look at it, staring at the long smooth petals until her heart had stopped pounding in her chest.

For all I know, she might have hated this. Heather took a long, slow breath. *Perhaps she would have hated all these flowers. Christ, maybe I should have brought rose hips.*

She waited, and eventually she heard the thin and wavering sound of a small group of people singing "Morning Has Broken," the hymn she had chosen to end the service. Shortly afterward, the crematorium doors opened and the vicar began ushering people out.

"Hev, are you all right?" Nikki came straight over to her, while her mother and auntie hovered anxiously behind. The small handful of mourners were moving out into the garden, pausing to thank the vicar as they did, but Heather couldn't help noticing that they were all taking little peeks at her.

"Sorry," she lifted her eyes to Mrs. Appiah and her sister so the apology took them in, too. "I just couldn't face it. I kept remembering dad's funeral, and the shock of everything . . ."

"It's understandable, honey," Mrs. Appiah waved her explanations away. "Your mother's at peace now, time for you to try and get some, too. Now, look at these beautiful flowers everyone sent. Colleen would have been very touched, I'm sure."

Heather nodded and obediently went back to the flowers, deciding that she would read each card and thank all the mourners personally. After all, they didn't know about her fraught relationship with her mother, and they had taken the time to come—it was the least she could do when she'd already caused such a spectacle. As she was bending to read the card on a posy of pale yellow flowers—the florist's handwriting was atrocious—Lillian appeared next to her, gloved hands folded around the handle of her handbag.

"A lovely service, *just* what Colleen would have wanted." Heather turned at the sound of her voice—was that a note of sarcasm? But Lillian looked as composed as ever. "Are you having a wake, dear?"

"At the King's Arms. I've rented the back room. I should have done it at the house I suppose, but . . ." She stopped. In truth there was no good reason. She just couldn't bear the idea of other people there, seeing where the dust had built up and peering into the fridge.

"No need to explain, I quite understand. It takes some of the pressure off, I imagine."

"And we've made some food." This was Nikki's aunt, who had appeared at Heather's elbow. "Sandwiches, cold cuts, sausage rolls. Plenty enough for everyone and more besides. I'll put some in a pot for you to take back, Heather."

Save me from the old women and their Tupperware, thought Heather, before noticing that Nikki's aunt was peering with curiosity at Lillian.

"Oh sorry. Shanice, this is Lillian. I guess you must know each other? Lillian is also, uh, was also a neighbor of Mum's."

"I don't think we've met," said Auntie Shanice, holding out one plump hand. "Whereabouts are you on the road, Lillian?"

"Up toward the school," said Lillian, before turning to Heather again. "Forgive me dear, but I must go—it really was a lovely service. I'll pop by later and bring you some of the butternut stew I'm making."

And with that she was gone. Shanice raised an eyebrow a touch, which Heather recognized as an extremely damning judgement on Lillian and the likes of Lillian, before heading back to her sister to make her report. Heather, her eyes caught by an unusually colorful bouquet, wandered down the far end to read the card. To her surprise, most of the flowers were familiar to her, because they were the sort you saw growing wild—violets, dog roses, daisies, foxgloves—and they were all carefully bound together in the shape of a wreath. She knelt and touched her fingers to the card—this handwriting at least was legible.

I know what you are, and I think you do too.

Her stomach dropped away in a sickening lurch. The card wasn't signed, and there were no other words on it—not even a little printed image of some flowers in the corner like most of the other cards. She snapped the card off the wreath and stood up, bile pressing at the back of her throat.

"Hev? What's wrong?"

She shook her head, unable to respond. Somewhere very distantly, a dog was barking, over and over.

I know what you are.

Someone out there—someone who knew all about her mother and the Red Wolf—was playing with her.

CHAPTER 29

THE WAKE WAS nightmarish. A dark backroom in a pub, platters of sandwiches and cocktail sausages—far more than necessary for the meager crowd—and glasses of sour red wine. Heather found that she couldn't focus on any of the faces, or follow the threads of any conversations; instead, she kept returning to the card, and its bitter little message: *I know what you are.*

Nikki checked in on her periodically, appearing with a paper plate loaded with cheese or a glass of coke, inserting herself into conversations that looked too painful or awkward, and Heather caught her eye more than once, surprised and touched by her friend's thoughtful actions. However, when an old man she dimly recognized as a neighbor of her mother's took hold of her arm and squeezed it, Nikki was on the far side of the room, having some sort of quiet argument with her aunt.

"Very sad to hear about yer mum, very sad." The old man squeezed her arm again, as if for emphasis. He had big blunt fingers, with fingernails that had been cut too close to the quick. "Do you know why she did it?"

I know what you are. Heather shook his hand off, but he didn't take the hint. Instead he continued to peer up at her. There were flakes of dried skin on the tops of his cheeks, and the capillaries on the bridge of his nose had burst long ago.

"You mean, do I know why she threw herself from the top of a cliff?" Her jaw felt stiff and her stomach was rolling again. She swallowed down the rest of her drink, and put the glass on a nearby table, with more force than was strictly necessary. "Tell me, do you really think that's a reasonable question to ask someone at a wake? A grieving daughter, no less."

"Well, I . . ." The man frowned dramatically. "There's no need to be like that about it."

"Isn't there? No need to be annoyed that you want me to drag out all my pain and misery for you to examine, *my mother's* pain and misery, just for your morbid curiosity?"

"That's not . . ."

"*Yes*, it *is*. God, I am so glad I got away from this shit hole when I had the chance. Can you believe I actually feel sorry for my mum, existing in this shower of vultures?' Her voice had risen, and she could see Nikki making her way across the room, her eyes wide. "Actually, sod this. I'll leave you to it."

Stepping out into the fresh air wasn't the relief she expected it to be. Instead, she felt hunted, exposed. She briefly thought about calling Ben Parker, sure that hearing his voice—warm and kind—would heal her somehow, but she was tearful, and the idea that she would sleep with him and then cry over the phone to him the next day was mortifying. There was a bus stop nearby with a bus just pulling up, so she jumped onto it without looking at the destination. It was only when she sat down, crashing slightly too heavily into the seat next to a startled looking teenager, that she realized the glass of wine she'd downed had gone to her head. A second later her phone pinged with a message from Nikki.

Where did you go? Are you alright?x

Heather looked at it for a long time before slipping the phone back into her pocket. She got off the bus when she caught sight of another pub, a peeling and battered sign painted with a red lion. It was a murky little place, with sticky floors and a handful of stunted old men in corners nursing pints of bitter. The landlady, who was short and brassy, gave her a pinched look as she came in, but didn't hesitate to pour the drink she ordered. Heather took her glass and a packet of potato chips, and set up at a small round table as far from the wide screen TV as possible, recognizing it as a beacon for men who enjoyed standing in groups making sudden loud honking and hooting noises at some sports related nonsense.

The rum was good and dark. With each sip she felt the sharp edges of her shock grow a little fuzzy, although she still couldn't help returning to the strange bouquet of wildflowers, and the note in the bathroom cabinet, with its little flurry of starling feathers as it fell into the sink. Then there was the trapped bird, flying around the landing crashing into walls, and the figure she thought she had seen standing on the edge of her mother's property—except hadn't Lillian seen it, too? She had asked about gentlemen callers, after all.

She downed the rest of the rum and ordered a coke. Her stomach was too empty for any more alcohol.

Perhaps the note in the cabinet really was from her mother. Perhaps Colleen had sent the flowers, too, arranging for them to be sent before she ended her own life. Was that even possible? If you paid the florist enough, if you had a pretty good idea where your predictable daughter would have your funeral, if you had clearly stipulated in your will that you wanted to be cremated. She might not know her mother as well as she'd thought—indeed, every day seemed to take her further away from who she thought her mother had been—but doing something like that would take a level of cruelty Heather couldn't quite believe she had. Had she been cold? Certainly. But malicious?

"This is insane." A pair of old men at the table next to her looked up at her, and she turned away from them. At the center of everything was the biscuit tin full of letters, a little time bomb full of unanswerable mysteries and terrible shadows. She thought of Michael Reave and his scarred hands, calmly telling her about wolves and women who ate raw flesh.

She got up to get another soft drink. On her way back to her seat, the news alert app on her phone beeped at her, and before she could look away, she caught the headline: THE LEGACY OF THE RED WOLF—SERIAL MURDERER INSPIRES NEW KILLINGS.

Heather blinked, her phone slipping through her fingers to clatter to the floor.

"Are you all right, love?"

"I'm fine."

Scampering after her phone, Heather scooped it up and returned to her table, feeling the eyes of everyone in the bar resting like dirty fingers on the back of her head. She glared around at them all, ignoring how difficult it was to focus, and went back to her phone.

The legacy of the Red Wolf.

It was from The Post, the newspaper Diane worked for. After taking a moment to steel herself against the worst, Heather opened the article and quickly read it through. There was Michael Reave's infamous mugshot, alongside a photograph of Fiona Graham, one of her standing with her students. The text included a quick rundown of everything that had happened so far, a summary of the historical murders and the details of all the victims, . . . and interspersed with that, everything she had given Diane: about Michael Reave being questioned and her impressions of him, the missing hearts, the flowers in the victims' mouths, the fact that the police were examining the cards Fiona Graham's students had given her for her birthday . . . It was all there. Diane hadn't waited for the full story—she had taken the juicy scraps Heather had given her and woven them into a larger piece. She could see the joins. Here was a paragraph that was hers, word for word. And another two sections after that. Because what she had sent Diane had been a rough draft, a great deal of what Ben had told her was there unchanged, verbatim. Heather stared at her own words, and they winked up at her like razor blades.

"*Fuck* you, Diane."

She could well imagine how it had happened. Diane reading over what she had sent, taking it to the other editors, and then, with every other paper leading with the copycat murders, the chance to whip the ground out from under their feet had simply been too delicious to resist. She could picture Diane nodding, agreeing. *There's no way we can sit on this.*

Heather sat with her fingers pressed to her lips, her heart thumping too loudly in her chest.

He'll know, she thought, staring at the bright little square of her phone screen. *When Ben sees this, he'll know I've spoken to the paper. He'll know what I am.*

For the longest moment, she was paralyzed with indecision. Should she call Diane, demand the whole thing be taken down?

Should she call Ben, try and explain things before he even saw it? Or, should she order a bottle of rum from the bar and start making her way through it? In the end, her paralysis was broken by her phone ringing. The number was Ben Parker's.

Fuck.

"Ben?"

"Heather . . ." There was a tone in his voice she hadn't heard before. Her stomach did a slow somersault.

"Listen, I can explain— "

"You know what I'm calling about then." He sighed, and somehow that was even worse. His anger she could cope with, but instead he sounded tired, disappointed. "It was you."

"Look, I spoke to a friend about what was happening. I didn't think she would— "

"You didn't think Diane Hobart, assistant editor of one of our biggest newspapers, would write a story about the Red Wolf? You know what, don't bother, please. I'm an idiot." She could hear him moving, as though passing the phone from one ear to the other. She pictured him in his office, perhaps glancing through the glass at his colleagues. "I shouldn't have told you anything. It's my fault, really. I know you're a journalist, Heather."

"Ex-journalist. If you've looked me up, you know that much, too." She bit her lip briefly, furious with herself and with everything. "I wasn't taking the piss, okay? Last night . . . I really enjoyed myself. I genuinely like you, Ben. Please don't take this to mean something it doesn't."

"I think it means I'm a fool who has jeopardized an investigation. Which means I've put lives in danger." He paused, and when he spoke again, she sensed him trying to distance himself. "Look, I'm really just calling to say I've canceled any further visitations with Michael Reave. I think it's best, for you and the investigation, if you keep away from it all for now. We'll be in touch if we need anything else."

Heather opened her mouth, not sure what she was going to say, but all she heard was another sigh, and a sharp electronic whine as he broke the connection.

* * *

Heather sat in silence, the hand holding her phone lying on her lap. She found herself picturing the walls in the bedroom of the first flat she lived in when she left home—when she ran away from home, really. The wallpaper had been cheap and peeling, and once she had torn off a strip, curious to see what was underneath. It hadn't been worth it—her landlord had been furious, and underneath there had only been patchy blue paint, the color of cornflowers. But what if she had peeled it off to reveal something darker, some terrible landscape full of truths that were too horrific to look at. And they had been there all the time, lurking under the surface.

She came back to herself abruptly to find a florid-looking man in a football shirt standing over her table. He had a pint of lager in one hand and was looking down at her with glittering, too lively eyes.

"Cheer up, love, it might never happen."

"What?"

He shrugged, glancing back at a crowd of mates, who were mostly watching the football. The pub had filled up quite a bit in the last hour.

"Got a face like a smacked ass on you, innit? Just saying, you'll feel better if you have a little smile."

Heather's face grew hot all at once, and her heart skipped and stuttered. She stood up, and as she did something else seemed to flow into her, boiling up from the roots.

"I beg your fucking pardon?"

The man pulled his chin in, a ludicrously offended expression on his shining red face.

"No need to be like that, love, I was just —"

"You were just fucking WHAT?"

Heather threw her full weight into the side of the table, sending it crashing into the man's thighs with enough force to scatter the empty glasses. There was a bright tinkling crash as two of them smashed to pieces on the floor, followed by the traditional cheer from the side of the pub that couldn't see what was happening.

"Oi, you mad bitch!" The man staggered back, remnants of coke splashed brown against his cream-colored slacks. Heather walked around the table toward him, feeling like she was floating, filled up as she was with something dark and light. Almost as an afterthought, she picked up one of the empty glasses that was still standing, thinking to smash it against his giant, thick head.

"You're fucking right I am," she said, pleased with how calm her voice sounded. The bloke's mates were all looking at her now, a few moving forward with their hands held up. "I am one mad fucking bitch, you hideous little prick."

She lifted the hand with the glass, but then the brassy little landlady was there, hissing in her face to get out.

"None of that, thank you very much! Go on, get out, we don't want that in here."

Heather boggled down at the woman, and whatever had been inside her—some quick, calm, awful thing that had also been there on her last day in the newspaper offices—seeped away. She cast one more look at the bloke, who, with the landlady now safely in front of him, was calling her every name under the sun.

"What is it about men?" she said to the landlady, her voice soft. "Can't even have a quiet drink without them ruining it."

The woman gave her a sour look, and then Heather was back out on an unfamiliar street. It had been a bright afternoon when she'd gone inside the Red Lion, and now it was early evening, cold and dark, with a miserable light rain moving through the freezing air. Heather stood, breathing it in. As her temperature dropped, the adrenaline washed out of her blood, leaving her ashamed and tired and slightly numb.

Stumbling slightly, she made her way back to the bus stop.

* * *

Back at her mother's garden gate, Heather paused to send off a final text to Nikki. They had exchanged texts all the way home; most of Nikki's sounded worried, all of Heather's were apologetic. She had promised, somewhat rashly, to make dinner for Nikki's mum and Aunt Shanice in an attempt to say thank you for their kindness, and her head was full of how many people she owed apologies when she opened the front door. She clicked the hall light on and stopped, staring at the floor.

Petals, as red as droplets of arterial blood in the dim light, were scattered across her mother's biscuit-colored carpet, leading across the hall and up the stairs. There was also a smell, a hot stench like old garbage or meat left in the sun too long. Heart in her throat, Heather made her way up the stairs, trying not to think of fairy tales where children followed a trail of breadcrumbs into the darkest part of the forest. Did Michael Reave have a version of that story? Of course he did.

The trail led into her mother's bedroom, and there on the dressing table was a small crumpled pile of darkness. A bird—a starling, in fact. A very dead one. The small cavity of its chest had been split open, and inside it, glistening unpleasantly, Heather could just make out more of the petals. They were the delicate pink of dog roses, just like on the wreath at the funeral.

CHAPTER

30

CATHY STOOD IN the entrance to the pub, for a brief moment uncertain what to do. Compulsively she took out her phone from her pocket and glanced at the screen, just in case a notification there could poke her into one direction or another. There was nothing.

Okay, she thought to herself, a hand resting on the door. *Turn around and go home now, if you want, get back on the bus and send her a message saying you couldn't make it after all. But if you do that, you'll always wonder what she was like. Forever. That's not really a choice at all, is it?*

The door opened and a man stepped out, pulling his collar up against the cold. He glanced at Cathy curiously, then he was past her. The glimpse she got of the pub interior was warm and cozy, so after taking a second to push her hair out of her face, Cathy stepped inside. Almost immediately she spotted the woman, whose name was Jane Bailey.

My mother. My birth mother, anyway.

She walked over to the table, and the woman looked up. Cathy felt a smile break out on her face even as she felt like crying.

"Hello, uh, I'm Cathy. Wow. I can't . . . I mean, it's amazing to meet you."

The woman didn't look amazed. Mostly, she looked pained, and she met Cathy's gaze only for a handful of seconds before gesturing to the chair across from her at the table. Cathy hesitated. Shouldn't they hug? Wouldn't there be a tearful embrace? She reminded herself of what her husband, David, had said; that this might be difficult in ways she couldn't predict, and that went doubly for her birth mother. She sat down.

"Here." There was an extra glass on the table. The woman picked up the bottle of white wine she'd been working her way through and poured a glass. "White okay? I suspect we could both do with a drink."

"White's fine, thanks." Cathy took a moment to study Jane Bailey. She was a little older than she'd been expecting, maybe a few years older than her mum had been when she'd passed away. She was well dressed, with an expensive looking navy-blue turtleneck jumper and white jeans, and she had gold hoops in her ears. Her hair was an unlikely shade of purple-red—something out of a packet. "And thank you for meeting me. I understand that it can't have been easy, but it means a lot to me."

"I won't lie to you, part of me didn't want to come at all. I thought all that . . ." Jane paused, fiddled with a thick gold band on one slightly pudgy finger. "Well, I thought it was all behind me. That was sort of the point. How did you find me, anyway?"

"My mum passed away. Well. I mean . . ."

"I know what you mean. And I'm sorry for your loss."

Cathy nodded briefly, trying to gather herself. The cold tone from the other woman was throwing her.

"Before she died, she told me I was adopted. It was a bit of a shock, to put it lightly. I never had the slightest inkling." She paused and took a gulp of her wine. "She also told me it was a private adoption, no official records or anything, which was partly why they never told me. It all seemed mad to me. Still does."

"It goes on more than you think." Jane Bailey had crossed her legs, and was leaning forward over her knee, although she was looking at some point beyond Cathy. "Especially then."

"She gave me the name of the woman who had arranged it, and . . . well, she took a lot of finding, is the short version of the story. When I found her, she did not want to talk to me at all.

Like, *at all.* It was only when I threatened to get the police involved . . . and I'm not proud of that."

Jane Bailey sat up, the color dropping from her face.

"You did what?"

"Nothing! Nothing came of that at all, I was just desperate. I wanted to know who you were. And she did tell me. So, I thought . . ."

"Look. Cathy. What do you want from me?" Her mother put her wine glass down on the table, and Cathy couldn't help noticing her fingers were trembling.

"What do I want? What do you think I want?" Cathy gritted her teeth, forced herself to slow down. None of this was going how she'd expected. "I want some idea *why.* I wanted to know who you were, and why you didn't want me. I guess that's the heart of it."

For a minute or so there was a silence between them. The television in the corner of the pub was playing a news report, black bars of subtitles flicking up and away before it was possible to make sense of them. The radio was playing some old '80s song that Cathy couldn't quite place.

"Cathy . . ." Her mother took a deep, slightly shaky breath. "I don't have the answers for you, I'm afraid. When I had you, I was young. Too young. And I was . . . unwell. I barely knew what I was doing back then, and it's not a time in my life I like to even think about, let alone talk about. And especially to a stranger. I'm sorry, sweetheart, but that's who you are to me."

"What about my real father? Are you still with him? Can you tell me who that is?"

Jane Bailey looked down at her hands, her sallow cheeks suddenly flushed with color.

"No, I can't tell you that. I don't know. Listen, this isn't a good idea for either of us, all right? I think it's best if—"

"You have grandchildren! Don't you even want to know about them?" Cathy pulled her phone out and with a couple of presses summoned pictures of Harry and Rosie—she passed it across the table and then when Jane didn't take it, flicked through the pictures herself. There were images of Harry's third birthday, when he'd had a cake in the shape of a truck; photos of Rosie at the park, her wellies splattered with mud. She came to baby photos of the both of them, looking nearly identical with their tiny screwed up pink faces. At these Jane looked pained. She reached behind her and picked up her coat.

"What are you—?"

"I'm sorry. I can't do this. Don't contact me again." She shrugged on her coat in a series of jerky movements, and picked up her handbag. "I mean it. Finish off the wine if you like, it's paid for."

With that she was gone.

* * *

Later, after a brief crying spell on a bus and a visit to the supermarket toilets to clean up her face, Cathy walked up her own road, feeling marginally better. So, that hadn't gone how she had hoped it would. There had been no tearful reunion, no sense of two families coming together—just an older woman who felt like she was having her privacy invaded. As David had pointed out beforehand, all the important things were still there in her life; Harry and Rosie, their lives together, and her memories of her own mum and dad.

I'll get over it, she told herself. *Jane Bailey isn't worth the trouble, it turns out.*

The lights were on in the living room, throwing yellow light onto the front lawn. It revealed a pair of scooters—pink and purple in daylight, but gray and orange in the shadows. Harry and Rosie were angels in many respects, but they did have a somewhat casual attitude to tidying up after themselves. Smiling to herself, Cathy picked up a scooter in each hand and instead of going to the front door, went to the side gate—always open when someone was home—and went around to the back garden. The lights weren't on in the kitchen, so the long and narrow garden was thick with shadows, and she could barely make out the shed at the very bottom. Still, she knew it well enough to get there in the dark.

"All right, from tomorrow, they put these away after themselves or I lock them in here for good." Cathy dropped the scooters and opened the shed door. There was a smell, bad enough that she instinctively covered her nose. "Christ. Something died in here."

With one hand she felt around for the light switch, but when she flicked it, nothing happened.

Sod it. This is a job for Dave. I keep telling him to clear this place out.

The idea of putting the scooters in the shed with something rotting was repulsive. Rubbing her hands on the front of her coat, Cathy turned to go, but not before she heard something—a small intake of breath, a sniff from someone suddenly very close. A shudder moved through her whole body.

"Who —?"

Something leapt at her from the dark, and Cathy went down hard, smacking the back of her head against the small gravel path. The night sky lit up with multicolored stars, before they were blacked out by a shape leaning over her. Hard, strong hands closed around her neck.

"I'm here now." The voice in her ear was soft, almost friendly. "I'm here to take you home."

Cathy squirmed, trying to throw the stranger off, but every movement summoned a bright flower of pain from the back of her head. Desperately, she turned her head away from her attacker, looking back at the house. Someone upstairs had turned a light on. She willed them to open the curtains. Look out the window. *Look out the window.*

"I *am* home," she croaked. "This is my home . . ."

CHAPTER

31

IT WAS LATE, and cold, and raining.

The police station existed in its own little oasis of light. Heather stood in the car park with her biggest coat on, her hood up against the persistent wet, and tried not to feel like a criminal.

She knew he was in the station. She also knew, logically, that he would have to come out to his car eventually, but as the hours passed by this piece of reasoning looked shakier and shakier. Perhaps he was pulling an all-nighter, perhaps the case had broken in some way and he'd already left, slipping out and leaving in a police car when she was looking in the wrong direction. Yet, every time she thought about giving up and leaving, she remembered their night in the kitchen, and the shape and the warm weight of him in the dark. She thought of how he brought her wine and laughed at her terrible jokes over Chinese food.

"There might not be anything left to salvage," she murmured to herself, her hands thrust deep inside her pockets. "But I at least owe him a proper apology."

To her own mild dismay, she recognized his silhouette as soon as he appeared at the big double doors. He paused there, in conversation with a colleague, then came down the steps, pulling his coat collar up against the cold. As he came to his car, Heather stepped out of the shadows.

"Hey."

He stopped, his shoulders dropping, before glancing back toward the well-lit station.

"Heather, I can't really talk to you right now." He sighed. "And it's pissing down out here. Have you been waiting all night?"

"Listen, I just wanted to say sorry properly, okay? Explain myself a bit maybe." She pulled her hood down, ignoring the fat drops of freezing rain that immediately began dribbling down the back of her neck.

"You mean, see what else you can wring out of me for your article?"

She winced, the guilt in her stomach gaining weight.

"I deserve that, I know. I just want a couple of minutes. Then you can tell me to piss off, I promise."

He sighed and pulled a key fob from his pocket. The car blinked into life.

"Get in."

He didn't look at her once they were in the car. It was as untidy as it had been the last time, a crumpled-up McDonald's wrapper in the footwell.

"I'll drive you back to your mum's," he said, his voice terse. "You really shouldn't have come here today."

"No, listen, I don't want to go there. Can we go somewhere else?" Heather rubbed her hands over her face. "You don't owe me anything at this point, obviously, but I really can't face that place at the moment. Is there somewhere else we can go?"

For a long time he didn't say anything at all, but as they drove Heather gradually realized that they weren't driving toward Balesford. Instead they were heading east, toward Hoxton way, and she bit down several caustic comments about hipsters and man buns. Eventually, they drew up outside a smart block of new build flats, a few doors down from a 24-hour bagel shop. Ben took his hands off the wheel, and spoke, still not looking at her.

"This is my place. If you want, you can come in for ten minutes, say whatever it is you need to say. You can have a cup of tea, or coffee, if I have any. And then I'll drive you back, and that has to be the end of it. Okay?"

"It's more than I deserve." She smiled at him hesitantly, but he didn't return it.

Inside, the flat was tiny and about as untidy as his car, but in Heather's eyes it was the good kind of untidy: books strewn all over the place, papers stacked randomly on corners, empty coffee cups left abandoned like beacons on every surface. The living room shared space with an open kitchen, and there were lots of interesting food gadgets crammed on the sideboard—this was a man who enjoyed cooking. Heather felt another pang of regret. *I've really fucked up here. He's perfect.*

"Tea? Coffee?"

"Whatever you're having."

He shrugged off his coat and chucked it on the sofa. Heather didn't bother taking hers off. After a couple of minutes, he handed her a steaming mug of tea, which she curled her fingers around gratefully.

"So. Right." She sipped at the tea even though it was too hot. Parker leaned against the kitchen top, his own tea untouched. "You know this wasn't some big scheme, okay? Yes, I did go to my old editor and tell her that I might have a story she would be interested in, but I told her I wanted full control over it, that I wanted to write it once this bastard was caught. I'd never have willingly put the investigation back in any way. Diane fucked me over, printed what I'd told her without my permission. And what happened the other night . . ."

"I asked you what you did for a living," said Parker, evenly. "And you told me you were a writer."

"Which isn't untrue."

He half laughed and shook his head, but there was no humor in it at all. Heather felt her heart sink.

"I suppose that makes it okay then. I know what happened at your old job, too." He looked at her, his hazel eyes steady. "I should have looked more closely at your background before now, of course, but I've had a lot on my plate."

She steadied herself against a kitchen stool. "What happened at the newspaper . . . You don't know how I was provoked."

"I guess not."

"I got into a fight with a colleague."

"A fight normally suggests two people attempting to do physical harm to each other."

"Do you have any idea how much you sound like a police officer sometimes?" Heather sighed. "Look, journalism is still crawling with the sort of men who are in shock that women have ventured out of the kitchens. It was, you know, a fractious environment."

Parker said nothing.

"There was this man, his name was Tristan. We were covering one of those stories, a model claiming she had been assaulted by a football player, and Tristan was all over it—raving on about what a gold-digger she was, how the man's career was ruined, blah blah. He said she was losing her looks, of course she was going to pull this. How else would she get column inches?"

"Right." Parker had put his tea down. As far as she could tell, he still hadn't touched it.

"He was always saying shit like that, usually to get a reaction from me, and, idiot that I am, I almost always rose to it. This time I told him I'd call him a cunt, except he didn't have the warmth or depth."

Parker turned his head away, but not before she caught the half smile on his face.

"Well. He came over to my desk and leaned on it, smirking. He opened his mouth to say something else and . . . I just lost it."

Heather paused, looking down at her mug of tea.

"You don't have to tell me any of this, you know."

"Yeah, well. Maybe I do." Heather took a sip of tea, remembering. "You have to put up with a lot of shit in that job, it's the only way to survive it. I hate that term "being one of the lads" but that's part of it—pretending you're not bothered by their crap, that it could never reach you or make you react. But just then, it all boiled up. How unfair it was that this little prick stain could strut about saying whatever he liked and I just had to eat it all up, and that no one would ever tell him he couldn't do it. I . . . I picked up my pen and I rammed it through his hand into the table."

Parker cleared his throat.

"It was pretty bad. Blood everywhere. He screamed blue murder, and while he did, I threw my hot coffee in his face." She looked away from Ben, not wanting to see the expression on his face just then. She didn't mention the shroud of cold that had settled over her just before she'd done it, or the pure, beautiful sensation that this little man did not matter, and that she could hurt him if she wanted to—the *pleasure* his pain had brought her. She did not mention the satisfaction of hearing him holler, or how the sight of his blood on her desk had pleased her. The image of it was still very vivid. "All hell broke loose, of course. Ultimately, though, I just got the sack. I could have made it very difficult for them, you see. Bringing up institutionalized sexism in the current climate would have gone down like a giant sack of shit, so they talked him into not pressing charges and I just left."

Outside, an ambulance wailed its way down the road, throwing up a brief flash of blue light across rain spattered windows.

"Listen, Ben, I'm a shit person, okay? I'm a mess, always have been. God," she swallowed past the bitter laughter that was bubbling up her throat. "Yeah, I wanted to get my career back, I wanted to try and understand a serial killer, maybe stop something dreadful from happening, but I can also stand here and say, yes, I also wanted you, and I didn't make that up. I *was* glad you turned up on my doorstep, and I'm *not* sorry you ended up in my bed." She looked down into her tea, furious that she was suddenly close to crying. "That night was the only bright spot in what has been a pretty hideous fucking month."

"Heather," Ben took a step toward her and then stopped, seeming to think better of it. "Heather, this taints the investigation. It's not like I'm investigating some shoplifting here, or tax evasion. People are dying. And I've been led down the garden path by someone who was looking for information, for juicy details that she can use to spice up a newspaper article. I have a duty to the victims and by letting you do this I have failed them." He stopped and ran both hands through his hair. There was less anger now; instead he seemed tired, and sad. "Someone else has gone missing, a woman with two little kids, I . . ." He shook his head ruefully. "You'd think I'd have learned my lesson about telling you this stuff, right? The point is, I don't have time for it. Not if I want to stop this bastard."

"I'm sorry, Ben."

"Yeah, well. I'm sorry, too."

He offered to drive her back to Balesford, but she refused; the idea of another entirely silent car journey with him was too much. Instead she called for a cab and stood out by the bagel shop waiting for it. When it came, she gave the driver her mother's address, and then sat in the back seat, peering out at the rain smeared streets as they went. When they passed an off license with all its lights still on, she got the cab to stop and nipped inside, returning to the car with a bottle of vodka and a packet of paracetamol.

If she had to go back to her mum's house, it wasn't going to be sober.

* * *

Later, a few vodkas into the evening and feeling both sick and very tired, Heather was curled up on her mother's sofa with Pamela Whittaker's album on her lap. Whether it was the alcohol or the effects of a very rough couple of days, Heather was finding each image more unsettling than the last—and there were so many of them. Pamela might have regretted her time at Fiddler's Mill, but it had certainly inspired her; there were photographs and images packed in so thickly that in some places Heather found several images hidden under another, crammed in like grisly pressed leaves.

The forest featured a lot, as did the big old house, and the sky at sunrise or sunset. There were fewer photographs of the other people at the commune, but each of these Heather scrutinized carefully, scanning every face for something familiar. Each time she failed to find anything she felt the tension thrumming through her lessen a little.

And then she turned a page a little too quickly, and several photographs slid out, fanning across her leg as though they were eager for her to see them. One of them caught her eye immediately.

It was her mother. Painfully young, and dressed in a bulky winter coat that came right up to her chin, but it was her all right. It was a shot of a crowd, gathered around a smoky fire, and there were lots of other people crowding close to the camera, but there was no mistaking her really—the only thing Heather didn't recognize was the carefree expression on her face; her whole face lit up with the idea of freedom. And in the background, on the top of a hill, the big house lurked. She had been at Fiddler's Mill. There was no avoiding it.

"I have to go there." The idea had a finality to it that both frightened and excited her. "I have to see this place."

CHAPTER 32

BEFORE

THE BLOOD HAD turned his sleeve into a sodden red mass. Michael found his eyes drawn to it again and again, taking his attention from the road often enough that eventually he pulled over, parking the van in a little gravel layby.

She had cut him. The bitch had cut him.

Jerkily, he opened the van door and stepped out into the summer's night. He was on one of the winding country roads that ran back to Fiddler's Mill, and it was utterly dark, with no street lights in sight. Overhead, the stars were bright and clear, and the moon was not quite full. Normally he would have taken a great deal of pleasure in such an evening—he could smell all the good green smells, and somewhere in the distance a vixen was screeching for her mate—but the pain in his arm blotted all that out, made it irrelevant.

Again, uselessly, he replayed what had happened in his mind, looking for his mistake. He had followed the woman as she walked back from the pub, far enough back that he was certain she had been unaware of him, at least at first. She had taken a path along a canal, poorly lit and deserted, and when she had done that he had been certain; this woman would be coming with him. Her heart would go deep into the black earth of Fiddler's Woods, and the rest of her he would cover in flowers. But when he had caught up with her, laying one strong arm across her shoulders, the face she'd turned on him hadn't been rigid with terror or surprise—she hadn't gasped or screamed. The face she'd turned on him had been angry. *Furious.*

On the quiet road, Michael walked around to the back of the van, thinking.

The woman had fought him. He was the barghest, he was the wolf, but she had pulled a boxcutter, of all things, from her bag and slashed at him with it, tearing through his thin shirt and across the skin underneath. It had only taken him a moment to strike it from her hands, and she only managed to cut him that once, but . . . What did it mean, if the barghest bled? Had he chosen the wrong one? Was that possible?

In another, more logical part of his mind, Michael wondered if people had been paying attention to the news lately, and had noted the number of women going missing in the area. Perhaps this one wasn't the only girl to go out walking with a blade in her handbag.

He had had the sense to pick the boxcutter up and take it with him, at least.

Casting a glance back down the road to make sure there were no lights approaching, he opened the back doors of the van. Her body was a crumpled form in the back, her hands and her face pale shapes in the gloom. One of her shoes had come off, and her foot was thrust out at him. In the struggle, her tights had been laddered all over.

This was all wrong, of course. The rules were very clear about this—he never brought their bodies back to Fiddler's Mill. It was unthinkable. The fact that he had come this far with it only demonstrated that the entire evening was a mistake, that there was something discordant in the night air. Abruptly, he wasn't the barghest at all, he wasn't the Wolf, he was just a man with a knife and a sleeve turning stiff and tacky with his own blood. If he wasn't the wolf, then was he anything at all?

He slammed the backdoors shut and got back into the van. He drove. Once he was back within his woods, he knew that his mind would clear. When he walked back over his graves, and felt their hearts singing there, things would seem normal again.

But when he got back to Fiddler's Mill, he found his way thwarted; the young people had sprawled their dwellings over one of the main access roads. He could see their lights and hear their voices, and a slow kind of panic began to grow in his chest; the panic of a prey animal, realizing that they had made a mistake, that they were trapped. He couldn't get to his woods, he couldn't get to the House. He was bleeding. He had brought a body back with him. This had to be where it all ended.

Michael was leaning over the steering wheel, convinced that the walls were closing in on him, that he could smell the musty cupboard and feel his sister's hands taking hold of him, when a white face appeared at the open window.

"Michael? What's the matter? Are you . . . are you bleeding?"

It was Colleen. She leaned through the window into the cab, her blonde hair falling forward over her face. In the light from the campfires, her hair glittered gold and copper.

"I had an accident." For some reason, the pure concern on her face had chased away his anxiety. Suddenly it was easier to think. "I was out clearing away rubbish for some people. You know, just a dirty job to make some easy money." He made himself smile. "But there was broken glass in the dump, didn't see it until it was too late." His arm, when he held it up, looked awful, and he saw her recoil. "It's not as bad as it looks, honestly."

"Jesus, Michael, I think maybe you should go to the hospital." But she said it doubtfully. No one at Fiddler's Mill was very keen on hospitals. The hospital might find out what drugs you'd been taking; the hospital might try to contact your parents, or the police. "Here, come out here where I can see it." She held up a plastic battery powered torch—a lot of the young people carried them, for the woods at night.

When he was standing by the van, Colleen bent her head over his arm, shining the white light over his tattered sleeve. She made a small noise of sympathy and tugged at a piece of the material. Michael grunted with pain.

"Ok. All right. Do you trust me, Michael?"

"What?"

She looked up at him, smiling shyly. Again, he was struck by the delicacy of her.

"I have a first aid kit back in my camper. I can try and see if I, uh, can make it better? But I'll have to cut your sleeve off I think, because it's stuck in the wound. Although I think you'll have to give up on this shirt anyway."

Somewhere nearby, someone began plucking notes on a guitar, only to be laughingly shouted down by several others. For a moment, Michael found he couldn't speak. Colleen still had her hand on his arm, apparently untroubled by the blood, and a few feet away, inside the van, a woman lay on a coarse blanket, her eyes staring sightlessly at nothing. It all seemed impossible. Colleen smiled encouragingly.

What is she?

"Come on, my camper's not far."

She was parked up a little way from the others, which Michael was glad of. Inside, it was cramped and untidy, with all the chaos that indicated it was home to at least two young women who kept unsociable hours. Colleen made him sit on the thinly cushioned seat that ran along one wall, and then pulled down a green plastic box from one of the cupboards. As she did so, a packet of plasters shed its contents all over the sink.

"Oh, whoops."

Then she fetched some water and scraps of dry cloth, and a pair of huge fabric scissors. Seeing the look he gave them, she held them up, smiling.

"They're Charlie's. She makes her own clothes."

For the next few minutes, they fell into an awkward silence as Colleen cut his sleeve away, peeling the fabric back from his tacky skin. Next, she wet one of the cloths and used it to wipe the blood away. As she did so, he watched the soft curve of her pale neck as a thin blush of pink moved up it.

"There, it's not so bad, actually. Bit ragged, but . . ." She opened a small, brown bottle and the stink of antiseptic flooded the small space. She wrinkled her nose. "Ugh. Hold still."

She swiped a cloth over the wound, and it burned fiercely for a few seconds, but Michael barely noticed. In here, with Colleen, all of his misery and fright had fled. In here, he was strong again. The knowledge that he could, if he wanted, take the scissors from her and cut her—that he could place his hands around her slim neck and push the life out of her—was comforting. It also increased his feelings of protectiveness for her. She was the one good thing. She was his alone.

"Colleen." She looked up at him, and he saw that the blush had turned her cheeks quite pink. He knew then that she felt it, too. "What would I do without you?"

CHAPTER

33

"I NEED TO GET out of here for a bit. Do you want to come with me?"

Nikki clearly hadn't been home long as her shopping was still on the kitchen counter and she had kicked her tights off in the hallway, replacing them with a pair of fluffy pink slippers that looked especially quirky with her sober navy blue shirt.

"Where were you thinking of going?" She shifted the shopping out of the way and began filling the kettle. "Cup of tea?"

"Got anything stronger?"

Nikki looked pointedly at her watch, but nevertheless went to the fridge instead and liberated a half full bottle of white wine.

"Hev, you look like you've been up all night. What's going on?"

Heather shook her head and accepted the glass of wine, taking three deliciously cold gulps before answering.

"I've had enough of that house, Nikki. It's, uh, it's sending me round the bend. I was thinking of driving up to Lancashire, going to this Fiddler's Mill place, having a look around. Why not? Call it a tribute to my mum, call it closure, whatever."

Nikki joined her at the kitchen counter, a glass in her hand.

"And what about your visits with Michael Reave?"

"They're over. After the article, I, . . ."

"Hmm. You haven't heard from the detective, then?" Nikki's face was carefully blank. She knew all about Heather's night with Ben Parker, thanks to a hushed chat before her mother's funeral, and so, inevitably, Heather had texted her the ignominious details of the end of the whole thing, too.

"I think, I can safely assume I've lost my chance there, in more ways than one." Heather forced herself to smile, hoping to cover up exactly how painful those words were. "A trip to the countryside is what I need now. It won't be completely terrible, I promise. The big old building is a spa now, and there's a nice cottage where we can stay, in the grounds. Fresh air, long walks, and I could do with some company. Stuck inside that house by myself, it's not healthy." She thought of the petals on the stairs, the heart on the terracotta pot. "Diane might have fucked me over with the Red Wolf story, but that doesn't mean I can't eventually write my own version of it. And this would be great background—absorb the atmosphere of the place. And maybe get a massage at the spa, I don't know."

Nikki swirled the wine in her glass, frowning into its depths.

"And, okay, mostly I am just curious to see the place. Pamela Whittaker said it was *evil.*" Heather smiled as Nikki rolled her eyes. "I want to see this miserable patch of grass my mum apparently thought was so amazing. Where this all started. I'm sure that . . . I'm sure that if I want to know more about her, I have to go to this place and see it for myself."

"This place is in Lancashire, isn't it?"

"Yup."

"Lancashire, where they recently found bits of a woman's body shoved inside a tree."

"Come on, it's the same *county.* It's not like the murderer is on the welcoming committee as you drive up the M6." For a moment, an image of the petals and the dead bird floated across her mind. She could still smell the blood. Guiltily, she pushed it away.

"Hmm." Nikki, who had been nursing the wine rather than drinking it, took a long swallow of her drink, then shrugged. "All right. I have some time off owing. And apparently, I have nothing better to do."

* * *

Heather had always liked long car journeys. They put her in mind of her earliest childhood, when her dad was still alive and he would get a sudden urge to drive to the coast. Her mother would give her a big bag of barley sugars to settle her stomach—never forgetting the incident where she had vomited noisily out the window while they were on the motorway—and she would spend hours sucking sweets and looking out the window at stretches of green and brown, smears and smudges of places she would never know. Sometimes she would play games with her dad, iterations of I-spy or word games based on number plates, and when they got to their destination, she would always be faintly disappointed. There was something precious and strange about having both her parents' undivided attention for so long.

Nikki looked less excited about the journey, repeatedly fiddling with her phone in its holder on the dashboard, which was serving as a sat-nav. Factoring in breaks, it was a good five hour drive to Lancashire and they had set off in the late morning, shunting and winding around the slow-moving traffic of London, and now they were out beyond the M25, free of the city's shackles. Hours passed, and anonymous fields and stretches of vegetation zipped by on both sides of the motorway, the sky overhead gray and nondescript.

They got to the borders of Lancashire just as the last of the sun was bleeding from the sky. Heather had been dozing in the passenger seat, but something woke her as they turned down a country road. She sat up, blinking and trying to recapture the specific sensation. A voice saying her name? Had she been dreaming?

"Oh good, you're awake," Nikki sounded distracted. "Can you keep an eye on the map for me? These roads are all really twisty, and this place is in the middle of bloody nowhere."

Heather nodded and peered at the electronic map. They drove for another hour or so, trundling up and down roads boxed in with trees and low stone walls, until it was completely dark. There were very few lights out here, and more than once Heather found herself staring out into the night, at the yawning blackness of the fields.

"When I was a kid," she said, "I used to imagine how scary it would be to suddenly be transported somewhere like this. If you were just at home, watching television in your pajamas, and then suddenly you were in the middle of a field at night, no idea where you were, no way to contact home. Cold and alone, no idea what might be in the woods. I used to imagine that a lot."

"Do we take the next left? No wait, I've got it . . ." Nikki nodded toward the windscreen. "There it is, look. There's the entrance."

Their headlights caught it—a flash of white in the night. It was a big shiny board, advertising the Fiddler's Mill Spa Complex in an ostentatious green font. Underneath it was a big stylized acorn with the words Oak Leaf written through it, and beyond the sign they could make out a long, smooth road, helpfully lit with discrete lamps. Somewhere out in the dark, up a gradually sloping hill, Fiddler's Mill House lurked. Heather squinted at the windscreen, thinking it would be possible to see lights in its windows perhaps, but the glow from the car cast everything beyond the road into a blank kind of darkness.

"Our cottage should be left of here," Heather leaned back. "It's a little way from the big house."

Dutifully they turned left, and after about twenty minutes of driving through more fields and trees, they came to another signpost, discreetly lit with a softly glowing lamp. It displayed directions to five holiday properties, each of which had been given their own name: Herne, Titania, Puck, Woden, and Frig.

"We're staying in Herne, apparently."

They drove on, following a narrow country road that seemed to hug the edges of a sprawling field, until a cottage loomed up in their headlights, box-shaped and oddly inert looking. Heather retrieved the keys from the lock box by the side of the front door, and together they brought their stuff in; suitcases, a bag of food and drink. Inside, all was cozy and neutral, and Heather found that she was oddly relieved. This was a place designed to be inoffensive, palatable to any holiday maker—no personality required. There were biscuit-colored sofas, deep red rugs, and discreet modern lighting, hidden among the beams that crossed the ceiling. No chance here, she told herself, of coming across sheets of paper from the notebook your mother used for her suicide note, no danger of some innocuous object rousing some long-forgotten trauma. Whatever was haunting her in Balesford could stay there.

Someone had thoughtfully left a small pile of the day's newspapers on the central table along with a pair of empty wine glasses, a bottle of wine, and a box of posh biscuits. Nikki went to the small open kitchen and began unpacking food, while Heather searched for a corkscrew.

"This isn't so bad," Heather said as they were ensconced on the sofa, sipping from glasses of wine. Nikki had her legs tucked under her, one of the local newspapers spread on her lap. "I could easily put up with four days of this." She slipped her phone out of her pocket. No messages from Ben Parker, but then, there was no phone signal either. She resolved to text him the next time she saw some stable bars on the screen, just to see how he was—it might not make any difference to how he felt about her, but it could ease some of her own guilt.

"What's your plan?"

"Hmm? Oh, eat a lot of crap, sleep a lot."

"How is that different from usual?"

"Ha ha ha." Heather swirled the wine in her glass. "So. This is the place my mum ran to when she was a teenager. Maybe I'll never understand what she did, but perhaps I can get a bit closer to understanding *her*." It was also the place where she met a man who she maintained a bond with for the rest of her life, despite what and who he turned out to be. She remembered what Pamela Whittaker had said about the land soaking up memories, keeping them to itself. She remembered Anna's face, how it had crumpled in on itself when she thought of her missing baby. There was something bad here, and the land remembered, deep in its bones. She had to find out what it was. What did she have to lose, at this point? "I'll have a look around tomorrow."

Nikki lifted the paper from her lap and turned it to show Heather the front page. There was a photograph there, blown up slightly too big so that the edges of the woman's smiling face were blurred, and across the top the headline screamed "LATEST VICTIM OF THE RED WOLF?"

"Whatever you say, we're in his territory now, Hev. Be careful with your snooping, yeah?"

Heather raised her glass. "I'll drink to that."

CHAPTER

34

BEFORE

COLLEEN'S CAMPERVAN WAS set back from the main crowd of tents and vans, and as Michael drove toward it, he noted that the windows were all filled with brittle yellow light—she wasn't alone tonight. Getting out of his van, he quickly looked himself over in the wing mirror, pushing his hair out of his face impatiently. The shower at the B&B had been cramped and tiny, and he had worn the soap down to a nub. He was more careful than he'd ever been these days, but it never hurt to check again—flecks of blood had a habit of finding the places that you missed with the flannel.

Satisfied, he went up to the campervan, opening the door onto their small, patchouli smelling living space. Three women looked up at him, clearly startled; there was Colleen, wearing a long, slightly threadbare maxi dress and a pink flower in her hair—a dog rose, he thought—and there was another woman he only vaguely knew, sprawled in the corner seat he liked to take for himself. She was heavily pregnant, her vastly swollen belly pushing against a yellow t-shirt that was much too small for her, and she peered up at him through a haze of tobacco smoke. The third woman was one of the Bickerstaff sisters; Michael wasn't sure which one. In comparison to the pregnant woman, she looked too alert, and she raised her eyebrows at him archly.

"Look at what the cat dragged in," she said.

Michael closed the door behind him, caught for a long second between two images: the girl he had left in a field outside Eccleston, her jumper soaked red and her mouth full of pansies, and the three women in the campervan, as they appeared to him then—Colleen the maiden, biting her pink lower lip, the unknown pregnant woman on the cusp of motherhood, and the Bickerstaff sister, her face young and unlined yet as knowing as any crone. The girl's heart was in the wood now at least. He reminded himself of that, and it calmed him.

"Mike, I didn't think you were coming back tonight." Colleen stood and came over to him awkwardly, slipping her arms around his waist and squeezing him. "We were just having a girl's night in."

"How nice." It was difficult to speak, the words lodged and dry in his throat. It always was after he had returned someone to the woods, as though part of him had gone back to the cupboard, to the time when he did not utter any words.

"Have you seen the news?" The Bickerstaff woman—her name was Lizbet or Beryl—slid a folded newspaper toward him. It was one of the red tops, the headline screaming "FIFTH SUSPECTED VICTIM OF THE RED WOLF" and underneath it was a fuzzy photograph of a stocky woman with thick, curly hair. The photo had been taken at a wedding, and she was dressed in a particularly unflattering peach-colored bridesmaid dress. She hadn't been wearing that when Michael saw her last. Lizbet or Beryl turned her lips down at the corners. "Nasty stuff, isn't it? What a monster he must be. What do you think, Janie?"

She elbowed the pregnant woman next to her, who took a good three seconds to react. Her head wobbled up, and she struggled to focus on the newsprint. Michael watched her trying to figure it out, and eventually she shrugged and turned away, stubbing out her cigarette in an overflowing ashtray. *Drugs.*

"It's scary," said Colleen, with feeling. "I wish they wouldn't use these names for them, it just makes it all seem, I don't know, glamorous or something."

"The Red Wolf," repeated the Bickerstaff woman. Then she grinned, and leaning over suddenly, rubbed at the pregnant woman's distended belly. "No big bad wolves in your bedtime stories, little one?"

This seemed to wake the girl in the yellow t-shirt up a little. "Do you have anything for me, Beryl?"

"Beryl and Lizbet are nurses," said Colleen. She looked up at Michael, as though trying to convince him of something. "They're keeping a special eye on Janie."

"A natural birth," said Beryl, gazing fondly at Janie. "A child born under the stars. Won't that be something?"

Michael shrugged. He knew already that the Bickerstaffs were providing the contraceptive pill to many women in the commune, knew that Colleen was diligently taking it. He didn't ask what other drugs the Bickerstaff sisters were doling out, or why the pregnant Janie was clearly chain-smoking her way through packets of Lambert and Butler. Instead he gently unhooked Colleen's arms from his waist and stepped back toward the flimsy door.

"Don't go," said Colleen quickly. "We were just . . ."

"I'll be back in a little bit, I just need some more fresh air." He didn't miss the look Beryl Bickerstaff gave him as he stepped out—flat and calculating, like a cat trying to decide if a mouse was worth the effort.

After just a few minutes inside the smoky campervan the night air tasted sweet and welcoming, and he walked back toward the house gratefully even as he felt a pang of regret at leaving Colleen behind. She did not like the big house, wouldn't stay in it overnight, although she'd never been especially clear on why—it was an attitude that mystified Michael. After all, it wasn't a run-down farmhouse surrounded by bleak fields, it wasn't a suffocating cupboard. Halfway up the hill he came across the man coming down. The dog was nowhere to be seen.

"Good night, lad?" It was too dark to see his face clearly, but Michael heard the grin in his voice all the same.

"The Bickerstaff sisters. What do they know?"

The man turned away, and a slither of moonlight picked out his features in beaten silver; the big nose, an old man's expansive ears, the dull sheen of his false eye. He was still grinning.

"They're useful," was all he said.

Michael nodded, although he didn't agree. After a moment he said, "I wish you hadn't made me leave that note."

"Why not? Why shouldn't they know your name?"

"The Red Wolf." Speaking it aloud was thrilling, but it also gave him a deeper, unhappier ache that he couldn't explain. It was coming too close to talking about the things they never talked about, and once they named it, he felt certain everything would vanish, like a soap bubble. "The papers have taken it. And they don't understand. Not really."

The man snorted. "That's our burden, lad. To never be understood."

For some time, Michael didn't move or speak. He could hear voices laughing and talking some distance away, and there were points of orange light from campfires away to his right, but up here on the hill it was cold, and the darkness of Fiddler's Woods seemed to tug at him eagerly. He longed to go there with the images that were still fresh in his head, visit the hearts that beat under the earth for him, but the thought of Colleen held him back.

"What are you doing here? With them?" He gestured down the hill even as he regretted the question.

But the man didn't seem concerned. He bared his long teeth in a grin, looking eerily like his own dog.

"The things I do for you, lad. For my little barghest. I've always looked after you, haven't I? Always provided for you?"

Michael nodded. He couldn't argue with that.

"Then trust me."

The man left, jogging lightly down the hill like a man much younger than his years. Michael watched him go, breathing in the dark scent of the night.

CHAPTER

35

THE MORNING WAS bright and cold, a sheer blue sheet for a sky with only a few wispy hints of clouds to the east. Heather and Nikki came out of the cottage slowly, full of the natural caution of city people suddenly faced with a great deal of quiet. Nikki was carrying a glossy map of the grounds, which had also been left on the table for them.

"You know, this place is huge, and really spread out. The nearest cottage is miles away."

The wind picked up, chasing old dead leaves across the small drive. Heather sniffed, and fiddled with the collar of her jacket. For the first time in weeks, she had slept the whole night through, and the hot shower had been powerful enough that she felt like she'd already had a massage. *This is better*, she thought, glancing around at the grass and trees. *I should have known staying in that house would make me unwell.* She looked at the map Nikki was brandishing at her and raised her eyebrows.

"Countryside people," she said eventually, "are really keen on walking, aren't they?"

"Good news is, although we're not guests of the spa, we can go up to their restaurant and have breakfast. What do you reckon?"

They got back in the car and followed the smooth roads back up toward the main entrance. It was a reasonably long way,

Heather noted—walking would have to take at least an hour. Eventually the main building of Fiddler's Mill loomed into sight, looking very much like all the paintings and photographs Heather had seen at whytewitch's flat. It had been given new, energy saving windows and a new gravel drive, but the dark stones of the House itself, looking like a rainy afternoon given weight and heft, were still intact. In the sprawling carpark to one side were only a handful of cars, and the big central doors were closed.

Nikki parked and they got out, standing for a moment looking down the hill. Back past the way they had come was a thick band of woods, looking impenetrable at this distance. Heather couldn't see anyone else about.

"I guess it's a bit late in the year for this, really," she said. "Anyone with any sense and this much money has buggered off abroad for the winter."

"Come on, let's get inside."

The reception area was spacious and tasteful and somewhat ruined by a series of tall white signs detailing all the spa treatments available within Fiddler's Mill House. A young orange woman with yellow hair beamed at them from behind a desk.

"Can I help you?"

"We'd like to have breakfast please," said Nikki. "Is your restaurant open?"

"Yes of course." The young woman slid a pamphlet across the counter to them. It had a picture of an avocado on the front and not, as Heather might have hoped, bacon and eggs. "Here is the menu. The restaurant is just through the arch to your right. Have a lovely day."

"Could I ask you a couple of questions?"' Heather leaned on the counter top, folding her arms.

"Of course," the receptionist dialed down the smile from satisfied customer to query incoming.

"Do you know anything about the history of this place? Specifically about the commune that was on the site during the '70s and '80s?'

The woman nodded carefully and retrieved another pamphlet from a drawer on the desk. This one had a black and white photo of the House on the front. "There you go. Fiddler's Mill was built in the late 1700s, and has had an interesting history since then. The main points are highlighted in the pamphlet there."

"Interesting history." Heather nodded slowly, looking at the leaflet. "What about the rumors that the Red Wolf used to live around here? Do you know anything about that? About Michael Reave?"

The smile vanished. "What?"

"I have it on good authority he was a part of the commune here from the '70s onwards . . ."

"I don't know anything about that."

"Are you sure? Because —"

"No seriously, I don't." The woman leaned forward. "They tell us to play down the commune stuff, because of all the drug taking and that," she glanced around briefly, as if her manager might be looming, "but I've never heard anything about the Red Wolf. Are you serious?"

"Is there much left on the grounds from that time? Could you tell me that?"

The woman grimaced and leaned back. Now, as she glanced around the reception, it was clear she was seeking someone else to deal with them. Heather lowered her voice. She could feel Nikki's discomfort next to her.

"I just want to know about the stuff that dates from then. How many people do you have staying here at the moment? Not many, I suppose, but there are cars in the car park—do you think they'd want to know about the history of this house? That the Red Wolf spent time in these fields in between dismembering bodies? Now, there are people that would be over the moon to hear that, but I doubt it's the same people who would pay eight hundred quid a night for peace and quiet and hot stone treatments. Especially not when a particular fan of the Red Wolf is apparently causing trouble again."

The receptionist took a slow breath, then picked up another pamphlet off the desk. This one was the same as the one Nikki already had. She picked up a ballpoint pen and began to make hurried additions to the map.

"Look, there's not much left on the grounds from that time, save for the House itself, and a few private properties in the northwest of the estate. A few old houses that are falling to pieces, a strip of land with a caravan on it—they are mostly still occupied." She made a couple more marks and then handed the map over, her mouth pursed. "I only know about it because I was here when they were building the new roads—they had to get agreements from the residents still living on the larger properties."

"Thank you." Heather took the pamphlet and tucked it away in her pocket. "Who owns it, anyway? This spa?"

"Can't you bloody google that?" The receptionist shook her head slightly, visibly retrieving her customer service skills. "It's part of a chain of spas, which are partly owned by a private individual and partly by an environmental charity."

"Oak Leaf," Heather remembered the acorn logo on the welcome sign.

Nikki frowned. "A green charity? Why would they own a spa?"

"It's a good way to keep the land from being built on," said Heather, stepping back from the counter. "Otherwise I imagine it would all get sold up in bits and pieces and made into several shopping centers." She smiled warmly at the receptionist. "Thank you, we'll go and have our breakfast now, I promise."

* * *

"Can you believe," said Heather, around half an hour later, "that they didn't even have any sausages?"

"They did," said Nikki, mildly. "They had vegan sausages."

"That is not a sausage, it is a tube of sadness and regret."

They were making their way down the hill, having left Nikki's car in the car park. According to the newly scribbled-on map, some of the private properties were only accessible by foot, or if you had the sort of four-wheel drive vehicle that positively embraces mud.

"What do you want to do?" asked Nikki as they continued to trudge down the hill. It was still a bright morning, but the wind was picking up.

"I just want to have a look around. Get a feel for the place. And it would be interesting to see if we can find some of the places our white witch painted." Inside her bag were copies of most of

Pamela Whittakers' paintings and photos—the photo that featured her mother, she had hidden deep in her bag. "Or even find the locations of her photographs. It would be interesting to know exactly where this commune was set up."

"Well if we encounter any "get off my land" types, I will let you deal with them. You were fairly mean to that receptionist, you know."

Heather gave Nikki a look. "Fair enough."

They walked on, both lapsing into silence. The quiet was oppressive, so full of the whistle of the wind and the quiet music of birdsong it felt like a physical weight. Heather found herself reluctant to speak, as though to do so would be to expose herself; although to what, she did not know. Eventually they passed over the neatly kept grasses and roads and came to a strip of trees, a single rough path leading through them. Despite the bright morning, the trees were a solid clump of darkness, seeming to hold their own shadows close around their trunks and branches. On the edge of it, Nikki hesitated.

"Are you sure this is the right way?"

"I am," Heather indicated the map. "See? And this bit doesn't last for long, there's a clearing beyond, and the first of the old houses. This is just a small branch of the larger Fiddler's Wood."

Nikki turned and looked back up the hill, where the House was now a squat gray box. More people were arriving in the car park.

"Let's get it over with."

Under the trees, winter felt oddly close, with a dampness in the air that spoke of frosts and late-night mists. The dirt track they followed was riddled with muddy puddles, and Heather found herself concentrating so hard on walking on the drier areas that it was a surprise when they emerged out under the sky again. The grass was thick and overgrown, quickly turning the cuffs of Heather's jeans dark with moisture. As they approached the trees on the far side, they saw that the woods were much thicker and darker, the path a little more overgrown. All of which made it something of a surprise, ten minutes later, to emerge onto a neatly manicured lawn with a well-maintained house sitting at the heart of it. More trees curled around the back of the house, which was built with dark stone similar to that of Fiddler's Mill House itself, and on the gravel drive out front stood a sturdy looking green Landrover, mud on its wheels. Next to it was a smaller, more modern car, and as they watched, the front door of the house opened and an older woman emerged dressed in a dark green raincoat, a large carry-all clutched in both hands. She looked straight at them, clearly startled, and then leaned back in the door. They heard her speak, but did not catch what she said, and then the woman climbed into the smaller yellow car and drove away—there was a proper paved road on the far side of the grounds, disappearing into more trees.

"We've been spotted," said Heather, unnecessarily.

As they walked toward the house, a shadow appeared at the door, not quite emerging into the light. When they were on the gravel drive, Heather could see it was a hunched old man, much older than the woman who had disappeared in the yellow car. He was watching them come, while leaning on a walking stick. There was a linoleum floor in the hallway; a green vine pattern against a sickly yellow background.

"Good morning!" She lifted her hand in greeting, but the man's only response was to tip his head slightly to one side. Next to her, Nikki leaned in close and murmured in her ear.

"Let's just keep walking and go up that road. I don't think they like strangers round here."

"Come on, just a quick chat. He might have known the area in the '70s and '80s—he certainly looks old enough." They came to the door and the man shuffled out a little further to meet them. As the brittle morning light fell on their faces, she saw him frown abruptly, his gnarled hands clenching over the end of his walking stick. He was clearly ancient, his thin, creased skin speckled with moles and liver spots, encasing a head that had lost all but some of its hair, and he had oversized nose and ears, in the way of elderly men. His shoulders were rounded, almost seeming to push at the back of his balding head, and he wore a hearing aid, the beige nub of plastic sitting neatly within his ear.

"Hello," Heather said again, deciding to front it out. "We're from up the hill. Just having a wander about really. This is a beautiful piece of land."

For a long moment, the old man didn't respond—Heather had the strangest sensation they had frozen him solid with surprise—and then he seemed to jerk into life. He shuffled out the door, his head tipped to one side still so that he was peering up at them through one slightly bloodshot eye.

"It is, it is, and you've chosen a beautiful morning to explore it on." His voice was friendly, warmed slightly with a hint of the local accent. "The woods really sing when the sun is out."

"Do you know much about the area? About the old house on the hill?" Heather smiled. "I'm interested in local history, you see. I like to learn a little bit wherever I go."

The man paused then, squinting at them in the bright light. There was something about the way he looked at her, as though he saw through her lies without even trying, that brought all Heather's misgivings back in a rush. Then, dragging himself and the stick with obvious effort, he moved to one side and indicated the darkened hallway.

"Ladies, you've come to the right place, and it just so happens that Linda put a brew on before she left. Join an old man for a cup of tea?"

Heather glanced at Nikki, saw the tiniest shrug of her shoulder, and turned back to the old man.

"We'd love to, thank you."

He shuffled back inside and they followed him down the shadowy hallway. Heather caught sight of various black and white photographs in frames hanging on the walls and an old, chintzy style wallpaper, and then they were turning right into a large living room. There were prints and paintings on the walls, and a large set of windows looking out across a wild lawn leading down into the woods.

"This is a lovely house," said Nikki, who went over to the window to look out. "It must be a very peaceful place to live."

"It is, it is at that. I'm Bert, by the way—it'll be nice to have some company this morning. Linda, bless her heart, likes to tell me all the cleaning lady gossip but half the time I don't know what she's harpin' on about."

They both introduced themselves, and Heather felt a little flurry of unreality; standing in a stranger's home, her mother's house—and her ghosts—far behind her. The feeling was compounded when she turned to sit on the nearest sofa and spotted an enormous black dog in the corner of the room. He was huge and shaggy, with a long wolfish face like an Alsatian, and he was sprawled on top of a dog bed that was much too small for him. Heather looked back to Bert to ask about the dog—what sort was he, what was his name, would he be likely to eat them both—but the old man had pottered back down the corridor. Instead, she looked at Nikki, who was peering at the prints on the walls.

"Isn't that a photo of the House?"

Heather looked where Nikki was nodding, and saw it; a very similar image to the ones whytewitch had had in her album, only this looked much older. A long row of men and women in a variety of servant's uniforms stood outside, lined up on the gravel path, and standing slightly awkwardly next to them, a handful of people dressed in old fashioned clothes. Heather guessed it was from the '20s or '30s, judging by the fashions and the rear end of an extremely antiquated car peeking into shot.

"Before it was invaded by the great unwashed," murmured Heather. A moment later, Bert reappeared at the door carrying a tea tray loaded with a teapot and cups. Nikki jumped up and helped him to wrestle it onto the low coffee table. When they were settled, with cups of tea warming up chilled hands, Bert leaned forward, his voice suddenly much more direct.

"What is it you wanted to know?"

Heather sipped her tea and shrugged. "There was a commune here in the '70s, wasn't there? Did you know the place then?"

The old man nodded slowly, not looking at them, as if confirming something to himself.

"Oh aye, yes, I knew it. It was lively, very lively. I remember when it was at its peak, when things were really *jumping*." He smiled again, baring his long teeth.

"Do you know who was living in the big house at the time?" Nikki smiled to lessen the baldness of her question. "It's just interesting to think of the history of the place, you know, while we're staying there."

"In the big house, are you?" said Bert, and Heather had the strangest idea that he knew that was a lie. Nevertheless, she nodded. He rubbed his thumb over the handle of his tea cup, back and forth, back and forth. "I don't rightly recall. It belonged to the same family for generations, but they dwindled, as big families sometimes do." His free hand clutched at his knee convulsively, and something about the movement made Heather shiver; it reminded her of a crab, sidewinding its way across some barren stretch of beach. "There was a lot of gossip about them, that family, most of it quite vicious." He grinned briefly, then it was gone. "Eventually the house was sold to the company that own it now, and I'm sure they were glad to be shot of it. It's hard maintaining a place like that, you know."

"What do you remember about the commune?"

He sniffed and nodded, leaning back in his chair. "A lot of noise, they made a lot of noise, and they got up to some strange things in the woods. Some of it would have turned my father's hair white, but then we live in a different age now, don't we? Quite different." He looked toward the window, sunlight shining off of his scalp. "I don't pretend I understood much of it, but I would help them where I could. Brought them groceries, sometimes, taught them which mushrooms were safe to eat." He smiled. "Although some of them were interested in the less-than-safe varieties, if you get what I mean."

He put the tea cup down, and for the first time Heather noticed that there were dark reddish-brown rings under his finger nails, as if he'd been digging in the dirt. Without really knowing why, she looked back toward the dog, and wasn't surprised to see that it was staring at her, brown eyes luminous in a shaft of sunlight.

"Did you get to know them well?" asked Heather. "The young people, I mean? My mum knows a lady called Pamela who said she stayed out here for a time—did you know her at all?" Outside, the sun passed behind some clouds, and the sunny living room grew dimmer. Something about that made her feel uneasy. The lawn through the window looked suddenly dreary, and the woods at the bottom seemed to promise horrors.

"Lots of young people came here, looking to get away from their parents and live more interesting, freer lives. They wanted to know the country, to live closer to the wild, but most of them found they didn't like it much when the winter came, and it got cold. They started to miss their parents' central heating." Bert smiled again, and it pinched his eyes into networks of wrinkles. "Some were committed though. A few really loved this land. Gave themselves to it. Can't remember individual names though, I'm afraid." He tapped the side of his head. "Not as sprightly up here as I was, more's the pity."

"It sounds like you spent quite a lot of time there," said Nikki.

"I just helped them, is all. Can't pretend I understood it, what they were up to," said Bert, all the decisiveness leaking from his voice. Suddenly Heather felt guilty, seeing Bert as he was: a very elderly man, living alone in an isolated house.

"Anything else you can tell us about the area?"

He brightened at that. "Oh yes, there's lots of history around here." He stood up, almost looming over them, and Heather realized that before his back started to bend him in two he had been very tall. He shuffled over to a nearby cabinet and picked up some papers, which he brought back over to the coffee table. Unlike the slick pamphlets from the spa, these were printed in black and white, and on cheap paper.

"A civil war battle, a mile or so down the road." Bert picked up one of the leaflets and passed it to Heather. There was a drawing of a Roundhead soldier on the front, clearly photocopied from some history book. "An especially bloody one, apparently. There's nothing to see there now, of course, but you could always have a look there, soak up the atmosphere. Course, local legend says its haunted."

"Haunted?" asked Nikki.

Bert smiled, as if amused at the ludicrousness of it all. "Go there on a moonless night and you'll hear the sounds of battle. There's lots of stuff like that up here, you'll find. The lady in white who haunts the back roads, and the barghest that stalks the fields and the lanes, all the lonely places."

"Barghest?" Heather took a sip of her tea. It had an unpleasantly grassy flavor. "What's that?"

"It's a word for a phantom dog," said Bert. "You get versions of the legend all over the country. Black Shuck, Gyrtrash, Padfoot. Demonic hounds. Very popular bit of British folklore, that. Blazing eyes and slathering jaws." He chuckled warmly.

Heather felt another tingle of unease, thinking of her mother's suicide note: *monsters in the wood.* The old man was poking through the leaflets again, apparently intent on finding something. Despite the tea, she felt cold, and she realized that she didn't like Bert. She didn't like him at all, yet she couldn't have said why. He nodded as he found what he was after, and passed Nikki a photograph. It showed a dense wood in spring, full of golden early morning light and dusted with bluebells.

"It's beautiful," said Nikki. Bert nodded seriously.

"These woods—the Fiddler's Woods, which you would have walked through a small section of to get to my house—are ancient woods. Did you know that?"

"Aren't all woods pretty old?" said Heather.

"Oh no," Bert leaned back in his chair, his hands on the tops of his legs and his elbows pointing out, as though he were about to give them a painful estimate on an MOT. He sucked air in through his yellow teeth and shook his head. "Oh no. Trees were planted, you see, forests have been planned. But ancient woodland has been here a very long time. Longer than many of us have been here." He shot a quick look at Nikki, and Heather stiffened, but he didn't elaborate. "Ancient woodlands are forests that existed before 1600. If they were around before 1600, then it's likely no one planted them—that they grew here, naturally. That they have always been a part of the landscape." He leaned forward and tapped the photo with a slightly overlong fingernail. "Bluebells are often a sign that the wood is an ancient one. Wood anemone, primroses, too. We have them all in Fiddler's Wood." He said it with obvious pride, and Heather fought down an urge to ask if he'd planted the woods in his youth—he looked old enough, after all.

"Where was this taken? Is it nearby?"

Nikki had picked up another photograph. This one was of a cold-looking beach, the sky a flat gray and the sea a steely band flecked with white foam. There was a rugged romance to the scene, and an odd building sat off to one side. Heather took it from her friend to get a closer look.

"Ah," Bert raised his eyebrows. "It is, it is. Beyond Fiddler's Wood, if you go far enough."

"And what's this?" Heather tapped the building. It was a tall structure of warm brownish stone, marked here and there with narrow leaded windows. It stood alone, a tower on the edge of the land.

"Fiddler's Folly, they call it round here. The family up at the big house was responsible for it, and there were lots of rumors about it, what it was for, why they built it." He grinned, looking at them with his head tipped to one side. "But no one knows, not really. It's standing empty now."

When they'd finished their tea, Bert walked them to the front door. The sunshine had gone, to be replaced with a blanket of thick clouds, dark with potential rain.

The old man peered up at the sky, smiling faintly. "Well, it looks like the sun is over for you." He turned back to look at Heather. "Take care, won't you?"

CHAPTER

36

THEY MADE IT through the first stretch of woods and then it began to rain heavily, in the steady sort of way that suggests it is planning to hang around all day. Deciding to try a short cut, umbrellas brandished above them, they walked through another, sparser set of trees, and came across an ancient looking caravan. Once it had been white with a red and a brown stripe along the side, but now it was camouflaged with patches of rust and a thick covering of dead leaves and forest debris. At some point someone had attempted to fence the thing off with wire panels, but those had mostly fallen down, and thick tangled bushes had grown up around its wheels.

"Hey, that's got to be from the commune. Do you want to have a look inside?"

Nikki grimaced. The rain was getting stronger all the time, the ground under their boots rapidly turning into mud. "Can we come back later? We should go and get the car."

"You go. I'll join you in a bit."

"Are you sure?"

Heather nodded. "Go on. I just want to have a quick poke around, and then I'll head back to the cottage. I think our exploring is done for the day."

When Nikki had trudged away toward the clearing, Heather picked her way across the wild undergrowth until she reached the flimsy looking door. It came open with one fairly solid kick, and, collapsing her umbrella, she stepped inside.

It was dark, the only light filtered through a series of small, dirty windows, and it smelt powerfully of damp and moldy clothes. Heather took out her phone and turned on the torch function, slowly turning around to take in the whole scene. There was a kind of sitting room, seats with padding that could be flipped to turn into beds, storage units and a fold down table. Further back was a tiny sink, with more cupboards lining the available wall space, and then at the far end, a closed door leading into another room. Here and there she could see more evidence that the place was more than forty years old—orange and brown wallpaper with a familiar ornate flower pattern; stickers on the cupboard doors that demanded the government "ban the bomb," several on the fridge that were of the Smurfs, their blue faces mottled with damp. More interestingly, there were signs that the owners had been interested in an alternative lifestyle of sorts. Heather spotted what could only have been a very old bong lying sideways in the sink, and an ancient poster on the wall detailed the months and signs of the zodiac, as well as phases of the moon and other esoteric advice.

Heather moved down through the van, the stench of the place coating the back of her throat. The rain was growing heavier, drumming on the roof in a persistent roar. She opened one of the little cupboards with her free hand and grimaced at the thick spiderwebs inside, but the cupboard above that one was full of small brown glass bottles with white tops. Bringing the phone closer, she tried to read some of the labels, but they were all blurred and warped with age. She did see several needles at the back, old-fashioned-looking bulky things, plastic packets of what looked like condoms and ancient plasters.

"You'd think kids would have been in here and had all this stuff years ago." She paused, thinking better of it. "Mind you, maybe kids aren't that stupid."

Moving down the small space she came to the little work area next to the sink. Here, a stained wooden chopping board had been left, its surface crisscrossed with deep knife marks. On the floor next to it was a big tea chest, painted with pentagrams and runes in paint that had probably been silver once. Heather smiled slightly, imagining the hippies that had once lived in this cramped little space, and reached down to open the lid. Disappointingly it was empty, but just as she was flipping it closed again Heather spotted a tiny corner of white sticking up from the bottom panel. She leaned down and took hold of it with her fingernails. When she tugged, a false panel in the base of the chest popped up, revealing a small recess filled with old Rizla papers and bits of foil. Underneath the old drug paraphernalia were a couple of Polaroids, their familiar white borders catching Heather with an unexpected stab of nostalgia. She fished them out and took them over to the closest window to take advantage of the weak natural light.

They were both of babies, both very young, their faces still quite red and raw looking. One was laying on a yellow blanket, wearing a white baby grow that was too big for it—the sock ends were flat where the baby's tiny feet did not quite reach them—and the other was being held by a woman whose head ended at the chin, cut off by the framing. The baby was wrapped in a blue and pink knitted blanket, and it was looking up at the camera with the particular expression of annoyed confusion special to all very small children. There were tiny wisps of ginger hair on its downy scalp.

Heather stood very still. There was nothing especially sinister about this, she told herself. People loved to take photos of babies. Judging by her Facebook feed, it was a pastime destined to be forever popular. But her mind kept returning to Anna in the visiting room, touching a hand to her stomach, saying "they took my baby." And the more she looked at the photo of the woman, the stranger it was to her that the photographer had cut her head off—if they'd taken a step back, they could have got mother and baby both in the picture easily enough.

And why were the photos still here? And hidden?

She turned the Polaroids over. On the backside of each, someone had drawn a tiny heart in red felt tip.

Taking a stumbling step backwards, Heather's boot landed on something soft and yielding. She lifted her foot and made a small noise in the back of her throat. It was a dead bird, quite a large one. Maggots moved busily under and around the feathers, a tiny squirming civilization.

Just a coincidence, Heather told herself as she stuffed the photos in her pocket. *Just a coincidence, just a coincidence.*

At that moment, there was a loud scuffling noise from the room at the end. Something threw itself against the door, and Heather turned and ran, jumping over the dead bird and flying out the door into the rain. She kept going, through the grass and into the tree line. There was a flat crashing sound as something threw the caravan door open, but she didn't look back. In seconds, she was deeper into the woods, the sound of her own breathing too loud, and even as she tried to convince herself she was fine—*it was just a fox, a fox made a den in there, that's all*—the sense that someone was running after her was irresistible.

Disorientated by the rough ground, she stumbled to a stop, leaning against a tree trunk, and she forced herself to hold her breath, and listen.

Rain pattered down through the trees, creating a cocoon of noise that shrouded everything else.

"Shit." Heather took a slow breath. Somewhere back toward the caravan, she could hear something—a crackle of twigs being broken underfoot, perhaps. Somewhere nearby, a bird cried out, making her jump.

Maybe not a fox. She stared in the direction of the noises, although she could see no one in the gloom. *Maybe a tramp. Someone who has been using it to get out of the rain.*

She waited, so tense her back began to ache, but nothing materialized from between the trees. As if on cue, the rain began to fall more heavily, and reasoning that the noise would hide her movements from anyone listening, Heather began to pick her way through the woods toward the cottage.

* * *

When Heather got back, she found Nikki bustling about, a dustpan and brush in one hand.

"We've been here less than a day, you can't have found anything to tidy up yet." She kicked her boots off, cringing at the overly casual sound of her voice. She felt tainted by the caravan and her panicky run from it, as though she'd brought back its fusty, rotten atmosphere to this cozy space. She wanted to have a shower.

"Oh. Well." Nikki paused in the kitchenette, looking at the floor critically. "We must have left a window open or something because a bird got in. Feathers all over the place."

"What?"

"It's all right, I got most of them I think." Nikki banged the pan against the bin, and Heather could just see a little pile of soft brown feathers disappearing into the binbag. "The bird itself must have done a circuit of the cottage and flown back out again, the little sod . . . Hev, are you all right? You look like you're going to be sick."

She turned away as she took her coat off, so that Nikki wouldn't see her face. *What has followed me here? And how could it?*

"Did you look in all the rooms? For the bird, I mean?"

"Yup, no sign. Are you sure you're okay?"

"I'm fine," Heather joined her friend in the kitchen, retrieving a bottle of wine from the side and pouring herself a glass. *It's probably nothing*, she told herself, although the sick feeling in her stomach only seemed to increase. *If you tell her, you'll be scaring her for no reason.* "Listen, I am a bit tired though. How about we call it a day and have a rest? I want to drink a glass of wine, have a hot bath or something." She took out her phone from her pocket and glanced at the screen, but still no messages from Ben. The idea of calling to complain that someone was leaving feathers in her holiday home only made her feel worse.

"Sure." Nikki smiled, although Heather could see the little crease between her eyebrows that meant she was worrying about something. "It's raining too hard to go for a walk now anyway. We'll pick up where we left off tomorrow."

CHAPTER

37

BEFORE

BONES, WHITE AGAINST the black earth.

Michael knelt, curious, pushing away clods of mud and pieces of mulch until a shape emerged: empty eye sockets, long toothy snout. It was the skull of a fox, he was fairly certain, and it had been here a good long time. Long enough to lose all its flesh, to simmer away its fur under the forest floor and then emerge this morning, clean and somehow alert, fitting so neatly into his hands.

There were bones all over his piece of Fiddler's Woods, and he knew the location of most of them, but of the women he brought back only their hearts nestled in the mud—that was the rule. This skull felt like a message of some sort, but he couldn't have said what it was. A warning? A blessing? Were the woods trying to speak to him directly?

He had just placed it back into the dark earth, turning it so that its eyes looked up to the trees, when an alien noise made him sit up. It took him a moment to place it—a baby, not crying yet, but whinging in that pitiful way that babies do when something isn't quite to their liking.

"Hello?"

He stood up and moved away from the skull, wiping his hands on his trousers. It was a warm day, and the midges were thick in the air. The closer he got to the sound of the baby, the more he picked up other, more reassuring noises: there was Colleen, her voice pitched higher than usual as she tried to settle the child, and there was the voice of someone else, talking to her. A moment after he recognized her voice he saw her, walking an old woodland path with one of the Bickerstaff sisters. She was wearing a short-sleeved shirt with tiny purple roses on it, and the baby was wrapped in a yellow blanket. Every now and then she rocked it in her arms, trying to get it to quieten down, but the whinging was edging close to crying now.

"Babysitting, are we?"

Both women looked up at the sound of his voice. Neither of them had heard him coming.

"Oh, Mike." Colleen smiled. Strands of her blonde hair were plastered to her high forehead with sweat. "Just giving Eileen a break. This little one," she pressed one hand briefly to the baby's cheek, "is teething, we think. Walking them about sometimes calms them down."

"Bit of brandy in the milk works, too," said the Bickerstaff woman. "That's what our mother used to do."

Colleen looked faintly scandalized. "Everyone's a bit frazzled at the commune, so I thought we'd best take our walk where it's quiet." She grinned suddenly. "This is the second spring baby!"

Now that he was next to them, Michael peered down at the baby's face; Colleen, pleased he was taking an interest, pulled the blanket back a little so he could see better. The small face was mottled and pink, and he could see a few curls of carroty hair sprouting from a downy scalp.

"Two babies and another on the way." He looked up at the Bickerstaff woman. It was Lizbet. "Are you sure those contraceptive pills aren't duds, lass?"

Lizbet scowled at him openly. "It's not our fault that girls are forgetting to take them, is it? You should be grateful you don't have to think about it, Michael. God knows where we would be if men had to take some responsibility for what they keep in their trousers, filthy beasts."

Filthy. Beast.

Michael swallowed hard. Something about his demeanor must have changed, because he saw a look of pure alarm pass over Colleen's face.

"She's just joking, Mike, that's all."

He could do it. He could reach out and snap Lizbet's neck like a twig; it would only take moments. His mother, who had called him dirty and monstrous had died in seconds, too, and then she had moldered away inside the ice house, her doughy flesh turning into brown sticks. But Lizbet was smiling at him, her eyes full of a knowledge she shouldn't have, and the moment passed.

"Take the baby up by the stream," he said eventually, not looking at either of them. "The sound of the water there makes it peaceful. That might calm her down."

CHAPTER

38

IT WAS, HEATHER had to admit, a beautiful stretch of land. Gentle hills in the distance, clumps of wild, dark trees held apart by empty fields, alive with the movement of long grasses. In the summer, she imagined it was magnificent—and at this end of the year, with most of the red and gold leaves around their ankles rather than on the trees, there was a pleasing bleakness to it all. And there was the silence. If it weren't for the constant calling of the birds, it might even have been possible for her to put aside the feeling that she was haunted—the sense that far from escaping the ghosts and horrors of her mother's house, that she had simply brought it all with her.

I'm getting closer, though. It was easier to put her worries to one side when the truth about her mother—and the Red Wolf—felt like it was just around the corner.

"Here, what's that?"

They had reached one of the little country lanes and on the corner of a turn there was, standing half hidden in a bush, a strange figure of twisted metal. Heather and Nikki wandered over for a closer look.

"I didn't expect to see something like this up here. I mean, wandering down Peckham Road, you're falling over stuff like this, but here?"

It was about five feet tall, and made of graceful twists of silver and copper-colored metal. The figure stood with its hands held out in front of it, each curving finger like a melting knife.

"Look, there's a sign." Nikki reached out and tapped the palm of the left hand: there was a small metal tag there, letters neatly pressed into it. She read it out loud. "The Shifting Man, a work by Harry Bozen-Smith. Commissions accepted. Follow the signs to my studio."

Heather straightened up and looked down the turning. The road there was narrower, the bare trees crowding in on either side, but she could already see the next "sign"—another figure of metal, this one with its arms raised and body bent, like a ballerina stretching.

"Let's go and have a look."

They wandered down the narrow lane, spotting another three figures made from metal before they found another turn off. This one led straight into a field, the grass snipped down to make a tidy path, and in the middle of it was a caravan and a shed. The shed doors were open wide, and it was possible to see a jumble of machinery and tools, half-finished statues and what appeared to be a very elderly car in the midst of being reduced to its parts. The caravan was old, too, but clean and shiny, with a neat sign on the side: Harry Bozen-Smith, Artist.

"Hello?" Heather called, and after a moment a man emerged from the shed, wearing a pair of dungarees streaked with oil and paint, and a black t-shirt. He was rubbing his hands on a rag, and as he emerged into the daylight, Heather glanced quickly at Nikki, catching her raised eyebrow.

Harry Bozen-Smith was unreasonably attractive. He had untidy dark hair, a carefully trimmed beard, and large brown eyes framed by a pair of thick expressive eyebrows. His arms, as he moved to throw the rag into a bucket, were firmly muscled, although not excessively so. Seeing them both, he smiled—a dreamy Disney prince sort of smile.

"Holy shit," muttered Nikki.

"Are we in a jeans advert?" muttered Heather back.

"Hello!" He walked down to meet them. He was wearing a battered pair of Dr Marten boots, and had a tattoo that circled the top of his bicep, almost hidden under his t-shirt. "Can I help? Have you come to buy something? You'd make my day."

"We saw your man on the corner," said Heather. "Harry, is it?"

The man nodded. "Don't see many people around here this time of year."

"You work out here by yourself?"

Harry Bozen-Smith shrugged. "Live out here, really, at the moment. Did you want to look at my work?"

Nikki nodded and stepped up to follow him, while Heather battled a sinking feeling—she'd been to enough final shows at art colleges to dread this sort of thing, but when he led them around the back of the caravan, she was pleasantly surprised. There was a small awning attached to the caravan, and underneath were a series of shapes and figures, all pieced together from junk or unidentifiable pieces of metal. She saw a great copper hare, his eye a shining bicycle light, and a crowd of bats, their tight formation held together by pieces of wire. The most striking piece was a great snarling wolf made of silver and black metal. Heather leaned down to look more closely, and caught sight of her reflection in its shining flank. *I know what you are, and I think you do too.* She looked away hurriedly.

Nikki knelt to examine a crow more closely—the black metal had been treated with oil somehow, so that its feathers shone rainbow-like even in the shadows.

"This is incredible," she said. "You take your inspiration from the landscape?"

Harry beamed, his hands in his pockets. "I do. This place . . ." he looked away, across the field. "This place is full of strangeness."

"We're trying to find out more about it, actually," said Heather. "Do you know much of the history of Fiddler's Mill?" She tucked a stray bit of hair behind her ear; the wind was picking up, and the awning caught the flat sound of the first few drops of rain. "We met a chap yesterday who said there's a haunted field around here somewhere."

"There is, that's true. I've been there. I didn't see any ghosts . . ." Heather glanced at him, but couldn't tell if he was joking. "Some powerful energies though. Very powerful."

"And there was the hippy commune up at Fiddler's Mill House. Did you hear about that?"

Harry straightened up. For the first time, Heather thought to wonder at his bare arms—it was hardly a warm day.

"You know that's infamous around here." He grinned. "I grew up in the little village down the road, and my mum used to talk about it with the neighbors when I were a lad. Enough scandal to keep them talking for decades."

Nikki returned his smile. "Scandal? Do tell."

"Oh, you know." Harry shrugged. "Nothing especially scandalous to people from London, I'll bet, but up here? Drugs and drinking and loose women. I always preferred my nana's stories about Fiddler's Mill—she was more about ghosts and that, fairies and witches, you know. I always . . ."

His words were lost in a gust of wind, and the pair of them shuffled further under the awning.

"Sorry?" Heather nodded encouragingly. "Please, local folklore is a special interest of mine."

Harry looked faintly embarrassed now, and he rubbed the back of his neck with one hand. "Aye well. She said there was a woman who haunted the woods around here, a woman wearing a red coat. Swore her life on it, she did. You've heard why it's called Fiddler's Mill, have you?"

"No?" Heather wrapped her arms around herself and glanced out across the grass. The line of dark woods continued there, waiting for them.

"Well," Harry said, "There was a mill, a long time ago, but that was named after the woods, you see. And the woods were said to belong to the fiddler, a man who came to the village with a magical fiddle. When he played it, the children became so caught up in the music, so absorbed in it, they would do whatever he wanted them to do. He took them away, to his secret home in the woods, and they never came back."

"What?" Heather ignored the look of surprise Nikki shot her. "What are you talking about?"

"The wood," said Harry, mildly enough. "The villagers got angry, and when he came back to collect more of their children, they chased him into the trees but lost him there. He never came back, and neither did any of their kids." He shrugged. "It's a creepy story, but you love stuff like that when you're a kid, don't you? I was always getting my nana to tell me that one."

"It's fascinating," said Nikki seriously. "Like the Pied Piper legend, but a local variety. Harry, I work at a college teaching English. I reckon my students would get a kick out of a proper old piece of folklore like this. I'd love to write about this story, if you wouldn't mind?"

"Uh, sure, knock yourself out." He looked bemused now. "Here, look, take my card." He fished a slightly bent business card out of his pocket and handed it over to Nikki. "Call me. You know. If you want to know more old stories.' He grinned. "Or you want to buy a giant crow."

As they walked away, back down the twisting paths, Heather elbowed her friend in the side.

"So smooth," she said. "You always were a player, Nikki Appiah."

"Oh, shut up." But Nikki was laughing while she said it, her eyes bright. For a moment, Heather felt a genuine measure of contentment—it felt good to be teasing her friend, just like she did when they were kids in the school playground. When the rain picked up, however, the pattering of the rain on their umbrellas made her think of the abandoned caravan, and the lost and tiny faces of the children in the photographs, and all feelings of warmth and safety seemed to drain away into the soil.

* * *

They spent the rest of the afternoon wandering the countryside, taking photos here and there and sitting on low stone walls. Heather brought out her folder of Pamela Whittaker's paintings every now and then, trying to match the images with the landscape around them, but she was never quite convinced she had got it right. She realized gradually that she was trying to pin the place down, as though it could be captured on Google street view, skewered like a butterfly on a board to be better examined, but Fiddler's Mill and its environs were ever changing; in a constant state of flux, eroded into change by the seasons and wildlife and weather. It was an unknowable place—unless, perhaps, you were prepared to live under its bare skies for a while, like the commune had. She tried to picture her mother out here, living with a bunch of long-haired bath-dodgers, but it was difficult. It was difficult to even imagine her mother being happy.

Nikki was a good sport about it, wandering wherever Heather's vague impulses directed them, but she noticed that her friend spent a lot of time looking at her phone, and any time there was a flicker of signal her fingers would fly across the screen. Giving into her nosier instincts, Heather peeped over Nikki's shoulder at one point and saw enough of her phone screen to know that she was already engaged in a lively text conversation with Harry the artist. She looked away, smiling. It made her think of Ben Parker and his tousled sandy hair—but of course there was little chance he would reply to her text messages, and she could hardly be surprised at that.

When the light began to seep from the sky, they conceded defeat, heading back to the cottage with sore feet and empty stomachs. Once inside, Nikki began cooking a chili, neatly laying out her ingredients on the side before browning some mince in a pan.

"So," Heather leaned on the kitchen counter, trying not to look at the darkness beyond the windows. "Harry the artist then. What's your progress?"

Nikki continued chopping onions. "What do you mean, what's your progress?"

Heather snorted. "Do me a favor, Nikki. I am an investigative journalist, remember?"

"Is that what you call it?" Nikki shot her a rueful look before sliding the onions into the pan with the edge of her knife. "I dunno, I'm thinking of asking him to do me a commission."

"Oh, is *that* what you call it?"

Nikki threw a tea towel at her.

"We're only here for a few days, aren't we? But," she shrugged, and Heather knew she'd won. "We did talk about going out for a drink tomorrow. There's a place he knows a short drive from here, they do a really good fish pie." When she met Heather's eyes, she looked abashed. "I won't go though, if you want me to stay, of course."

Heather rolled her eyes at her. "Who am I to stand in the way of true love? And those muscles." When Nikki opened her mouth to protest, Heather shook her head. "No honestly, go. I'm glad you might actually have some real fun on this little jaunt, rather than just traipsing around in the mud with me all day."

"It's just an evening thing, and . . ." Nikki sighed. "I am worried about you though, Hev. Do you really think you should be alone at all? With everything that's happened?"

"Oh god, don't start. I'm fine." She thought of the dead bird on her mother's dressing table, the petals like drops of blood leading up the staircase. She forced a smile on her face. "Honestly. It's doing me good, to be away. Maybe my mum was right about this place. It's peaceful."

"If you're sure." Nikki went to the cupboard and retrieved a can of chopped tomatoes. "Did we have another bottle of red? It'd go better with the chili than the white."

"I think I've still got one in my case."

The shadows in her room were already the deep shades of night. Heather flicked the light on and began rummaging around in her case, trying to retrieve the bottle of wine that was nestled beneath her discarded socks and t-shirts. Her fingers had just closed around the neck when she saw a dark shape sitting neatly in the center of her pillow. She dropped the wine and straightened up, her heart skipping sickly in her chest.

Although it wasn't the right size or shape at all, for an awful instant she was sure it was a dead bird, even as her eyes confirmed the truth—it was an old Polaroid photograph, very much like the two she had found in the abandoned caravan. The photo showed a typical scene between two lovers—a man and a woman on a beach, the sea a burnished strip of blue behind them, the man with his arm draped possessively around the woman's narrow shoulders. They were both wearing coats and hats, their cheeks pink with the cold. The woman's face was coyly turned inward, nuzzling a little at the man's broad chest, and her left hand was tucked snugly between the man's knees. She was grinning, her eyes shining. She looked very young. There was no question that these two people were a couple, and it was almost charming in its simplicity—a couple on a beach, enjoying themselves, very much in love.

Except that the man was a notorious serial killer, and the woman was her mum.

Heather snatched the photo off the pillow. Her breathing sounded too loud, whistling in and out like a kettle boiling. She shook the photo and pressed her fingers to the shiny surface in the strange and slightly desperate hope that it would prove to be a fake—something crafted in photoshop and printed on fancy paper. But she'd handled enough photos in the newspaper's archive to know what it was. It was real. A real photograph of Michael Reave and Colleen Evans, cozied up with their arms around each other. Her mother even had on the same thick winter coat she had been wearing in Pamela's photo.

She turned it over. On the back were two scraps of writing, each written in a different hand with a different color pen. The first one, written in black ballpoint pen, said:

Fresh air!! March 27th, 1983

The second, in red ink and a familiar, blocky font, read:

I know what you are, and I think you do too.

For long, elastic minutes, Heather couldn't do anything at all. She stood with the Polaroid clutched between her fingers. She couldn't stop looking at the date.

March the 27th, in 1983. Heather's birthday was in October of that year.

No.

If the date was correct, then her mother was already pregnant in this picture. Had been pregnant for maybe six or seven weeks.

No.

Reluctantly, she turned the photo over and looked again at her mother, this girl-child image that she had never seen before. There was no way of telling, with the big coat covering her lap, but then some women didn't show until fairly late in their pregnancy, especially when it was their first child. And hadn't her mum and dad gotten married when she was a toddler? Why had she never questioned that? They had always told her they had known each other since school, that they had started dating when Colleen was nineteen, but that had to have been a lie. An image of her dad floated into her mind, his round, easily flushed face, the strawberry blond hair that edged into straight-up ginger near his ears, or when he grew a beard.

I look nothing like him. I never did.

"No."

She didn't realize she'd spoken aloud until she heard Nikki call out from the living room.

"Hev? Are you ever getting that bottle or what?"

Reluctantly, her eyes were drawn back to the picture of Michael Reave. He was young here, even handsome, his face as yet free of the lines that would be etched there by his time in prison. She couldn't help noticing his dark hair, the particular shape of his cheekbones, the line of his nose.

"Hev?"

Nikki's voice was closer, as though she was standing in the little hall that led to the bedroom.

"Coming, sorry, just got distracted!"

She looked around the room, but nothing else seemed out of place. The window was shut and locked, as she'd left it, and the little dressing table was littered with the usual junk she took out of her pockets every night—receipts, loose change, sweet wrappers. Everything was normal, except . . .

She turned back to the bed, a cold hand walking down her back. The bed was made, the covers pulled up neatly to the pillow, which was itself straight and freshly plumped up. The only time Heather ever made the bed was just before she got into it herself, and then it was really only a case of tucking in the under sheet again, or retrieving a pillow. Whoever had left the photo had also made her bed.

For a horrible, suffocating second she thought she was going to laugh. And then she heard Nikki's footsteps going back to the kitchen and the compulsion passed. Instead, she slipped the photo into her pocket, snatched up the bottle of wine, and closed the door firmly behind her.

CHAPTER

39

BEFORE

He remembered where each of them was so clearly that often he felt like he could almost see them. Women sitting on the edge of the stream with their feet in the water, or women up in the trees, their souls taken up in the roots and spreading through the leaves. He could almost hear them sighing as he walked through the woods, and the gentle thrum of their hearts was ever present. Their bodies were far away, arranged with precision and care in distant green places, but they were here really, with him, in Fiddler's Wood. They all wore red coats.

It was raining on the day he lost Colleen, and although it was only around six in the evening the woods were rushing eagerly toward darkness. Michael moved through the shadows contentedly, listening to the graves and the patter of raindrops against leaves and mud, when he heard a sudden, piercing scream. He stopped and held himself very still, the hair raising on the backs of his arms. Screaming held no terrors for him—how could it?—And he was by now used to the noise generated by the commune, but this was a noise out of place, a noise that shouldn't have been there. A few seconds passed, and there was another scream, somehow more desperate and then abruptly cut off.

He left the woods, stepping into the downpour that the trees had been sheltering him from, and ran toward the big house. On the way there, he saw two figures hurrying away down the hill, and he moved to intercept them. It was both the Bickerstaff sisters, looking oddly similar to how they had on the first day he had seen them; their heads touching, walking with their sides pressed together, although now one of them held a shawl over their heads, and the other was clasping some small bundle to her chest. When they saw it was him, she gathered the little shape closer to her so he could not see it. One of them—Lizbet, he thought—levelled her cold gray gaze at him, but did not speak. The rain picked up, and Michael realized that the path beneath their feet was pinkish with watery blood, blood that was washing off of them.

'What's happening?'

They drew closer together. Beyond them, the fields and hedgerows looked hazy and indistinct as the rain blurred their edges.

'He wanted to see it,' said Beryl, as if that explained anything. 'When it came into the world.'

"What is it?"

Michael took a step forward to get a look at the thing they were carrying, but the two sisters exchanged a look of disgust between them, as though he was a dirty child at their feet.

"You'll see it again soon enough," said Lizbet.

"Who was screaming?"

"Anna isn't feeling herself. Go on up and have a look, if you're so worried."

"Where's Colleen?"

The two women smiled identical, icy smiles. "She's a good one, isn't she? Too good for the likes of you."

"I don't know what you mean."

"You didn't think you could keep her, did you, Michael?" Despite the shawl, Beryl's face was wet, shining unhealthily. "What a fool you are."

With that they hurried away from him, heading down the hill and back toward the commune, leaving a trail of watery blood behind them. Michael looked up at the big house. There were lamps burning in the living room windows, casting squares of brash yellow light out onto the gravel drive. The house had always seemed like a haven, a place where he could exist fully. He had slept with the lights on all night; had eaten dinners in a silence that wasn't challenged; had washed blood from his hands and clothes, over and over and over. Yet tonight it did not feel safe. Tonight, he looked at it and saw what Colleen saw—an empty place that housed a monster, perhaps several monsters. He knew suddenly that if he went back there, if he went and opened the door now, his sister would be waiting for him with her kindly smile and her red coat. She wasn't dead at all—none of the hearts buried in the woods belonged to her, not really, and she could still have him, if she wanted him.

He turned and ran back down the hill. The Bickerstaff sisters were already out of sight, vanishing into the cluster of tents, cars, and vans that littered the commune, but it wasn't them he was looking for. There were a few people about, despite the rain. He caught glimpses of pale, uncertain faces, some of them slack from drugs and drink, others looking alarmingly sharp, their eyes going again and again to the big house, where the screaming had come from. Once or twice he thought he saw the big black dog running alongside him, a shape flitting across the spaces between caravans.

Colleen kept her campervan on the very edge of the gathering, but he already knew what he was going to find before he got there. He skidded to a halt, the taste of something foul in the back of his throat. The screaming red landscape shivered and beckoned, making the fields and the woods look insubstantial and dream-like.

The campervan was gone, along with the little tent just outside it where she liked to sleep sometimes. In its place there was a patch of yellowed dead grass and a light scattering of damp cigarette butts.

Colleen was gone.

CHAPTER

40

THAT NIGHT, HEATHER did not go to bed. When they went off to their separate rooms, she waited half an hour or so for Nikki to go to sleep, and then she crept back down the hall to the living room, where she sat with her phone in her lap and her legs tucked up under her for the rest of the night. She listened, and she looked at Ben Parker's number on the small electronic screen. There was no signal, but she could use the phone at the cottage to call him. As easy as that. Despite the late hour, she was almost sure he would answer.

But instead she stayed awake, one small lamp on next to her and a knife from the kitchen lying in easy grabbing distance on the sofa. She listened and watched, her body thrumming with tension like electricity through a wire. Someone here knew who she was. Someone here was playing with her. Why? What did they want?

Was the new Red Wolf watching her?

By the time Nikki got up the next morning, Heather had brewed a pot of coffee and put the knife away. In the daylight, the crisp green landscape around them seemed less threatening, and all the horrors of the previous night—*whose daughter am I exactly*—seemed ludicrous.

"You're up early." Nikki yawned hugely, taking the cup of coffee in both hands. "Raring to go?"

Heather smiled, although it felt sickly and false on her face. "Not exactly. My head is killing me."

Nikki sat on one of the kitchen stools, her mouth turning down at the corners. "A migraine?"

Heather nodded and sipped from her own cup, ignoring the slippery feeling of guilt in her chest.

"Bloody hell. Do you want to go to a doctor or something?"

"No, but I think I'm just going to lay low for the day. Maybe you could move your date with Harry forward a bit? Spend the day with him."

"But . . ."

"Don't worry about me, honestly. It's hardly fair to drag you all the way up here then doom you to a day of tedium because I've got a migraine, is it? Just test the water, see what he says."

"If you're sure."

When Nikki had vanished from sight in the car, Heather went and got dressed, and stood for a moment with the Polaroid in her hands. Someone was fucking with her. Someone who had followed her from London, someone who knew more about her mother's history than she did. Despite everything, she found it hard to believe that the person responsible for the photograph was the new Red Wolf—he had been far too busy dismembering women in Lancashire to be the person leaving notes at her mother's house in outer London—but she was aware that as rational as this assumption was, it was still a dangerous one. Her most concrete link to this person, whoever they were, was the photo that had been left on her pillow. Time to see what she could find out about it.

It was cold and gray again when she stepped outside, the chill taking her breath away. Nikki having taken the car was annoying, as it meant she was stuck walking everywhere for the day, but once she started across the fields she was almost glad—the cold and the freshness of the air chased away the lingering effects of her sleepless night, and she felt stronger, more focused.

And perhaps it was more than just a feeling. Halfway up the hill that led to the imposing form of Fiddler's Mill House, she realized that she had seen the odd building in the back of the photograph before, on a coffee table. The old man called Bert had said it was Fiddler's Folly, a building belonging to the family who had once lived in the old house—and like all follies, it was a place with no obvious use or purpose. That meant that the photo had been taken here, on the coast.

She stopped where she was, ignoring the gusts of freezing wind, and wrestled the map out of her coat pocket. It was clearly produced with tourists in mind, covering the natural nearby attractions and the stretches of wild countryside, but it did just about reach the coast, at the very outer edge of the map. Heather squinted at it, looking for something likely to be the Folly, but she couldn't spot it. Either it had been named something else, or they'd simply left it off. Frowning slightly, she folded the map and continued heading up the hill. She needed a reliable Internet connection.

"Oh. Can I help you?"

The orange woman with yellow hair looked pained at the sight of her. Heather stamped off some of the water onto the slick marble floor of the foyer and summoned her most winning smile.

"Hi, yeah. I was wondering if I could use your wi-fi?"

The woman frowned theatrically and appeared to consult a sheet of paper on her desk.

"Are you a guest here currently?"

"You know I'm not." Heather leant on the desk, then thought better of it. "I'm sorry, I don't mean to be a pain in the ass. Don't you have a café or something? I'll buy a coffee, a sandwich, whatever you like. The place where we're staying is located in some sort of technological black hole, and I desperately need to get something sent off for work. Deadlines, you know how it is."

The woman narrowed her eyes. "How do I know you're not going to start, I don't know, mouthing off to our guests about murders, and drugs, and so on?"

Heather held her hands up. "I've no interest in doing that, I promise. You've been really helpful so far—I'll mention you personally on my Tripadvisor review." She looked at the name badge on the woman's shirt. "Melanie."

"Fine." Melanie turned back to her computer screen. "The café is to the right. You get the wi-fi password on your receipt when you buy something. So, you *will* have to buy something."

In minutes Heather had a cup of coffee and a plate of crushed avocado on toast, her laptop set up at a small table and her browser open. Very quickly she found Fiddler's Folly on Google maps, although now it was called The Heron Look and it was owned by the same environmental charity that partly owned the Fiddler's Mill spa. That was interesting, but as far as Heather could tell the building was still standing empty, and she could find no information about whether it was now used as a hotel, storage, or some sort of headquarters for the charity. Looking a little deeper, she found a number of references to the "rumors" the old man Bert had mentioned, although they were all annoyingly vague. The family that had built it had dwindled and died off, but she got the impression they weren't thought of with any affection by the locals.

Eventually, she gave up on Fiddler's Folly—she now knew, at least, where exactly the photo of her mother and Michael Reave had been taken—and began looking up Polaroid websites. Through these, she discovered that it was possible to figure out the rough date the Polaroid film had been manufactured, if not the date the photo had been taken. A long string of numbers on the back, very faded and almost impossible to read, revealed that the Polaroid film had been made in April 1982, which certainly fitted with the date scribbled in black ink. According to the website, back then instant film had been very expensive, and many families with Polaroid cameras would save their shots for important occasions. Feeling the coffee turn to a sour slick in her stomach, she imagined someone—possibly Michael Reave—buying the film, perhaps smiling over all the "special" moments he would capture with it.

She looked at the photo, which was lying next to her on the table. There must, she reasoned, be thousands like it—quick snaps of couples on beaches, their arms around each other. Very few, she suspected, would have such a dark history surrounding them.

She retrieved the photographs of the babies she'd found in the caravan from her bag, keeping them face down and on her lap, for reasons she couldn't quite explain. It didn't take long to figure out that, yes, these photos were from the same film run that had produced the photo of Reave and her mother. The film was produced on the same day in the same year, according to the codes on the back. It even told her on which shift the film was made.

Thinking of photographs, she remembered the one she had given to Ben Parker, of the fete and the red-headed girl who would grow up to be a PE teacher. Parker had said Fiona was there to pick up a certificate for some sort of nature scheme—on a whim, she put Young Nature Walkers Prize into the search engine. The scheme had ended some twenty years ago, but there were still a few remnants of it left online; someone had put the bare bones of a Wikipedia page together for it, logging the sorts of activities the children had to complete to get their certificate, things like rambling, pressing flowers, making a corn dolly. The scheme had been sponsored by Oak Leaf, the same environmental charity that had a hand in the very spa she was sitting in.

"More fucking coincidences."

Except they couldn't be. Heather sat back in her seat, ignoring her lunch. What did it mean? Did it mean anything at all? Inevitably her eyes were drawn back to the photo of her mother on the beach. Was it possible she had been *with* Michael Reave—her stomach turned over at the thought—while also seeing her dad at the same time? That could mean that the man who raised her *was* her dad, but she had no memory of her dad ever mentioning a commune in the north, and the idea of her mother playing two men off against each other felt wrong . . . But then, a lot of what she had thought she'd known about Colleen Evans had turned out to be a lie.

The other option was almost too horrible to contemplate.

"Doing more local research, Heather?"

She jumped. Bert, the old man who had made tea for them the other day, had appeared at her shoulder. Outside of his house and in the bright lights of the spa café he looked even more wizened, and he was peering at her with his head cocked, just as he had when they'd first met him.

"Uh, hello, Bert. Just, you know, getting a bit of work done while I'm here."

He raised an eyebrow at that, and just as Heather was trying to sneak it back in her pocket, he saw the Polaroid.

"Is that of the beach? May I have a look?"

Heather froze. In that long awkward moment, she could think of no good reason not to hand the Polaroid over, so she passed it to him, feeling her face flush crimson. She was certain he would recognize Michael Reave. After all, he had one of the most infamous mugshots in British criminal history, and it was clearly the same person, down to the little flash of white hair at his temple. And then he would ask what on earth she was doing with such a photo . . . But instead, he just stared at it, his face very still. Eventually he nodded.

"Yes. How interesting. The Folly was in a bit of a state back then," he said. "It went through an extensive restoration at one point, and I'm pleased to say it's less of an eyesore now."

"Do you know when that was? The restoration work, I mean?"

"Oh, in the mid-eighties, I think. Yes, that's right." He smiled, stretching dry lips across his long teeth. "They made the place habitable again." He looked like he was about to glance at the back of the photo, but instead he passed it back to her politely. "Discovering you have history here, are you?"

Heather looked up at him sharply. "Why do you say that?"

He shrugged, a one-sided movement with his crooked back. "You said your mother's friend was here at one point. Is that not her? In the photo."

"Oh. Oh yeah, that's right. Pamela." She smiled. "To be honest with you, Bert, I just like looking at old photos."

He tipped his head to one side, a motion that wasn't quite a nod.

"Well. I'll be letting you get back on with it then, lass."

When he'd shuffled some distance away, Heather turned to watch him go. He didn't seem like a typical spa customer, and she couldn't imagine why he had dragged himself all the way up the hill on a rainy day, but as he reached the foyer she saw the blond woman come out from behind the desk to greet him, and watched as they chatted together for a few minutes. Perhaps, she reasoned, the receptionist was a relation—a granddaughter, or a niece.

She stayed in the café for another couple of hours, digging deeper into forums about counter-culture, about drug use and the history of Fiddler's Mill, but didn't find anything that suggested who might be trying to mess with her. Eventually, she packed up her things and left, heading out into a day that had grown a little brighter. The clouds overhead were breaking up, letting through tantalizing glimpses of a soft, dreamy blue sky, and she walked out across the grass with no clear thought as to where to go next. Nikki, at least, was away from the cottage and safe with Harry. They were probably downing pints in some quaint country pub by now, talking about old ghost stories and eating a ploughman's lunch. The thought was a comforting one and she clung to it. Better to think about that than worry about what she might find when she got back—another note, a dead bird. Something worse.

She was so lost in those thoughts that when her phone rang it took her a few seconds to recognize the sound. Heather pulled the phone out, assuming it must be Nikki or even Ben, but instead it showed a withheld number. She pressed receive, and an automated voice told her she had an incoming call from HMP Belmarsh, and that she should stay on the line if she wished to be connected.

All at once, she felt exposed again. She looked around, but she was alone. The line of Fiddler's Woods marched off to her right, and the big house was a small shape far behind her. Not sure what else to do, she waited to be connected.

"Hello?"

She knew his voice immediately. A surge of conflicted emotions made her look at her feet; he sounded worried. Did serial killers get worried? It seemed like too human a reaction.

"Mr. Reave? Why are you phoning me?" She paused, and shook her head. "How do you even have my phone number? I seriously doubt the police gave it to you."

"Listen." But he didn't continue, and she could just hear his breathing, slow and measured.

"What is it?" Abruptly she felt furious, outraged that he could call her in the middle of the day and cause her stomach to tighten with what was undeniably fear. She wanted to hit something. Hit someone. "What do you bloody want?"

"Where are you?" There was a scuffling noise, and she pictured him transferring the receiver to the other ear. "Aren't you in London?"

"It's none of your business where I am."

"I wish you hadn't done that. God, I wish you hadn't."

Some of her anger seeped away then. He sounded more than worried, he sounded scared. And what could scare a murderer? The wind picked up, reminding her that she was alone. *I could just ask him*, she thought. *How well did you know my mum, really? Why were you so keen to talk to me?* And *am I the daughter of a serial killer?* But she had a terrible feeling she already knew the answers— and to hear it from him would make it real.

"Michael, if you know something —"

"I knew they couldn't leave well enough alone. I knew it was a mistake, to drive them away like that. They're just like her, they see everything."

"Like who?" His voice began to break up, tugged into electronic fragments by the fragile signal. "Like *who*? Who are you talking about?' She glanced at her phone. The symbols showing the signal strength were down to a single bar. It was a miracle that he'd got through to her at all.

"They want to hurt me, like she did. You have to leave, are you listening? Get back to—" There was a strangled blast of pops and static. ". . . back to the ground, it's harvest . . ."

"Michael?"

She heard a couple more disjointed words in the roaring electronic fuzz—"red," perhaps, and "punishment"—and then the call dropped.

CHAPTER

41

IT WAS GROWING dark, and no one knew where Heather was.

It was a strange feeling, and more comforting than she would have expected. She headed for a strip of ancient woods that she was fairly sure ran along the back of the holiday cottage—a short cut through the trees, a chance to think about things. The scents of the earth, rich and thick, filled her nostrils, and she breathed deeply, as if by doing so she could cleanse herself of it all. Out in the woods, it didn't matter who her father was, or what her mother had or hadn't done.

The crunch of undergrowth beneath her feet, the rustling movement of small things, the murmur of wind. With each step she felt better.

She walked on, listening to the crisp noises of her footfalls, tasting the clean air on her tongue. She came to a large tree and stopped. The cottage should be close now—she should at least be able to see lights from its windows—but the woods ahead of her promised no such thing. And a darker interior voice was asking why she wanted to hurry back at all. What would she find back at the cottage? More letters, more feathers? Reave had sounded shaken on the phone, but should she trust him? Someone was certainly trying to frighten her, but why would Michael Reave care about that? Unless what the Polaroid suggested was true. She brushed her fingers against the bark of the tree, and saw that someone had carved a shape into it, probably with a knife. It took her a second to recognize what it was.

A heart.

It was cold and she was alone; she wasn't safe, she was in danger, and terribly exposed.

"Fuck. What am I even doing here?"

She fumbled her phone out of her pocket and pressed it into life. The light from the screen display dazzled her, lighting up the bare trees and undergrowth in a painful fizzle of artificial glow. She blinked rapidly, alarmed at how little she could see, and turned the phone out into the night. No figures lurched into sight, but she was suddenly very aware of how large the woods were, and how tiny her light.

There was a crump of noise off to her left, like something heavy moving rapidly through the undergrowth, and Heather put her back to it and began to run, as best she could in the dark, the light from her phone weaving back and forth to summon an endless crowd of chaotic shadows. The noise behind her increased as whatever it was came after her, and Heather heard herself make a small noise of terror. She was in a nightmare, the earliest nightmare, the one where you were running from something terrible but your legs were hopelessly slow. Against her will she thought of the stories Michael Reave had told her, and Pamela Whittaker's paintings. The woods are dangerous. The woods are where the wolf waits.

She stormed up a slope, crashing into and through small bushes. Twigs and thorns caught at her skin and clothes, pulling her back as though the very woods were against her. Reaching the top of the slope, where she hoped to be able to figure out where she was, she stumbled, going to her knees in the mud. There was a smell, a combination of the wild, dark earth and another scent that seemed older, and stranger. She scrambled back to her feet, and there was a new sound very close—panting, quick and hot.

The barghest. Black Shuck. The hound that haunts the lonely places.

All thoughts of finding a path driven from her mind, Heather threw herself back down the small hill, careening forward with her arms held up to ward off the blow she was sure must be coming. Now, she was certain that several things were after her—creatures that ran on four legs, that could smell her fear—and they were on all sides, chasing her down. *Drink from the river*, she thought wildly, *drink from the river and become a wolf.*

The ground dropped away below her and before she could react Heather sprawled headlong into the wet and busy earth. All the air knocked out from her, she could do nothing but lay there for a long moment, the mud seeping into her jeans. She'd fallen partly into a bush, and the leaves were pricking her through her coat, as though she lay in broken glass. The noises had stopped, but as she picked herself up and looked around, the sense that she was being watched had increased tenfold. Eyes in the forest, watching.

"What do you want?" her voice wavered, untrustworthy. "Who are you?"

Silence. It was a deeper silence than that she had experienced before; no small animals moved through the undergrowth, no night birds called—even the wind seemed to have stopped. Something was listening. Much to her own surprise, she realized she was still holding her phone; when she'd fallen, some instinct had caused her to clasp it close to her chest. She held it up, activating the screen, and slowly turned the small oblong of light back and forth, all around her. The empty forest looked back at her, full of distrust and lies.

"I know you're there," she said. Anger, familiar and comforting, began to seep through her limbs. She was cold, wet, and frightened, she had been scratched all over and her right knee had taken a serious knock, and all because someone was playing silly buggers in the woods. "Say something, or piss off. All right?"

There was no reply, but in the corner of her eye Heather caught the slightest movement in the shadows. She spun the light toward it but whatever it had been was gone. However, it was possible now to see the path, and even beyond that, the clearing that led to their cottage.

She headed that way gladly, wincing as various cuts and bruises made themselves known. The cottage stood in its own cocoon of silence, soft lamplight glowing at the window. Heather was still some distance from it when she thought she saw the figure again—someone was standing at the back of the cottage, near one of the bedroom windows. She gasped in a breath, ready to shout, but in another heartbeat the shape was gone again, if it had ever been there in the first place.

Heather ran the rest of the way back to the cottage, crashing in through the door, half convinced she would find the shadowy figure in the kitchen, blood dripping from his hands, but instead she found it empty. The cups from that morning's coffee were still on the table; the lamp she had left on was still casting it's soft, yellowish light. Half convinced that this quiet scene of domestic contentment must be hiding something, she did a quick search through every room in the cottage: no notes, no feathers, no photographs. The windows and doors were locked. She poured herself a glass of wine in the kitchen, and fired off a series of messages to Nikki while she sipped at it. *Hey where are you? Are you staying with Harry? Pls let me know!*

She hesitated, then added: *I think someone chased me in the woods tonight. When you get this message, pls give me a ring.*

Heather put the glass of wine down and went to her own room. She shrugged her coat off, grimacing at the mud on her hands and face. Although it seemed incredibly likely that Nikki's date with Harry had just lasted longer than they had predicted, the empty cottage had left her deeply unnerved. Did they even know who Harry was really? He was basically a stranger, and she had let her friend go off with him. Again, she thought of calling DI Parker, but when she glanced down at her phone, she saw that all her messages to Nikki had failed to go through. Still no phone signal.

"All right." She pulled her jumper up over her head and threw it on the floor; there was mud on her hat, too. "I'll have a shower and try again. No need to panic yet."

Wincing from half a dozen new bruises, Heather went into the small en suite bathroom to have the hottest shower she could summon.

CHAPTER

42

HEATHER WOKE IN the night with a start, her heart thumping. She had been sure she wouldn't be able to sleep, so she had laid down on the bed after her shower, thinking only to rest her aching limbs for a moment. Yet, now she had the sense of having been ripped from a very deep sleep, a sleep populated with vivid dreams of the woods at night, and . . .

She heard it again. The sound of something heavy moving outside, the crunch of footsteps on fallen leaves. Not, she noted, the loud and casual stomping of someone—Harry, for example—making their way home, but the careful tread of someone who didn't want to be heard.

In an instant she was up, pulling on the last of the clean clothes from her suitcase. Once she put on her boots, she headed out into the hallway toward the kitchen. She had no clear idea what time it was, or how long she'd been asleep, but the living room was empty, and all the lights were off. Nikki's bedroom door was slightly open and a quick peek inside confirmed her bed was unslept in. Heather's stomach dropped.

"Christ, Nikki, where are you?"

She checked her phone to see if her messages had been received. They hadn't. All at once the idea that Nikki had simply stayed out late without telling her seemed ludicrous. She had brought Nikki into danger, and now she was gone. Heather went to the kitchen drawers and pulled out the biggest, sharpest kitchen knife she could find, feeling the weight of it in her hand.

Well, fuck this.

Heather went to the front door and eased it open. For a handful of seconds, she stood very still. She could see nothing else from where she was, but somewhere to her right she could hear those slow, methodical steps. The wind gusted in her direction, and she even heard the soft noise of nylon brushing against nylon.

Holding the knife low by her hip, Heather stepped out into the dark, keeping close to the wall of the cottage. When she rounded the corner, she froze, sure that whoever it was would see her, but she saw almost immediately that she had been lucky; the figure had its back to her, and it appeared to be heading back into the woods. Wearing a thickly padded winter coat, this tall figure had its head covered in a hood, appearing little more than a dark shape. As she watched, the figure turned its head slightly, clearly glancing at the windows of the cottage.

Fear vanished. She didn't even feel the cold. Instead, a hot, dry landscape of anger opened up inside Heather, just as it had the day she had slammed a pen through a man's hand. Here, undoubtedly, was the person who had been terrorizing her these last few weeks. And they were still at it, creeping about in the dark, looking for a place to leave more of their notes and feathers.

Before she even knew she was moving, Heather had crossed the short space between them and thrown herself at the stranger's back. They collided and fell together with an *oof*, crashing into the leaves and mud with more force than Heather realized she was capable of.

"Who the fuck *are* you? What do you want?"

The figure scrambled, trying to buck her off violently, but Heather drove her knee into its back, and they slumped into the dirt again. Grabbing the coat by the shoulder, she yanked the mysterious figure around to face her, bringing her knife up to the throat.

Lillian glared back at her, with her teeth bared.

Heather blinked, her hand growing loose around the knife. She couldn't make sense of what she was seeing; it was her mother's neighbor, except it wasn't. There were more lines on her long face, and there was a deep scar on one cheek, white and puckered-looking in the gloom.

"Lillian?"

The woman underneath her grinned, her body going slack. She looked, abruptly, unhinged.

"God, look at you," she spat. "Exactly as much of an idiot as the rest of your pathetic family."

"What?"

Taking advantage of Heather's surprise, the woman shook her off and scrambled to her feet. The hood fell back, and Heather saw that her hair was a shade darker than Lillian's, and her face was a subtly different shape; the nose a little longer, the jaw a little narrower. She stood up, the knife back at her waist.

"Who are you?"

The woman shook her head in disgust. "My sister did say you were weak minded. So easy to manipulate. You're asking all the wrong questions, Heather Reave."

"Shut up!" Heather brought the knife up, the moonlight flashing along the blade. "What do you know about that?"

"Make up your mind." The woman grinned again, dots of spittle on her lips glinting wetly. "Do I shut up or explain everything?" Before Heather could reply, she continued. "You don't have time, anyway."

"What are you talking about?"

The woman who was not Lillian nodded back toward the cottage. "Go inside and find out. Don't call the police or go running off to get help—I can tell you now that your friend doesn't have time for nonsense like that."

"Where the fuck is Nikki?" For a dangerous second, the edges of Heather's vision turned dark. She sucked in a breath and clenched her fist around the handle of the knife. Her knuckles were turning white. "What the fuck have you done?"

The woman stepped backwards. "Always the wrong questions. It's not what *I've* done that you need to worry about. I—"

"Where is she?"

"Oh, you know where she is. I practically told you, you *fool*. He's waiting for you. Hurry up now, little wolf."

With that she dashed back into the tree line. Heather jerked, her whole body singing with the need to go after her, but . . .

"*Nikki*."

She crashed back through the cottage door, wanting more than anything to see her friend standing in the kitchen, yawning in her pajamas and complaining about the noise, but the place was dark and silent.

"Nikki?"

The bathroom was on the way to Nikki's bedroom, so she kicked the door open as she went; nothing, an empty bath, the brief flash of her reflection staring back at her, pale and wild. As she came up the hallway to the room on the far end, she caught sight of dark smudges on the pale, biscuit-colored carpet which she hadn't noticed before. *Mud,* she thought, *it's mud, it has to be mud.*

The last room was the utilities room at the back, with the washing machine and dryer. There was a back door here, and racks for hikers to leave their muddy boots, but she and Nikki had barely used it. When she opened the door to it, there was a thick, mineral smell, the smell of a butcher's shop in high summer, and Heather felt some of the strength leach out of her legs. She slammed on the light, throwing everything into a hectic, yellow glow.

I brought her here, she thought. *I brought her up here, said it was safe. Oh god, I brought her here.*

Her bones heavy with dread, she crept to the far end of the room. Slumped in the space between the washer and the door was a body. It was difficult, for a moment, in the midst of her shock and the sheer amount of blood, to recognize that it wasn't Nikki at all, but eventually her mind caught up with what her eyes were seeing; it was a man in his boxer shorts, those parts of his skin not covered in blood painfully white. His neck was gaping open. It was Harry. Harry the artist, his hands lying palms up on his thighs and his face turned up to the ceiling, looking a little like a martyr in a sixteenth-century painting.

"Fuck. *Fuck*."

Heather ran back to the living room and snatched up the phone. There was no dial tone. Picking up the unit itself, she saw that the wires had been cut, ending a handspan before they reached the wall. She fumbled her phone out, but of course there was no signal. Outside, Nikki's car was still missing from the drive way. She was stuck.

She sank down against the cottage wall. It was the middle of the night. Somewhere out there was a killer—someone who had murdered a man, perhaps while she had been sleeping in the same house, and taken her friend. She could not call the police. The nearest neighbor was a good hour's walk away. *You know where.*

That was what the woman had said. She had said she knew where, that she had already told her.

"She called me a fool." Heather thought of the Polaroid, with the beach in the background. The Folly, standing empty behind them—the Folly that was owned by the same environmental charity that partly owned this land. Something about this tickled at the back of her mind, but she dismissed it. There was no time. If she headed out through the woods, she would get there eventually. Right now, she was Nikki's best hope of getting away alive. And more than that, she had the sense that this was exactly what she had been heading toward all along. Walking into these woods with murder on her mind—it would be a kind of coming home.

Heather went back into the cottage and retrieved her knife. She put on her coat, tucked the blade into an inner pocket, and ran out into the darkness.

CHAPTER

43

HEATHER HEARD THE ocean long before she could see it; a huge, hissing roar, both loud and quiet, the canvas that all the other noises were painted on—the crunch of dry leaves underfoot, her own labored breathing, the wind in the trees.

The woods had been dark, yet she had not felt afraid. Instead, she'd had the strangest feeling of being watched—not by enemies, or by this monster she was currently chasing, but by a warm silent presence that urged her on. When she emerged from the tree line she stood still, letting her eyes adjust to the moonlight glinting off the vast stretch of sea, to the pale sand that seemed to contain its own luminescence. To the right was the Folly, a darker shape pointing up into the night sky. She could see no lights there, no glow from the narrow windows, but there was a smaller shape crouched at the base of it. The small, dilapidated house had been missing from the images she had seen of the beach, and she suspected people had been careful to crop it from their photographs. Squat and covered in cheap pebbledash, it quite ruined the bleak romance of the shoreline and the wind-blasted tower.

There was no one in sight, and no movement to be seen anywhere. Checking once more that the knife was still in her coat, Heather began to climb down the rocky bluff that separated the forest from the beach, until she stood on the plain of shingle that led down to the sand. Something about the angle had changed her view of the house, and she could now see a tiny slither of light emerging from under the blind of one window.

"Bastard."

She curled one hand around the handle of the knife. Fear still felt like a very distant thing. Instead, the dry kindling feeling of rage that had nestled in her chest when she'd slammed the pen through her colleague's hand was back. It didn't matter what happened next, because she was *right*. This person she was chasing, the person she intended to hurt, was a monster, and she couldn't be feeling guilty for wanting to hurt him. And perhaps she would find the woman who looked like Lillian and hurt her, too. The sensation was incredibly liberating.

As she drew closer to the Folly and the house, she got a better idea of the layout of the place. The Folly didn't sit directly on the sand—she supposed that would have been a very unstable foundation—but on a spur of rock that had been laid, spiking out from the forested area toward the sea. There was a rough sort of road leading away from it, curling away into the dark somewhere out of sight, and the house crouched within its shadow, a strange sort of afterthought.

She had just stepped onto the rock when the thin line of light under the window blind vanished. Stopping where she was, Heather waited, expecting to see another light come on elsewhere in the house, but several long minutes passed and the darkness remained complete. She listened, too, desperate to get some sense of where this person was, or where Nikki was, but no voices were carried to her on the wind, no slamming doors or footsteps. Everything was eerily quiet. With the knife now held at her hip, Heather circled the place until she found a back door, a short flight of steps leading up to it. In the dark, everything was colorless.

Wait. Wait, wait, wait. She screwed her eyes up tight, trying to concentrate on the small voice of reason. *Try your phone again. You have to. You could be about to get both yourself and Nikki killed, idiot.*

Half a bar of signal. It might be enough, but then again, she might get a few words out before she lost the connection, and then what? She quickly texted Ben: Fiddler's Folly. Red Wolf found. He has Nikki. Help.

She didn't wait to see if it had gone through or try to call him. The monster inside this place would get a good early warning that she was here, and that could doom Nikki. *Better to go in quiet now,* Heather told herself. *Better to take the chance.*

The door was unlocked. Heather stepped into a small, filthy kitchen, thick with shadows. A square window let in enough moonlight for her to see a sink filled with dirty plates, an old wooden table riddled with burn marks and scratches, a packet of breakfast cereal open on the counter. There was an old-fashioned radio sitting on a cupboard shelf, and the wallpaper was peeling away in long, moldy strips. The place was old and badly maintained, but also clearly still inhabited.

She moved out into the hallway beyond, which led at the far end to a staircase that turned back on itself. There was a door to either side—one, which was standing open, revealed a room used as both a living space and bedroom. She could see a vast lumpy sofa covered with sheets, a coffee table littered with cups, and as she moved into the room itself, piles of dirty clothes just thrown all over the floor. Her heart in her mouth, she checked in every corner, but the place was empty.

Perhaps he's gone, she thought suddenly. *Saw me coming and left. He could have left through the door I couldn't see when I was walking across the beach.*

Or, suggested a darker part of her mind, *perhaps this is a perfectly innocent house. Perhaps you have broken into the home of some poor, lonely soul, and you're about to frighten the living shit out of them because you've lost touch with reality.*

Heather backed out of the room and went to the closed door. Her hand on the door knob, she paused as a painting on the wall next to it caught her eye. It was difficult to see in the gloom, but something about it made her fish out the phone from her pocket again, letting the screen light up the canvas briefly. It depicted a strange, red landscape, a flat and arid place with soft hills clouding the horizon. In the foreground, there was a single stunted tree, so twisted and black it almost looked like a crack in the arid ground, its sharp branches reaching like fingers. Heather swallowed and looked away. The painting frightened her.

As quietly as she could, she opened the door. Beyond it was a sheet of utter darkness, so she illuminated her phone again and cast the light ahead of her. There was a set of concrete steps leading down into a basement, and a strong smell of salt and bleach. Her stomach cramped.

Heather made her way down the steps, tipping her makeshift torch into the room ahead. The floor was bare and stained, and a long sturdy table stood on one side, much newer and better cared for than the one in the kitchen. There was a large plastic storage box in one corner, filled with big industrial bottles of cleaning fluids and other things she didn't recognize, and next to the table there was a metal trolley, littered with tools.

Still think this is the wrong place? Part of her asked mockingly.

The light dawdled over the trolley, winking off of scalpels, knives, and small saws with tiny jagged teeth. There were other things there, too— razor blades, ice picks, a long length of nylon rope, dark brown glass bottles with white paper labels. On the corner of the thing something dark and gelatinous clung; it had hair coming out of it, long strands of slightly curly red hair. Heather backed up rapidly, her heels striking the front of the last step and making her jump.

"Fuck. *Fuck.*"

All of her previous certainty seemed to flee her. Grinding her teeth together to keep from crying out, Heather ran back up the steps and into the hallway, the light from her phone jumping and flashing. For a few seconds she stood at the kitchen entrance, quite ready to run back outside and across the beach, when she heard someone moving upstairs.

It was the briefest sound—half a footstep, the shifting of a shoe against carpet—but it was enough to stop her dead.

Nikki, she told herself. *Nikki could be up there.*

She went to the stairs and climbed them, wincing at every creak of the floorboards. At the top was a wide landing, the carpet stripped up and rolled against the walls. There were three doors that she could see, one standing open to reveal a tiny, dismal looking bathroom. She opened the door closest to her, the knife held high. The blinds in this room were drawn tight, and she could barely see anything save for a vague impression of some bulky furniture; a bed, a wardrobe perhaps?

"Nikki?" No response.

She lifted the phone light again and had a brief glimpse of a big mirror on the other side of the room. She saw her own face, pale and gaunt, her dark hair strewn haphazardly across her forehead—and then watched in shock as the face blinked and held up both hands to shield its eyes.

"What—?"

The figure lunged at her, throwing her down and to the floor with a crash. Heather cried out, the knife flying from her hand, and then the figure had both hands around her throat. It was a man, she belatedly realized; a man who had her face, her stature, her hair. He crashed her head against the floorboards, and her vision filled with static.

"I am the wolf," the man shouted. "I am the wolf!"

With some difficultly, Heather bucked him off, causing him to smash his head into the door frame. For a second he was stunned, and she took the opportunity to scramble away.

"Who are you? Where's Nikki?" The knife was by her foot, so she snatched it up. She had dropped the phone, but to her surprise he stood up and flicked a light switch in the bedroom, casting them both into a harsh artificial glow. "I . . . who *are* you?"

He stood unmoving, watching her. Now that there was more light, she could see that they weren't identical after all, of course they weren't. He had a wider jaw and thicker eyebrows, and there were scars, lots of them, crisscrossing their way up his forearms. His hair, too, was shorter. But other than that, the resemblance was uncanny—there was little doubt who he was, not really. For a strange, horrible few seconds, Heather found she wanted to laugh, or be sick; she wasn't sure which.

"Why do you look like me?" He sounded petulant almost, a child angry because he was confused. His hand crept up to his head, touching the place where he had struck it on the door jamb.

"I'm your sister." Heather paused and made a strangled noise, somewhere between a laugh and a sob. "I'm your bloody sister, aren't I? Who's your dad?"

He looked confused by the question. Instead, he took out a knife from his back pocket. It was slim and lethal, and not clean. As he held it up, Heather found herself noticing other details about him; his hands had spots of blood on them, and his shirt, which was a dark navy blue, had darker patches on it.

"Listen," he said. "Listen." He shook the knife at her. "I am the wolf. *I* am the barghest. There can't be two of us. It's my job."

"What is? What is your job?"

He took a step forward, and Heather held her own knife up in front of her. If she got up and fled down the stairs, she'd have to turn her back on him, and she still didn't know where Nikki was.

"To take them *home*." The last word was filled with such longing, such raw emotion, that Heather found herself bewildered. Tears were running freely down his gaunt face. "They were born here, they belong to the woods, so I'm just bringing them back to their home. I can't let you stop me from doing that, because it's what I was made for."

"What do you mean, they were born here?" With a shudder, Heather remembered Anna in the hospital, her hands hovering over her stomach. How she had shouted about the baby—the baby taken from her. "Fucking hell. The babies born on the commune, is that what you mean? They would be my age now, or older, and you're . . ." The sea roared in the silence. "What's your name?"

"My name?"

"Yes, your fucking name. You're my brother, I should at least know your bloody name."

"I am the wolf, I am—"

"*Your name.*"

Her flash of anger seemed to startle him.

"Lyle," he said in a quiet voice. "My name is Lyle, Lyle Reave, and I am the barghest, the new Red Wolf. It's what I was made for."

"Listen to me, Lyle. My friend Nikki, who you took, she wasn't born here. She wasn't born in Fiddler's Woods, okay? She hasn't got anything to do with this, all right? Let me take her away from here. That's all. And I'll leave you be."

"No." He said it softly. "No, it's a bit late for that."

"What do you mean? Where is she, Lyle?"

"She's in the Folly," he said, coming forward again. "With the other one. That's why she can't go, because she's seen her, and she's seen me. And anyway, the old wolf is there now." He seemed to brighten. "But maybe this is right. If you're my sister, then you belong to the woods, too. I can take you there."

"No!"

He came forward, the knife raised. Heather sprang at him, trying with everything she had to push him over, but he was too strong. Instead, he shoved her roughly toward the bannister, which struck her across the middle of her back, and then slashed at her with the knife. Heather threw herself out of the way just in time to avoid a blow that would have struck her in the chest, but he came straight after her. A thin line of agony moved down her left arm and she knew he'd got her.

"Stop it!" She swung her own knife around, but it seemed hopelessly inelegant in the face of his wicked little blade, and the flat of it bounced off his arm. "Do you think Michael Reave would want you to kill me? Your own sister?"

But his face was closed, masklike. There was nothing behind his eyes now but a terrible flatness that made her think of the red painting downstairs. His knife flashed again, this time slicing across her belly, and she screamed thinly, horrified by the immediate hot wetness soaking into her jumper. The stairs were directly behind her now, and she clasped onto the newel post for balance, her fingers slippery with her own blood.

"It's good that you came," he said. His cheeks were still wet from his tears. "This is how it should be. I am the wolf."

"Oh *fuck* you," Heather spat through her teeth. "You're nothing but a murderer, a desperate sad waste of space. Every woman you've killed is worth ten of you!"

For the first time, a flicker of some alien emotion passed over his face, and Heather was reminded of the time she had seen Michael Reave lose his temper—*the truth*, she thought bitterly. *He doesn't want to hear it.*

"There's nothing grand or mysterious about you," she said, and she laughed, genuinely amused. Her head felt very light. "Just a little man hurting women because it's the only way you feel powerful. God, losers like you are ten a penny."

His face twisted and he leapt at her again. This time, Heather embraced him, ignoring the bright white agony as the knife tore across her midriff, and pivoted herself. When she had gravity back on her side, she pushed with everything she had left, and Lyle Reave fell away from her, into the dark space filling the stairs.

There was a shout and series of thumps, and then silence. Heather stood very still, waiting.

Later, Heather wouldn't be able to say how long she had stood at the top of the stairs, bleeding from three knife wounds and staring down into the dark, waiting for her brother to come charging back up. When she thought of that time, she remembered the sound of the sea, somewhere beyond the windows, and the steady drip of her blood splashing onto bare floorboards.

Eventually the spell, whatever it was, broke, and she snatched up her phone and the knife before heading, very slowly, downstairs. At the bottom she found a light switch, which she flicked on, and there was Lyle Reave, lying in a heap just to one side of the final step. Gritting her teeth, Heather pressed her fingers to his throat—she thought, for a moment, she felt a flicker there, some movement in his blood, but then she seemed to lose it; it was difficult to tell if he was alive or not, over the thumping in her own head and the pain in her arm and stomach.

Nikki.

Nikki was in the Folly, possibly with another woman, possibly under the care of something Lyle had called "the old wolf." Heather had no idea who that could be—it couldn't be Michael Reave, who was, presumably, still safely locked up—but whoever they were, they would be expecting Lyle. Lyle could get into the Folly, could probably even get to the women. It was where he was supposed to be.

As quickly as she could, Heather stripped off his stained shirt and his jeans—underneath them he was lean and scarred, little round marks on his thighs and stomach suggesting that someone had once used him as an ashtray—and, dumping her own clothes on the floor, dressed in them herself. They were a little large, but not significantly so, and she rolled down the sleeves of the dark shirt to cover the wound on her arm. With the wicked little knife, which had landed on the stairs, she stood and cut raggedly at the back of her hair, chopping off the last three inches or so that curled at her neck and at the sides of her face. Feathery pieces of dark hair fell across her brother's face and chest as she did so.

With her phone and the big knife shoved into the jeans pocket and the lethal blade in her hand, Heather stepped back into the night.

CHAPTER

44

BEFORE

SHE HAD THOUGHT she was safe. She had thought she had walked away from it all, had left that dark time behind her.

Yes, she had made a mistake. It was about as bad a mistake as anyone could make, that was true, but they happened. Colleen had always been a trusting girl, an optimist; the sort to believe the best about everyone. It was a good thing, surely, to be so sure that people were good at heart? She still thought that. Or at least, most of the time she did. When she stumbled from her bed at 3AM, both babies screaming fit to bring down the heavens, and she sat with their warm little shapes curled under her breast, her mind would return inevitably to the babies born at Fiddler's Mill, and the women who had vanished over the last few years. Her *inherent goodness*, her *relentless optimism* hadn't saved them. There would be a price to pay for her weakness.

So, perhaps that was why, deep down in her bones, she wasn't surprised when she opened her door one night to see them both standing there. Michael, looking not so much angry as bewildered—he had lost weight since she'd seen him last, there were hollow places on his cheeks—and the old man, his eyes gleaming with triumph. She made a noise in her throat and went to slam the door shut, but Michael pushed his boot in the gap, holding it open easily.

"You were pregnant?" was all he said.

She lifted her chin, setting her face into an expression of determination she didn't feel. "Oh? And I was the only one with secrets, was I?"

Michael didn't move. He looked hurt, and ludicrously, she felt a pang of sorrow. Once, she had genuinely loved him—had thought of him as her wild, country boy, had craved his rough, scarred hands and every moment they had spent alone in the woods together. When she had missed her first period, she'd experienced a trembling moment of euphoria. This baby, she had thought, would be blessed—born of love and raised to have a love of nature . . . it had all seemed perfect. And then she had seen the inside of his van.

"That child belongs to Fiddler's Mill." The old man elbowed his way in front of Michael. "More than any of them. It's ours."

"Come back," said Michael simply. "Please, I want to see my child. To know them. Was it a boy or a girl? Please, Colleen."

"I'll call the police," she said, glancing past them at the road. It was late on a school night, and the little cul-de-sac was empty. She was renting the tiny house for a pittance; a favor from the owner of the women's refuge, and no one knew where she was. Too late, she realized, what a mistake that was. "I'll call them right now. You can't threaten me like this."

"Do you think the police can keep you safe, lass?" The old man grinned, baring all his long, yellow teeth. "You know better than that, I reckon. The child is ours. Give it to us, now, and think no more of it. I know you ran away and had that baby in secret. Who even knows about it? Not your parents, I reckon."

Colleen looked at Michael, hoping that he would be outraged by this obvious threat to her life, but he was looking at his feet. He had also, she noticed, moved so that his body was blocking the door. How far would she get if she ran back inside? He would be on her in moments. She had always admired his easy strength, his grace. Now, the thought made her want to be sick.

"How am I to know you won't come back for me? How do I know . . ." She paused to gasp in a panicky breath, "that you won't just show up here one night, with your *van*."

"I swear it." He met her eyes then. "Give us the child, and we'll go. You'll never see me again. I'll keep my distance." His green eyes flashed. "But I'll write. And you'll write to me. That's all. I love you, Colleen. I just want what's mine."

"Yours." She laughed a little, although tears were streaming down her cheeks.

"He'll write, and you'll write back," added the old man, "and we'll know where you are at all times. Do you understand me, lass? You keep on writing to my boy here, because we'll need to know you're on side. Just in case you start feeling the need to unburden yourself. You never speak of this child to anyone. To you, they no longer exist. And for that, we'll keep our distance. *I* can promise you that." He lifted his lips in a sneer. "What are you sniveling about? You can have more babies. That's what women do, isn't it?"

Michael turned to look at the older man, a scowl briefly darkening his brow. "That's enough."

"What will you do? With the baby?"

"Raise him, Colleen. He's my boy." Michael smiled slightly, and quite abruptly she hated him with every part of her, a hate to shake the stars down from the sky. "Or girl. I'll look after him. It might even, you know, help me. To be . . ."

He licked his lips and looked down at his feet again.

"To be less of a monster?" Colleen provided. He gave her that hurt look again, and suddenly she couldn't stand it. She raised her hand. "You will stay here. You will wait here, and not come inside my home, or I swear to god I will kill the baby myself before you get to us. Do you understand?"

The old man looked like he might argue, but Michael nodded. Colleen went back down the hall to the little spare room she had been using as a makeshift nursery, trying with every step not to be sick. The twins were in matching basinets, snug in tiny yellow and white baby grows, their little pink faces scrunched up tight with sleep. She stood over them, knowing that she had no time, no time at all—the foul old man would get impatient, would come after her, then they would all be lost—but still, it was hard to look away, knowing this would be the last time she saw them together.

Over all the long years to come, Colleen would often look back on the moment she had decided, looking for reasons, for the truth. Hours spent awake as dawn stained the net curtains yellow. Every time she took Heather to the park and watched little kids playing on the slides or pushing each other into the dirt—always the question was hanging over her. But the truth was that when she bent down and plucked the little boy from his crib, she wasn't thinking at all. Her mind was a terrifying blank, all comfort and hope blasted from it in one searing moment.

She carried him back down the hall and gave him to the monsters.

CHAPTER

45

Outside the sky had changed color. The inky darkness of the middle of the night had gone, to be replaced with a kind of dark silvery mauve. Heather looked at it for a moment, confused. How long had it taken her to run through the woods? How long had she been in the house? It seemed only minutes ago that she had found Harry's body in the cottage, and now dawn was edging over the horizon.

As she rounded the base of the Folly, looking for a way in, she spotted an old-fashioned car parked up on the far side, with two figures standing next to it. One of them raised its hand to its eyes, clearly peering at her with interest. A voice she recognized floated toward her.

"Lyle!"

Heather nodded and waved, and began to jog over to them. It was Lillian, and the woman she had caught outside the cottage, her sister. Now that they stood next to each other, it was clear she was a few years older than Lillian, or had had a rougher life. Lillian was wearing a long camel hair coat, the collar turned up, and her gray hair was whipped by the wind, while the other still wore the heavy parker. It was Lillian who stepped forward, a wide grin splitting her face.

"Did you catch her, Lyle? Did you kill her?"

Heather, who was still in the deeper shadow of the Folly, turned her face away and down, keen that they should not recognize her until the very last moment. Lillian though, seemed unconcerned, stepping toward her with her arms open.

"Little wolf, your father will be *so* pleased."

Heather grabbed the older woman by the shoulders and slammed her backwards into the car. She squawked like a chicken, while her sister shouted something Heather didn't catch.

"*Who are you?*" Heather brought the lethal little knife up to Lillian's throat and pressed it there. When the other woman moved, she shook her head. "Another step and she's dead. I bloody promise you."

"Calm down, Heather, dear," said Lillian. She cleared her throat. "We're old friends of your father. You know who that is now, don't you?"

"Why? All that stuff with the house, the funeral. You wanted me to come up here. Why?"

"A little family reunion." Lillian grimaced. "We thought Lyle should know about his sister."

"We raised that boy," spat the other one. Heather spared her a glance. She looked furious, hectic points of color in the middle of her gray cheeks. "When your idiot father got caught, we became everything to that little lad—his mothers, his sisters. We kept him out here, safe from the world. But when he was old enough, suddenly . . ."

"Suddenly we weren't good enough anymore. Cast out," Lillian continued. "I ask you, Heather, is that fair? After all the work we'd done, the hours we'd put in? All these years we've kept track of the children of Fiddler's Mill. We've practically been like second parents to them. And apparently your father approved of our dismissal. He agreed that we should be removed from the boy's life, even as he himself sat moldering in prison." She grunted. "When we realized that dear, sweet Colleen had lied all along, well, we thought wouldn't that make a fitting little present for Michael?"

"The daughter he didn't know, murdered by his precious son," the other woman grinned. "Although of course he hasn't fucking managed it. Should know better than to trust men to do anything right."

"What do you know about my mother?"

Lillian bared her teeth. "Everything. We've always known where she was. We thought of her fondly, of course. We went to see her, didn't we, Lizbet? Once we realized what she'd done, what she'd been getting away with all these years. We asked her about it, about you, and all the years in between, and she told us everything. After a fashion. After a little . . . *encouragement*. She told us about the man who raised you, the birds, how you pushed him to death's door . . ."

"Fuck you."

"And we told her some things, too—about the upcoming harvest, and the role she'd played in it. I have to admit, I wasn't dreadfully surprised when I heard she'd killed herself. No one wants to find out they birthed a monster. Or a pair of them."

Heather didn't move. She couldn't look away from the point of the knife where it pressed into Lillian's sagging neck. A little more pressure, just a little, and this revolting woman would never utter another word. Somewhere above them, a seagull cried out, and she moved back, horrified at what she had almost done.

"This is all insane," she told them. "*You* are all insane. I'm going in there to get my friend. If you come after me, if I ever see your twisted old faces again, I will kill you."

Something about this answer pleased the women. She saw them exchange a glance; their eyes bright.

"Like father like daughter," Lillian said.

Heather left them standing by the car. On the far side, facing the woods, she found the door to the Folly standing open. Inside there was a curiously empty space; flagstones dusted with sand and dead leaves, and curling up the inside of the tower, a set of spiraling stone steps. The smell of salt and blood hung heavy in the air, a silvery kind of light filtering in through dirty windows. She had her foot on the first step when she spotted a pile of old hessian mats in the corner—the furthest one was half folded over, as if someone had thrown them over something in a hurry. The knife still held in one fist, she left the stairs and went over to the mats, dragging them away to reveal a trap door flush with the flag stones.

It revealed another staircase, this one spiraling downwards. There were bright, modern electric lights fitted to the walls, and from somewhere far below, she could hear soft noises—someone moving, the faint sound of crying.

"Nikki?"

Her voice sank into nothing, but below her the noises increased. Heather headed down, one hand braced against the wall, until she came to a nondescript wooden door. Beyond it was a dank, cold little room, and in it Nikki and another woman she didn't know huddled together on the floor. At the sight of her, the other woman moaned, a desperate, terrified noise, but Nikki sat up, her eyes very wide. They were both bound with nylon rope, hands cinched tightly behind their backs and gags around their mouths, and Nikki was sitting slightly in front of the other woman, as though to shield her from something.

"Christ." Heather went to them, bringing up the wicked little knife, and the woman behind Nikki wailed behind her gag. "It's all right, I'm just going to cut you loose."

There was a noise on the staircase behind her. Heather turned, the knife held up again.

"Here you are, lass. I suppose it was inevitable you'd get here eventually." It was the old man who had given them tea; the small, bent old man who peered at them out of one eye and had seemed so frail and fragile. Now, standing in the doorway and blocking the staircase, he did not look frail at all. His dog, the huge shaggy black creature, was standing at his knee. Bert smiled and nodded, as though confirming something. "Jesus wept, but you look like him. Like both of them. Where is my boy, eh? What have you done with him?"

"He's dead," said Heather. "Who are you, really?"

The old man shrugged, taking a further step into the room. Behind her, the two women were silent.

"You can't save them," he said quietly. "Especially not my Cathy. Cathy belongs here, do you understand? She belongs to me." The eerie contentment on his face began to fade, to be replaced by something else. "I *made* her. I brought her parents here, I gave them this free world to live in, and the fruits of that are mine. All of them . . ."

"The women were all born here, at Fiddler's Mill. And then what? Taken away? Adopted out?"

Bert smiled. "The Bickerstaff sisters you just met were nurses, did you know that? Or at least, nurses in training. I'm not sure they ever qualified though, or whatever you might call it. They knew the drugs to use, they knew how to deliver babies onto pure, black earth. Very persuasive, the Bickerstaff sisters. The children of Fiddler's Woods went off to their new families, and we've waited until now. Until the *harvest*."

"You are out of your fucking mind." Heather swallowed hard. Standing up felt like the hardest thing in the world, and there was a ringing noise in her ears. Distantly she was aware of blood pooling inside her jeans, and every time she moved fresh lines of pain encircled her body. "All of you."

Bert pursed his lips together. Now that he was looking at her dead on, she could see that one of his eyes was false; it looked dull under the fierce white lights.

"Michael, he didn't care who he took. He was always so primitive, that one. That little beast. But I was interested in the perfect victim, one bred for the very purpose of dying. Don't you see how *fine* that is? How *apt*? Livestock, ready for the culling." He grinned, revealing his long teeth. "We raised the boy to have more refined tastes. And if the police started to think that perhaps they hadn't got the real Red Wolf, all those years ago, well . . . The lad was keen to see his father again. A boy like Lyle, he can't exactly go visiting people, as I'm sure you'll agree."

"You mad old bastard. Haven't you got it yet? This is the end of your nonsense. Your weapon is dead, and me and Nikki and Cathy are bloody walking out of here right now."

He cocked his head to one side again. The dog sat up, its ears pricked.

"You have to get through me, lass. You'll have to kill me. And you don't have what it takes to do that, because your blood is weak. Michael was a suggestible idiot, easily molded into what I wanted him to be, and in the end, Lyle was even worse, tainted by the blood of your mother. And what are you? Just some other little offshoot of a damaged, incestuous family." Seeing the look of surprise that passed over her face, he grinned a little wider. "You wouldn't know, of course, but the woman Michael killed when he was a child wasn't his real mother. Ask him sometime about the woman in the red coat. Ask him what she did to him."

"Enough." Heather raised the knife. "Get out of my way. Now."

"I told you, you'll have to kill me." He raised his hands up, palms flat. "And you don't have it in you, little girl."

Behind her, Heather heard Nikki moving against the concrete, but sounds in the square concrete room were growing distant and distorted. She could see the old man in front of her, his sneering expression of disgust twisting his face into something goblinlike, but hanging over him and obscuring him was a stark, red landscape—a place that beckoned to her, that called her home. She held the knife up.

"You don't know me at all."

She slammed the knife into his chest. A fierce bolt of joy passed through her, and briefly all the pain from her own wounds was wiped out. The old goblin made a strangled noise and he seemed to crumple in front of her. There was a dog barking, somewhere.

Heather, Heather, Heather.

And then reality crashed back into her in a rush. At some point, she had pulled the knife back out again—she had stabbed him in the upper part of his chest, not far from his collar bone—and bright spurts of his blood covered her hands and arms. In a shudder of revulsion and horror she dropped the knife, and it clanged against the concrete floor.

"Fuck!"

"I knew it," he croaked. "All of you, so weak." He pressed one gnarled hand to the wound turning his shirt black. "Why . . . do I even . . . waste . . . my time?"

"I can't . . ." Heather glanced at the knife, then back to the old man. "I'm not —"

From the shadowy stairwell behind him, an arm reached out of the dark and circled his neck. The old man was yanked backwards, and this time he did scream, just before something shiny and lethal ripped his throat into a giant gaping mouth. There was a brief struggle, Bert's arms flapping at nothing, and then he fell back to the floor in a rapidly expanding pool of blood. Heather had a glimpse of the figure on the stairs—he wore her face, though his eyes were not human, not human at all—and then Lyle was gone. His footsteps were light scuffles on the steps, and there was the crash of a door opening and closing. Gone.

With some difficulty, Heather reached down and plucked the knife from the floor, then staggered back to Nikki and the woman called Cathy. She tugged away her friend's gag, then used the last of her strength to cut the bonds around her hands.

"Hev? Are you all right? Christ, you're bleeding all over."

Heather nodded dumbly. She sat down, and she now had the distinct feeling she couldn't get back up. Nikki was still looking at her even as she untied the other woman.

Heather looked slowly around the room. It was growing darker. "Hey, where's the dog? I didn't see where the dog went."

"What dog?" Nikki took her arm then and shook it. "Stay awake, Hev. What dog? There wasn't any dog. Hev?"

CHAPTER

46

BEFORE

THE NIGHTMARE OF Fiddler's Mill retreated for Colleen, but only so far. The creatures she had left behind in the woods didn't forget about her, after all—and all her life, she felt them watching.

There was the summer fête, where she had seen the Oak Leaf symbol on an awning, where small children were queuing to pick up their prizes. It was *his* company, his way of keeping track, and although he wasn't there, it was as though she could smell his fetid old man breath on the back of her neck. In a blind panic, she had scooped Heather up into her arms and turned toward the carpark.

There was the card, left outside their front door. When she thought how close they had come then to finding out the truth, it had knocked all the strength from her.

And then, eventually, there came the Bickerstaff sisters, creeping around her door and pushing their way inside. All of Colleen's careful defenses, built up over so many years, were tattered into pieces over that long, horrific afternoon. She learned the fate of her long-lost child, of the harvest that was coming, and still they kept her pinned in place with the worst threat of all: tell anyone, and we'll come for your daughter, too.

When they finally left her—after they'd extracted every painful secret she'd ever held close to her heart—Colleen went and fetched her nicest notepad, the one she had never used to write to Michael. She sat down at her own kitchen table and, just like her daughter, she tried to find the words.

CHAPTER

47

THE FOREST DID not seem darker with him in it. The birds still sang, the sunlight still filtered down through the branches, a dappled blessing on the earth and grass. Michael Reave walked with his face turned up, trying to take it all in, and Heather watched him closely. It seemed wrong that Fiddler's Woods did not recoil from him, that the skies didn't turn black and the trees die, but then, she reminded herself, he was their creature. He had fed the roots and nourished the ground, in his own way.

"Heather?" He turned to face her, smiling. "Look, do you see that there?" He nodded toward a hole next to a small mound of fresh earth. "That's the entrance to a badger sett. I used to see them sometimes, but they're shy animals. They can have big families living inside them, the larger setts. A clever little network of tunnels."

"This isn't a nature walk."

"No, lass." He put his smile away, and his eyes drifted up to look over her shoulder. "No, you're right there."

Behind her, she knew he could see the police gathered, DI Ben Parker among them. They were never far behind.

So far, Michael Reave had led them to the remains of four women, one of which, he said, had never been listed as one of his official victims. Identifying them was going to be difficult—he had only ever buried what he called "the soft parts" of them within the woods, although he had sometimes included other things—trinkets, items from their purses, or hairclips, even a shoe. He had agreed to do this as long as Heather continued to visit him and came with him on these little jaunts to Fiddler's Woods. With the death of Albert "Bert" Froame and the capture of Lyle Reave, all his pretenses of innocence had vanished.

"You're happy here." It wasn't a question.

"Aye. I was happy here, once." He stopped, so she stopped. His hands were bound behind his back with steel cuffs, and he had made no threats toward her, but she still didn't like to get too close. "Before it all really started . . ." He shrugged. "There was a bit of time where I thought I was free, and I spent it here, with these trees. Those were good memories."

She nodded. She supposed, that if you didn't know what was buried here, it could seem like a peaceful place.

"I wanted to ask you . . ." Heather glanced back to the police, both making sure they were close enough to help, and far away enough not to hear. "About the woman in the red coat."

Michael Reave straightened up. He took a long, wavering breath in, then held it for a moment. His eyes were too bright.

"My sister," he said eventually. "My older sister. Only she wasn't just that. My father, your granddad, was a sick man, and he infected the whole house with his sickness. My sister was born in 1947, her name was . . . Evie." He stopped. Saying her name seemed to cause him some physical pain. "And then when she got a little older, when she'd just turned thirteen, Evie had me."

Heather looked down at her hands, feeling sick. She thought of Ben Parker telling her that killers had almost always experienced abuse.

"The woman who called herself my mother, she hated me for it," continued Reave. "I was a sign of everything that was wrong with our family, lass, do you see? And Evie, I think she tried to make up for it, for how much her mother hated me. But she only knew one way of expressing that. Because of what had been done to her. She would come to me, at night." He paused, shuddering. "I still remember her standing in my bedroom door, in her red coat. Smiling. She said she just wanted to love me."

"What happened to her? To Evie?"

"She died. Long after I ran to Fiddler's Mill, she drifted away to live with some bad people. The house she was staying in burned down while she was in it. I only heard about it because it was in a newspaper." When he looked at Heather again, he had composed himself. "And . . . I don't think you should hear any more about it. It's not healthy, lass."

Somewhere in the trees above them, a magpie was making a racket. He looked up into the branches, smiling again.

"I would like to tell you another story," he said.

Heather shrugged.

"Once upon a time, there was a rich man who had spent all his life doing evil deeds. He had been mean, never shared his wealth, and had watched as others starved. He had hurt people for his own pleasure and enjoyed it. Then one day he had a change of heart. When his neighbor, a poor man with hungry children, came calling at his house, he promised that the poor man could have half his food and wealth if, when he died, he watched over his grave for three nights in a row. He was worried . . ." Michael Reave paused, his face slack. "He was worried that the devil would come for his soul."

For a long time, Reave didn't say anything more, although Heather was sure that wasn't the end of the story. They walked a little further, with the soft trample of the police coming along behind.

"This doesn't change anything, you know," Heather said eventually. "It doesn't change who you are, or what you did."

"No," he said. "It doesn't." He turned to look at her, and not for the first time Heather felt a shiver of discomfort; it was as though he looked straight to the heart of her. As though he could see down to her bones.

"What is it?"

"I was just thinking." He smiled, that rueful almost-smile made so famous by his mugshot. "I was just thinking that Colleen should have given me you, instead of Lyle. There's so much more of me in you."

* * *

It was spring. The dog roses on the cliff path were all in bloom, their soft pink and yellow heads nodding in the freshening sea breeze. Heather brushed her fingers against the petals as she passed them, plucking one or two blooms and thinking of nothing in particular until she came to the cliff's edge. Yawning away below her was the drop, and the solid blue sea—the last thing her mother had ever seen, probably.

Colleen Evans had been faced with a terrible decision—the worst decision, perhaps, that anyone could have to make—and, ultimately, she hadn't been able to live with it. Certainly not when the Bickerstaff sisters had come sniffing around her door, not when the time had come for the dark harvest of Fiddler's Wood. Such a decision had broken her, twisted her into something sharp and cold, and Heather wondered if Lyle, sitting in his prison cell, deserved to know that: if he deserved to know how it had broken their mother, to give him to the monsters. She thought, all in all, that it was a mercy he hadn't earned. However small a mercy it was.

"I think I'm more like you, actually." She said it forcefully, but the wind picked up her words and snatched them out to sea. "I really do think that. I'm sorry I didn't see it sooner, Mum." A seagull cried overhead, a clear and hopeful sound. "I'm sorry."

Heather scattered the dog rose petals where she stood and walked away from the cliff's edge.

ACKNOWLEDGEMENTS

This book essentially owes its entire existence to my brilliant agent and friend, Juliet Mushens. We had long shared an interest in true crime, swapping stories and Wikipedia links, and one day, when I joked about passing off all my dodgy internet activity as book research, she fixed her eye upon me – via Whatsapp – and said, 'well why don't you write a thriller, Sennifer?'. Thank you, Juliet, for being the kick up the bum I needed, and of course for being one of my dearest, wisest friends.

So, A Dark and Secret Place was a new genre for me, and never has a single book taught me so much. I've been lucky enough to have an extraordinary team of excellent minds to lead me through it and very kindly teach me all the things I needed to learn. Huge thanks to Natasha Bardon at HarperFiction, who saw through to the bones of this book immediately and made it work. Enormous gratitude also to the team at Crooked Lane Books, who made me feel so welcome and have kept on top of everything with such enthusiasm – Faith Black Ross, Melissa Rechter and Madeline Rathle, you all rock. Many thanks also to Jenny Bent, another agent who has had my back at every step.

I happen to be writing these acknowledgements in the middle of a worldwide pandemic, which is certainly not a sentence I ever expected to write, to say the least. We've been in lockdown for around three months now, and it's not an easy time to do anything creative, let alone write fiction. The two brilliant bookshops where I work, Clapham Books and Herne Hill Books, haven't seen me for a while, but my colleagues have been so supportive and brilliant during a period that has not been the best of times (for various reasons). Nikki, Ed, Sophie and Roy – thank you so much.

As ever, I am grateful to have had the backup, moral support and effervescent company of a bunch of writer friends. Den Patrick, Andrew Reid, Adam Christopher, Alasdair Stuart, and Peter Newman – thank you for being the best sounding boards and drinking buddies. I would also like to give a shout out to the Onesies; I hope to get back to adventuring with you soon. And, of course, unending gratitude and love to my mum and the rest of my family, some of whom might even read this book because it has murders rather than dragons!

Lastly, all my love to Marty Perrett, my partner and best friend, who I think has always been slightly concerned by my interest in missing persons and body disposal. It turns out it was all for a book, after all. Love you babe.